"Since evolution became fashionable, the glorification of Man has taken on a new form . . . Science, which has always had to fight its way against popular beliefs, now has one of its most difficult battles in the sphere of psychology."

—Bertrand Russell, *The Basic Writings of Bertrand Russell, Volume 10*

"Nothing is more dangerous than a dogmatic worldview—nothing more constraining, more blinding to innovation, more destructive of openness to novelty."

—Stephen Jay Gould, *Dinosaur in a Haystack*

"A new scientific truth does not triumph by convincing its opponents and making them see the light, but rather because its opponents eventually die, and a new generation grows up that is familiar with it."

—Max Planck, *Scientific Autobiography and Other Papers*

"One question keeps haunting me as a scientist. One query's answer eludes me. I ask and ask, search and search, research and research, and not one scientist can give me a definitive answer. I posed the question when researching the Scopes Monkey Trial as a graduate student. I inquired when 'Little Lucy' was unearthed. I have combed the halls of academia, scoured the journals of science, and questioned leading experts searching for the answer to this question: Of what or whom is evolution afraid? If time is on the side of truth, then there is nothing to fear if it is truly truth we seek."

—Evelyn Sims, PhD, "Biospheres and Bios-Fears: Keeping an Open Mind in a World and Time of Scientific Discovery," *Journal of Marine Paleontology*, Vol. 12, pp. 17-32.

THE SERPENT'S GRASP

C. KEVIN THOMPSON

Hallway Publishing

45 Lafayette Road #114

North Hampton, NH 03862

www.hallwaypublishing.com

Contact Information: info@hallwaypublishing.com

The Serpent's Grasp

Second Edition, July 2017

Cover Design by Hallway Publishing

Typesetting by Odyssey Publishing

ISBN: 978-1-941058-67-1

Published in the United States of America

They exchanged the truth of God for a lie, and worshiped and served created things rather than the Creator—who is forever praised. Amen.

—Romans 1:25 (NIV)

For Cindy

Remember when the "angel" approached us on that cold, snowy, winter's day in one of our darkest hours and said we were destined for great things?

I believe he was correct.

CHAPTER ONE

Wednesday, 1:57 a.m.
Atlantic Ocean
Approximately 11 Nautical Miles East/Northeast of Fort Pierce, Florida

Tethered to the ocean floor for hours, an eighty-five-foot schooner floated in rhythm with the gentle swells of the Atlantic. The masts, standing vigil in the shadows of the night sky with their sails battened tight, rocked back and forth as solitary sentinels. Under a veil of thin cirrus clouds, the moon beamed a brilliant but dispersed glow upon the vessel whose white underbelly glistened against the backdrop of the watery depths.

A soft breeze, mixing with the smell of salt and sea life, wafted across the deck, carrying the mounting sounds of a quarrel that emanated from the quarters below.

"I don't care about all that. But obviously you do," the woman said, putting on her clothes.

The man flopped over onto his back and sighed. "Why does that bother you?"

"It's becoming clear that our relationship is important when we can have our little trysts, but when it comes to disrupting your cash flow, then whoa, wait a minute. You've suddenly got to think it through."

"That's not fair, Regina, and you know it. If I divorce Evelyn, she'll want half. Do you know what that means?"

Regina crossed her arms and shrugged.

"I'd have to sell the business. That's what it means. All that I've worked for would be gone. I'd be left with our rental in Fort Lauderdale, this boat if I'm lucky, and a whopping alimony payment."

Regina closed her eyes and dropped her chin to her chest. "So *our* relationship is based on *your* financial future? Wonderful."

David Sims sat up on the edge of the bed and snatched his polo shirt off the floor. "Look, this is not what I had in mind." He thrust his arms through the sleeves. "If we're gonna fight, I might as well go home."

"I've got to know this is going somewhere." She lifted her gaze and watched him get dressed. "If you're not willing to leave your wife, then all I am is a plaything, and I can't live like that."

David sat for several awkward moments before speaking. "What about your husband? Is it that cut and dry for you? Don't you feel a little remorse when we're together?"

"Sure, I do." Regina unfolded her arms and slipped her hands into the pockets of her shorts. "You know, you're not the only one destined to lose something in this."

"But you're the woman. You should get a healthy chunk of your husband's money." David chuckled. "Maybe that would help make our lives easier after the dust settles."

"Well, I hate to paint a bleak picture for you, Dave, but I won't."

"You won't what?"

"Get anything from my husband."

"You didn't."

Regina nodded. "I signed a pre-nup. If I hadn't signed it, Robert wouldn't have married me."

"You get nothing if you get divorced?"

"Not exactly. Only if I have an affair . . ."

David stared at the wall. "So, you're losing everything with Robert and gaining everything with me."

"No. It would appear I'm only getting half of everything with you, and I'm not sure that's enough. For you, that is."

David fell silent again. He hated it, but her display of nobility—warped though it was—made him feel defenseless. "Okay. I'll file the papers when we get back."

"Are you sure that's what you want? Do you love me enough to leave your wife and suffer the consequences?"

"Regina, all I know is—"

Before David could answer, his body launched off the side of the bed. He slammed to the floor with horrendous force, striking his head on the corner of the coffee table halfway across the room. Lying on an oriental rug, the trauma from the blow caused him to black out for a split-second.

Regina, as if someone had tackled her from behind, flew from the corner of the room. She smashed into the foot of the bed.

The eighty-five-foot vessel rocked in a violent fashion, sending loose items crashing to the floor.

Kneeling against the bed, holding her rib cage, Regina gasped in pain. "David? What was that?"

David struggled to his hands and knees. Blood trickled down his temple as he staggered to his feet. "I don't know. A whale . . . maybe? A . . . a wave?" Using the coffee table as a crutch, he grimaced in pain, holding the side of his head. He looked at his hand. Blood covered his palm. "I need to get topside."

"I'm coming with you."

David teetered up the stairs with Regina on his heels. He flipped on the *Greenback*'s underwater diving lights before engaging the flood-lights positioned at the bow and stern. On the starboard side of the craft, a huge churning of water made itself obvious amongst the temperate waves. They both edged near the railing, straining to see anything that might lend them a clue as to the cause of the disturbance. The last vestiges of an abnormal swell blended into the cadenced movement of the ocean.

Regina pointed at the water. "What's that?"

"I don't know."

Then, in the distance, beyond the reach of the floodlights, a loud splashing originated about a hundred yards away.

David motioned out into the inky blackness as the moon's light dissipated behind a bank of clouds. "Did that sound like a whale to you?"

"I've never heard one in real life. Only on TV."

"Hurry. Go get the movie camera. We might be able to catch a good shot if it comes close again."

"But won't all the lights scare it off?"

"You might be right." David strolled over and flipped the switches.

The two were plunged into an eerie gloom. A spew of light from the quarters below mixed with the last rays of the moon to produce an odd, oily feel to the night air.

"Grab the big flashlight, too. We're gonna need it up here."

Regina nodded and disappeared below deck.

"Flashlight, flashlight, flashlight." Regina mumbled, repeating the word in a nervous chant while searching the cabin's teakwood cabinets and drawers. Pulling on every pewter handle and exhausting every conceivable hiding place she could imagine, she gave up, snatched the movie camera from the dining room table, and proceeded topside.

"Did you find it?" David called from above.

Regina fumbled with the unfamiliar camera case as she emerged from below. "Can you give me a hand opening this? I think the zipper's stuck." She exhaled in frustration and looked up in his direction.

But her distressed eyes never met his.

Her mind never did register his question.

Her breathing, heavy when she attained the main level, became syncopated, staccato-like. Her pupils widened in horror. Starting to convulse, she dropped the case just as David reached for it. The camera smacked the deck with a crunch. She then bellowed an almost inhuman screech.

"Regina, what's wrong?"

Her mouth was numb.

Her thoughts, scrambled.

Her body, frozen.

Her eyes fixed on something over David.

Behind him.

Beyond him, past where he stood.

David swung around on a pivot as it materialized out of the darkness.

A head.

A neck.

Teeth.

And large, menacing black eyes.

The creature emitted a roar like that of an angry lion mixed with the piercing shriek of an eagle about to pounce on its prey.

In one swift motion, the creature lurched at David, snatching him off the deck with precision. The large head crashed into a mast on its way up, snapping it in two like a dry twig.

Regina stood stone-still. She had witnessed it but couldn't believe her eyes. She heard David yell. His voice hit an octave unlike anything from a man as the creature latched onto him.

Then his shout of terror became muffled.

Distant.

Fading.

Until all she heard was the growling, gurgling sound of the monster somewhere in the dark distance.

In a hellish instant, her lover had vanished.

Now, standing motionless and confused, she became at once aware of her ghastly isolation.

She was alone on a boat.

One she could not navigate.

With a monster somewhere out there that knew she was still on board.

Her breathing escalated, and bile rose in her throat. She vomited on the deck, coughing and gagging in a struggle to breathe. She then heard a thrashing in the distance and breathing like that of a whale when it surfaces.

Her convulsions intensified as she stumbled down the teakwood stairs, half-dazed, clutching onto the railing.

She staggered into the main quarters of the boat and looked in all directions, trying to figure out where she could hide. She dashed for the bedroom, jumped into the bed, and covered herself with the sheets, killing off the light in the process, hoping the monster would just disappear.

Several anxious minutes passed before she felt a brutal bump. She grabbed the sheets to keep from falling over the edge of the bed and let out a stifled scream.

She yelled at herself in a hushed tone, "Shut up! If it hears you, it'll tear this ship apart until—"

Another wicked jolt. This time, however, the push came from underneath, throwing Regina into the air a foot off the mattress. She heard something raking against metal, reverberating like fingers on a blackboard.

"Oh, no. It's going to sink the boat. Oh, please, God, please. Somebody help me."

Regina shot sideways. Not her body only, but the entire yacht. The creature struck the water craft with appalling force, knocking her out of bed. Hitting the floor and rolling onto her back, she smashed against the coffee table David had struck with his head moments earlier.

She groaned in agony. Frantic, she searched the room for something, anything that could be helpful.

She spied movement outside, shadows sliding past the window. Just then, an eye appeared in the porthole, peering into the cabin.

Regina closed her eyes and lay on the floor, tremulous.

It was then she remembered the boat's radio at the far end of the cabin. She opened her eyes. The porthole was empty.

Working up enough courage, she rocked back and forth before jumping up and bolting across the cabin. In an apprehensive motion, she snatched the handset from its cradle and pressed the button.

"Mayday! Mayday! Is anybody there?"

Silence.

Is this thing working? She fumbled with the knobs. Static all at once filled the speaker.

"Mayday! Mayday! This is the *Greenback*. Mayday!"

Silence.

Another wicked pounding pummeled the schooner, smashing Regina's shoulder into the wall.

"Mayday!" Her voice squeaked in fear. A full-blown sob began to resonate. "Someone, please help me!"

CHAPTER TWO

Wednesday, 2:24 a.m.
Atlantic Ocean
Approximately 35 Nautical Miles East/Southeast of Fort Pierce, Florida

Micah Gregson sat on the bridge of the *USCGC Cormorant*, peering out the windows at the watery darkness. The Coast Guard cutter was heading for a stretch of water between Florida and the Bahamas—an expanse known for illegal activity on several levels. He wished some stupid drug runner would jet by in a racing boat so he could get his adrenaline pumping at the thrill of the chase. But he knew that wasn't going to happen. Runners were too sophisticated these days, too high-tech. For all Micah knew, the *Cormorant* was probably being surveilled right now via satellite by the very people they were looking for.

For several days in a row, sleep had been a slippery rascal to catch for Micah. Getting to bed at a decent hour was not an issue. Falling asleep was also not a problem. His head would hit the pillow, and the lights would go out, both literally and figuratively. The quandary occurred four to five hours later. It was as if someone tossed freezing cold water in his face. Three months into this foray now, fatigue was starting to take its toll.

It also was affecting his role as Commanding Officer. Coast Guard officers were like firemen and policemen wrapped into one while displaying their abilities on the high seas. It was a rewarding job and a challenging one, too. An officer had to be alert, especially the CO. That's what made this early morning shift so difficult.

Taking a deep breath, he tried to summon some strength before standing and stretching. "Wellman, you've got the Conn."

"Aye, sir. Where you headin'?"

"I just need to get some fresh air."

"Still havin' trouble sleepin'?"

Micah nodded. "I've got my radio if you need me."

He stepped outside the bridge and found his way down to the bow. Lying down on the deck with his arms crossed behind his head, he allowed the crisp night air to bathe his sleepy soul.

For over twenty minutes he enjoyed this bliss until his chief boatswain's mate, Richard Wellman, started wrapping his knuckles on the bridge window to get his attention.

Micah lifted his radio without opening his eyes. "What is it?"

"Sir, we've got a live one," Wellman said. "We just received a distress call from a capsized yacht. Sounds legit."

"Ten-four," Micah said. Not moving, he opened his eyes. He turned his head and searched for stars. In the distance to the south, some were still visible, winking in the night sky. He gazed at them and wondered if there were any alien life forms on faraway planets putting themselves in harm's way, needing to be rescued before they died.

Probably not.

Captain Micah Gregson entered the bridge. "Status report."

"We received a distress call from a woman on board a yacht called the *Greenback*, sir. We're running the registry now."

"What's her location?"

"We don't know. She has been unable to tell us."

Micah grabbed the handset. "This is the U.S. Coast Guard. Captain Micah Gregson speaking. What is your emergency?"

The woman's voice was shrill. "I told you! I'm being attacked!"

"Who is attacking you?"

"I don't know."

"Ma'am, is it a person? A group of people? Is it another boat?"

"No, it's a thing. A large, ugly monster."

Micah looked at his second-in-command and rolled his eyes. "Ma'am, can I have your name, please?"

"Regina. Regina Fleming."

"Regina, can you give us your coordinates?"

"I don't know where I am. Dave was the one driving the boat."

"Who is Dave?"

"He was on the boat with me, but that thing killed him. He's gone. Dave's gone. You've got to help me!"

"Okay, Regina, calm down. Do you have any idea at all where you are? What port did you sail out of?"

"Fort Pierce."

"Good," the captain said. "Now, do you know in what direction you sailed from Fort Pierce?"

"East. We headed straight into the sun."

Micah looked at Wellman. "That would be east, northeast. Get Jensen in here, and let's try to plot her coordinates."

The captain pressed the mic button. "So you must have set sail yesterday morning then?"

"Yes, about seven o'clock."

"What's the name of your vessel?"

"The *Greenback*."

"And who is the owner of the boat, Regina?"

"David Sims. Well, actually, David and Evelyn Sims."

"Good." The captain released the handset button. "Wellman, how are we comin' on that vessel's information? I want to know all about who owns that boat—occupation, criminal history, bank accounts, hair color, what kind of car they drive, everything."

"Aye, Captain."

Micah continued. "Okay, Regina, do you happen to know how far you sailed?"

"Dave said something about twelve miles, but I don't know if we traveled that far or not."

"That's okay, Regina, you've already helped us a great deal. Are there any other vessels in the area?"

"No."

"Can you see any lights on shore? Are there any lights at all around you?"

"I don't know if there are any or not. And I'm not going out to look either."

"That's okay. Are you anchored now?"

"We were, but I'm not sure now. That thing's slapped this boat around a lot."

Micah's demeanor grew more concerned. "Can you hang on just a minute?"

Regina's voice increased in pitch again. "I don't know. Please don't leave me."

"Regina, I'll be listening, but I need to talk to my crew. You just yell if anything happens, okay?"

"Okay."

Micah turned to the bridge crew. "Triangulate that signal and get a fix on her position. Contact Sector Miami and apprise them of the situation. And where is Jensen? I want to see if this ship was set up for SARSAT detection before her battery dies and she can't contact us anymore."

Petty Officer Marc Jensen entered the room just as Micah was concluding his sentence. "Captain, there's a cold front moving in. It'll make triangulation more difficult, sir. SARSAT is our best bet."

Micah paused and scanned the face of every other bridge crew member. "Is there an echo in here?"

The rest of the bridge crew snickered.

"An echo?" Petty Officer Jensen said.

"Seaman, if you had been on the bridge, you would have already heard me say that."

"Say what, sir?"

The bridge crew snickered again.

Micah closed his eyes. Times like these made him long for the private sector. "Never mind, Jensen. Just let me know when SARSAT detection is made and we've got a fix on that ship's position so we can set a course and get a chopper up."

"Aye, sir."

Officer Wellman stepped over to his commanding officer. He spoke in a hushed tone out of the side of his mouth. "Captain, what about the . . . *onster-may?*"

"What about it?"

"A *monster,* sir? Ate the only man on board? Is she drunk or on drugs?"

Micah raised his eyebrows. "Or did she kill him, and now she's going stark-raving mad? Or maybe she's luring us in for the kill . . . maybe we are the target."

"Nice," Wellman said. "I'm tryin' to be serious, and you're the one crackin' jokes."

"So, we reversed roles for once. We've got to have a little fun on this job, Richard. Otherwise, the plight of mankind will drive us insane."

Wellman shrugged. "In that case, maybe the monster is really a terrorist organization that killed the man and is now holding her hostage, making her say all these things."

"Could be. And we would be the target in that scenario, too, wouldn't we?"

"Either way, Captain, crazy story or not, she's unstable."

"I'm not worried about a lunatic so long as she's alone on a boat in the middle of the Atlantic. Besides, if she did commit a crime, the last thing you would expect her to do is call for help, right?'

Wellman wrinkled his face. "Sometimes guilt can be a powerful motivator."

Micah agreed and spoke into the mic while his eyes were still on Wellman. "Regina, can you describe the monster for me?"

"It was huge. Its head was as wide as our boat, maybe bigger. Its teeth were enormous. And it had a long neck."

"Sounds like a freakin' sea dragon," Officer Wellman said.

Starting to respond, Micah let go of the microphone button like it was a hot potato and glared at his second-in-command. "Do you mind?"

Wellman raised both hands in a gesture of surrender and backed away. "I'll just go review the emergency handbook. Section Twelve, I think it is. How to Take Down Aquatic Terrorists."

Micah eyed Wellman like he was looking over a pair of glasses. "Regina," he continued, "what about the rest of the monster's body?"

"I don't know. It's dark outsi—"

Just then, Regina screamed, and the mic cut off mid-shriek.

"Regina, what's happening?" Micah said.

"It's back! It's trying to sink the boat! Help me!"

The strident notes in her voice sent shivers up Captain Gregson's spine. In the background, beyond the wailing of Regina Fleming, he could hear the sound of metal twisting, contorting. If he didn't know any better, he would have thought the vessel had run aground. "Okay, Regina, we're coming for you. In the meantime, we need you to turn on the lights you have. Turn on all the lights. This will make it easier for us to spot you."

"But what about the monster? The lights might attract it."

"They may scare it off, too. But if you don't turn on those lights, Regina, it might be daybreak before we find you."

"That'll be too late."

"Then, please, turn on the lights. Okay? If you want, just turn on the outside lights."

Regina's breathing intensified. "Okay."

"Regina, it's going to be all right."

She didn't acknowledge him.

"Keep the channel open, and come back and let us know when you're finished. All right?"

"Okay."

Regina Fleming set the handset down and moved deliberately toward the staircase. She felt like a fish in a fish bowl. The hungry cat was outside, licking its lips, and now, at the Coast Guard's request, the fish had to jump out of the bowl to turn on some ridiculous lights.

She was a wreck when she reached the top step. Peering above deck in all directions, she listened for that dreaded breathing of a whale. Not hearing anything but the lapping of water against the boat, she bolted over to the console.

When she reached the switch panel, she groped for the switches and banged her knuckles on the metal railing. She wanted to scream, wanted to swear, wanted to yell. Expanding masses of pent-up fear, anger, and frustration oozed from her, about to explode. However, the thought of the creature lurking, waiting for the slightest noise or movement, was enough to keep her emotions in check.

She reached again for the switches, found them, flipped them on, and then scampered downstairs to the radio. Out of breath, she grabbed the mic. "Okay, they're on."

"Very good, Regina," Micah said. "Now, did the monster go away?"

"I don't know."

"Keep the channel open. It will take some time, but we should locate you soon. Thanks for keeping the lights on for us."

Regina, flustered and shaking, missed the intended pun. "No problem."

Micah Gregson sat down in the chair next to the radio. "Well, ladies and gentlemen? Any news for me?"

"Captain," Wellman said, "the *Greenback* is an eighty-five-foot

Nordia Classic Staysail Schooner registered to a David Louis Sims. He is the owner/proprietor of DLS Properties, LLC, of Miami Beach, Florida. It looks like he's a commercial real-estate broker."

"Whew, eighty-five-footer? That's about our size, guys. And she claims this monster of hers is slapping that boat around like a baby in a bathtub? What's the weight of that vessel?"

"According to the Nordia website, Captain, displacement is sixty-six tons."

"Come again?"

"Displacement is sixty-six tons, sir. Full weight is registered at a hundred and forty-five thousand, five hundred pounds."

"And that's before being prepared for departure?"

"Yes, sir."

"Wow," Micah said, "this David Sims is a rich guy. I know I can't afford a ride like that."

Through the speaker of the radio, the Coast Guard crew heard Regina Fleming yell. Her words were slurred by her sobbing.

"Get me out of here! It's going to sink the boat! It's grabbing the front and trying to pull it underwater. There's water in the cabin now. Help me! I'm gonna drown!"

"Regina, hang on. We're on our way." Micah turned to another crew member. "Anything on that radio signal yet?"

"I do have an initial line of bearing, sir. Waiting for exact coordinates."

"Jensen, do we have SARSAT?"

"Still searching for a registry, sir. It's going to take a couple more minutes."

Micah growled, "I want to know where that boat is in one minute, people. Got it?"

"Captain," Petty Officer Jensen said, "the ship does have a locator beacon. I'm attempting to access the satellite now."

"Good. Now, let's hope it was activated before they left port."

Officer Wellman stepped next to Micah. "What if we can't find her in time, Captain?"

Captain Gregson's face, with his eyebrows furrowed, was all the answer his second-in-command needed.

They both listened to the radio speaker. Micah grew more disturbed when they heard Regina scream for help while another grisly yowl blared in the background. Cracking mixed with the monster's long-winded bellow. The captain turned his ear toward the speaker. "What's that noise?"

"Sir, the only things on that vessel that could make that kind of sound are the masts," Wellman said. "There's two. One's midship, and the other's toward the stern. Both are made of wood."

Another hideous noise blasted from the speaker. A roar mixed with a high-pitched shrill.

Regina shouted into the mic. "Help me, please! Somebody help me!" Her screams turned to incessant sobbing.

Beyond the bawling of Regina Fleming, a loud thud and the wrenching of metal was heard.

Regina shrieked again. "Oh, no! The boat's leaning! It's tipping! I can't hold on! The boat's tipping over!"

The monster's sickening howl overpowered Regina's failing voice.

In an instant, the speaker ceased to radiate anything but static and a high-pitched squeal.

Desperate, Captain Micah Gregson fiddled with the knobs to no avail.

All radio communication with the *Greenback* had been lost.

CHAPTER THREE

Wednesday, 8:43 a.m.
National Marine Institute
Miami, Florida

Dr. Evelyn Sims never went home.

Refreshed from a few hours of sleep on a cot in the back of her office and a hot morning shower, she stood in front of a large window. Through the glass—Plexiglas to be precise—circulated over ninety-six thousand cubic feet of salt water. This particular salt water was the makeshift home to twenty-seven different varieties of shark and eel. It was part of a research-based grant for an obscure French company interested in the effects of global warming on marine life. *A waste of United Nations funds,* Evelyn thought as she watched the sharks swim in a carefree fashion around the tank on what appeared to be an invisible track. Nevertheless, money was money, she concluded, and in their business, U.N. monies spent just as well as anybody else's.

"I hate that we have to place these animals on display," Evelyn said. Her hands were in her pockets; her right hand possessing her cell phone. "I came to Florida to study these animals, not parade them—especially for money."

"I understand your disgust, Dr. Sims, and I empathize." Evelyn Sims's assistant, John Spencer, was standing next to her, hands on his hips. "But you know as well as I do that part of this dirty little business means showing off the product for pecuniary purposes."

"You say that so matter-of-factly, John. It doesn't bother you?"

"Of course it does. But I also know that the kind of government grants you desire are hard to acquire in our post-9/11 world, especially as an independent lab. Besides, if you weren't here, where would you go? Where could you go to study animals like this?"

Evelyn sighed. Her expression was one of weariness. "You know, John, you would think we wouldn't have to go anywhere. After all these years in the business with numerous awards for our work, documentaries by noteworthy news outlets, and the development of new scientific technology for studying marine life, you'd think we would have *carte blanche* whenever we needed it, within reason, of course. I mean, for Pete's sake, Oprah did her show here."

"Well, that might have been more of a hindrance than a help."

Evelyn slapped John on the shoulder. "Stop it, you goon. Here I am trying to be serious, and all you can do is crack jokes."

"You know I'm the comic relief in this relationship. Now that I think about it, I'm the comic relief in this whole complex. Without me, this place is like, you know . . ." he said with a shrug. "Work."

Evelyn nodded and smiled, looking back at the tank. "That's the only reason you're still here."

"Thanks, I think."

"You're not just funny, John. You make a good gopher, too. Which reminds me, I need a cup of coffee. Lots of cream, one packet of sweetener, no sugar. I'm on a diet."

"Again?"

"Just get me my coffee, gopher."

John placed his hands together and bowed at the waist before he darted off toward the employee canteen. "You know," he said as he walked away, "I would have thought that getting my doctorate would account for something besides being your manservant."

"It does, John. You're now the Assistant Director of Operations. Now, go operate the coffee machine."

John threw his hands up in the air and shook his head. "I knew I should have gone into international politics. Would have been easier."

Dr. Sims chuckled and turned to face the tank once more, wondering what her next move should be when her cell phone rang. She looked at the screen and smiled.

"Good morning, Bud."

"Hi, Evie."

"So, what's up?"

"I think you need to come up here and see this for yourself."

"What's wrong?"

"Evelyn, I can't explain it. You just need to get up here . . . now."

"Okay, I'll be right there."

CHAPTER FOUR

Wednesday, 9:00 a.m.
National Marine Institute
Miami, Florida

Hours earlier, while the sun was still hiding behind the horizon and before Evelyn Sims was called up to Bud Kensington's office, the *USCGC Cormorant*, an eighty-seven-foot Marine Protector Class Patrol Boat, had located the *Greenback* drifting to the north at the will of the current. The only way they were able to locate the capsized boat in the hours before dawn was with the Search and Rescue Satellite (SARSAT) of the National Oceanic and Atmospheric Administration. The signal radiating from the overturned vessel had grown weak but was still pulsating—a lone heartbeat in a vast wilderness of wind and water.

At the break of dawn, an HH-65A Dolphin short-range recovery helicopter had been sent from Sector Miami to assist in the search for survivors. When the chopper arrived, the crew spotted a drenched woman standing on the bottom of the vessel, clinging to the keel. Hovering over the schooner, they lowered a ladder and expected the frazzled woman to lunge at it. But when the ladder almost smacked her in the head and instead struck the side of the keel, she didn't budge.

"Grab the ladder, lady." The swimmer looked down and shook his head as he positioned the ladder once more.

"She's not going to grab it. You're gonna have to go down and get her," the hoist operator said to the swimmer at the top of the rungs, shouting over the rotors.

"Roger that." The rescue swimmer swung around and scurried down the ladder like a monkey on a branch.

The sun's presence had started to creep over the horizon, creating a strange reflection that shimmered off the water. Ominous shadows danced across the surface of the deep. The wind from the chopper's rotors added apropos sound effects to an already peculiar setting.

When the swimmer reached the bottom of the ladder, he called out to the woman. She was looking the other way, her blank gaze fixed on the ocean. "Ma'am, grab the ladder. I need you to grab the ladder for me."

No response. The woman, still staring at the water, never acknowledged his arrival. Her face was ashen. She didn't blink.

"Ma'am, I'm with the Coast Guard. We need to get you off this boat."

Still no reaction.

The swimmer looked up the ladder. "She's unresponsive. I'm gonna have to get on the boat with her and talk her through this."

"Roger that. Be careful," the hoist operator said. "She could be a screwball for all we know."

"Aye." The swimmer gave the chopper a thumbs-up sign.

The pilot, throttling down a smidgen, set the swimmer on the aluminum hull of the *Greenback*.

The swimmer released the ladder and headed straight for the woman when something caught his eye. Bending down, he saw four grooves running parallel with one another, at least four feet in length. He squatted down to get a closer look. "What in the world . . . ?"

"What's the matter?" the hoist operator said.

"I'm not sure. This hull is all scratched up."

"Could be anything. Let's get this woman and go home, Franky."

The swimmer jumped to his feet. "Roger that."

Still in the same position as before, Regina Fleming's eyes appeared hollow. It was clear to the swimmer now that she was in shock.

When the swimmer reached her, he placed a hand on her shoulder. Before he could say anything, Regina jerked away, spun around, and started uttering crazed, nonsensical phrases.

"It's okay, ma'am. I'm Lieutenant Adams; I'm with the Coast Guard. Settle down."

Screaming as the lieutenant spoke, Regina started to inch away from the stranger, circling the keel, keeping it between her and the swimmer. Her knuckles, white and bloody, grasped the keel in a death grip. Her eyes, wide and paranoid, said it all.

"Hey, we've got a real problem down here," Adams said, keeping his eyes on Regina.

"I see that, Franky. You're gonna have to talk her through it."

"Aye. What was her name again?"

"Regina Fleming."

He turned to the woman once more. "Regina Fleming, listen to me. I am First Class Aviation Survival Technician Franklin Adams with the U.S. Coast Guard. I've been dispatched to rescue you. I need you to climb this ladder with me so we can get you to a hospital."

Regina heard his words, but it was like they were in a dream . . . like she was in a fog . . . or was it a nightmare? She stopped screaming and stared at the lieutenant with quizzical eyes, as if searching his soul. "Who are you?"

Then, without warning, her eyes lifted, above the crewman, behind him.

It rose out of the water.

The long neck.

The eyes.

The teeth.

The water dripping from its enormous frame.

Regina screamed with her hoarse voice and ducked behind the keel. She pointed a shaking hand toward the ocean, but now her voice could no longer emit a warning.

Lieutenant Adams spun around and surveyed the ocean. The chopper's rotors created windswept, circular ripples, but he didn't see anything else. Nothing unusual. He turned back to face the woman. "Regina, there's nothing there. It's okay."

Regina remained hidden, shaking.

Adams looked up. "Hey, we've got a real Signal Twenty here."

"Franky, try it one more time. Use ultimatums if you have to," the pilot said. "We don't have much time left."

"Ultimatums?" Adams said to himself. "Oh, ultimatums." He stepped close to the keel. "Regina, I am with the U.S. Coast Guard. We were sent to rescue you. If you do not cooperate, we will have to leave you here."

Regina focused on the water. "Rescue me? You're too late. It's over. It already got Dave. The monster is coming back. Now it'll get us both. You waited too long."

"Not if we leave now, Regina. We need to hurry before the monster does come back."

Regina shot him a look of horror. Before he could say any more, she lurched at him and grabbed him around the shoulders. "Get us out of here before it comes back! Hurry! Hurry!"

The swimmer moved them both away from the keel, giving her specific directions. He motioned to the chopper to bring the ladder in close. They latched on to it and were reeled in by the other three crew members on board.

A tugboat from the Riptide Recovery Company had been dispatched from Fort Lauderdale, rigged with inflatable braces for supporting the *Greenback* once she was attained. Divers for the company secured metal towing lines two inches in diameter along with the braces before the tug began its slow trip back to the mainland with its catch in tow. The Coast Guard cutter ran alongside, giving aid as needed.

It was this image, broadcast over the major news networks, that Henry "Bud" Kensington was watching when Evelyn Sims entered his office.

"Evelyn, you had better sit down."

Puzzled, she did so. "Bud, you're scaring me. What's going on?"

Bud just pointed to the television that sat on an old cart whose wheels had seized up with rust years ago.

Evelyn began watching as Bud snatched the remote from his desk and turned up the volume.

"As you can see by the picture here," the news anchor said, "the boat is completely capsized. Government officials have told us they will not be able to determine the extent of the damage until they can get the vessel into port. However, we have learned that the yacht, registered under the name *Greenback*, was owned and operated by David Louis Sims, a commercial real-estate broker out of Miami Beach. We have also learned that David Sims was not on the boat when the lone survivor, an unidentified woman, was rescued earlier this morning. David Sims was married, but the whereabouts of his wife are also unknown at this time. The cause of the accident is also undetermined, but officials have not ruled out foul play."

Bewildered, Evelyn retrieved her cell phone and dialed her husband's number.

Voice mail.

She dialed David's hotel in Bermuda—the one where David told her a series of meetings were being held that would land him some huge real-estate deal on the island. He was to be there for a couple of days.

"Good morning, The Reefs at Southampton. This is Jacqueline. How may I direct your call?"

"Yes, this is Dr. Evelyn Sims. My husband, David Sims, is a guest there, and I really need to speak with him. I tried his cell phone, but it must not be getting service right now. Is there any way I can speak with him? It's an emergency."

"I'm sorry, but we cannot give out patron information. I can take a message and have him call you. Would you like me to do that?"

"Jacqueline, please. I can't wait for hours hoping he'll get the message soon. This is extremely urgent."

"I'm sorry, ma'am, but I am sure you can understand our policy. It is for our patrons' safety and security."

"But that's why I'm calling. He may be in danger."

"What kind of danger? Should I call the authorities?"

"No. It's not there; it's here. That's why I need to speak with him before he leaves."

"I wish I could help, but what I can do is put an alert on his account so that if he does not get his messages before he checks out, he will get them then. That's the best we can do at this time."

"You can't send someone to his room and have him come to the front desk to speak with me?" Evelyn said.

Evelyn heard a sigh on the other end. "What was your husband's name again?"

"David L. Sims. S-I-M-S."

Evelyn could hear fingernails tapping computer keys and voices in the background talking and laughing.

"I'm sorry, Mrs. Sims, but we do not have anyone registered here under that name. Is there another name he might have used?"

"What? No. Are you sure he's not registered there?"

"Yes, ma'am. I have no David Sims registered here. Are you sure you have the correct hotel?"

"Yes. He always stays there."

More computer keys were tapped. "Ah, yes, I do have a record of stays for a David L. Sims, Miami, Florida. He does stay here a great deal. But his last stay was over three months ago, according to our records."

Evelyn sat in a stupor. *What does she mean he hasn't been there in three months?* "Are you sure? He was supposed to have stayed there two weeks ago."

"I'm sorry, Mrs. Sims. The last time he stayed was three months and twelve days ago."

Evelyn's voice became distant. "Thank you."

"Is there anything else I may help you with, Mrs. Sims?"

"No. No."

"Have a good day."

Evelyn didn't respond. Instead, she tapped the screen on her phone and stared at the floor before lifting her eyes to the television once more. The tugboat was still dragging a boat behind it. From that vantage point, Evelyn couldn't tell if it was their boat or not. There was one thing she did know, however. David was not supposed to be on a boat. He told her he was *flying* to Bermuda. *But maybe I misunderstood. He could have changed his plans and taken the boat instead. He's done that before.*

Evelyn tapped at her phone again and raised it to her ear.

"DLS Enterprises, Jane speaking. How may I help you?"

"Jane, this is Evelyn."

"Oh, hi, Mrs. Sims. What can I do for you?"

"Do you have a number where my husband can be reached? I really need to speak with him, and his cell is turned off."

"I'm sorry, Mrs. Sims, but he's not here."

"I know that, Jane. He's in Bermuda, right? He was supposed to call me last night, but he didn't. So I expected him to call this morning, but he didn't do that either."

"Uh, Bermuda, no. Not to my knowledge. He hasn't been to Bermuda in weeks. He told me he was going up to Fort Pierce to check on a deal. He left the day before yesterday and said he'd be back later today."

Evelyn felt sick. "When did he leave the office?"

"The day before yesterday. Around noon, I think."

"Okay, Jane. Thank you." Evelyn hung up before Jane could respond. Jane had already said enough.

Evelyn looked up at Bud. Her eyes were wet. She nodded toward the television. "Where did they find it?"

"Fifteen miles northeast of Fort Pierce, drifting with the current."

Evelyn closed her eyes. She dropped her head and gripped her forehead with her left hand. She slowly started to rock back and forth.

And that's when the tears fell.

CHAPTER FIVE

Wednesday, 10:32 a.m.
NMI—Director's Office
Miami, Florida

Evelyn Sims still wept a little. Visions of capsized yachts and hotel desk clerks claiming they hadn't seen her husband in months haunted her.

The office, as drab as one might think for an ex-government billet, was much smaller than Evelyn envisioned when she arrived at NMI. The concrete block walls were painted an ascetic bone color. A typical drop ceiling with acoustic tiles stained in various places from leaks small and large were darkened by years of accumulated dust around the A/C vents. A conference table, stacked with piles of files and rolls of blueprints for expansion plans long since forgotten, sat in the corner with four chairs crammed around it. Straining under the load of thick, scientific books, two bookcases leaned against the wall for some relief while three rusty filing cabinets stood at ease behind Bud Kensington's small, paper-laden desk. His computer, the one technological bright spot in the disparaging dungeon he referred to as his home away from home, sat upon his desk, blinking its flat-screened eye, each wink displaying a new picture of the sea.

Bud sat in his old, beat up office chair. The wheels had been replaced twice, and the right armrest was held together with several strips of duct tape. The casualty of a fit of rage over a fiscal cutback, the chair was a monument to the man sitting in it. When asked if he was going to ever replace the eyesore, his reply was always, "It fits my fat *derriere* just right. Why would I want to break in a new one?"

He had given Evelyn a box of tissues eighteen tissues ago and was now sitting in silence, watching his friend suffer . . . feeling helpless.

"I'm sorry for all this, Bud."

"Sorry for what? You couldn't have known all this was going on."

"I should have. All the signs were there."

"Listen to me. The only Evelyn Sims I've ever known since I hired you six years ago is a tough, reserved, no-nonsense professional. Whenever there's a crisis, I know you can handle it. That's why I hired you. Donald DeMint, the guy you replaced, wilted every time a bill was past due."

Evelyn managed a slight chuckle.

"It's true. Don was a nice guy and all, but he didn't have a head for the business part of this park. He couldn't take the heat. He always said he hated showcasing the animals in a pen for someone else's enjoyment."

Evelyn sniffed. *Sounds familiar.* "I understand what he meant."

"Oh, I do, too. Trust me. But if you want to help these creatures, you have to study them. And it's a lot easier to study them in a pen than in the ocean. Either way, it takes money."

Evelyn nodded. She knew Bud was right, but philosophical arguments were not at the top of her agenda right now. She grew silent and allowed his comment to linger.

"Evie, is there anything I can do?"

Evelyn wiped her eyes. "Just tell me this," she said, still looking at the floor, "why do men do these kinds of things?"

Bud repositioned himself and cleared his throat. The way he squirmed in his seat told Evelyn how uncomfortable he was with the question. "What 'kinds of things' are you talking about, Evie?"

Evelyn looked up at him with an *Are-you-that-stupid?* facial expression.

"Okay, okay," Bud said, "so I do know what you're talking about."

Evelyn continued to glare at him.

"Evie, that's a hard one to answer. There isn't just one reason men —or women for that matter—have affairs. For me, it was loneliness. Out at sea for months at a time makes you do some pretty stupid things. I have three failed marriages because of loneliness. The first two garnered me two illegitimate children in Europe."

"I didn't know you had kids."

Bud frowned. "I'd appreciate it if you didn't broadcast that. No one here knows. Well, no one except you now."

"You know I won't, Bud, but that's why I asked you. You had affairs."

Bud snorted. "Of course, ask the resident adulterer. Maybe he'll give some insight into the minds of those leeches."

"You are the resident expert."

"That's not fair, Evie."

Evelyn dropped her head and started crying again. "I'm sorry. It's just . . . I always had a dream of what my marriage would be like. That's not to say it's unfolded exactly as I imagined it, but . . ." Evelyn yanked another tissue from the box. "Who was that woman on the boat?"

"I don't know, but I have John making some phone calls to try and get that answered."

Evelyn looked up at the TV again. CNN was replaying the scene of the Coast Guard cutter escorting the tugboat that was towing the capsized vessel. Maps of the east coast of Florida in relation to the location of the boat when it was found flashed on the monitor. Ex-naval personnel, in studio as the network experts on such matters, sat behind news desks, dressed in suits and ties, extrapolating their theories of how an eighty-five-foot boat could have capsized.

It was during one of the admiral's conjectures when Evelyn pointed at the TV. "Did you see that?"

"See what?"

"Look at the hull."

Bud leaned forward and squinted. "Where?"

"Port side. Next to the yellow thingy."

"You mean the inflatable brace?"

"Don't get technical with me."

Bud snickered. "I see it. Looks like they ran up on a reef or something."

Evelyn gave Bud an incredulous look. "Are there reefs that shallow fifteen miles out in the Atlantic?"

"No. Fifteen miles out, that direction, the waters are probably thirty, thirty-five meters deep, give or take."

Evelyn stood. She walked over and grabbed a chair from the conference table, pulling it up in front of the television. "Bud, you're not only the affair expert around here, you're also the whale expert. Would a whale act aggressively enough to cause that kind of damage?"

"An Orca could be aggressive enough, but those gashes are way too big to fit the biting radius of an Orca. Besides, a pod of twenty Orcas couldn't capsize a boat that size unless they all jumped on the same side at the same time."

"What about other whales?"

"Sperm Whales have been known to attack people and boats, like the Peleg Nye incident back in 1863 and the attack on the Essex out in the Pacific. But I don't see why one would attack this boat unless they provoked it somehow."

"Maybe they shot at one for some weird reason or hit it with the boat accidentally."

"Evie," Bud said, pausing to get her attention, "stop fishing. You'll get your answers soon enough."

Evelyn's eyes returned to the television. She stared at the four gashes on the hull. Just then, the picture disappeared, and a commercial about feminine products blared through the speaker.

"Just great." Evelyn whirled about. "Where's the remote?"

Bud pointed to his desk.

Evelyn retrieved it and changed the channel. Fox News had similar pictures of the towed vessel. So did MSNBC and several local news stations. Local reporters stated that they were investigating the story and would have coverage on their noon broadcast.

Evelyn sighed. "You know what that means?"

"Already got it covered."

Evelyn's eyes pinched together.

"The doors are locked. The institute has been shut down for the day, and we have security guards manning the gates to keep all the news hounds out. John and I both guessed it wouldn't take long for those reporters to figure out where you worked."

Evelyn smiled. "Thank you."

"Least I could do."

Evelyn stepped closer to the television and stared at the screen. The eyes of the wife in her were beginning to give way to the eyes of the marine biologist. "Bud, I want to go see the boat when it gets into port."

"Are you sure that's a good idea?"

"No, but I want to see the hull, up close, and . . ." Evelyn inhaled.

Bud put his hands up in a halting gesture. "Evie, don't do anything that will make matters worse for you. You'll get to meet her soon enough."

CHAPTER SIX

Wednesday, 4:59 p.m.
Station Fort Pierce
Fort Pierce, Florida

It was late afternoon before the *Greenback* found itself hoisted onto dry land with a boom and derrick ferried in from Port Canaveral. The parking lot between the dock and the building that comprised the headquarters for Station Fort Pierce had been cordoned with police tape and converted into an improvised examination area.

Federal agents from the FBI and ATF, along with agents from the Florida Department of Law Enforcement, local police officers and sheriff's deputies, were everywhere. The scene was reminiscent of an ant mound being disturbed from its slumber. People with badges and guns maneuvered here and there. Some carried clipboards. Others talked into walkie-talkies. Everyone appeared to have his or her own agenda, not caring about what the other people were doing.

Initial examination of the vessel seemed to indicate no foul play occurred, although any evidence, such as blood, fingerprints, and the like, were all washed away. Everything not bolted down or fastened to the walls of the schooner was gone, finding itself a home at the bottom of the Atlantic.

Every government official present believed that the woman's story of the boat being capsized end-for-end could not be confirmed . . . or denied. Neither could her sanity.

Captain Micah Gregson and his second-in-command, Boatswain's Mate Richard Wellman, stood on the bridge of the *Cormorant*, staring at the *Greenback* as it rested on a makeshift dry dock.

"What do you make of it?" Micah Gregson said.

"Not sure," Wellman said. "It does look like something slapped it around a bit. Look at those masts, for example. What could break 'em off like that? They must be eight inches 'round, maybe twelve."

Micah's eyes focused on the commotion surrounding the boat. "You know, the FBI believes Regina Fleming killed David Sims."

"I wouldn't be surprised."

"So, I guess she capsized the boat, too?"

Wellman squinted. "I'm sure she didn't do all that damage by herself."

Micah smiled. "Seriously, what happened? I mean, look at all those agents. I know this David Sims was a big shot from Miami . . . lived the millionaire, playboy lifestyle . . . but why all the hoopla?"

"I asked about that when they interviewed me, Captain. They said it was routine."

The skipper leveled his eyes at his second-in-command. "Routine?"

"Yeah. Can you believe that? The FBI agent told me it was routine—'international waters and all that jazz,'" Wellman said, mimicking the interviewing agent's deep voice.

"We found the *Greenback* about fifteen miles out, Wellman. Those are contiguous waters, not international waters."

"You know, I never caught that."

Micah raised an eyebrow. "That's why I'm the Commanding Officer, and you're just the Mate, Mate. So, did our misinformed FBI agent say anything else?"

"I told him that we were the Coast Guard, and that I had never seen so many Feds unless it involved a famous person or some big-time drug smuggler."

"What'd he say to that?"

Wellman bowed up and lowered his voice. "'You've been watching too many episodes of *CSI: Miami*, son.' That's what he said."

"No way. He actually said that?"

Wellman held up his fingers. "Scouts' honor."

"Unbelievable. And he called you *son*?"

"Sure did. It took everything in me to keep from saying what came to mind."

"Well, maybe Regina Fleming is famous," Micah said. "That would warrant all the LEOs."

"Yeah," Wellman chuckled, "and I'm gonna bring sexy back better than Justin Timberlake, too."

"You know how the chicks dig a man in uniform."

Officer Wellman straightened his stance and adjusted his collar. "I do make this look good."

Micah began searching the crowd. "I want to talk to Regina Fleming and examine that boat myself."

Officer Wellman pointed toward the wrecked vessel. "Better get in line."

Regina Fleming sat on the hood of one of the FBI sedans in front of the *Greenback*. Her feet rested on the bumper, and a beach towel was draped around her.

Encircling her were dozens of law enforcement personnel, asking her questions like a presser at the White House.

Stinking vultures, Micah thought.

Micah retrieved his set of binoculars and scanned the scene below.

The agents and officers would ask questions and then look at each other in bewilderment.

Regina Fleming was unresponsive. Her hair was still a tangled mess, and her eyes were hollow. Fixed on something directly in front of her.

Micah thought it looked like she was gazing through the agents, past them, into another world where sound and sight no longer exists and only visions lurked to haunt a ravaged soul.

He continued to examine the crowd when he saw an ambulance snaking its way through the masses of bodies—law enforcement agents, press, emergency personnel—and stopped a few yards from the enclave encompassing Regina Fleming. Two paramedics hopped out of the cab, neither seeming rushed. They pulled a stretcher out of the back of the vehicle and made their way over to the shell-shocked woman whose cold stare had not changed.

"Great," Micah said. "They're taking her to the hospital."

"Maybe you can interview her there."

Micah lowered the binoculars and leaned on the railing again. "I'll go tomorrow. Maybe all the commotion will have died down by then. Did you notice how she didn't say anything when they were asking her questions?"

Wellman patted his CO on the shoulder. "Why don't we go look at the boat? We're Coast Guard. Who better to help ascertain what happened? Right?"

Gregson turned and looked at Wellman. "Why not?"

"I'm sorry, sir, but we'll need you and your officer to remain behind the yellow tape," the FDLE agent said.

"I'm sorry, I didn't get your name," Captain Gregson said.

"That's because I didn't give it," the agent said, sizing up Captain Gregson with a sneer. "But my name is Detective Williams."

"Well, Detective Williams, it was our ship, that one right over there," Micah said, pointing at the *Cormorant*, "that rescued that lady who was just escorted to the hospital. It was our people who risked their lives—as they do every day—retrieving her from this capsized schooner. So I think that at least entitles us to a general look-see, don't you? Besides, who better to help you figure out what happened than two Coast Guard officers who know these waters better than anyone here?"

"I have my orders, sir."

"From who?"

Detective Williams eyed the personnel darting here and there and then pointed. "Over there. Agent Jackson. The one with the glasses and the ball cap."

"Thank you, and remember, Detective Williams, smiling is free." Micah gave the detective a wink as he and Officer Wellman headed in the direction of Agent Jackson.

"But sir, you can't cross the—"

The two Coast Guard officers ignored him and kept walking, ducking under the yellow police tape.

"Gentlemen!" Detective Williams followed them.

Micah turned slightly but continued walking. "You had better not leave your post, Detective Williams. Someone could walk right up to that boat now, and you'd never know it."

"Gentlemen, stop!"

Micah heard the detective unholster his weapon. He reached out, placing his arm in front of Officer Wellman and turned to face the agitated, armed agent.

"Keep your hands where I can see them, gentlemen."

"You're joking, right? We're not armed, Detective."

Wellman lifted his hands above his head.

A voice came from behind the two Coast Guard officers. "What's going on here?"

Micah turned to find an agent wearing glasses and an FBI ball cap coming toward them. "Agent Jackson?"

The agent eyeballed the two men, glancing at the sleeves of their uniforms. "You must be Captain Gregson and Chief Boatswain's Mate Wellman."

Micah looked at Officer Wellman, wondering how Agent Jackson knew their names and rank. "Yes, sir; that's us."

Agent Jackson motioned with his hand. "You can holster your weapon, Detective. I'll take it from here."

"Very good, sir." The detective turned and walked back to his post.

Agent Jackson removed his cap, slicked his hair back, and repositioned the cap on his head with a sigh. "What do you gentlemen need? As you can see, we're extremely busy here. Lunch was five hours ago, and I missed it. Now, it's supper time, and my stomach thinks my throat's been cut."

"We wanted to examine the boat and try to help you figure out what went wrong," Micah said.

"I appreciate your offer, Captain, but we have some experts coming soon to examine it. Thanks anyway." Agent Jackson turned away.

"Wait a minute." Micah grabbed Jackson's arm.

The agent stopped and glared at Micah's hand. "Sir, I suggest you remove your hand, or I'll have you arrested for battery on a law enforcement officer."

Micah let go and stepped in front of the agent. "Now, just one minute. We're on the same team, right? We work for the same government, right? So let us help."

The agent stared at Micah, emotion being something he didn't seem to enjoy. "You were in Naval Intelligence, weren't you?"

Micah cocked his head. "Yeah. How did you know?"

"It's my job, Captain." The agent turned to Officer Wellman. "What about you?"

"Who? Me? Naval Intelligence?" Wellman shook his head. "I know the government needs all the intelligence it can get, but I have never had the privilege of adding mine to the mix."

The agent rolled his eyes and sighed again. "What is it you want to look for specifically, Captain?"

"Nothing in particular. We just want to help solve the mystery of this ship's capsizing. That's all."

"Well, you were the first ones to contact the Fleming woman, correct? And Riptide Recovery's divers completed the investigation at sea, isn't that right?"

"Yes, that's correct."

"And I've read your report, Captain."

"Already? Man, that was fast."

"I'm good at what I do, Captain."

"I'm sure you are."

Agent Jackson thought for a minute, creating an awkward, anxious atmosphere. He sighed one last time, as if wanting his annoyed state known. "Come with me, though I don't know what you'll find that we haven't already."

The three men strode over to another agent who looked as excited to be there as Agent Jackson. He was holding a clipboard in his left hand. A pencil rested behind his right ear. He stood, swinging the clipboard back and forth, smacking his right hand against its back, looking bored.

"Agent Lowery, this is Captain Micah Gregson and Chief Boatswain's Mate Richard Wellman," Agent Jackson said. "I am giving them authorization to help search the boat for evidence."

"Very well, sir."

Agent Jackson turned to face Micah. "Any evidence you find is to be given to Agent Lowery. Understood? Nothing leaves this crime scene."

"Who said it was a crime scene?" Micah said.

"I did, Captain. Nothing leaves. Understood? Otherwise, I cannot allow you on this boat."

Micah didn't appreciate the agent's condescending tone one bit. "Got it."

"Good. Now, if you'll excuse me?" Jackson gave a slight nod before walking away.

The three men waited for Agent Jackson to round the corner and disappear behind a cluster of people.

"I wonder what's got his panties in a wad," Officer Wellman said.

"Tell me about it," Agent Lowery said. "He hates cases like this. So don't feel too special. He treats us all like that."

Micah was perplexed. "Cases like this?"

"Yeah, giant sea monster. Bigfoot. Abominable Snowman.

Chupacabra. Loch Ness Monster. You know . . . 'Oh my, it's Bigfoot,'" Agent Lowery said, mimicking a fictitious person with an effeminate voice. "'He attacked our dog and trashed our campsite.'" Lowery frowned. "And then it turns out to be a brown bear lookin' for chocolate. That's why he hates these cases, yet they stick him on all of 'em."

"I thought the FBI had field offices that serve their own jurisdiction?"

"For the most part, that's true. They help each other when needed. But Agent Jackson and our team, we're a special unit. We only work cases like this one."

"*X-Files*," Officer Wellman said.

The agent chortled. "Yeah, right. I call us the *Y-Files*. Why do we have to do all these cases? Can't we share the wealth once in a while?"

Micah and Officer Wellman both chuckled.

"So, if Agent Jackson and the team hate cases like this so much, why doesn't the FBI 'share the wealth'? Break up the monotony?" Micah said.

"No way. Agent Jackson's been working these cases since the team was formed over four years ago. He knows more about these creatures than anyone in the Bureau. If the Bureau did that, it would take the replacing agent years to learn what he knows. Besides, I think—and this is between you, me, and the boat here," the agent said, nodding at the vessel, "Agent Jackson groans and complains because all the cases we've covered so far have been bogus or unexplainable. Yet, I think he keeps doing them because there's a glimmer of hope in that rock-hard personality of his that believes one day we'll hit the jackpot. Then, all the hours we've spent will be worth it."

"So, Agent Jackson thinks what? Some natural explanation caused this?" Officer Wellman said.

"He hasn't said. He always keeps things close to the vest in the initial stages of an investigation. But my money's on a big wave. Not a tsunami, mind you. Too sensational. Just a big wave. One big enough to capsize the boat but small enough to eventually die off, flatten out, disappear without a trace."

Wellman peered up at the boat, his face twisted in thought. "A wave? To capsize a boat this size, you'd need a wave at least ten to fifteen feet high, maybe higher, and it would have to strike the boat from the side at just the right angle."

"Right," Micah said, "and that still doesn't explain the broken masts and the four congruent gouges in the hull detected by the rescue swimmers."

The agent tried to justify his reasoning. "The masts could've broken when the boat turned over. Too much force too fast; not enough give to withstand the pressure. Snap!" The agent simulated a stick breaking with his fists.

"Unlikely, but possible, I guess," Wellman said. "But how do you explain the gouges and the woman's testimony of the owner being killed by a monster?"

"The gouges? Possibly by the masts after they broke."

Wellman frowned. "One big gouge or a big puncture, yes. Four gouges parallel to one another, two-to-four inches deep each? Not a chance."

"Maybe they ran aground on something."

"In thirty meters of water?"

Agent Lowery shrugged. "Okay, so the gouges are a mystery."

"What about the woman's testimony?" Micah said.

"Lover's triangle," the agent said. "We see it all the time in this business. Revenge for being used. That David Sims guy? He was a player. Now, he's fish food."

"Lover's triangle?" Officer Wellman scowled at his captain.

Micah shrugged.

The agent cocked his head. "You haven't heard?"

"Heard what?"

"The man and woman on that boat weren't married to each other. They were havin' an affair."

"Of course. We figured that part out," Micah said. "His name was Sims. Her name was Fleming. But that doesn't mean they were having an affair. Maybe they were dating."

The agent shook his head. "We ran 'em both." He flipped through the pages of his clipboard. "David Louis Sims was married to a Dr. Evelyn Sims, marine biologist at the National Marine Institute in Miami. Regina Fleming was, or rather still is, married to a Robert Fleming, a manager of a department store in North Miami."

"Huh," Micah said. "Learn something new every day."

"You see, gentlemen, he's wealthy. She's not. She gets used. He won't leave his wife. It's a classic case, guys. It's *Fatal Attraction* meets *Psycho*, or some weird deal like that."

Micah's eyebrows popped up. "Interesting theory. So, does she kill him in a fit of rage, or was it premeditated?"

"Not sure yet. Since nearly all the evidence has been lost, I'm leaning toward premeditated."

"No doubt, you're onto something." Micah nudged Officer Wellman. "Mind if we have a look around, Agent Lowery?"

"Just remember, gentlemen, notice anything, let me know."

"Roger that."

As the two officers rounded the boat out of sight of Agent Lowery, Officer Wellman put the index finger of his right hand up to his temple and drew circles with it. "Can you believe that guy, Captain? *Fatal Attraction* meets *Psycho*? Takes one to know one."

"It does make you wonder what the FBI sees in some of these guys. How they get through the Academy is beyond me."

"How much of that stuff did you buy back there?"

Micah started up the steps that led to the deck of the *Greenback*. "Listen, Wellman, and maybe you can replace Agent Know-It-All someday. God knows our government can use all the intelligence it can get."

Wellman followed Micah up the stairs. "I'm all ears, *Capitaine*."

"You and I both know that rogue waves big enough to capsize this vessel would come from something detectable. Earthquake, hurricane, whatever. Yet, there were no storms and nothing on the Richter scale in the northern or western hemispheres." They both stepped onto the deck of the *Greenback*. "We also know the seas were calm last night, and variable winds were primarily blowing off the ocean and heading inland. There would have been nothing to stop a twenty-foot wave from making it to shore. And if it had, it would have made news. Right?"

"Uh-huh."

"We can also surmise that the death of David Sims was accidental or involved some unexplained phenomena—"

"Like a sea monster."

"Yes, like a sea monster or some other large creature like a giant squid, for example."

"Aye, the Kraken," Wellman said in a raspy pirate's voice.

Micah shook his head, then pointed his index and middle finger at his eyes. "Stay focused, Richard."

"Sorry."

"Now, David Sims's death couldn't have been premeditated." Micah paused. "Why?"

Wellman thought for a moment and then shrugged. "Uhh, I got nothin'."

"Think about it, Richard. Did anyone know they were out there?"

"Apparently not."

"Exactly. No one knew they were out there except them. If you're having an affair, secrecy is paramount. So, if you're planning to 'off' your lover and no one else knows where you are, why kill him, dump his body overboard, then be left aboard a boat you have no idea how to operate or navigate?"

"It could've been an act of murder precipitated by a fit of rage? They get into an argument, she loses it, she shoots him or stabs him."

"That is a possibility . . . and that would explain her distraught nature."

"Or she could have been playing the dumb blonde routine . . . as a brunette?"

Micah leveled his eyes at Wellman. "Maybe I was wrong about you replacing Agent Lowery after all."

"Hey, that was below the belt."

"C'est la vie."

"I hate it when you speak foreign languages."

"Come on, Wellman. Did that woman we pulled off this boat look like a cold, calculating killer? Or even a woman who would fly off the handle and murder her lover?"

"No, sir. Unless you think it could have been a lover turned psycho ordeal like Agent Lowery suggested."

"No. I've seen psychos, Wellman. I've caught them before. She didn't have the eyes of a killer. She had the eyes of someone scared to death."

"So what now?"

Micah gestured toward the boat. "What are we looking for, Chief Boatswain's Mate?"

"Anything that will show us how the boat was capsized. Find the answer to that, and you have your killer."

Micah smiled. "Houston, we have lift-off."

CHAPTER SEVEN

Wednesday, 5:22 p.m. (EST)
Brennine Pharmaceuticals, Ltd.
London, England

Three men, hundreds of miles away, dressed in immaculate business suits and seeming rather priggish for such a late hour, sat around an African mahogany coffee table sipping tea.

Lounging on a loveseat by himself, Eric Gilliam, the man who had initiated the meeting, was silent. Ensconced at one end, he rested his left elbow on the armrest. His long legs and short body concealed his six-foot-two frame, causing his appearance to be less than formidable when seated. His short jet-black hair, slicked back with gel, gave him a look from an era long past. A tan complexion, inconsistent for that part of the world at that time of the year, made him stand out even more. His green eyes were sunken, almost gaunt, and dark from years of staying up late and rising early, drinking scotch and soda, and stressing about his next move. Yet, although his temporary sagging posture exposed a venerable angst, nothing could diminish his air of authority.

His two visitors, sitting on the full-length couch, grasped their cups and saucers, lifting the cups to their lips while perpetuating the maladroit silence that had filled the room. They, too, were tired but were rapt and attuned to the gravity of the situation.

The man on the right broke the stillness as he set his cup and saucer down on the coffee table. "The reason I agreed to this meeting was because I am beginning to have second thoughts about our arrangement, Mr. Gilliam. What once sounded like a grand plan is now starting to become too complicated for my taste, I am afraid."

Gilliam listened, not showing much emotion. "I hate to be the bearer of dire tidings, Mr. Antonella, but I must remind you that all of us are in too deep now to turn back."

The pinstriped-Italian businessman leaned back, drawing in a measured breath. He crossed his legs, revealing his dark brown leather Testoni Norvagese shoes. "You may be, sir, but I am new to this game. I just stepped onto the field, as it were. I have not even come in contact with the *fútbol* yet. Therefore, I do not believe my coach should hold me accountable for the goals already scored against us."

The man on the left gave a nervous snicker.

"Besides, Mr. Gilliam," Antonella continued, "I have reason to believe I have not been made fully aware as to the nature of my company's involvement. All I know is that our technology in the field of DNA sequencing was a much-sought-after commodity and has been used in a variety of tests under your supervision.

"Now, there's a creature attacking boats that has captured the attention of the world and rattled the cages of my company's stockholders. As you can imagine, that makes me extremely nervous about moving forward. I must know everything, or I am afraid you will have to find another biotechnology company with which to do business."

"Mr. Antonella, I fully understand your . . . introversion? However, I would hate for you and your company to miss out on an extraordinary undertaking. Four years and thousands of man hours have been spent planning for every contingency. Adding companies like yours and others was always part of the original plan. Timing was crucial, though. Add too many at once, and we would have aroused suspicion. So, we bided our time and followed the plan, not deviating at all." Gilliam shrugged with an *Oh, well* grin. "How were we to know that dinosaurs still existed?"

"Isn't that the point?" said the third man in a hearty German accent. "How are we to be sure every contingency has been accounted for? How are we to know our companies are safe? Already one *surprise* has been uncovered. Who is to say more will not come to light?"

"Herr Schmitt, rest assured, we have everything under control," Gilliam said. "Even this 'unforeseen setback,' as you see it, was part of our contingency plans."

The look on Antonella's face was incredulous. "How can that be?"

Gilliam raised his right hand in a calming gesture. "Why don't I call our man in the field? He can give us an up-to-the-minute report. Maybe that will allay some of your fears."

The two men looked at each other, and with simultaneous nods, the German waved his hand.

Gilliam smiled and stood with intent. He walked over to his massive cherry desk and removed his cell phone from a custom-made wooden cradle from Brazil. Flipping it open, he accessed the number, plugged in a speaker, and set the apparatus down on the coffee table.

The three men waited as the connection was made. A noise crackled from the speaker like a rushing wind colliding with a microphone at a concert. "Mr. Gilliam, what a surprise. I have to admit, when I saw who was calling, I was a bit shocked, but what with everything going on, I can understand it. I suppose you've been watching the news, eh?"

"Indeed I have, Dr. Fontaine. Indeed, *we* have, actually. Sitting here with me is Mr. Antonella and Mr. Schmitt. You remember them, don't you, Anthony?" Gilliam cast a knowing wink at his two companions.

"I sure do, sir. How are you two gentlemen doing?" Fontaine said.

"They are doing well, Anthony. They wanted me to call and have you give an update on your expedition. We want to be sure that the advent of this creature you are investigating will not endanger our endeavors."

"Absolutely not, sir. We're in good shape. I've been allowed to get into the necessary restricted areas and make sure no one will ever be able to figure out what happened. If there are any conclusions drawn from this ordeal, they will not point in our direction, sir. I can make certain of that."

Gilliam nodded and looked at the two men. "Satisfied?"

Antonella pointed to the phone. "May I?"

"By all means," Gilliam said.

"Dr. Fontaine, this is Cesare Antonella."

"How are you, sir?"

"I'm quite well, Doctor. I have some questions about this creature."

"I'll do my best to answer them."

"First, is there any way this incident could cause government or U.N. officials to begin questioning scientific theory concerning evolution? In other words, will they think it is somehow flawed in its present state? And will this cause the religious ranks to cry foul?"

"To answer your first question, Cesare, no. Not a chance. Even if this thing turns out to be a bona-fide, true-blue dinosaur, there are enough studies in place to explain its existence within the evolutionary framework. It can easily be used to bolster our work.

"In answer to your second question, religious fanatics are always looking for a chink in evolution's armor. Let them look. Let them cry foul. Their voices were silenced a long time ago. No credible scientific institution gives them the time of day anymore and neither does the press. We also have the university system in our hip pocket, gentlemen, so you have nothing to worry about. I assure you." Fontaine laughed. "You just keep the funding river flowing from the various governments and foundations, and I'll make sure no logs clog it up."

"One more question, if you please, Dr. Fontaine," Antonella said.

"Go ahead," Fontaine said.

"Are there government types snooping around that yacht, asking questions, getting meddlesome? Could our companies be in any kind of danger of exposure by association?"

"No, sir. I assure you, your companies are safe. As far as anyone here is concerned, they believe I am here on my own behalf and the behalf of my institution, which adds another layer of protection for you, gentlemen."

Antonella nodded and motioned to Gilliam that his inquiry had ended.

"Mr. Schmitt, do you have any questions for Dr. Fontaine?"

"*Nein.*"

"Anthony," Gilliam said, "what about the woman involved in this incident?"

"Which one, sir? There are actually two."

"Of course. The woman on the boat and the scientist who was married to the owner. I was referring to the marine biologist. Has her involvement complicated matters any?"

"Well, sir, I'd be lying if I said her involvement has not and will not complicate matters at all. However, she's not very popular or well-respected in the arena of marine biology. Her article in the Journal of Marine Paleontology really hurt her chances at gaining any true respect from the scientific community. So I'm not terribly concerned about anything she will have to say about her findings. But just to be on the safe side, I have someone watching her. If she makes any discoveries that seem dangerous to our cause, I'll be the first to know."

Gilliam peered at his two visitors. "Thank you, Anthony. That will be all. We'll keep in touch."

"Very well, sir."

Gilliam disconnected the phone and sat back in the loveseat with his hands clasped, fingers interlocked. "Gentlemen," he said, "as you well know, I have been able to use my company to help millions of people. We have invented new drugs and improved older drugs to save lives and ameliorate the overall quality of life for people who would have otherwise perished from this planet. In the process, Brennine Pharmaceuticals has made a great deal of money as well."

The other two men smiled and nodded.

Antonella rapped the German man with the back of his hand. "It has been a great ride, no?"

"I feel totally guilty," Schmitt said in a serious tone before losing his composure and breaking into a warm, welcomed laugh.

"Guilty enough to purchase your leading Austrian competitor," Gilliam said.

Schmitt gave a small shrug. "It is a dirty job, but somebody has to do it. Why not me?"

Gilliam chortled. "Gentlemen, this money of which we speak has been provided to us via the scientific efforts of our biologists. In turn, my company's twenty percent profit margin has been invested wisely as has your twenty-four percent margin, Cesare. These monies and others like them have been multiplied almost tenfold. We also have shown our employees we are truly committed to them by creating one of the best working environments on the planet. Our salary structures, benefits packages, and retirement plans are but a tip of the iceberg. The paid leave, vacation allocations, and family-oriented business model we employ ranks our employees number one in job satisfaction in an industry that is typically overworked, underpaid, and cycles through employees like a fast food chain. That is why we have, presently, ten thousand applications waiting to be processed with approximately two hundred and fifty coming in each week on average. Word is out, gentlemen. We own the companies everybody wants to work for within the European community.

"We have spent the last twelve years winning our employees' trust. Now, because of the trust we have engendered, strengthened even further by all the lobbying we do on their behalf for additional funding from governmental sources, institutional grants, and various foundations around the world, I am confident these same employees will continue to study areas we need them to study. They believe they are helping produce new drugs and therapies, and they would be correct.

"That, gentlemen, is the ultimate ruse.

"They indeed are doing just that. But they are unwittingly helping us with another endeavor. An endeavor I was going to tell you about . . . eventually . . . when the time was right. But it seems our prehistoric discovery in the Atlantic has sped up that timetable for us."

Gilliam stood and walked over to a floor-to-ceiling window. He gazed down upon the Thames River. "We are less than two years away from the beginning of one of the greatest revolutions in the history of mankind. All the pieces are now in place."

Gilliam turned slowly and looked at the two men. "Cesare, you and your company's expertise in the field of biotechnology was one of the last pieces of the puzzle. We now have twelve partners total in this endeavor of ours. Partners that are spread across the western hemisphere, lending their aid, their expertise, and their support. I purposefully never had all twelve meet together for fear that someone might take notice. That's why you two are here while no others join us. I have made it policy that I meet with no more than four partners at a time. But rest assured, we are all of one mind. We have the scientific know-how—a *savoir faire* which has covered out tracks quite nicely."

Gilliam pointed to the window. "Monumental breakthroughs have been made that will forever change the landscape of humanity, and we are the keepers of those secrets. The scientific community and the public still believe this technology is dangerous and in desperate need of refinement. Governments meet in their chambers to discuss and decide how far they will allow science to carry this torch and for what purposes. Little do they know, however, that we are light years ahead of any known research. I predict that by the end of Year Six, we will have amassed enough units to begin mass production on a grand scale, and by the time anyone ever figures out what is going on, it will be too late to stop us.

"But that's not all, gentlemen. We have the capital to fund this plan to its fruition and then some. Thanks to the United States government alone, there is a six hundred and fifty million-dollar pot to be stirred. I have been assured that we should garner the lion's share of that pot via our varied interests. Additionally, we should garner funds from pots all over the world as well. That's why I chose the twelve partners I did." Gilliam tapped to his head. "Strategy, gentlemen." He displayed a wry smile. "We also have the political backing of nearly every North American and European government, and even some from the regions of South America, the Middle East, and Asia."

"You're joking," Schmitt said.

"I am afraid not, Herr Schmitt." Gilliam bellowed a sinister laugh. "When people think you are working for the good of all humanity, they open their arms wide . . . and their wallets."

"So, you personally own two companies?" Antonella said.

"No. Just one. It is simply broken up into two entities. The one the world sees, and the one no one knows exists. I told you, gentlemen, this has been a dream of mine for nearly twenty years. Now that technology has caught up with my vision, I have worked feverishly for the last four years maneuvering all the pieces on the chess board. Everything from the pawns to the bishops to the queen herself."

Gilliam strolled over to the wall behind him and pressed a button hidden to the naked eye unless one knew where to look. Straight away, a hatch in the ceiling opened, and a large map unfurled like an overhead projector screen. "We have purchased large tracks of land on the island of Malta, several in the Caribbean chain, and one in Brazil," he said, pointing to the areas in question. "We have been granted a plot of land in Germany, per Herr Schmitt's diligence, one here in England, compliments of the queen, and one enormous parcel—some three thousand acres—in the backwoods of Canada's Yukon territory. On these plots of land facilities are being built that will house in upwards of six hundred thousand people total. And, of course, if we need more land, we will surely get it."

Antonella slid forward. "You never told me all this, Gilliam."

"I didn't want to scare you, Cesare. A plan this grand must be eased into like a bubbling hot tub. Throw you in all at once, and you'll just get burned and jump out."

Antonella was hesitant. "So, for what purpose are these facilities being built?"

Gilliam paused and smiled. "I was afraid you were going to ask that. But I anticipated it as well."

"Afraid? Why *afraid*?"

"Because, if you get this information all at once, it could be too much."

"Try me, Mr. Gilliam. I did not develop my father's little back room laboratory into the largest biotechnology company in Italy by being timid . . . or in the words of my friend here, a *dummkopf*. So, again I ask, what is the purpose of these facilities?"

Gilliam braced himself. "They are training facilities."

"Training? For what?"

"Military training."

"I am sorry, but I do not see how getting involved in military matters concerns us, or more specifically, my company."

"You will. In time."

Antonella faced Schmitt and studied his friend.

Schmitt remained quiet.

"There is something you both are not telling me. And if you wish to keep this alliance we have formed, I suggest I be brought into the inner circle quickly. I have little patience when it comes to people threatening my company's well-being."

Gilliam and Schmitt exchanged glances.

"One last chance, Mr. Gilliam," Antonella said. "What are the facilities for?"

"The better question would be, *Who* are they for?"

Antonella lifted his hands in exasperation. "All right. Who, then?"

Gilliam offered a half-baked smile. "The clones, of course."

Antonella cocked his head, befuddled. He shot a look at Schmitt to see his reaction before turning back to Gilliam.

Schmitt remained motionless, allowing Gilliam to explain.

Gilliam's eyes narrowed, their lean gaze disturbing. "How did you think we were going to overthrow the Middle East and Asia, Cesare? Just ask them for the keys to Mecca?"

Antonella's puzzlement grew. "You are planning an invasion?"

"Eventually, yes. It will be several years, of course. But when the time is right, when the clones have grown at their accelerated rate and their training is sufficient, then we will be ready to launch an assault, in cooperation with the armies of the western hemisphere, of course."

Antonella shot up out of his seat. "You are mad! Everyone knows that the nuclear transfer process for reproductive cloning is fraught with dangers. To produce your six hundred thousand clones, you would have to try the procedure one hundred times that amount. You are talking lunacy."

Gilliam held up his hands. "Cesare, calm down. You haven't heard the rest of the story."

"And what about the clones who make it to actual birth?" Antonella started to pace, ignoring Gilliam's request. "Odds are they will not be normal. They will have horrible, grotesque abnormalities. More than likely, none will make it that far anyway. And if one does, mammalian clones have just died for no apparent reason when appearing to be in excellent shape."

Gilliam walked over to his friend and placed his hands on Antonella's shoulders. "Cesare. Cesare. Let me explain."

"You are mad, Gilliam. You are completely insane." Antonella shook his head and then pulled away from Gilliam, pointing his finger at his host. "I want out. I will have no part in this."

Gilliam clenched his teeth before speaking. "Cesare, have you ever heard of reproductive twinning?"

"Twinning? Of course. Mother and father copulate, and a child is conceived. The cell divides and becomes two fetuses. They develop in the womb independently and are born minutes apart as either identical or fraternal twins. So?"

Gilliam feigned a smile. "Thanks for the human biology lesson, Cesare, but have you heard of *reproductive* twinning?"

"That's what I just explained, Mr. Gilliam."

Gilliam closed his eyes in frustration. He despised faulty communication.

Just then, Antonella's eyes lit up. His jaw dropped. "You're not talking about Dr. Seed and his craziness, are you?"

"No, Cesare," Gilliam said. He opened his eyes. His features creased into a tense expression. "I am talking about taking an in vitro embryo and actually causing it to twin, and even divide into triplets, quadruplets, and beyond."

Antonella's face made a precipitant switch from raw anger to cynical bewilderment. "That's never been tried in the way you are proposing."

"Are you so sure, Mr. Antonella? Two days ago, I bet you would have said that dinosaurs were extinct as well, but *voilà,* we have one attacking yachts in the Atlantic."

Schmitt leaned forward. "Okay, Mr. Gilliam, you have made your point."

Gilliam attempted to suppress his growing rage. "You see, gentlemen, geneticists and biologists have been trying to clone animals and people using cells from parts of their bodies, like skin cells, for example. Then they have to go through the outrageous process of nuclear transfer, like Cesare mentioned earlier. And he is correct. The process is fraught with dangers and raises serious ethical questions. The trick is to do the duplicating after the DNA sequencing has taken place. If they would just wait until the sperm meets the egg and the fireworks start, then the cloning becomes much easier."

Antonella shook his head. "But that is not true cloning."

"Isn't cloning, by definition, the taking of one living being and making, for all intents and purposes, at least one duplicate?"

"Technically, yes. Although some would argue the point."

"I'm not concerned about the point being argued. I'm concerned about creating an army large enough and formidable enough to defeat the powers of the East. It is simply a matter of survival of the fittest, old chap."

"How do you intend to bring these embryos to maturity?" Antonella said.

"There will be two primary ways. Simulated amniotic basins designed to replicate the mother's womb in every way right down to the playing of Brahms and Beethoven, and surrogate mothers dedicated to our cause. The latter being the preferred method, of course. The former will help bring production up to quotas."

Antonella began to pace again. "Where are you going to get all these developing embryos?"

Gilliam laughed. "It is easy, really. There are hundreds of thousands of embryos created every year in fertility clinics and laboratories around the world. They are frozen and left in stasis. They are unwanted and generally destroyed after a period of time. So I have contracted with several of these laboratories and clinics sympathetic to our cause, and they will be our initial suppliers. Our estimates are that we will have more frozen embryos than ways to gestate them in the beginning. However, once some of our female clones reach the appropriate age, they will be enlisted as human incubators as well."

"What about insubordinate clones?" Antonella said. "You know, as these clones mature, they will have minds of their own. Not all will wish to become cannon fodder once they find out their purpose in life."

Gilliam paused for effect. "Sixty-something years ago, a small country—Herr Schmitt could tell you about it better than a Brit—was on the verge of world domination. How did they do it? By enlistment. By socioeconomic and idealogic coercion. Why do you think so many conquered people raised their hands and shouted *Heil Hitler*? It was because they believed. They believed in what Nazi Germany was doing. They believed in their leader and his philosophies. They believed in his desires, his methods, and his madness, even his hatred. And now, we face a similar foe in radical Islam. Mohammed was not only a religious leader. He was also a military leader and a political leader. That is why the West will never defeat these terrorists with conventional means. The Muslims must be destroyed if the world wants peace. And it must happen before their royal caliphate is completed."

Gilliam managed a guileful grin. "So, to answer your question, Cesare, we will only use those clones that believe in our grand purpose. Our clones, and our other allies as well, for that matter, will be indoctrinated into our beliefs. But trust me, Cesare, in four years from now, with the onslaught of radical Islam marching across the face of the planet, people will be knocking down our doors to join forces with us."

"You still haven't answered my question, Mr. Gilliam. What will happen to those clones that do not believe, or do I even want to know?"

Gilliam pursed his lips. "That's the ugly thing about war. You are bound to have collateral damage no matter how well you aim. Those who do not wish to be part of the program will be . . . deprogrammed."

Antonella, massaging his forehead with the tips of his fingers, looked down at the floor. "Supposing your grand scheme works—although I have great reservations about this technology of which you think so highly—governments will not allow it. You will be annihilated before your clones leave your base camps, and that is if you can keep them concealed that long."

Gilliam strolled back to the loveseat. "Cesare, sit down, old friend. Do you think I would even attempt such an endeavor without covering everything? Didn't you hear me earlier? We have the backing of nearly every North American and European government."

"Ahh, but presidents and prime ministers change. Kings and queens die. You could meet strong opposition in the years to come."

Gilliam chuckled as he sat down once more. "Oh, Cesare, you do tickle me. You are where I was four years ago. You are where Schmitt was two years ago, isn't that so, Randolph?"

Schmitt nodded.

"I was there, Cesare. Trust me," Gilliam continued. "Worrying. Asking questions. What about this? What happens if that occurs? But four years later, those issues are dead. I do not trust in presidents and prime ministers for that very reason. They are too fickle, too imperious, and too momentary to rely upon unequivocally. Therefore, I enlisted those individuals who will be there when needed: military officials, intelligence personnel, scientists, backdoor life-long politicians, and the like. I sought out those who would be of like mind with us . . . who believe as we do . . . who are tired of their governments acquiescing to the demands of groups who want nothing more than to see our Western way of existence obliterated.

"And as an added bonus—and this makes my job of trying to sell our plan immensely easier—our enemies keep playing right into our hands. Suicide bombers. Terrorist attacks at public venues. Islamic terror groups forcing people to flee from their homeland, like those coming out of Syria. Economic clout from the Middle-Eastern oil industry willed upon suffering countries. Marxists embracing capitalism just enough to use it to their advantage, causing a major shift in the economic climate of our age." Gilliam tittered. "Nostradamus may be right after all. Worldwide catastrophe may be on the horizon. However, what he did not foresee was our alliance. By the time we are ready, the Western world will urge us on to victory and thank us for eliminating those countries that stand in the way of Western domination."

"How are you going to have an army ready in just a few years?" Antonella asked. "If I understand this new process correctly, a twin, once born, will have to develop like any other human being. Army age isn't usually until eighteen, correct?"

"I'm glad you brought that up, Cesare. I almost forgot to mention it. In the twinning process, one of our other companies has developed a method that involves the bathing of the embryos in some special solution that stimulates growth, thus accelerating the growth of the embryo. They predict that the age of eighteen would occur in four to six years. Eight at the most."

Antonella's look was one of skepticism. "You know you are going to start World War III. The people you plan on annihilating will not go quietly."

"We never expected them to. But several of our facilities will be built underground. Let them bomb if they choose. They know the radiation will harm them as much as it will us. That's why they won't.

"Don't you get it, Cesare? The leaders of radical Islam use weak-minded people to carry out their suicidal bombings, but the leaders never strap on a vest loaded with C-4. Why? Because they enjoy living too much. It is this weakness in their military planning that will serve our own ends.

"As the war rages on, we will still be creating replacement forces in our underground facilities while their armies are decimated. And if they choose to use nuclear weaponry, our contingency will be unscathed by the fallout. Our buildings have been designed with that in mind. Their caves? Not so much."

Antonella, who had seated himself, still rested on the edge of the sofa. His voice was soft and tentative, his energy spent. "What assurances can we have that everything will go as planned until the armies are ready?"

"We enlisted numerous scientists around the world, like our Dr. Fontaine, for example, to make sure the 'machine' runs properly. I also get periodic updates from key military personnel and political figures who have locked arms with us. There's not a day that goes by, Cesare —and I mean that literally—that I do not hear about an event long before the media gets ahold of it. Sometimes, they never do."

"I want to see these facilities you speak of, and for which I am paying," Antonella said. "I also want to see all the research you have on this reproductive twinning. If my company is to be at the forefront of this plan, I want to make sure we are not running down a road to destruction."

"In time, Cesare. In time. I will bring each of you to the facility in Malta soon. One at a time, of course. Once you see that one, you will have seen them all. They are identical in every way. That way, if we have to move a scientist from one facility to another, he or she will already know their way around."

"You have thought everything out, haven't you, Eric?" Schmitt said.

"You see, gentlemen, everything is in place. We are now waiting on facilities. Several are near completion as we speak. I have visited each and every site. Construction and clone development are proceeding as planned. We should be able to harvest our first recruits by the end of this year or the first quarter of next year at the very latest. They will become our generals and leaders."

Gilliam flopped back in his seat and raised his finger. "Oh, and by the way, the front portion of each facility will be used for biological research to continually enhance the cloning process. Think about the possibilities, gentlemen. A wife gets pregnant, and as an insurance policy, has the embryo twinned. Then, the twinned replication is frozen and stored indefinitely. The parents could have the twinned replication at a later date . . . you know, spread the children out by placing some years between them. Another possibility is that they could have the twinned replication frozen and then implanted into the mother's uterus and brought to maturity if something ever happened to the first child. The distraught parents could get their son or daughter back in a mere nine months." Gilliam shrugged. "The possibilities are endless, gentlemen. And who knows, this process may be the very deception we need to keep the plan hidden from the public's eye."

"How is that?" Schmitt said.

"They would view our companies as being on the cutting edge of science. Advancing mankind toward perfection. However, behind the scenes, an army of clones would be trained to assist existing armies from our North American and European allies. An army so large and terrifying, even the Chinese army with its incredible numbers would be astonished."

Schmitt and Antonella laughed nervously.

"You can go back and tell your constituents that all is well,"

Gilliam said. "Within three to eight years, the face of planet Earth will begin to change, and those who have joined forces with us will reap the benefit of the greatest land expansion the world has ever witnessed. Can you imagine how much money a two-story beach house on the coast of Dubai will fetch?"

The two men nodded; their eyes wondrous.

Gilliam's fiendish dark eyes sparkled. "Now, before we retire for the evening, can I get us some celebratory drinks?"

CHAPTER EIGHT

Wednesday 6:12 p.m.
En Route to Station Fort Pierce
Fort Pierce, Florida

Evelyn Sims yawned. "Bud, how much longer?"

Bud smirked. "You sound like a little kid. 'Are we there yet?'"

"I didn't get much sleep last night, and it looks like I won't be getting much tonight either."

Bud Kensington steered around a tractor-trailer. "I guess I should've deferred that phone call from the FBI to another marine facility, huh? So you could get your beauty sleep?"

"Did it have to be tonight? What's wrong with in the morning?"

"Science never sleeps, Evie. You know that."

She nodded and yawned. "Who called you anyway?"

"An Agent Archibald Jackson. He referred to this case as 'a delicate but urgent matter.'"

"I get it. Urgent because of the nature of the incident. Delicate because of me, right?"

"I figured we could kill the proverbial two birds if we went."

"I hope we can, Bud."

"I'm not sure what the FBI has to do with this, though."

"I was wondering the same thing earlier. Why would they be involved unless they think either David or that woman were into something illegal?"

"I'm sure we'll get some answers when we arrive."

Evelyn peered out her side window. She swiped at the tear trickling down her cheek.

Bud shot a quick glance at Evie. "You okay?"

"I'll be fine." Evelyn's words betrayed her heart. She inhaled and closed her eyes in an attempt to block the sorrow. Crying again in front of Bud was not an option. She wrestled with the tears, and little by little while she had been watching the mile markers whisk past, loneliness enveloped her like quicksand. *I'll be fine. Yeah. Right. What a ridiculous answer.*

You'll never be fine, Evelyn.

In the waning months of their troubled marriage, when David would work late or be on business trips to anywhere, Evelyn's job had become her lover, her saving grace on those abandoned nights when the forecast of going home to her empty house always seemed gloomy.

Her love for the ocean was why she had moved to Miami in the first place. That love was why she accepted the job at NMI. She had been a marine biologist first. Before becoming a wife.

In this stream of thought it came to her, on the trip to Fort Pierce. One very important thing rose to the fore: This assignment would be the only way to express her grief. Find closure. Obtain the answers eluding her and solve the mystery. Allow the marine biologist to help. Maybe she can save the grieving wife. Then, they both could cast their wounds into the ocean depths as well.

For right now, though, both were anything but "fine."

One felt all alone. The other had friends. Yet, although Bud and John had tried their level best to console and comfort, the chills of despair still saturated her body.

She was now the one alone on a capsized boat. The marine biologist and the wife. In the middle of an ocean of disbelief. Isolated. Gripping the keel. One looking to the ocean for a killer. The other looking into the soul for her husband. Both searching for answers. To questions neither will ever get to ask.

David was dead.

Micah Gregson and Richard Wellman had scoured the *Greenback* for over twenty minutes. The quarters below were in a shambles. Not surprising, considering the vessel's ordeal at sea. What was interesting to Micah, though, was the lack of evidence. He expected to see furniture strewn everywhere, anything that could be broken or shattered smashed into a million pieces, and saltwater stains in all the carpets and fabrics. Instead, the inside of the cabin appeared to have been cleaned and cleared of anything and everything wrecked and soiled.

There were signs of violence. A dangling handset from the onboard radio pulled beyond its corded limits. A crooked picture with the screws on one side yanked out of the wall. A kitchen cabinet door dangled, almost ripped from its hinges. The dining area table was bent upward, unable to retract to its normal station.

"You know," Micah said as he rummaged through the living room area, "I saw guys hauling out boxes of stuff earlier, and I thought they were taking evidence back to the crime lab. But this is different. If you and I came in here and boxed up anything that appeared to be evidence, there would still be pieces of broken glass, broken legs off this coffee table, torn lamp shades, wet clothes, food . . . something would have been left behind, wouldn't you think?"

Wellman opened the drawer in the living room armoire. "It's like they want this cleaned up so it can be sold tomorrow."

"Follow me," Micah said.

The two Coast Guard officers chugged up the stairs and onto the deck of the *Greenback*. "According to Regina Fleming's brief statement, they both came up here and heard noises off the starboard side." Micah strolled over to the side of the craft. "Then he sent her down to get a camera. When she came back up, that's when she saw whatever it was she saw." Micah grabbed Wellman by the arm. "Stand here."

Micah positioned Officer Wellman where he thought David Sims would have been standing. He then trotted back down the stairs out of sight. "Don't move, Wellman."

"Okay," Wellman muttered to himself. Then he said, "Hey, what are you doing, by the way?"

"Patience."

Micah, step by step, ascended the stairs, examining everything he could. "Now I've got the camera in my hand," he said, pretending to be Regina Fleming. "I'm looking down, fiddling with the zipper. I reach the top of the stairs and call you to come over and help. You come over to where you're standing now. Then I look up over your head and behind you."

Micah Gregson's mind replayed visions of his childhood. He had seen this monster a thousand times. He had battled it in the swimming pool of his parents' old house when he was ten, aboard a sailing vessel from the thirteenth century. He had outwitted it and had been outwitted by it. Struggling against it time and time again, he witnessed its medieval shape rise high into the air. Its glassy black eyes lifeless in their pursuit. Its teeth shimmering as the water dripped from their razor-like edges. Its skin, scaly and wet, writhed like a giant snake. Behind it, only visible for moments at a time, was the top of a large, powerful body, almost entirely submerged, wading, positioning the long neck for the kill.

"Wellman," Micah said, "squat down a little and turn around."

Officer Wellman raised one eyebrow. "Okay."

"Now," the captain said, "picture a sea monster with a neck about twenty to thirty feet long and a head as wide as this boat."

Officer Wellman squinted. He tried his best. "Okay, I think I've got the picture."

"Good. Now you are in David's position, although he would've been facing toward me. I'm in Regina's place. If a creature that big swooped down and latched onto you, he could easily engulf your body with his mouth, right?"

Shivers shot across the spine of Officer Wellman. "Uh, yeah, I guess so."

"Though, like any predatory creature, bald eagle, alligator, lion, you name it, they just want to grab you and secure you. They'll reposition you for their final kill once they feel they have you in a safer place and you're not kicking and screaming as much, right?"

"I guess," Wellman said, shooting his commanding officer a worried look.

Micah laughed. "Relax, Richard. I'm only trying to put two and two together so Agent Lowery will be proud."

Wellman saluted. "We're the Coast Guard. We aim to please."

"Right. Now, the monster grabs you, or if you like, David Sims—"

"Yes, let's use the dead guy. He won't feel a thing."

Micah rolled his eyes. "Okay, so David Sims gets snatched by this creature; the mouth closes down on him and only his legs are sticking out."

Wellman shivered again. "Do we have to be so . . . detailed?"

"Richard, that's the thing about working the ocean. You never know what you'll encounter. And like any crime scene, it's the details that make it so interesting. There's so much we don't know about the sea. That's what got me into all this years ago. The unknown of the ocean. I actually wanted to be a marine biologist growing up. Stories of sea monsters and the Loch Ness Monster and giant squid and overgrown sharks fascinated me. When other kids in my classes were reading Judy Blume and Gary Paulsen, I was reading *National Geographic* and everything I could find from the Cousteau Society. I thrive on the sea. That's why you'll never find me in some cubicle or living inland. I'd die."

Officer Wellman nodded, stared at his captain, and inhaled, trying to muster a stronger stomach. "So, where were we?"

"You were just eaten alive by a huge sea monster," Micah said, placing his right hand on Wellman's shoulder, "legs sticking out, twitching with an autonomic reflex. Quite gruesome."

Wellman's stomach announced its objection to any further scenarios. "Oh, no."

Micah laughed at the discomfort of his crewman. "I'm sorry. I'll keep the details to a minimum."

Wellman exhaled through his lips. "Thanks."

"Okay, now if I stand here," Micah motioned with his hands, "and you're there, that rear mast would have been right in the line of fire."

Officer Wellman turned and surveyed the scene. "She said its head was as wide as the boat, right?"

"Yes, and if that's true, when the creature grabbed Sims, it would've been able to see where it was going when it was attacking." Micah started using his hands to demonstrate. "Weave its head between or around the masts. While on the way up—"

"It *wouldn't* have been able to see," Wellman said.

"Exactly. If its body was out here," Micah said, pointing to an area on the starboard side, "and Sims started to walk over to help her with the camera, he'd be standing about here when he was grabbed. That would mean the creature would have had to reach around the mast to get him. That would be consistent with her report of seeing the head of the thing over and behind Sims. Then, when the creature started to back up, it could very well have clipped the rear mast."

Micah stepped over to what was left of the mast in question, moving around it as if positioning himself as the creature. Then he stepped back and used his hand like a golfer lining up the winning putt to determine where the mast would have fallen.

He marched over to the starboard side and began examining the boat. He searched for well over five minutes but saw nothing. "Huh.

That's not the way it happened. There would also be damage to the bridge or the starboard side of the boat if it was."

Officer Wellman frowned. "Maybe her story is just that, Captain. A story."

"Perhaps." Micah raised his right index finger. "But, what if . . ." He motioned for Officer Wellman to follow him. "Let's try this again."

He repositioned Wellman and himself back in the original places. "Now, what if the creature was farther out, and toward the front of the boat more? I was originally thinking it would come up almost perpendicular to the boat. But what if it stayed out farther? Say, ten to twenty feet off either the starboard bow or the port bow? That would fit the Fleming woman's story of it coming up from behind Sims's head, too. Then, when it lurched back after attacking Sims, it would have hit the midship mast and not the one in the aft."

"That makes for one long neck, Skip."

"Yeah. You're probably right. So maybe it came up alongside but was still parallel to the boat instead of perpendicular."

Micah turned toward the bow and lined up the midship mast as he did the rear mast minutes prior. Seeing something, he bolted to the bow. "Aha! See this, Wellman?" He touched the railing.

Knowing the situation—in this case, the capsizing of the boat, Micah surmised a dent like this particular one could have been, and no doubt was, attributed to something of considerable weight hitting the railing in a violent manner. Agent Lowery would have blamed a phantom wave. But the damage was too specific, for lodged in the rounded impression was another piece of wood unlike that of the railing. Micah reached into his pocket and pulled out his trusty Buck knife. He opened the blade and with a surgeon's precision extracted the evidence from the balustrade.

"Look at this," Micah said. He held the three-inch sliver of wood up to the waning rays of the evening sun.

Wellman came close and examined it with younger, more precise vision. "Looks like mast wood to me."

"Let's see." Micah ambled over to the mast's stump and held it out with the finished side facing out. "Perfect match," he said, shaking his head. "Isn't that amazing? This little piece of wood stayed in place through the entire trip back to port."

Wellman nodded. "So, the woman's story may not be a story after all."

"It would appear so."

"Do you realize what we're saying?"

Micah nodded. "That out there, somewhere in the depths of the Atlantic, is a sea monster?"

"Yes, Captain. Now go and report that to Sector Miami and see if they don't send you to McLean."

"McLean?"

"A psychiatric hospital from my neck of the woods. A lot of famous people go there. They have some real nut jobs, too. In their eyes, with that story, you'd fit right in."

"You think I'm crazy?"

"Let's put it this way. You had better come up with a whole lot more evidence than a little sliver of wood before you start telling people about medieval sea dragons. That's all."

Micah shook his head in dismay. "Wellman, did you actually think I was going to rush out and announce to the world that we had solved the case? This is merely the first piece of the puzzle that will either prove or disprove Regina Fleming's story." He started to walk away, then turned back around. "Wow, you've sure got a lot to learn."

Officer Wellman held out his hands, palms up. "Sorry, I just thought—"

"That's what you get for thinking, Wellman. Too much thinking and talking, not enough listening."

"Hey, that's another one below the belt."

"You work for the government, don't you? Get used to it."

"Are you going to turn that sliver of wood in to Agent Lowery?"

"Why? So he can throw it into a box and corroborate his wave theory? No."

"But Captain, this is a federal investigation. You're withholding evidence. That's a—"

"Thanks for the judicial lesson, Wellman. But sometimes—and you'll learn this if you stay in the service long enough—you have to play by the rules of engagement, not the rules of the game."

Wellman shrugged. "Meaning?"

"In a game, there are rules that both sides play by. If one team member breaks one of the rules, he or she gets penalized. However, the rules of engagement dictate that there are no hard and fast rules when the greater good is at stake. As a matter of fact, as is often the case, more rules get broken than followed."

Officer Wellman was still befuddled.

Micah sighed. "Richard, somebody's not playing by the rules. You saw that cabin. You're not supposed to sweep a crime scene clean like that. It's like there was evidence in there that someone *didn't* want others to see. Something else is going on here, and until we find out what, there's going to be two games played simultaneously. Understand now?"

Wellman winked. "Gotcha."

"Good. Now, let's go look at those scratches on the hull."

CHAPTER NINE

Wednesday, 8:10 p.m.
Station Fort Pierce
Fort Pierce, Florida

The National Marine Institute's Ford Explorer rolled up to the gate of the Coast Guard Station. It had been a long, emotional day already, yet, Evelyn Sims knew the day was just beginning.

An officer appeared out of the guard shack, holding up his right hand. A firearm rested in its holster, in clear view for even clearer reasons.

Bud lowered his window.

The officer leaned in to see Evelyn's face. "How may I help you, sir? Ma'am?"

"We're here at the request of the FBI." Bud handed the officer their credentials.

The officer took the information, held each piece up, and studied the faces on the driver's licenses and identification cards, glancing back and forth between the IDs and the visitors.

"Just a moment, please." The guard then stepped through the doorway of the guard shack, picking up the telephone.

In a minute, the officer handed their credentials back. "Agent Jackson is waiting for you. He said to pull up next to the boat." The officer motioned for them to proceed while another guard slid a heavy wooden barricade out of the way.

Evelyn noticed Bud glancing at her several times as they approached the *Greenback*. He monitored her expression while trying not to run over the myriad of people scattered across the dock. She also witnessed people, standing outside the police barricades to their right, pointing at their SUV, seeing the NMI insignia emboldened on the sides. *Great,* she thought. *Now the press knows I'm here.*

Melancholic, Evelyn didn't move as the Explorer came to a stop. Her eyes scanned the *Greenback* from bow to stern and back again. She drew in a shaky, measured breath and blew it out through her lips.

Bud's hands remained on the steering wheel. "You gonna be okay, kiddo?"

Evelyn sat silent for several seconds, then said, "We've been married six years, and I've only been on that boat once for a short trip from Miami to Key West and back. We had a great time." A slight smile emerged. "We snorkeled. We swam. I even got close enough to touch a dolphin before it bolted away."

"That's nice, Evie."

"It was a wonderful experience," she said, continuing as if Bud had never spoken. "I wanted to go on other trips, but David's business made it next to impossible. I thought David hadn't used the boat in months. But when I left NMI earlier, I didn't go home like I said I was going to. I went to David's office instead." Her eyes misted as she glanced at Bud. "I had to know."

"What did you find, if you don't mind me asking?"

"No less than thirty-seven times when David had used the boat in the last three years. And it didn't just make port in Miami, either. I found payments on three different slips. Three different ports. There may be more, but the one here in Fort Pierce was purchased over a year ago." She looked away and wiped her eyes.

"I'm so sorry, Evie."

"You don't have to be sorry." Evelyn swallowed hard, chasing back her emotions. "I just wonder what other disconcerting stories this boat's gonna tell us."

"Do you need a little more time?"

Evelyn shook her head, finding her vocal cords a little knotted.

"Let's go, then, shall we?" Bud said. "Let's get this over with."

They got out, grabbed their bags and equipment out of the back, and sauntered around to the front of the SUV, waiting for Agent Jackson. From behind them, they heard a voice. A man wearing glasses and a ball cap strode their way, hand extended.

"Dr. Kensington. Dr. Sims. I'm Agent Archibald Jackson, FBI. Boy, am I glad you're here. These news reporters are driving me insane. You gave me a good excuse to leave."

Bud shook the agent's hand. "Agent Jackson, we would really appreciate it if you could keep the press away from Dr. Sims. I'm sure you can understand why."

"Of course. Actually, it's already done. That's why they're back there behind the yellow tape."

"Thank you," Evelyn said.

"You're welcome," Agent Jackson said with a sorrowful smile. "I hesitated to even call you considering the circumstances. I almost contacted the Oregon Institute of Marine Biology. I've worked with them several times, but I felt it would be better to get an Atlantic Ocean institute instead." He touched Evelyn's arm and looked her squarely in the eye. "This incident won't be too difficult for you, will it, Dr. Sims?"

Evelyn lifted her chin. "I'm hoping that being here will help us both."

Agent Jackson nodded with a pursed lip. "Let's get started. Right this way."

As the three approached the vessel, a weary agent jumped up and assumed his post, standing at attention and clutching a clipboard.

"Agent Lowery, this is Dr. Kensington and Dr. Sims," Agent Jackson said. "They are from the National Marine Institute in Miami. They are to have anything and everything they need, understood?"

"Yes, sir."

"Agent Lowery, we will be top deck if you need us."

"Yes, sir."

Agent Jackson spoke as he escorted Evelyn and Bud to the steps. "Agent Lowery is responsible for logging in and out any evidence that is found as well as keeping some semblance of order when it comes to managing the number of people on and around the boat. That's why I introduced you to him. Anything and everybody who enters or leaves this boat must be cleared through him."

"Why all the security measures?" Bud said.

"It's routine when we have a case like this in international waters."

"International waters?" Evelyn said. "This boat wasn't found that far out to sea, was it?"

"That's right," Bud said. "I was told it was found about fifteen miles out."

"Where the boat was found is not officially international waters. But in matters like this, the government doesn't quibble about whether or not the vessel was found inside or outside the twenty-three-mile boundary of 'international waters.' Homeland Security changed that rule after 9/11. It makes it simpler for law enforcement purposes."

"I can understand law enforcement needing to monitor waters out farther than the established twenty-three," Evelyn said, "but what would that have to do with this boat or my husband?"

The agent stopped and sighed. "Dr. Sims, I don't know quite how to say this without appearing blunt."

"Don't waste your pleasantries on me, Agent Jackson. I'm a big girl. And today, I've grown up a whole lot more than I have in the last six years." Evelyn cocked her head at the agent. "Trust me."

Agent Jackson managed a diffident shake of his head. "I was hoping we wouldn't have to cross this bridge until later, but . . . here's go nothin'." He pulled his ball cap off and raked his fingers through his hair. "We've been monitoring your husband's activities over the last two years. Let's say his business dealings are not altogether stellar."

Evelyn grunted. "Surprise."

"We have linked him to the selling of properties in the Bahamas that were underworld-related. The proceeds of those sales were washed a few times, but they finally went straight to the Middle East and the backing of Islamic terrorist activity. And now that he's dead, we'll have to account for . . ." Jackson paused. "Well, I'm sure you can fit the pieces together."

"Oh, wonderful," Evelyn said. "You're going to be tearing my house apart now, aren't you?"

Agent Jackson offered an expression of feigned empathy. "That's next, yes. But trust me, Dr. Sims; I will be there to personally oversee the investigation. And I will make sure you are as well. That's one of the reasons I had you come with Dr. Kensington. If you had stayed, my supervisor would have wanted to search your house immediately. Instead, I was able to postpone that until I get there. In the meantime, we have agents staked outside your house to make sure no one gets in or out."

"Please believe me, Agent Jackson, when I say that even though David and I were married, for the last couple of years we lived almost separate lives. I knew nothing of his business dealings. Had I known, I probably would have turned him in myself."

Agent Jackson pivoted his head and peered at Evelyn out of the corner of his eye. "I believe you, Dr. Sims."

"You said that so matter-of-factly," Evelyn said.

"Suffice it to say that we've had your house and Mr. Sims's offices under surveillance for some time."

Evelyn sniffed and stared at Bud. "Unbelievable."

"It was part of our investigation."

"If you've been watching our house so closely, how did you *not* know David was out in the ocean sleeping around with some bimbo?"

Agent Jackson sighed again. "Your husband must have caught wind of our surveillance. He was able to elude our agents in a shopping mall two days ago. As a matter of fact, his car is on its way to our crime lab as we speak."

"She helped him escape, didn't she?"

"Dr. Sims, I'm really not at liberty to say at this time. Besides, at this point, it would all be conjecture, and that's not a good way to investigate anything. Now, if we can move on with our investigation of the boat, I'd like to show you the hull specifically."

Evelyn Sims straightened her stance. Her lips thinned. "Fine. Let's get this over with."

Bud placed his hand on her shoulder. "You okay, Evie?"

She glared at him before shaking her shoulder lose. "Do I look okay, Bud?"

That was all the answer Bud Kensington needed.

Micah Gregson and Richard Wellman walked back and forth, examining the hull, one on each side. Along the keel, about fifteen feet from the bow, four gouges, all parallel with one another, were detectable from a distance. The rest of the hull, except for a couple of dents here and there, was still in great shape despite its ordeal. The damaged area, unfeasible as it seemed, appeared at first glance to have been caused by the boat running aground on some jagged rocks or reef. The edge of each groove was frayed and ragged. No two gouges' edges looked identical. Each one differed somewhat from the others. It was as if claws had slashed at the *Greenback*'s belly, Micah thought.

Officer Wellman moseyed back to the area of the only real damage. "This is a pretty thick hull, Captain, for a schooner." He wrapped on the hull with his knuckles. "It would take some force to puncture it like this."

Micah Gregson, still scouring the hull for other signs of violence, tapped on the hull as well and then met up with Wellman. "That's what doesn't make any sense. About the only thing that could cause this would be sailing straight into a reef or a rocky shoreline. But we know that's impossible."

"Maybe there's a reef out there that we don't know about, Captain. It wouldn't be totally preposterous to have a reef develop undetected."

Micah craned his neck for a better view of the hull. "True, but could one grow ninety feet high in less than twenty-five years?"

"Probably not."

"My point exactly. Some pretty detailed maps were done in 1993 by the Department of Defense's mapping agency in cooperation with the Netherlands. That means a reef in that vicinity would've had to grow like a tower ninety feet high in about twenty-five years or so." Micah swiveled to meet his second-in-command's eyes. "Ain't happenin'."

"Okay, so, we have six-inch-deep gouges in the hull. Can't be a reef. Can't be rocks. Can't be a tsunami-like wave. There isn't any evidence of an explosion, so it can't be that. No evidence of the boat being hit by a torpedo or rammed by another boat, so that's out. Yet, there are four gouges in the hull." Wellman snorted. "It's got me stumped."

"Me, too." Micah grunted, trying to get a closer look at the damage without getting on his knees and sullying his uniform. "Hey, wait a minute. What's this?" He pulled out his pocketknife once more and started digging into the hull.

Officer Wellman bent over, trying to see. "Uh, Captain, I don't think the FBI will be too pleased if you ruin those gouges. That would be like contaminating a crime scene."

Micah groaned as his body became contorted even more. "I'm being very careful, Wellman. Hey, keep your eyes open, will ya? If you see someone coming, let me know."

Wellman stood with his palms turned upward. "Great. Now I'm an accomplice."

"We're not robbing a bank, Wellman."

"No." Wellman leaned over and whispered under the boat. "We're robbing a crime scene."

Micah snickered. "Didn't Agent Jackson say that if we found any evidence, we were to let them know? Give it to Agent Lowery?"

"Like you did with that sliver of wood?"

"What sliver of wood?"

Wellman smiled and scanned the area. "Oh, yeah. What sliver of wood?"

"You're learning."

Micah repositioned himself. His left leg was going to sleep. He dug a little more, scraping the hull with the knife.

Wellman's gaze skittered around the perimeter like a nervous juvenile lookout standing on the curb while his buddies committed the convenience store robbery. "That doesn't sound good."

"Ah, there it is," Micah said with a grunt.

Wellman squatted. "There's what?"

Micah moved out from under the boat and stood, grabbing his back. "I've got to get back in the gym." He then held up the object.

Officer Wellman stood with Micah and stepped closer. "That looks like a giant tooth."

Holding it up, Micah brought his pocket knife next to it, blade extended, making the knife five inches in length. "It's got to be eight inches long. And look at the serrated edge." He ran his finger along its length. "Ouch!" Micah looked at his finger; an infinitesimal amount of blood pooled on the surface. "That felt like a needle prick."

"I'm no marine biologist, Skip, but a tooth that big had to have come from one big mouth."

Micah laughed. "You think?"

At that juncture, three people's voices became audible. The two Coast Guard crewmen heard footsteps approaching the port side of the craft. Micah folded his knife and slid both the knife and the tooth into his pants pocket before brushing down his uniform.

Agent Jackson, seeing the legs of two people standing on the other side of the boat, bent down and called out, "Is that you, Captain Gregson?"

Micah Gregson and Officer Wellman both peered under the vessel.

"Oh, hi, Agent Jackson," Micah said. "You still here?"

"Where else would I be?"

"Oh, I don't know. Getting something to eat maybe?"

"Already done. Hey, Captain, can you come over here for a minute? I've got some people I'd like you to meet."

"Captain Micah Gregson," Agent Jackson said, pointing, "Chief Boatswain's Mate Richard Wellman, this is Dr. Henry Kensington and Dr. Evelyn Sims. Doctors, the captain and chief boatswain's mate were on the cutter that made first contact with the survivor. They also conducted the preliminary examination of the boat while still at sea."

Captain Micah Gregson extended his hand, but it was his eyes that were fixed on Evelyn Sims. "Nice to meet you." He shook her hand first and then Bud Kensington's.

Agent Jackson continued. "Dr. Kensington and Dr. Sims are here representing the National Marine Institute, and—"

Micah pointed at Evelyn. "NMI, out of Miami, right? You were the marine biologist a couple of years ago who experimented with the hyperbaric biosphere."

Evelyn blurted a nervous laugh, flattered that someone outside the field of marine science noticed. "That was me."

Micah reached out to shake her hand again. "Oh, I'm really glad to meet you. We've got to talk later."

Evelyn blushed. "Okay."

Then, as if Micah's eyes couldn't get any bigger, he pointed at Evelyn again. "Sims, not the Sims related to—" He pointed at the boat.

"Yes," Evelyn said. "David Sims was my husband."

"Dr. Sims," Micah said, "I—I'm so sorry."

Evelyn shrugged. "Don't be."

"Well, gentlemen," Bud said, "Agent Jackson was telling us that you had requested to examine the boat for evidence."

"We did," Micah said.

"Did you find anything?"

Officer Wellman cleared his throat.

Micah looked at him, wanting deep down to ring his neck. Instead, he smiled and turned back to Bud. "Well, yes and no, actually."

"And what does that mean exactly?" Agent Jackson said.

Micah stalled for time to organize his thoughts. "We examined the quarters down below first. What we found there was really all about what we didn't find."

Bud squinted. "Huh?"

"Everything has been cleaned up. I mean, there is still some damage visible, but everything that wasn't bolted down is gone. The curtains, carpets, and fabrics look like they haven't seen any salt water. It's weird."

Bud turned to Agent Jackson. "Is this true?"

"All the items Captain Gregson is referring to are now in the possession of the FBI. We've taken them to the crime lab at our Miami Bureau for further analysis."

"And what about the carpets and curtains?" Micah said.

"Those are just as we found them."

"So, you found them cleaned?"

Agitation rose in Agent Jackson's words. "Captain, let me remind you that this is an ongoing investigation, and you are here as guests, not as members of the investigative team."

"But what about Dr. Sims here? I'm sure she wants this investigated properly more than any of us."

Evelyn raised her left hand, setting her duffel bag down. "Look, gentlemen, I'm sure we all have my best interest at heart. I'm sure we all want to solve this mystery. Captain," Evelyn said, facing him, "Agent Jackson already told me that the investigation is going well, and that they have several leads and theories. Please, let's work together."

Micah inhaled and held it before letting it out. "Okay."

"Thank you," Evelyn said. "Now," she told Bud, "let's look at that gash in the hull."

Officer Wellman turned and stood at attention. "Captain, permission to be dismissed, sir?"

Micah straightened his stance and saluted. "Granted." He then turned toward Evelyn. "I think I'll retire for the evening as well. It was nice meeting you," he said with handshakes before leaving.

Walking away, Micah glanced over his shoulder for no other reason but to get one more glimpse of Evelyn Sims. He expected to see her examining the boat, searching for clues. But when he turned, their eyes met once more.

CHAPTER TEN

Thursday, 7:27 a.m.
Atlantic View Beach Club
Fort Pierce, Florida

Micah Gregson couldn't sleep. All night he tossed and turned in his beachfront condo along North Highway A1A. It was an opulent place, but the lavishness couldn't calm him. Many of his friends and colleagues often joked, saying Captain Gregson must have been muling drugs over the Mexican border in his California days to be able to afford such digs.

It was a witticism not well appreciated by the skipper, since the condo came at the expense of his paternal grandfather's death. Paid for, Grandpa G's place was easy to sell. The location didn't hurt either. Ocean View Boulevard in Pacific Grove was always coveted by real-estate hounds sniffing for a huge sale. Grandpa G's will ordered the sale of the house, with half of the money being split between his two children and the remaining half being split between his five grandchildren. When you sell a twenty-seven-million-dollar home on the Pacific Ocean, with its own eighteen-hole golf course designed by Lee Trevino, and then split half of that five ways, drug running is not needed to buy a condo in Fort Pierce.

On the balcony, overlooking the surf and sunrise in just a pair of shorts, Micah couldn't get the evidence on the *Greenback* out of his head. Getting a two-a.m. head start, he had drunk a full pot of coffee, and his former Naval Intelligence training was in full swing now. Things weren't adding up, though. Several items troubled him. The cleaned quarters of the *Greenback*. The damaged railing. The talk of international waters. The gouges in the hull.

And the tooth.

Micah stepped inside and picked it up. The tooth had sat dormant on the table for the better part of an hour. It was easier to examine now that the sun was up.

Earlier, with the tape measure still sitting on the table, he had measured it—eight and three quarters inches long, almost an inch and a half wide at the base. Micah wondered how long the tooth had been while still in the mouth of the beast, for the tooth looked like it had been broken off. The edge of the base wasn't smooth like a normal tooth is when it falls out to be replaced by another. Micah had seen shark teeth that came out by natural means. This one was different. The edge was higher on one side than the other, and the entire circumference was jagged.

Micah began talking to himself, working through the details, motioning with his right hand, pretending it was the mouth of the serpent. "If the creature bit the hull from underneath, then where are the other teeth marks?" He began replaying the scene from the night before. He was squatting under the boat. Wellman was standing next to the boat, looking more nervous than a scared rabbit in a den of wolves.

Then, without any forewarning, he envisioned Evelyn Sims. He saw her smile . . . her bright white smile . . . her shoulder-length hair with its crimped curls . . . her radiant hazel eyes . . . her glistening lips—

"Stop it!" he said to himself. "Just stop it."

In disgust, Micah grabbed an apple off the table. It had been the subject of an experiment over two hours ago. He gripped the fruit with his right hand. There were bite marks all over the skin of the fruit. *Whenever you bite down on something,* he thought, *there are two sets of teeth marks, top and bottom, but I didn't see a second set of marks.* He jumped up and went inside, snatching the phone from its cradle.

"Hello," came the sleepy voice on the other end of the phone.

"Richard, this is Micah. Did I wake you up?"

"Since we work through the night, like we did two nights ago," Wellman said, yawning, "and then don't get to bed until the following night, then yeah, I'm usually asleep at . . . oh, man, seven forty-five? Really?"

"Get over it, Wellman. You can sleep later."

"You've been up all night, haven't you?"

"How could you tell?"

"You're too perky. You're on a caffeine drip, aren't you?"

"No. Just one pot since midnight," Micah said. "Get dressed. We've got to go check something out on the *Greenback*. We missed something."

"What? No, I'm not getting dressed, and I'm not going with you to go check out the boat again. You just want to go see if that Evelyn doctor chick is there."

"That's not true. We did miss something. The tooth we found last night—there should have been more gouges than that."

"Huh?"

"I was eating an apple, and—"

"Hey, I'm glad to hear your Naval Intelligence is alive and well, and that your eating habits are improving, but I'm going back to sleep. We're off the clock. So, I'll call you later, when I'm better rested and really give a flip." Wellman hung up.

Micah stared at the phone, listening to the busy signal. "Oh, no you didn't. You wait, Officer Wellman. You know what they say about paybacks."

Clad in his uniform, Micah arrived at the dock of Station Fort Pierce, thinking he'd get farther wearing his dress whites than he would in civilian clothes. Strolling up to the *Greenback*, he was hoping he could just go to the hull, inspect it, and leave.

He scanned the area from the perimeter and noticed the total number of agents and press reporters had dwindled a great deal. Good news. Maybe interruptions would be minimized. Check-in, check-out. Get in, get out. With one last scan, he marched across the asphalt toward the boat.

"Captain, what brings you down here so early in the morning?" Agent Lowery stepped out from an improvised shelter comprised of pieces of wood, cardboard, and a beach towel. It sat in the same place the agent stood yesterday—an obvious crack at beating the sun. Micah never saw him.

Wow. I've been out of the NI game too long. "Me? What about you? Did you sleep down here last night?"

The agent chuckled. "I got three hours in the front seat of the car. What a life."

"Sorry to hear that," Micah said. *But it was more than I got last night.* "Hey, can I get one last look at the boat here? I was thinking about something and wanted to check it out."

"Sure. I take it you didn't find anything last night?"

"Nothing of consequence."

The agent squinted. "You never know, Captain. Sometimes it's the little things that crack a case wide open."

"Oh, you don't have to tell me. I used to work in Naval Intelligence."

"Well then, I'm preachin' to the choir."

Micah pointed toward the boat. "May I?"

"Yeah, sure, but hold on a second."

Micah cocked his head, trying not to appear bothered.

"You said you found 'nothing of consequence.' What exactly did you find?"

Micah paused. "We noticed that the quarters were all cleaned up. You know, carpets cleaned, curtains, et cetera. That seemed strange to me, what with this being investigated as a crime scene and all."

"Really? You see, I haven't been on board yet. Can't leave my post. Then, when I had the chance, I had to get some sleep. I was plum worn out. I still haven't seen the deck or the inside."

"Ahh. Well, it was a bit odd to find the quarters cleaned like that. However, we spoke with Agent Jackson last night about it. He explained it to us."

"What did he say?"

"I'll let him fill you in. I'm in a bit of a hurry." Micah nodded toward the boat once more.

Agent Lowery waved his hand. "Sure. Again, let me know if you find anything."

Micah pointed at the agent and gave him a wink.

Walking around the stern of the vessel, Micah searched the hull. Bright white when it was new, it was dulled by the time spent at sea and in port. There were little nicks and scratches here. A few more dings there. Judging by the location, he thought they were from the tow and subsequent lift out of the water. Larger dents on the sides were from the creature's impact . . . if there was a creature at all.

Micah arrived at the place where the gouges announced a terrible struggle. Remembering his apple at the condo, he searched the immediate area around the damage. Then he found it. It was no wonder everyone had missed it. No one would have dreamed of looking that far away.

The gouges, where he had found the tooth only hours earlier, ended not far from the keel. He pulled a small tape measure from his pocket. *Seven inches away from the keel, running at approximately a thirty-*

degree angle and just under four feet in length. Reaching into his other pocket and removing a pen and notepad, he scrawled some notes.

On the other side of the hull Micah found several puncture marks —the size of a quarter, maybe. They ran at an almost a perfect hundred and fifty-degree angle, lining up with the gouges. He measured the distance between the two punctured areas and whistled.

Twenty-seven feet.

Micah took several steps back to get a better overall picture. His mind filled with images. He could see the boat out on the ocean, getting pummeled by this creature. The creature's head slams into the boat. It smashes its body into the vessel's side. Then, like a predator, it attacks the underside, the belly, biting the hull. Thinking it to be flesh, it rips at the hull, expecting to severely injure its prey. Instead, the ripping motion yanks a tooth from its mouth. Furious and injured, the beast capsizes the boat.

But how?

Micah stepped back a couple of steps farther. He closed his eyes and started imagining himself as the creature. He replayed the entire scene once more, hoping to see clues in his mind's eye.

It slams into the boat . . . sees the vessel as a threat . . . a possible enemy . . . or, at least, a possible dinner.

This is its territory . . . it's the king of this part of the ocean. It slams into the boat again. All of a sudden, lights come on, and little things appear within easy reach.

It lunges at David Sims and snatches him from the deck . . . then re-submerges to finish his prey.

But it's not done. It knows there's more where that came from still on the boat, and it knows it bumped the boat and made them appear the first time, so why not try again?

It does. But this time nothing appears. On to Plan B . . . bite the belly . . . go for the soft spot if there's no neck to grab.

It does with such force that the woman on board thinks the boat is going down. Then, with a ripping motion, it jerks its head, expecting the flesh to come with it. Instead, a tooth gets yanked out.

Then, the picture crystallized for Micah.

"The other mast," he said in a whisper. His mind saw the creature, angry and in pain, elevate its head high into the air, another predatorial action, and grab the last remaining mast with its mouth. At that point, all it would have to do is pull down. The boat would overturn in a second as the mast sooner or later snapped in two. Then, thinking it had killed its enemy and exacted its revenge, the creature left.

That was the splitting of wood we heard before we lost radio contact. Micah glanced at his notes again. *That would have done it.*

A mouth at least twenty-seven feet wide when open. Micah pictured an enormous animal. Feverishly, he jotted down his thoughts, then began drawing a sketch of the hull with the location of the bite marks.

He glanced at his watch. *I wonder if Evelyn noticed this last night.*

Evelyn Sims perched on a leather barstool in her kitchen, held the morning paper. A glass of orange juice, half-finished and sweating onto a coaster, sparkled upon the dark green granite countertop.

Every so often, she would drop one side of the paper and run her fingers through her hair, placing it behind her ears. Her red silk pajamas, a gift from her mother some years ago, displayed her intentions of not going to work early. A regular custom. But of course, getting back at two in the morning from Fort Pierce helped her decide long before Bud Kensington made a similar suggestion.

Plastered across the front page was the story she knew all too well. Pictures of the ravaged boat in dock and of her husband, taken from his website, flashed like neon lights. She read every story on every page pertaining to the accident. There was nothing in the stories that she didn't already know or suspect. Yet, there was plenty she did know that the news reporters didn't.

Thank God, she thought.

She dropped the paper on the counter and gazed out into her beautiful backyard. Designed by one of the top builders in Miami, it had a swimming pool with a waterfall on one end, a butterfly garden, and dense, lush greenery surrounding the perimeter of the lot. This was the house she picked just before David proposed to her. So, despite the agitation she felt every time David's name surfaced, she found solace in the fact that the home was hers first.

Not much else was.

She peeked around the wall separating the kitchen from the living room. Peering out the front living room window, she could see yellow police tape imprisoning her property per the orders of Agent Jackson. She was told two undercover FBI agents had been monitoring her house for several weeks prior to the death of her husband. She hadn't noticed them until this morning. A grey sedan was parked a block away. Two men, acting like lost tourists, held up maps in plain sight. Coffee cups from a local convenience store could be seen from time to time.

Now, on the street side of the fragile tape, she could see at least twenty news reporters from various media venues being scrutinized by a minimum of four Dade County sheriff's deputies assuming their normal police presence stance.

Earlier, Evelyn had flipped on the television, only to see her house on MSNBC and the street upon which she lived closed with police barricades. As she lay in bed watching the news report, she wished she had purchased the modest French provincial in the gated community across town with the guard shack and the little old man who played a convincing sergeant major. *Hindsight's always 20/20.*

She made her way over to the refrigerator when the phone rang. She checked the caller ID. *I don't recognize that number.*

She allowed the answering machine to take it.

"Dr. Sims?" the voice said. "This is Captain Micah Gregson. We met last night after you arrived to inspect the *Greenback* at Station Fort Pierce? Well, I was just calling to discuss some evidence I uncovered this morn—"

Evelyn snatched the phone off the wall. "Uh, yes, Captain. Hi. I, uh, didn't recognize the phone number, and with all the news reporters standing outside my house right now, I had to start screening my calls."

"I totally get it."

"Thanks for being understanding."

She heard Micah take a deep breath and exhale. "So, uh, how are you holding up?"

Evelyn rocked her head back and forth. "Needless to say, I've been better."

"I'll bet you have."

A short awkward silence crept into the conversation. "So, Captain, how may I help you?"

"Well, I was wondering. What did you find last night when you examined the boat? Did you find anything . . . unusual?"

"Nothing that Agent Jackson didn't already know about."

"So you didn't take anything back to your lab at the institute?"

Evelyn paused. "Captain Gregson, is there something you need to tell me?"

Micah moaned something inaudible, like he was trying to find the right words. "Dr. Sims, what did you think of Agent Jackson?"

"Arrogant. Short-tempered. Already knew it all before we arrived." She huffed into the receiver. "On the way back to Miami, I wondered why he called us in the first place."

"Why did he ask you and your colleague to come?"

"He said he needed some experts to examine the boat."

"For what?"

"He said he needed us to confirm or negate an animal attack."

"An animal attack? Did he happen to mention what kind of animal?"

Evelyn wondered where this session of twenty questions was heading. "No. Captain, do you and Agent Jackson have some kind of rivalry going on that I need to be aware of? Why all the questions about him?"

"Dr. Sims, before I answer that, can I ask you one more question?"

"Okay. One."

"Did he tell you why your boat was cordoned off as a crime scene?"

Evelyn sighed.

"He did, didn't he?"

"Yes, he did," she said.

"And?"

"I'm not sure I'm at liberty to say at this point."

"I see. Well, that was my one question."

Evelyn switched the phone to her other ear. "Actually, that was two, but who's counting?"

"And you should know I have another to ask, too. Well, several really, but I'm a man of my word." He cleared his throat. "Between you and me, I do not trust Agent Jackson. I believe he's hiding something."

"You don't trust him?"

"Nope. I've seen his kind before. They march to the beat of their own drum, if you will, and they will step on your throat and press down if they get the chance."

"Oh, man, you don't know how happy I am to hear you say that."

"Happy to hear what, exactly?"

"I don't trust him either. He's a weasel. You should have seen him last night. He stood over our shoulders the whole time. I thought Bud was going to cuff him."

"He stood over your shoulder doing what?"

"Watching us. Asking questions. Asking about every procedure. He said he was curious because he wanted to learn more about our jobs."

"Bull."

"That's what we thought, too."

"Did he say why they cordoned off the boat?"

Evelyn plopped down in a chair at the dining room table. "He said my husband was involved in some kind of terrorist activity."

"What? How so?"

"Something about selling some land in the Bahamas . . . the money from the sale supposedly funded some Islamic terrorist group."

"Nice."

"What do you mean, 'Nice'?"

"What I mean is, that's a good story."

"You don't think it's true?"

"It's hard to say. I mean, your husband could've been involved without knowing it. He thought it was a genuine sale, made his fair share, done deal. No harm, no foul. He became the laundromat. Then the money gets laundered a ccuple more times before reaching its intended destination. He could very well have been merely a step in the process."

"I suppose that's true. I know David was many things, but he wasn't a traitor or a terrorist. Nor would he willingly help terrorists. He was living the American dream and would never freely scheme to hurt our country."

"That raises another possibility, Dr. Sims. He may have been forced to help against his will."

Evelyn shook her head. "No, David was a careful businessman. I find that hard to believe."

"Would you have thought of him as an adulterer?"

Evelyn's answer was quiet. "No."

"Dr. Sims, I'm sorry. That was, uh . . . incredibly insensitive on my part."

"No, Captain." Evelyn wiped her eyes. "You did what you had to do. Get me to see David in the proper light. He did lie to me. On more than one occasion, I might add." She paused. "There really is no telling what he was capable of doing."

"Before you throw anymore stones at his memory, think this through with me."

"Okay."

"You heard Agent Jackson skip around my question about the cabin of the boat? Did he say anything specific about the cabin quarters to you after we left?"

"Yeah. He said they cleaned up the evidence before I got there because they thought it would bother me too much."

"What would bother you too much?"

Evelyn held back a sob. "He told us there was a great deal of . . . blood in the cabin."

"Dr. Sims—"

"Please, Captain, call me Evelyn."

"Only if you call me Micah."

"Deal. Now, what were you going to say?"

"Agent Jackson said there was a great deal of blood in the cabin and that's why they cleaned it up?"

"Yes."

"Evelyn, that doesn't make any sense. The divers from the recovery company examined the boat after we rescued Regina Fleming. They said that if there was any evidence in the cabin, the salt water would have washed the majority of it away. There may have been some faint stains, spots here and there, so forth and so on, but I know there couldn't have been 'lots of blood.' Think about it. If the boat was capsized shortly after a killing, the forensic evidence would have been pretty fresh. The fresher it is, the easier it is to wash away, and that boat was dragged in the ocean for fifteen miles after being capsized and adrift from several hours."

"Of course." Evelyn exhaled in disgust. "How could I have been so stupid?"

"Because you were dealing with the death of your husband. Your mind was not on your work."

Evelyn closed her eyes. *No, it wasn't.* "All the way there last night I kept thinking I wanted to go and find out what really happened. But when I saw that boat and heard about what they thought David was involved in, all I wanted to do was leave."

"Evelyn, I need to show you something I found on the boat, but we can't tell Agent Jackson about it at all."

Evelyn's eyes widened. "You found something?"

"Yes."

"I can come up there this afternoon."

"I think it would be better if I came down there. We might need your lab to check it out."

"What is it?"

"I'd rather not say on the phone."

Evelyn smiled. Of course, surveillance. "Sure. I can be there after lunch." She gave him her cell number and asked him to call when he was on his way.

"Great," Micah said. "I've got one stop to make later this morning; then I'll call you."

CHAPTER ELEVEN

Thursday, 10:05 a.m.
St. Lucie Regional Medical Center
St. Lucie, Florida

Micah Gregson took a seat next to the bed in Room 245. He had a notepad, a pen, and a book from his personal library in his possession. If you would have asked him why he was there, he wouldn't have been able to give you a specific answer other than compulsion.

It was a mere impulse that forced him to drive across town. He felt it yesterday while standing aboard the *Cormorant*. He couldn't explain in words why he needed to speak with the woman found stranded on a capsized boat fifteen miles out in the Atlantic. He wasn't attracted to her in a physical sense, although he would've been the first to admit she was pretty. He didn't know if she could provide any additional information than what had already been given. He didn't believe she was a murderer; at least she didn't appear to be one—neither by the evidence nor her demeanor. He also didn't believe she had anything to do with the capsizing of the boat. Yet, while confident in his viewpoint, Micah also didn't have a clue who she was and why it was so important to be there. Nevertheless, there he sat, holding his notepad and pen. The book rested in his lap, the front cover facedown.

"I don't know what to say," Regina Fleming said, groggy from the heavy dose of clozapine given to her the night before. "I'm all alone now. My husband called me this morning and told me it's over. He's thrown my stuff out on the front porch. Told me I could come by and get it whenever." She frowned. "I don't have any family, either. So, yeah, I've got time, Captain. What do you need to know?"

"Mrs. Fleming, I'm sorry to hear about your circumstances. Please know that I'm not here to gather evidence against you. I'm here strictly to investigate what caused the capsizing of the *Greenback*. I firmly believe that determining what capsized the boat will shine a definitive light on what happened to the deceased, and you. So, don't be afraid to tell me anything you may remember. Any information you can offer would be greatly appreciated."

"You want me to recall what happened?" Regina Fleming shrugged. "I've already told the story twice. Once to you and your crew, and once to the FBI."

"Mrs. Fleming, sometimes in the retelling of events, especially traumatic events, some details get left out. As days pass, certain details are remembered that may not have been remembered before. Crucial details that might help break the case. It's very common."

"I can still remember everything, Captain." Regina's voice rang hollow. Void of the emotion Micah expected.

"Whatever you can, at your own pace. I'm not in any hurry."

Regina rubbed her eyes. "Where do you want me to start?"

"How about when you first encountered whatever attacked the boat?"

"I'll never forget it. Dave and I were having a big argument—"

"About what, if I may ask?"

"What else? What do people who are having an affair usually argue about?"

Micah forced an embarrassed smile. "I can't say that I know, for sure."

"Dave was getting cold feet."

"About . . . ?"

"Leaving his wife."

"Really?" Micah started writing things down.

"Yeah. It had to do with all the money he was going to lose in alimony."

Micah lifted one eyebrow.

"I told Dave it didn't matter to me how much money he had. He just needed to make a decision—me or his wife. We discussed things some more. Then he told me he'd made a decision. He was going to file the divorce papers when we got back to Miami." Regina stared at Micah before turning her head away. "I asked him if that was what he really wanted, but he never got to answer the question. That's when something hit the boat."

"And what happened next?"

"The force of the hit shoved me forward. I smacked my side into the edge of the bed. Dave was sitting on the other side of the bed. He was knocked to the floor. He hit his head on something, because when he stood up, I saw blood running down the side of his face." She pointed to the left side of her head. "It must have been the table that sat there in front of the loveseat."

There was a table in there? "Table? Was it connected to anything?"

"No. It wasn't bolted down, if that's what you mean."

Micah scribbled notes. "Did it open a pretty big gash on David's head?"

"Big gash? No."

"Did he bleed profusely all over the cabin?"

Regina shot a befuddled look at Micah. "No."

"Were you cut?"

"No."

"You weren't bleeding at all?"

"Why do you keep insisting there was blood?"

"According to one of the FBI agents," Micah said, "they supposedly found a lot of blood in the cabin."

"No, there wasn't. Who told you that?"

"I'm not sure I can divulge that information. But you can testify that there wasn't blood all over the cabin?"

"Absolutely. Dave just had a cut on his head, near his temple. I was going to ask him about it, but he said he needed to get upstairs to see what hit us."

"Did you go up, too?"

"Yes."

"And what did you both think it was at first?"

She gave an embarrassed chuckle. "A whale."

"What made you come to that conclusion?"

"It was Dave who said he thought it was a whale. By the time we got up there, all I saw was the water churning," she said, rolling her hands. "Dave said he thought he heard a whale surface out away from the boat. I don't know what I heard exactly."

"I see." Micah jotted down more details. "Now, when you saw the animal that attacked the boat, what did it look like?"

Regina's breathing increased. "I only saw its head and part of its neck. I never saw the whole thing."

"Just tell me about what you did see."

"The head looked kind of like an alligator's head, but wider . . . *a lot* wider, and its teeth were a lot longer, too."

"How wide do you think it was? You can use anything in this room to help you figure out how big it was. The width and length of the bed, the size of the room, the size of the other furniture, whatever helps."

Regina looked around the room before her eyes settled on the bed. She sat up, still shaky, and examined the bed in much more detail than Micah imagined she would. "Its head was at least as wide as this bed is long, but I think it was bigger than that."

Micah scribbled some notes down and then stood up. He stepped to the end of the bed and slid back another three to four feet. "About this big? From the head of the bed to here?"

Regina nodded, cautious at first, but seemed to become more convinced the longer she mused. "Yeah, that's about it."

Micah looked down at the floor, counting the shiny vinyl tiles. "So, its head was about ten feet wide. Correct?"

She shrugged. "I guess so."

Micah returned to his seat and flipped open the book he had brought. He skimmed the pages and stopped somewhere in the last third of the volume. He turned the book around so Regina could see.

On the page was a drawing of a plesiosaur.

"Regina," he said, "did the head of the creature look anything like this?"

She shook her head. "No. The head on that thing is about the same size as the neck. The thing I saw had a head that was bigger than the neck."

"Hmmm." Micah took the book back and flipping more pages. "What about this one?"

"*Kro-no-sau-rus queens-land-i-cus?*" She pointed to the picture of a man standing next to the fossil of the head. "Is this real?"

"Yes, that's a real picture taken at the Harvard Museum of Comparative Zoology of a man preparing the fossil for display at the museum."

"That size is pretty close. The one I saw, though, was probably a little bigger." She studied the picture. "If you took that man in the picture—" Regina's eyes spasmed as she fought tears. "And placed him in the mouth—" She closed the book and handed it back to Micah. "I can't do this."

"I understand." Micah took the book and placed it back on his lap. He waited while Regina gathered her composure. "Was the neck of *kronosaurus queenslandicus* also about the right size?"

Regina became more animated. "No. The monster I saw had a neck more like the other one you showed me, just . . . bigger . . . thicker . . .

wider." She gazed up at the ceiling. "And the sound it made—" She started to cry.

"You heard it make a sound? Besides that of a whale breathing?"

Regina nodded. "It was like a bear or a lion, but higher-pitched."

"Higher-pitched?"

Regina sighed. Micah could tell that trying to articulate the ineffable was frustrating her. "One second it sounded like a lion or a bear. The next second it sounded like a giant hawk." She shivered. "It also had a . . . a growl mixed in . . . kind of like a dog does when it's angry and watching your every move."

Micah scrawled more notes. "Mrs. Fleming, I saw you at the dock last night before the ambulance brought you here. Why didn't they take you straight to the hospital by chopper?"

"I was told I needed to be debriefed first before they brought me here and doped me up. Nice guys, huh?"

"But they could gave questioned you here."

"Not according to the FBI."

"I see," Micah said, jotting down more notes.

Regina let her eyes fall until they met the muted television fastened to the wall in the corner of the room. "Uh-oh."

"What?" Micah first looked at Regina, then followed her eyes to the TV.

On the screen was a special news report.

Regina fumbled for the control and turned up the volume.

". . . where it is being reported that a World Class Cruises ocean liner called the *Titan* has been attacked. Authorities are telling us that the incident took place in the early morning hours just north of Walker Cay in the Bahamas."

The reporter shrank into a box that slid to the left side of the screen. Another box appeared on the right, sporting a detailed map of the Bahamas and the ship's planned course.

"Initial reports are unconfirmed by authorities, but we are told that a distress call came in from the *Titan* as she was making her way around the north side of the Bahamas en route to St. Thomas in the Virgin Islands.

"The *Titan* sailed out of Port Canaveral, Florida, at approximately five thirty p.m. last night. With over four thousand passengers on board, the *Titan* was on a seven-day cruise from Port Canaveral to St. Thomas. From there, they were to travel to St. Maarten, back to Nassau, which you can see on the map is located due south of the Great Abaco Island, and then back to Port Canaveral.

"According to reports, there were a few people on deck when they spotted what one person referred to as a sea serpent. The passenger stated that the creature swam alongside the cruise ship for nearly two minutes before disappearing in the water. Then, about a minute later, the eyewitness said the creature reappeared near the front of the boat. The eyewitness also stated that the creature had positioned itself ahead of the ship, turning around to face it.

"Then, as the eyewitnesses watched, the creature attempted to snatch a woman off the deck before disappearing back into the ocean. But the creature couldn't reach the deck and instead crashed into the side of the boat. The ship stopped about five minutes later and made the distress call.

"At this time, it is unconfirmed if any passengers are missing. Also, we are still awaiting reports of any damage to the ship. We will stay on top of this late-breaking story. This is Marilyn Meadows, CNN, Port Canaveral, Florida."

A growing disturbance outside Regina Fleming's door interrupted Micah's train of thought. One of the voices sounded agitated. He could only hear bits and pieces of the conversation, but the tone signified threats to either livelihood or life in general . . . or both. The other voice sounded like the agent stationed outside earlier, assigned to guard the room.

Micah stood just as Agent Jackson stormed into the room.

"Captain Gregson, what're you doing here?"

"Hello, Agent Jackson. It's good to see you again, too."

"I'm going to ask politely one more time. What are you doing in this room?"

"Politely? Hmm, jury's still out on that one."

"Okay." Agent Jackson turned to the other agent standing inside the door. "Arrest him."

Micah held his hands up. "Whoa, wait a minute. First of all, Agent Jackson, your agent let me in here. I told him I wanted to speak to Mrs. Fleming. As you can see, that's what I've been doing. Second, this dear woman may be a witness to a crime, and then again, she may not. Therefore, until I see her in handcuffs, I will treat her as an accident victim and a hospital patient until otherwise charged. So, are you here to charge her with anything, Agent Jackson? Because if not, then she is entitled to visitors."

Agent Jackson took a step closer to Micah. "Captain," he said, looking over at Regina Fleming, "may I have a word with you out in the hall?"

"Certainly." Micah's pinned his eyes to the agent's eyes like a boxer in the ring right before a fight. Then he turned to Regina. "Mrs. Fleming, thank you for your time. Your help has been most valuable."

Regina looked at Agent Jackson first. Her eyes became daggers, and her gaze made Agent Jackson fidget. She then turned to Micah, and in an instant her face softened. She scanned Micah's person in a flirtatious manner. "Anytime, Captain," she said. Her voice deep and sultry on purpose.

Micah nodded and walked out of the room, followed by the two agents.

When the three men stepped into the hallway, Agent Jackson grabbed Micah by the arm.

Micah jerked away.

Agent Jackson threw his finger in Micah's face. "Listen here, Captain, you're in way over your pay grade."

Micah sneered, his eyes never leaving Jackson's. "How original."

"I suggest you go home, live your life, and leave this case alone."

"And if I don't?"

"You don't want to know."

"Ooo," Micah said. "You forget, Jackson, I'm part of the government, too. I've been in Naval Intelligence. I've been in the field. The battlefield, mind you. Have you, Agent Jackson? Have you ever been in battle?"

Agent Jackson remained silent. Micah could see how uncomfortable the agent grew with the comparison.

Micah leveled his eyes at Agent Jackson's. "Ever heard of the *USS Cole*?"

"Yes. What about it?"

"Do you know who was responsible for that attack?"

Agent Jackson rolled his eyes. "Everyone does. Al-Qaeda."

"But who helped them?"

Agent Jackson shrugged. "Who cares, Captain?"

Micah leaned forward into Jackson's face. "I do. That's who. I had two buddies killed in that attack. One of the guys was my best man."

"I'm sorry to hear that, Captain." Agent Jackson stepped back to allow a nurse with a medicine cart to pass.

"Yeah, I'll bet," Micah said, waiting for the RN to turn the corner. "Sudan, Agent Jackson. The Sudanese were involved."

"Okay, Captain. Great. Then let's go get those Sudanese dogs as soon as we're done with ISIS. What's your point?"

Micah took two steps forward and angrily backed Agent Jackson up against the wall outside Regina Fleming's room. He narrowed his eyes. "It's always good to know who your enemies are, isn't it, Agent Jackson?"

Agent Jackson returned the glare. "Yes," he said in a whisper, "it is."

Micah took several steps away before stopping. "Oh, yes. I forgot to tell you," he said before turning around. "I was the one who broke that case." Micah stared at Agent Jackson, letting the effect of his words percolate.

"Three months inside Sudanese territory, *in the field.* And I was alone. I went dark three days before I was captured by Islamic extremists. No one knew I was being held prisoner.

"Once my captors realized I was a military operative, I became a virtual gold mine to them for publicity purposes. They planned to decapitate me while broadcasting it over the Internet. Then, they were going to throw my body into the Red Sea while videotaping the whole thing.

"So that night, I overpowered my guard and escaped. By the time I left that compound, I had killed eleven extremists and maimed two more.

"It never made the news, Agent Jackson. There's no *Fox & Friends* interview or *Anderson Cooper 360* archive you can visit. However, you're FBI, so I'm sure you can get a warrant and take a peek at the classified files of the Navy, if you wish. When you do, look for Operation Dry Dock."

"What's you point, Captain?"

"My point, Agent Jackson, is not only that you need to know who your enemies are, but that I can take care of myself."

Micah gave Agent Jackson a mocking salute before spinning around and exiting through the large double doors at the end of the hall.

CHAPTER TWELVE

Thursday, 10:45 a.m.
St. Lucie Regional Medical Center
St. Lucie, Florida

Agent Archibald Jackson watched Micah Gregson disappear behind the two large wooden doors. Standing tense with his fists clenched, Agent Jackson's mind raced from one possible scenario to another, trying to concoct how Captain Gregson could be arrested, thrown into a dreary cell somewhere, and ditched until he was finished with this case. Out of sight, out of mind.

But he realized that the negative publicity from locking up a local Coast Guard officer would bring a great deal more attention to an already inundated dilemma. So he simply stood there—shaking—revealing his anger to the other agent who had seen it on more than one occasion.

Agent Jackson motioned for the other agent to step closer.

The agent took two steps and leaned forward while Agent

Jackson grabbed him by the shoulder and whispered something into his ear inaudible to the nearby nurse's station. The agent nodded, gave Agent Jackson a thumbs-up sign, and exited the hallway through the same double doors Micah Gregson had used moments prior.

Agent Jackson eyed the other agent until he also evanesced beyond the doors at the end of the hallway.

The tempo of Jackson's breathing increased. He had a mission to complete, and no one was going to stand in his way, especially some do-gooder Coast Guardsman from a podunk district of an auxiliary branch of the government. *I'm FBI,* he thought as he stood there in the hallway, still staring at the double doors.

FBI. F-B-I.

Agent Jackson nodded with confidence before reentering the hospital room.

Regina Fleming, who had been watching the news reports of the ocean liner attack, turned to see who was entering the room. Her eyes furrowed. "What do you want now?"

"Your cooperation, Mrs. Fleming."

"Didn't you already question me yesterday?"

Agent Jackson reached into his coat pocket and flashed his badge and identification. "You remember me. That's encouraging."

She ran her right hand through her hair, using it as a hairbrush. "Not really," she said.

But he knew she did. She was just trying to aggravate him.

"It's understandable if you don't. You were in a great deal of shock last night."

She stroked her hair again and looked away. "No kidding, Sherlock. Look, Agent Jackson, I'm really not in the mood right now to discuss anything. If you could come back tomorrow, then maybe I will be. I'm sure you understand."

Agent Jackson manufactured a polite smile. *You're not going to call any shots today, honey,* he thought as he sat in the chair next to the bed. "I do understand, Mrs. Fleming, but I hope you can understand when I tell you that it is paramount for us to find this creature and kill it before it causes any more harm. Your help will be—"

"Like I told you, Agent Jackson," Regina said, raising her voice and turning to face him all at once, "I'm not in the mood."

Agent Jackson simpered. Her attempt at a threatening demeanor almost made him snort in her face. Her eyes, though, not as menacing in their wildness as the night before, caused him to narrow his and not blink. "Mrs. Fleming, I'm not sure what Captain Gregson said to you or showed you while he was in here, but I will demand the same time and respect from you that you afforded him. Nothing less."

"You can demand all you want, but—"

Agent Jackson leapt from his chair, grabbing her by the throat with his left hand, pushing in and up with a pinching motion, restricting the trachea while forcing her jaw shut at the same time. He covered her mouth and nose with his right hand, pressing down with great force. "Scream, and I'll squeeze. You'll be dead long before any nurse gets in here, and I'll just say that's how I found you." Jackson paused and grinned devilishly. "I'm sure Captain Gregson will become a person of interest."

Regina began to struggle at first, grabbing for his hair and clawing at his face and arms, but when she heard his words, she stopped. Her lungs shrieked for air. She nodded, and then the clench of the agent's hand eased. A sudden flow of air rushed in as she gasped, causing her to cough and choke.

He leaned in close to her ear. "Will you cooperate, Mrs. Fleming, or do I need to retain my grip?"

Regina, reacting to the stench of the agent's cigarette-laced breath, winced before nodding in the affirmative.

"No funny business, Mrs. Fleming. I promise I will not be long." He released her throat and mouth, standing erect but not moving yet. He didn't trust her. *She has already proven to be an unfaithful wife,* he thought. *If she can do that, she can without a doubt double-cross me.*

Regina Fleming placed her left hand over her throat and coughed again. "What do you want?" she said in a raspy voice.

"Just some information, Mrs. Fleming."

She eyed Agent Jackson as he sat back down in the chair next to the bed. "What kind of information?"

"About the attack."

"I already told you everything last night."

"Ah, but sometimes details come back at later times. For example, was there anything you told Captain Gregson that you forgot to mention to us last night?"

Regina massaged her neck and closed her eyes. A tear welled up at the corner of her right eye. "I told him mostly what I told you. Except he brought a book in with him. It had some pictures in it of some dinosaurs. Old fossils. Black and white photos. That kind of stuff."

"Do you recall what the pictures looked like?"

"One picture was of a huge dinosaur. There was a man standing in the picture. The head of that thing was as big as the man."

Agent Jackson cocked his head, reaching up with his left hand to scratch his cheek. "Did the man in the picture have a lab coat on by chance? You know, the white kind with the little pockets?"

"Yes, I think so."

Agent Jackson studied Regina's face. "Why did Captain Gregson show you that picture?"

Regina shrugged. "He was trying to figure out what it was I saw. He first showed me a picture of a dinosaur that had a neck and head that was kind of like a large snake. But I told him that the one I saw had a thicker neck than the one on the picture, and the head was a lot bigger than the neck."

Agent Jackson retrieved a small pad of paper from his coat pocket and snatched a pen from shirt pocket. He started drawing a rough sketch of what she was describing.

Regina watched as Agent Jackson's pen scratched and scribbled on the notepad page. "What are you doing?"

Agent Jackson didn't answer at first. He was trying to concentrate on his dimensions, trying to draw it to scale. He was also attempting to blot out the face of Captain Gregson. That ex-Navy twerp had horned in on his territory. He was liable to compromise very sensitive evidence conducting his lackadaisical interviews and impromptu investigation.

After several minutes, Agent Jackson turned his notepad around and held it up for Regina to examine. "Does this look anything like what you saw?"

Regina squinted and reached out for the picture. Agent Jackson allowed her to take it for a closer look. She began to nod. "The head was bigger . . . and I think its neck is longer than this."

Agent Jackson's eyes widened as he chuckled. "You're kidding, right?"

Regina nodded and shivered. She then grabbed her forehead, squeezing with her right hand while handing him the note pad. "No, I'm not, Agent Jackson. All I want to do is forget. Forget what happened. Forget that thing. That creature. Forget David screaming. But I know it will be years, if ever, before that happens. Every time I close my eyes, I see it. The teeth. The mouth. The eyes."

Her breathing started to grow heavy. "It snatched him off the deck like he was an insect." She blinked her eyes, opening and closing them, squirming, turning her head back and forth as if trying to escape a nightmare.

"David's legs, they just stuck out." She started to cry and became convulsive. "David screamed, but he never had a chance. I think the thing could have swallowed him whole. I can hear it . . . gurgling, growling. I can see the teeth pierce his—"

She started to scream. "Get away! Get away!" She grabbed Agent Jackson by the coat, almost falling on the floor. "Help me! It's coming for me! It's going to get me! I can see its eye! It's looking in through the window!" She began to cry, peering over his shoulder with a manic gape.

Agent Jackson stood and grabbed both of Regina's wrists, attempting to break her grip. Her adrenaline was flowing, however. She was much stronger than before.

"Mrs. Fleming, let go."

"Help me!" Her hands gripped him tighter. Her eyes became possessed. Her pupils turned to black holes. The whites of her eyes drained of color. She wasn't blinking now. Her hands began twisting the agent's coat into a gnarled mass. Beads of sweat popped out all over her pallid face. "Don't leave me!"

Agent Jackson, struggling to remain standing, looked over his shoulder to see one sizable nurse breeze through the door holding a syringe. The flash of her face gave Agent Jackson the impression this was a common occurrence.

"Calm down, Regina." The nurse snatched the clear tube hanging from an IV bag on a hook.

"Help me," Regina said. Still clutching Agent Jackson's coat, her eyes now bored holes through him. "It's going to sink the boat."

"I am, Regina. I'm going to help you right now." In one nimble movement, the nurse stabbed the needle into the IV port and thrust the plunger forward, emptying the contents into the steady drip of saline solution.

At once, Regina Fleming's grip loosened as the mixture of fluphenazine hydrochloride, thorazine, lithium, and haloperidol invaded her body. Agent Jackson held on to her arms as she fell limp.

The nurse slipped the empty syringe into her pocket and grabbed Regina Fleming, repositioning her. With several nudges and jerks, she had the patient lying straight on the bed once more before tucking in the sheet.

"How much did you give her?"

"Enough," the nurse said. "Trust me. Enough."

CHAPTER THIRTEEN

Thursday, 11:47 a.m.
I-95, Southbound Lane
Near the Hobe Sound Exit

Micah Gregson left the hospital enraged. He never wanted to punch anyone more than he did standing there in front of Room 245. Agent Jackson represented everything Micah despised about working for the government.

Arrogance.

Lying.

Dishonesty.

The government thought they knew more than everybody else. They thought they were better than everyone else, too. Politicians and military brass loved to tell the masses stories and make wild promises in order to placate fears, win votes, and gain control. Then, while behind closed doors, those same slimy rascals would cut deals with evil cunning and reprehensible forethought.

It seemed that nice people—gracious people, people he'd known—had to check their brains at the door when they arrived at work in order to become indoctrinated drones for Uncle Sam. This infuriated Micah. He fought it with every ounce of his being every day he was on the job.

He and his wife had talked at length on the subject while she was still alive. They had both agreed that if one started to act "governmental," the other would start saluting with the hand reversed and turned palm up. One salute would send them both into peals of laughter. That was, of course, if they were honest with themselves.

That salute, with the palm turned upward, was the gesture he flipped Agent Jackson before he vacated the hallway in front of Room 245. Agent Jackson had "gone governmental" on him. *Becky would have been proud,* he thought.

A half-hour later, after returning to his condo to retrieve some items of interest, Micah headed south on I-95 to see Dr. Sims at the Marine Institute. Trying to keep his eyes on the road, he pulled out his cell phone and dialed the number scribbled on a sticky note adhered to his steering wheel.

"Hello?"

"Dr. Sims, this is Captain Gregson."

"Oh, hi, Micah, how are you?"

"I'm fine. I just wanted to let you know I'm on my way to Miami and should be at the institute in about two hours."

"You've already left?"

"I'm on I-95 now."

"That's not good."

"Why not?"

"The FBI hasn't shown up yet. They were supposed to be here already."

Micah grimaced. "I had a run-in with Agent Jackson this morning, so if he was the one who was supposed to come to your house, he'll be awhile."

"Great. You had a run-in with him, huh? Anything I can thank you for?"

Micah chuckled. "Not really. I was at the hospital interviewing Regina Fleming. She told me some interesting things about the creature she saw." Micah snapped his fingers. "Oh, that reminds me, have you been watching the news this morning?"

"No. I didn't want to see my house on television."

"You've got a lot of reporters there, eh?"

"Only about thirty."

"Unbelievable."

"So, what's on the news?"

"There was another attack last night. A cruise ship was heading for the eastern Caribbean and was attacked just north of the Bahamas."

Evelyn headed for the bedroom. "A cruise ship? Are you kidding me? Was it a normal-sized ship?"

"Sounds like it. They said there were over four thousand passengers on board. They didn't have any pictures to show, but the report said it tried to grab a woman off the deck but couldn't reach her."

Evelyn's gait accelerated. "Depending on the size of the ship, the main deck would be what? Thirty to fifty feet above sea level?"

"Sounds about right. Let's hope this ship was a smaller one with a thirty-foot-high deck."

She grabbed the remote on her bedroom night table. "I've got the TV on now. They're showing it."

"Anything new?"

"Just a minute." She pulled the phone away so she could hear. At the bottom of the TV screen the caption read: "DINOSAUR OR HOAX? Cruise Ship *Titan* Attacked."

She turned the volume up and flopped down on the foot of the king-size bed.

". . . to recap the information about the attack on the cruise ship

Titan bound for St. Thomas in the Virgin Islands. The *Titan* is owned and operated by World Class Cruises, Incorporated, out of Los Angeles, California, and is one of eleven ships owned and operated by this international company here in the United States. We have tried to reach a spokesperson for World Class Cruises, but the company says they have no comment at this time," the news anchor said before looking off camera.

"Sorry for the interruption, folks, but I'm receiving new information concerning some late-breaking developments." Someone handed the reporter a sheet of paper. "According to Associated Press sources, some pictures are just coming in from the cruise ship. It appears someone on the ship had a camera phone with them at the time of the attack and was able to capture some images."

The anchor continued, holding her earpiece, "I believe we're ready to show these pictures?" The anchor looked off camera once more. "But let me caution the viewers. These pictures may not be suitable for young children."

On the screen, the blurred image of a twenty-seven-second video shot from a cell phone was difficult to see. The night sky, illuminated by what appeared to be a full moon and lack of outside lights, made the figures morph and blend into an amalgamation of baleful shadows. One second the deck was visible. The next second the water below shimmered. It was as if the camera was having trouble focusing on just one target.

Evelyn could hear voices talking; it was clear to her they were the recorded voices of people near the photographer. People were shouting "There it is!" and "It's coming back!"

Then, right at the very end of the clip, an image grew large, coming into focus. A head like that of a giant snake. Teeth, staggered and long. A mouth, open wide.

The image froze.

Evelyn, staring at the television, wasn't listening to the anchor as she spoke about the quality of the images and what experts thought it all meant. All she saw was the mouth . . . and gasped.

"Evelyn? Are you still there?"

Stunned, Evelyn picked up the receiver. "Micah, have you seen that?"

"Seen what?"

"They just showed an image taken on the cruise ship with a camera phone."

"No, they didn't have any pictures earlier."

"Well, they do now. Micah, this thing is enormous. That cruise ship deck, at least what I thought looked like the deck, must have been at least forty feet above sea level. That creature almost reached it when it lunged out of the water. It couldn't have been any more than ten feet from the railing. It's a wonder the person didn't drop the phone."

Micah turned his radio up and scanned for news stations. "That's what we've got to talk about, Evelyn. There's something out there. Something big and dangerous. Possibly right out of Conan Doyle's *The Lost World*. When can you get to the institute?"

Evelyn sighed. "Not until the FBI leaves . . . if they ever get here. And no telling how long it will take 'em."

"Can you call me when you're ready to leave your house? I'll head on down, and if I don't hear from you, I'll stop and grab a bite." Micah paused, realizing his poor choice of words. "And wait for your call."

"Okay. I can do that."

Micah scanned the radio dial for anything related to the attack on the cruise ship *Titan*. He must have looked like a drunk driver at times as he weaved back and forth in his lane, fumbling with the buttons. He would glance up into the rearview mirror and side mirrors to make sure he wasn't going to side-swipe someone with his brand-new Ford Mustang Cobra.

"I can't believe there are no news stations covering this." Frustrated with the hair-loss commercial and its silly little jingle, he slammed his hand down on the steering wheel. "You would think every station would be all over this." He switched back and forth from AM to FM. No luck. *I wish I hadn't allowed my satellite radio subscription to expire now.*

Peeking in his rearview mirror after rounding the dial a fourth time, he noticed a nondescript black sedan, American-made, lingering about the length of a football field behind him. He hadn't paid any attention before. He was too engrossed in his phone conversation with Evelyn at first. Then he was too preoccupied with the radio. Now he wondered if the car really was following him, or if he was just being paranoid.

There's only one way to find out.

Micah accelerated until his speedometer read eighty mph. He peered into his mirror, expecting to see the black sedan become an ever-decreasing speck. Instead, the car kept pace.

He repositioned himself in his seat. "Oh, I see how it is, now."

He sped up even more until he reached an old, decrepit exit. He exited the interstate but didn't slow down as much as the signs demanded. When he neared the end of the exit ramp, the light turned green. He jerked the steering wheel to the right, careening around the corner, tires squealing.

The black sedan raced down the ramp but had to swerve to miss a slow-moving semi that had just appeared from under the overpass. The driver lost control. The back end of the sedan spun around to the left, causing the sedan to almost complete a hundred-and-eighty-degree u-turn. The driver righted his car and continued the chase.

Micah darted down the road about a half-mile before whipping the car into the oncoming lane, spinning the back of the car around like a stunt driver. He doubled back, wanting to see the driver of the black sedan.

The sedan sprinted down the road until the driver caught sight of the red Mustang. He slammed on his brakes.

Micah slowed and peered through the window. Through the tinted glass, he saw a face. "Lowery." Micah gunned the Mustang, laying down two tracks of rubber and creating a cloud of smoke. He jumped back on the interstate.

Agent Lowery turned around through a gas station parking lot, using the entrance and exit. He sped up and caught a glimpse of a red Mustang at the top of the entrance ramp.

Micah was incensed, and he was driving that way, too. He bolted into the left lane and honked at anyone who wasn't traveling a hundred miles per hour. "Agent Jackson had me tailed. I can't believe it. No, wait. Yes, I can."

The black sedan made up ground on the Mustang as Micah kept getting cut off by slower-moving traffic. Micah saw Lowery in his mirror and the upcoming exit off to his right. In a festinating move, Micah whipped over in front of a delivery truck and dashed down the ramp. He looked in both directions, and when he hit the intersection, he yanked the steering wheel hard to the right.

From the ramp, he saw an abandoned gas station and headed straight for it. Entering the premises, he flew around the corner and behind the dilapidated building, skidding to a stop.

Micah jumped out of his car, having already pulled his MK23 Mod 0 SOCOM from the glove box. As he ran to the corner of the building and waited for the black sedan, he attached the suppressor.

Lowery, trying not to kill himself and any other drivers while at the same time not losing the Mustang, slowed down. He turned into the abandoned parking lot. When he didn't see the Mustang on the east side of the building, he slowly drove around to see behind the structure.

Micah stepped out from around the corner and trained his gun on Lowery's forehead through the front windshield of the agent's car. "Get out of the car! And keep your hands where I can see them!"

The sedan screeched to a halt, and the driver's door opened. Two frantic waving hands appeared. "Don't shoot! It's me, Captain Gregson. Agent Lowery."

Micah stepped closer, his gun still trained on the agent's head. "Get out of the car with your hands behind your head."

Agent Lowery did as he was instructed. "Captain, it's okay. I wasn't sent to hurt you or anything. I was only supposed to find out where you were going."

"Come over here behind the building and get down on the ground. Interlace your fingers behind your head."

"Please, Captain." Lowery did as he was asked and lowered himself into the dirt. "I was only doing my job."

Micah stepped closer until he stood over the agent. "Who sent you? Let me guess. Jackson."

"Yeah, Agent Jackson sent me to follow you."

"Why?"

"I already told you. He wanted to know where you were going."

Micah bristled at the agent's dullness. He jammed the barrel of his weapon into Lowery's neck. "Why?"

"He didn't say why. He never does. He just tells us to do something, and we do it."

Mindless, indoctrinated drones, Micah thought. "Where is Jackson now?"

"He was on his way to interview Evelyn Sims."

"Well, Agent Lowery, this is what you're going to tell Agent Jackson, okay?" Micah then turned and aimed his pistol at the agent's car. With one shot, he blew out the black sedan's front left tire.

Agent Lowery jumped, shocked by the swift spurt of metal and the noisy blast of air leaking from his tire. "What are you doing?"

"You're going to tell Agent Jackson that I went to Sector Miami—

my headquarters—to speak with my superiors. That's it. Nothing else. It's routine. Happens all the time. If Agent Jackson asks where I went after that, you are to tell him that I visited what appeared to be some friends for the afternoon. You didn't recognize any of them. Then I went to a nightclub with a couple of those friends and had a few drinks while enjoying the company of a beautiful woman whose name you did not get. Is that understood?"

"Uh, yeah. Sector Miami, superiors, friends, bar, woman with no name. Got it."

"No, not a bar. A nightclub, Agent Lowery."

"Who cares?"

Micah straddled the agent and pressed the gun barrel into Lowery's neck again. "I do."

"Would you stop threatening me? You know that's assault and battery, right?"

Micah leaned over and spoke into the agent's ear, continuing to jam the gun barrel into Lowery's neck. It was bound to leave an imprint. "Agent Lowery, just remember this. If Agent Jackson finds out from you where I'm really going, I'm coming after you."

"Meaning?"

"Do you know what happened to Jimmy Hoffa, Lowery?"

"No. No one does, except the people who offed him."

"Exactly."

"Oh, now you're threatening me with bodily harm? That's a form of extortion."

"Call it what you want. If you don't want to be part of the foundation for a new football stadium, then I suggest you do as I have requested."

Lowery sighed, his breath creating a miniature dust cloud. Sand was stuck to his lips and the side of his face. "Can I get up now?"

"After I drive away." Micah stood and backed away from Agent Lowery. He had lowered his gun to his side but was ready to present it in a split second. His nerves were on edge. He was ready for a fight.

Micah got into his car and laid down two tracks that trailed off somewhere in the middle of the sandy parking lot. He looked back in time to see Agent Lowery kick his front tire and shout something in his general direction.

"You're welcome, Agent Lowery. It could've been worse."

CHAPTER FOURTEEN

Thursday, 11:51 a.m.
South-Central Atlantic Ocean
Approximately 200 Kilometers Northeast of Nassau, Bahamas

One hundred meters below the surface, cruising at fifteen knots, a Russian submarine snaked its way toward the Caribbean island chain of the Bahamas. The *Kirov*, a Dolphin-class sub, eleven days prior, had performed a successful test-firing of a ballistic missile—an RSM-54—at a target on the Kamchatka peninsula. What made this feat so monumental was the fact that the *Kirov* launched the missile from the Kara Sea—over two thousand miles away.

The RSM-54 hit its designated target with staggering accuracy. It was the second such deployment in a week as part of the Ministry of Defense's initiative to develop answers to other country's antimissile defense system capabilities.

Now, as part of the "agreement" between the Ministry of Defense and the crew of the *Kirov*, the captain had been instructed to reward his crew with a trip to Venezuela to enjoy all the pleasures South American life had to offer. But while en route there was one more drill scheduled to which only the captain and the defense minister were privy. It involved an exercise with the *Kirov*, its sixteen intercontinental ballistic missiles, and several cities along the eastern seaboard of the United States and one notable city on the West Coast.

The helmsman spoke in Russian, checking the dials in front of him. "Captain, we are approximately two hundred kilometers from Nassau. Our course is two-one-zero. Our speed is fifteen knots."

The captain, with hands clasped behind his back and exhibiting a proud expression, peered at his crew. He surveyed them as if about to give a speech. "Very good, gentlemen. It is time." He patted his lieutenant on the back. "Maintain course and speed. Ascend at a five degree bow plane and bring us to periscope depth."

The lieutenant barked out the captain's orders, and several men from the helmsman to the engine room responded, repeating the orders like Pavlov's dogs.

"Once we reach the surface, gentlemen," the captain said, "we have one more exercise to complete before our mission is done. Once it is finished, then we shall head for the Port of Guanta, find some female companionship, and do things that would make our mothers blush, no?"

The men on the bridge howled in laughter at the captain's comments. Some growled and barked like animals, anticipating what awaited them.

The air on the bridge was light and happy. It had been a good mission thus far. The motherland was proud of her fleet's son as he plowed ahead through the dark, murky waters of the Atlantic.

The lieutenant pulled his superior aside while the rest of the bridge crew discussed their plans for Venezuela. "Captain, what is this last mission you mentioned? I was unaware of any additional exercises. I thought our test on Kamchatka was the last."

The captain lowered his voice and leaned in close. "No one knows but me and Minister Nikitin. It is a top-secret mission. Therefore, I cannot tell even you until the time is here."

"I understand, Captain. When can I anticipate the beginning of it, if you can tell me that, sir?"

"Once we reach the surface, my friend. Once we reach the surface. But I can tell you this." The captain leaned closer to his second-in-command. "This mission is comprised of things destined to start a war."

The lieutenant formed a malevolent smile. "Glory to the Motherland."

The captain slapped his second-in-command on the back and showcased an infernal grin. "Man your station."

"Aye, Captain."

The petty officer operating the sonar began waving his arms, motioning for the captain to come. "Captain. Captain."

The captain sauntered over to the sonar screen. "What do you have for me?"

"I am not sure, sir. Sonar picked up something below us just moments ago, and our portside camera picked up an image. Take a look at this."

The sailor tapped a few computer keys. On the monitor was a picture of a large, dark . . . something.

"What do you make of this, Lieutenant?" the captain said.

The lieutenant stepped over and gazed at the image, cocking his head from side to side. "If I did not know any better, Captain, I would say it is a flipper."

The captain peered at his second-in-command as if he was a lunatic. "That is one big flipper, yes?"

The lieutenant frowned with his shoulders raised. "You asked me. I answered. That is what it looks like to me."

"Dispatch this to High Command," the captain said. "We will let them chew on it for a while, eh? Once we get to port, I will have President Maduro call our defense minister to ascertain their response while we chew on something other than a flipper."

The lieutenant and petty officer both let out a raucous laugh.

Then, without warning, something walloped the Dolphin-class submarine with a vicious jolt to the starboard side. The lights on the bridge flickered and went out briefly.

"Emergency lights! Battle stations!" the captain said. "Status report!"

"There has been a hull breach, Captain," the helmsman said. "We are taking on water in the engine room."

The captain spun on his heels as the red claxons began flashing. "What hit us, Lieutenant?"

"Uncertain, Captain. We are not deep enough for it to be a reef. The closest mountainous range is to our west. Twenty kilometers away."

"Is there another ship in the area?"

"Sonar," the lieutenant said. "Have you detected another ship in the vicinity?"

"No, sir. There is nothing being detected."

Before the captain could respond, another ferocious strike came from underneath the *Kirov*. The momentum of the hit sent every standing member of the bridge crew into the air. Every sailor not holding on to something came down with a thud. Areas of the hull began to spew water as the pressure of the *thwack* became too much to bear.

"Emergency blow!" the captain said. "Hit the surface now! Engine room, full throttle!"

Frantic, the captain, the lieutenant, and three other sailors began cranking pressure valves and punching buttons on the consoles. Having twisted downward because of the last hit, the nose of the sub began to rise once more.

"We are heading upward, Captain," the helmsman said. "Two hundred and fifty meters . . . two hundred and twenty meters . . . two hundred meters . . ."

"Sonar, can you detect anything out there?" The captain trotted over to the station.

"Sir, for a moment, I heard a noise, but then it was gone."

"What did it sound like? A torpedo? Another sub?"

"No, sir. Nothing man-made. It sounded like . . . a whale."

The captain frowned as he turned to look at his lieutenant. "A whale?"

"Yes, sir. It sounded like the call of a whale but at a much higher pitch. I will—"

Another horrific stab from the port side. The joggle was so sadistic the water leaking into the engine room became a river.

"Report!" the captain shouted in a shrill tone.

"Captain, I have lost contact with the engine room," the lieutenant said.

"Go see what is happening, Lieutenant."

"Aye, sir," the lieutenant said. But before he reached the first bulkhead, the *Kirov* lost power. The nose began to dive, and the lights flickered.

The captain motioned for the lieutenant to run and grabbed the hand mic all in one motion. "Engine room! Engine room!"

No answer.

"Helmsman, get this ship back online, or we are all dead men."

"Sir, the helm is not responding. The engines are offline."

"What is our depth?"

The helmsman spun back around and checked the console. "Three hundred meters and falling fast, sir."

"Launch the emergency beacon!"

"All power to the beacon is offline, sir."

The captain clutched the hand mic with white knuckles. "Engine Room! Respond! Lieutenant! Respond!"

A crackling came over the speaker. "Sir," the lieutenant said, "the engine room is completely flooded! I repeat, the engine room is completely flooded! The water is moving forward. I have sealed off the bulkhead, but I am afraid we have taken on too much water for the ballasts to do any good."

The captain leaned against the wall, frigid salt water spraying him in the torso. His mind raced through every inch of the submarine, through every protocol and procedure, through every conceivable solution, but to no avail. Picturing his vessel plummeting five thousand meters to the icy ocean floor, being crushed on the descent like an empty aluminum can in the hands of a thirsty man, he knew now, full well, the meaning of the Scripture he had heard his grandmother read that morning when he was a boy of ten years old, kneeling in the little Russian Orthodox Church on the outskirts of Minsk:

"And the sea gave up the dead which were in it . . ."

CHAPTER FIFTEEN

Thursday, 1:22 p.m.
The Home of Evelyn Sims
Normandy Island, Miami Beach, Florida

Evelyn Sims had changed from her red silk pajamas into a pair of Gloria Vanderbilt jeans and a beige blouse some time ago. She thought Agent Jackson and his cronies would have been there already. That's why she was up at eight a.m., sitting bleary-eyed at the kitchen bar, listening to the sharp ringing in her ears that was drowning out the chirps of cicadas and cardinals outside her window.

She never had been one for functioning on little sleep. She liked her sleep. She used to be an eight-hour-a-night girl. Had been since elementary school. Seldom would you find Evelyn Sims awake past ten at night unless there was no other alternative.

Until her marriage started to fizzle. Then the alternatives became excuses. The more David was away on business, the more Evelyn remained at the institute—staying late, going in early, pushing herself to break into the scientific limelight.

Now, here she was—about as scientifically illuminated as she cared to be—wishing she was the no-name marine biologist from several days earlier.

Her phone call from Micah Gregson seemed eons ago. She had been in the bedroom watching the news report on the *Titan*, but had to move out into the kitchen to stay conscious. It was a mistake to lie back on the bed to watch the news. Not that the news wasn't interesting. It was right up her alley. It was the commercials that caused her to close her eyes "just for a moment." Fifteen minutes later, the sharp sound of a flute advertising a prescription medication alerted her to the obvious—get up. Now.

So, she sat in her kitchen. The place where she loved to experiment with exotic dishes had now become a jail cell. She couldn't go into the backyard, sit by the pool and read. She'd discovered that earlier, realizing that a picture of her in those red silk pajamas, taken by a photographer with what seemed to be a lens fit for shooting cheetahs in the Serengeti, would soon be plastered all over the front page of countless newspapers, or worse, the Internet. She couldn't go into the living room unless she wanted to feel like a fish in a fish bowl. Once reporters realized she was that close to the front of the house, their incessant calls from the sidewalk, begging her to come outside to answer "just a few questions," would never cease. It would make the living room an annoying place to be.

That left the back office, the bedrooms, and the kitchen.

Another fifteen minutes passed before someone rang the doorbell.

Bothered by the waiting, she peered through the peephole before opening the door, staying out of the sight of cameras. "Agent Jackson, it's about time."

Agent Jackson, not wearing his ball cap but instead sporting a blue long-sleeve dress shirt, a tie, and some black slacks, had arrived with two other agents Evie had never seen. "I'm sorry we're late," he said.

He and the two officers entered the house not appearing to be sorry at all.

The two other agents carried metal cases. Evelyn had seen enough episodes of *CSI* to know what they were.

"Mrs. Sims, this is Agent Fredericks and Agent Solomon," Jackson said, pointing to each man in turn. "They're going to search your house, looking for anything that might help us with our investigation of your husband's business dealings."

"That's fine," she said, "but I doubt you'll find much here. He hardly ever brought his work home. He preferred staying late at his office."

"Ahh, the late-at-the-office routine. Telling."

Evelyn feigned a smile. "I guess that does take on new meaning now, doesn't it?"

"Sure does."

Agent Jackson nodded at the two officers who returned his nod and split up—one heading for the hallway leading to the bedrooms, the other moseying into the kitchen.

"Mrs. Sims, may I have a word with you? I have some questions I need to ask."

Evelyn motioned to the couch and recliner.

Agent Jackson strolled over to the curtains and drew them shut before sitting down on the couch and pulling out a legal pad and a pencil. "The reason I was late, Mrs. Sims, is because I had to stop by the hospital and see Mrs. Fleming."

Evelyn, having sat down in the chair, straightened. That was twice her dead husband's lover had been mentioned within a couple of hours. Just hearing her name made Evelyn's blood boil.

"Mrs. Sims, how well do you know Captain Micah Gregson?"

Evelyn's left eyebrow arched in a mystified look. "Captain Gregson? I met him last night for the first time. You introduced us."

"Have you spoken with him at all, besides last night when I introduced you?"

"He called me this morning. He had a couple of questions about the boat." Evelyn could see Agent Jackson's interest pique.

"What kinds of questions?"

"How long we had owned it. Uh, did we like it? Questions like that. He said he was in the market."

"In the market?"

"You know, he's looking to buy a boat and wanted to know what I thought of our schooner." She knew Jackson wasn't buying it. It was a lame excuse, and she knew it. But he caught her off guard.

"Captain Gregson's in the market for a million-dollar yacht? On a Coast Guard salary?"

"I didn't question him about his finances, Agent Jackson. Maybe he won the lottery."

"I doubt it." Agent Jackson set his jaw. "Was that all he called about?"

"Pretty much."

Agent Jackson studied her face for a moment before rifling through the pages of his notepad. He finally came to one specific page and paused. "Mrs. Sims, I've been doing some reading. As you get to know me, you'll find that I'm an avid reader. I'm not a television person. I couldn't tell you what kinds of shows are on the tube these days."

"You don't watch TV at all?"

"Don't even own one."

Evelyn couldn't believe that in a technological age like this—where people his age and younger were techno-savvy, even techno-saturated—a man like Jackson didn't watch it at all. "What about when you stay in hotels? You must travel a great deal in your line of work. You mean to tell me you don't flip on the television late at night just to unwind? Catch the news?"

"Nope. I unwind with a good book instead. And the news I need to know about is always handed to me in manila folders and envelopes, if you know what I mean."

Evelyn pursed her lips but didn't respond.

"Mrs. Sims, a few years ago, three to be exact, you developed a hyperbaric biosphere for the National Marine Institute, correct?"

"Yes. You know what it is?"

"Yes, Mrs. Sims. Reading. Remember?"

"Of course." She wondered where these questions were leading.

"Can you tell me a little about that project?"

"I thought you already read about it, Agent Jackson. What else is there to tell?"

"I'm sure you didn't put everything in your paper."

Evelyn flashed a bogus smile. "You're right. I didn't. I'm assuming you're referring to the paper that appeared in the *Journal of Marine Paleontology*?"

"Yes. I did read your paper, and it was my understanding that your article was the laughingstock of the year—archaeologically speaking, of course."

Evelyn's pleasant, tolerant demeanor eroded. "Agent Jackson, that paper may have been the laughingstock of the *Journal of Marine Paleontology*'s community. They thought the project extremely comical because it was rejected by every foundation out there for grant purposes. Too many of our scientific communities are nothing more than stuffy, self-absorbed ivory towers writing and reading their own papers. When someone comes along and upsets their philosophical apple cart, they attack those ideas. But that's okay, because the project garnered enough funding from private industry to fund our institute's research endeavors for the last three years. That's more support for one project than anything the institute has ever done. And, I might add, substantially more than the grants would have given us."

"I know, Mrs. Sims. There were some large corporations involved in the private funding of the project, weren't there?"

"I'm not at liberty to say, Agent Jackson, but I'm sure you can finagle your little hands into the right cookie jars to get the answer to that question, can't you?"

Jackson fleered. "What else can you tell me about the project?"

"I'm sure there's not much to tell that you don't already know."

"Why don't you go ahead and amuse me, nevertheless."

Evelyn tucked her hair behind her ears. "The project was an experiment to see how many atmospheres of pressure it took to totally oxygenate blood."

Agent Jackson's eyes lifted from his notepad to Evelyn. "And?"

"The Earth's atmosphere is comprised of twenty-one percent oxygen and seventy-eight percent nitrogen. The other one percent is made up of other various gases. This concentration remains virtually unchanged regardless of altitude. Whether you're at sea level or standing on top of Mt. Kilimanjaro, it's the same. So, it's a misnomer to say the oxygen is thinner at high altitudes. It has to do with pressure and density, not oxygen levels.

"It was this fact that forced us to study pressure and density.

"As a result of this study, we found that human blood became totally oxygenated at two point one four atmospheres of pressure. The oxygen content in the blood increased from twenty-three percent—which is today's average amount—to thirty-five percent. The carbon dioxide increased by ten times the normal amount. We theorized that this level of atmospheric pressure would be perfect for not only mankind, but also for all forms of life on the surface of the Earth, including plant life."

"Meaning?"

Evelyn shrugged. "At that atmospheric pressure, a person could run a hundred miles and never get tired. A tomato plant can grow thirty feet tall and produce tomatoes the size of basketballs . . ." Evelyn stopped. She was going to say more. The scientist in her wanted to plow ahead with information she loved to discuss. But she remembered to whom she was speaking.

Agent Jackson leaned back on the couch, his notepad and pencil dropping in his lap. "You're joking, right?"

"Do you run, Agent Jackson? Jog? You know, to keep in shape?"

"I used to jog. I can't anymore. Knees," he said, tapping his right knee with his pencil.

Evelyn nodded, not offering any sympathy. "When you ran, did you ever get tired and out of breath?"

"Of course."

"You got tired from running because your body required more oxygen than your lungs could deliver to your vital organs and muscles at our current atmospheric pressure."

"Which is fourteen point seven pounds per square inch."

Evelyn scrutinized the man sitting in her living room. "Which is the equivalent of one atmosphere of pressure, yes. Your high school science teachers would be proud."

Jackson ignored Evelyn's jibe and began scribbling numbers on his notepad. "But, at two point one-four atmospheres of pressure, or at thirty-one point four-five-eight pounds per square inch, I wouldn't get tired at all? Is that what you're saying?"

"Yes. Because the oxygen forced back into your lungs as you breathe would be richer in oxygen content. The higher content would then be transferred into the bloodstream, where it would be distributed to all your vital organs that would normally be suffering from oxygen deprivation at fourteen point seven pounds per square inch."

"But what about the higher levels of carbon dioxide? Wouldn't that have an adverse effect, negating the effects of the increased oxygen? I mean, that's one of the leading causes of global warming and the greenhouse effect."

Evelyn scoffed. "Global warming . . . right. You can believe that if you wish, Agent Jackson, with all its erroneous science and political tentacles. But at two point one-four atmospheres of pressure, the richer CO2 content would actually help the plants grow larger and produce *more* oxygen."

Agent Jackson wasn't laughing. "You don't believe in global warming, Mrs. Sims?"

"I didn't say that, so don't put words in my mouth, Agent Jackson. Let's just say that global warming or climate change or whatever you want to call it today is science terribly misguided and leave it at that, shall we?"

Agent Jackson, bothered by her answer, continued. "What other benefits would there be by an increased atmospheric pressure?"

Evelyn grew suspicious. *How much should I tell? Try to stay within the parameters of the paper. Don't give any more details than the paper mentions.* She shifted in her chair. "You would also heal faster, and bites from insects and certain animals would not be harmful. They would actually be a good thing."

Jackson, jotting down notes as Evelyn spoke, glanced up at her with startled eyes. "Wait a minute. All these benefits are because of increased atmospheric pressure?"

"Yes. Oxygen heals, Agent Jackson. Haven't you ever heard the phrase, 'Life is in the blood'?"

Agent Jackson's eyes became antagonistic. "Yes."

"When the blood is totally oxygenated, the red and white blood cells are at their optimum levels. For example, if your body is not struggling to breathe, say while digging a ditch six feet deep and one hundred feet long, then if you cut your hand, your body can focus solely on the cut. Thus, healing occurs quicker than what we are accustomed to seeing."

"That doesn't explain how bites can be beneficial."

Evelyn tucked her hair once more. "Insect bites and snake bites, for example—and we are particularly talking about ones that are poisonous—are comprised of a complex blend of proteins, peptides, enzymes, and toxins. The reason they become toxic to humans is simply because our bodies cannot assimilate the nutrients fast enough. Therefore, the nutrients in their super-concentrated state are toxic, poisonous. It would be like overdosing on vitamins. Something that was intended to be good for you becomes harmful.

"We've known this for years, Agent Jackson. Years ago, Christian missionaries out in the field developed a machine that disperses the toxins using an electric pulse similar to a defibrillator. It ran at a high voltage but with no amps. The theory was that if you could disperse the toxins quickly while at the same time giving the patient oxygen, the bite would not kill the person. Of course, it works on less potent bites better than more lethal ones. However, if we lived in two point one-four atmospheres of pressure as opposed to just one atmosphere of pressure, the nutrients would be assimilated easily and would be beneficial."

Agent Jackson lifted an eyebrow. "You mean to tell me mosquito bites would be beneficial?"

"Correct. That's why they're so annoying. We can't assimilate the nutrients fast enough. So they become toxic and make the skin itch."

"And that explains why a bite from the Brown Recluse spider does so much damage?"

Evelyn shot him a perplexed look.

"My nephew was bitten by one a few years ago. He nearly lost his hand."

Evelyn's puzzlement softened. "Sorry to hear that. The Brown Recluse does have one of the more potent insect poisons. It sits in the tissue for days, even weeks, and destroys the flesh. However, at two point one-four atmospheres, it would be like drinking an energy drink—one that was good for you, that is.

"Did you know doctors, right now, as we speak, are working with snake venom, looking for a cure for cancer? The answer is the hyperbaric biosphere with the right dosage of venom."

Agent Jackson scribbled down more notes. "Mrs. Sims, what would finding out this information have to do with your line of work?"

Evelyn shrugged. "There are several different applications," she said, not wanting to reveal too much. "For example, finding out about what sea life was like thousands of years ago can help us understand sea life today."

"I still don't see the correlation."

Evelyn sighed. "Just as there is atmospheric pressure above sea level, there is also pressure in the water. We call it hydrostatic pressure. The deeper you go, the more pressure you encounter. Understanding how this works above sea level may help us understand how it works in the ocean."

"How?"

"Ever wonder how giant squid can live so deep and survive?"

"Can't say I have."

"When humans dive—say scuba diving, for example—the deeper they go, the less time they can stay down. A tank of air lasts longer if you stay shallow. But why does hydrostatic pressure affect humans negatively while it seems to have little effect on giant squid?"

"Okay, okay. So your experiments with the biosphere were simply to aid your work at the institute?"

"Well, yes. What else would they be for?"

Agent Jackson studied Evelyn. "Oh, nothing, I suppose. Although I have heard and read of people using studies like yours to try and discredit Darwin's evolutionary theories."

Evelyn wrinkled her brow a little. "And how would that concern the FBI, Agent Jackson?"

"It wouldn't, I guess. I just recall reading a review of your article, and that was the biggest concern raised by the scientific community, from what I could surmise. And as you know, I'm not a scientist, so such things confuse me when I read them if they get to technical. All that jargon starts to put me to sleep."

"That's understandable. I'd probably feel the same way about FBI matters."

Agent Jackson offered a rigid smile. "But you still didn't answer my question."

"I suppose," Evelyn said, feigning deep thought, "if one believed Darwin's theory was flawed, they could use this information in an attempt to discredit it. It's a possibility."

"But that's not why you're studying such things, is it, Dr. Sims?"

"No," she said, ashamed of her answer. "I'm just searching for the truth, Agent Jackson, in all its forms. Where the chips fall is what science is all about, isn't it? Create theories. Prove or disprove those theories. Get to the bottom of it. Approach such topics with objectivity?" She smiled. "Wouldn't you agree?"

CHAPTER SIXTEEN

Thursday, 4:31 p.m.
National Marine Institute
Miami, Florida

Deciding to trek over to the marine institute after he ate lunch, Micah paid his seven-dollar parking fee and pulled into Space 52 in the Crustacean section of the lot.

Then he waited.

Fifteen minutes later, with his windows rolled down, a nice breeze drifting off the ocean, and a full belly, the reclined driver's seat beckoned him to catch up on lost sleep from the many previous nights of restless slumber. He accepted, for over an hour, until his cell phone rang.

It took the better part of sixteen measures of the theme from *Jaws* to awaken him from his impromptu nap. Groggy and disoriented, he fumbled with his phone. "Hello?"

"Micah, it's Evelyn. Where are you?"

Micah yawned. "I'm in the Crustacean section of the parking lot at the National Marine Institute."

Evelyn laughed. "You're already here?"

"I fell asleep waiting for you to call."

"Must be nice."

"It was. Wasn't long enough, though. I'm not a power-nap kind of guy."

"Do you want to go back to sleep or come on in?"

"You're already here?"

"Yes. So, what'll it be?"

"I'm on my way."

"Don't you want to know where to meet me?"

Micah stretched his limbs while still trying to orient himself. "Probably would be a good idea."

"I'll be waiting at the front gate. Just go straight to Gate 12 on the right side of the main entrance and bypass all the ticket booths."

Micah rolled his windows up, opened his car door, and crawled out. "I thought you were going to call me when you left your house?"

"I guess you thought wrong."

"That's what you told me." He looked up, searching for Gate 12.

"I changed my mind. A woman's prerogative."

"A woman's way to control the situation, you mean."

"Po-tay-to, po-tot-to." Evelyn giggled. "Gate 12, Micah. Your other right."

Micah turned and saw a beautiful woman in a white lab coat waving with a cell phone pressed against her ear. "Oh, there you are. That sign was blocked. I couldn't see Gate 12 from where I was."

"Sure. Whatever you say, Captain Gregson."

"It's the truth, Doctor." He clipped his phone to his belt and smiled. *I could get used to this.*

Evelyn escorted Micah through some back doors marked "Authorized Personnel Only." They weaved their way through hallways and in-between buildings before marching down some stairs into what appeared to Micah to be an army bunker.

At the bottom of the stairs, a metal door on rusty hinges created a dead end of sorts. Centered in the top half of the door was a small window with wire mesh embedded in the glass. The door's chrome handle exposed much of the brass underneath, well-worn from years of being grabbed with grubby hands.

Evelyn opened the door. "This way."

"Are you sure it's okay for me to be here? This seems 'official,'" he said, mimicking quotations marks with his hands.

"I'm the director of operations for the research side of the institute. Bud Kensington, the man who was with me last night, is the only one over me . . . actually, our shareholders are over all of us, but you get my meaning."

Micah straightened his stance. "Well, I'm impressed."

Evelyn smiled, her eyes brilliant in the dark corridor. "Good. You were supposed to be."

Poured concrete walls, painted a stale off-white, met a ceiling of reinforced concrete girders that gave the underbelly of the complex a tomb-like aspect. The solid concrete floors had been surfaced with polyurethane, which had yellowed with time. Along the edges of the floor, and every so often down the height of the wall, water trickled, sounding to Micah like those miniature waterfalls many people had in their living rooms, setting on a table, dribbling their little songs over and over again.

"I think you have a leak," Micah said, acting concerned.

Evelyn stopped and turned to face Micah. "It's perfectly fine. You are now under the shallow end of the dolphin tank. There are over two hundred thousand gallons of sea water directly overhead." She waited, watching Micah's expression. "With another six hundred thousand gallons connected to that."

Micah pointed upward. "You mean there are dolphins directly overhead, performing tricks for the audience as we speak?"

Evelyn laughed. "I'm kidding. The dolphin tanks are clear over on the other side of the park."

Micah blew a big sigh through his lips. "So, what's really above us? The tank for the blue whales? Great white sharks? Stingrays?"

"Orcas."

Micah squinted and studied Evelyn's face. "Really?"

"No, not really."

"You're a piece of work. You know that?"

Evelyn smiled once more. It was clear she loved the company.

Micah pointed at the wall. "So, where's the water coming from?"

"We're in Florida. Water table's high. That's why we don't have basements here. Besides, these walls were built back in the late Sixties. It's a wonder they haven't cracked to pieces by now."

"This has always been a marine institute?"

"Not one open to the public. The military built this place years ago as a research laboratory."

"Ah, my first impressions were correct. I thought this place had a military feel to it."

Evelyn motioned for him to follow. "This was one of the Naval facilities used by the government to train dolphins to retrieve bombs and other such craziness."

"I didn't realize they had a facility here."

"Very few did, I guess. Anyway, the Navy abandoned it in the late Eighties, and it sat vacant for about a year. A group of investors bought it and turned it into a marine institute. Bud came on as head director in the mid-Nineties, and I came along about ten years later."

"And you've been here how long?"

"Going on ten years."

"And how long were you married?"

"About nine years."

Micah gave Evelyn a confounded frown while acting like he was counting with his fingers.

"Yeah, yeah. I know. Whirlwind romance."

"Really?"

"Really. I met my husband while trying to find a place to live." She blushed. "He was my real-estate agent."

"You married your real-estate agent?"

Evelyn managed an afflictive smile.

Micah's eyebrows arched. "That gives a whole new meaning to the term 'closing costs.'"

Evelyn's mouth flew open. She smacked Micah on the shoulder with the back of her hand.

"I'm sorry," Micah said, still chuckling inside. "Foot-in-mouth disease. It's always been a problem in my family."

They sauntered through two more doorways, another set of stairs, and a short hallway before they entered a large laboratory that reminded Micah of his high school science classes. Fluorescent lighting illuminated a room with multiple tables topped with black epoxy resin. White boards lined one wall, and a bank of computers lined another.

"How long had you known your husband?"

"We met on my third day in Florida. Then we dated about two months before getting married."

"That sounds kind of quick."

Evelyn gave a heavy sigh. "It was. I was on the rebound . . . and just plain stupid."

She sat on a stool next to one of the well-worn wooden tables. Looking up at Micah with girlish eyes, she patted the stool next to her.

Micah's interest piqued as he sat down. "Rebound?"

Evelyn peered at the ceiling before closing her eyes in embarrassment. "I was engaged back in California."

"You were in California? Where?"

"San Diego. Scripps Institute."

"No way," Micah said. "I was stationed at Point Loma for years."

"Small world, huh?"

"Really."

Evelyn pointed to Micah's left hand. "I see you're married."

"I was. My wife was killed in an automobile accident a few years ago back in Point Loma. Drunk driver. T-boned her car at an intersection. She was on her way back from the grocery store." Micah hesitated. "I kissed her goodbye and told her I'd start supper. I never saw her again."

Evelyn's bright eyes sank, apologetic for striking such a solemn chord. "I'm sorry, Micah. I didn't know."

Micah played with the ring. "How could you? I wear it because I loved my wife, and I don't want to forget her."

Evelyn grasped Micah's hand. "That's so sweet. She must have been special."

Micah didn't pull his hand away. "She was."

Evelyn peered into Micah's eyes, examining how attractive they were right down to the pupils. "She was a lucky woman."

Micah straightened a little. He slid his hand away. "Your husband was a lucky man, too." His voice became a little tremulous. "I'm sure you're really hurt by all the events of the last couple of days."

Evelyn stiffened and shook her head. "Oh, Lord, please forgive me," she said before her eyes began to well up.

"What's wrong?"

"You must think I'm a monster."

Puzzled, Micah said, "A monster? Why?"

"Here you are, years removed from your wife's death. You still wear your wedding ring because you don't want to forget her. And here I am, one day from the news of my husband's death, and I'm coming on to you like some middle-school girl with a crush." Evelyn shook her head in disgust, stood, and walked to a large stainless steel sink along the north wall of the laboratory. She placed both hands on the sink's edge and started to cry.

Micah got up and followed her. "Evelyn, it's okay."

"No, it's not okay." Her sobbing made the words slur together. "I know we weren't close. David and I never should have gotten married. But he was my husband." She tried to stifle her weeping. "You would think I would feel remorse . . . that I would be hurt or sorry or sad . . .

but I don't. I'm not." She looked at Micah with pleading eyes. "I feel . . . relieved instead. How horrible is that?"

"Evelyn, I'm not here to judge you."

Her gaze remained on him. "I didn't want it to turn out like this."

Micah nodded. "I'm sure you didn't."

"I used to pray it would work out, but I gave up praying about three years ago." Evelyn dropped her head again and turned away. "It was then I realized I had run away from God and into the arms of a man I hardly knew."

Micah placed his hand on her back, trying to console her. "We all make bad decisions from time to time."

Evelyn choked back a sob. "Yeah, but I knew that running to Miami wasn't the answer. But when my fiancé dropped me, I went berserk. It was so sudden. We had just booked a cruise for our honeymoon. All the plans for the wedding were being finalized. Everything seemed perfect."

She gripped the edge of the sink tighter with one hand while wiping her face with the other. "Then, a month before the wedding, he calls me up and says we need to talk. We met for dinner, and he tells me he's reconsidered. Doesn't want to get married now. Says he's really sorry," Evelyn said with a swaying of her neck. The anger in her voice rose. "And that he'll take care of the cruise. Then he throws some money down on the table to cover the check and walks out." Evelyn turned and looked back up at Micah. "He never even said goodbye."

Micah was speechless.

Evelyn shifted her feet and returned her gaze to the sink. "I ran to Miami and NMI. I was hurt and lonely, and David was just at the right place at the right time."

"Or possibly the wrong place at the wrong time."

Evelyn glanced up again. Clearly she was puzzled, but she appeared to be calculating his words. "It definitely was all wrong."

Micah placed his hands on Evelyn's shoulders as she released the sink. "Let's sit down and talk."

As Evelyn stood straight and met Micah's eyes, her heart began to flutter, to waver, to almost palpitate. Her hands felt sweaty. A sudden flush flowed from her torso to her neck and head. Her breathing quickened. Her muscles tensed, and the point where his hands touched her shoulders became a focal point of multi-faceted sensations.

Is this what love feels like? she thought. *Or am I just an emotional mess?*

Frazzled, she allowed Micah to escort her back to the table.

CHAPTER SEVENTEEN

Thursday, 4:45 p.m.
Location: CLASSIFIED

A man, whose face remained indeterminate in the shadows of the large oak tree, flipped open his cell phone and pushed the number six on the keypad.

Another male voice answered, sounding annoyed by the interruption. "Hello?"

The first man spoke in almost a whisper. His voice sounded altered, like a robot. "Are you alone?"

The second man lowered his tone to a near whisper as well. "Yes, but I thought you were not supposed to call me unless it's at the appointed time."

"Don't tell me how to run this operation. Remember, you work for us, not the other way around."

"Sorry. Just like to know when protocol changes, that's all."

"Unless you haven't noticed, there is no protocol. It's my show, my call. Whatever I deem necessary is what gets done. Understood? If you have a problem with that, then I can easily find someone else to do your job."

"Look, I understand, but—"

"Good," interrupted the first man, "because circumstances have escalated to such a degree that waiting for our scheduled time was no longer an option."

"What's so pressing that it can't wait until tonight?"

"There's been another incident. The Russians lost contact with one of their subs. It was due to check in four hours ago."

"Where?"

"Central Atlantic, we think."

"How far out?"

"We're not sure. They were on their way to Venezuela according to the ministry of defense. A transmission was received just prior to the sub going dark. They sent a copy of a photograph. It is undetermined what the photo is, but in the transmission from the submarine, there was mention of a 'flipper.' Now, they are asking for assistance from our government with finding the locator beacon."

The second man's voice changed pitch with excitement. "Do you know what this means? This creature is expanding its territory."

"What?"

"Animals are territorial by nature. They do that to protect their young primarily, but I've always believed it is a safety issue as well. Humans do it, too, albeit our reasons may have more complexities. We call it conquering."

The first man shook his head. "But that sub was a Dolphin-class sub. It's a hundred and eighty-eight freakin' feet long. What in the world could attack a ship that big?"

The second man snorted. "I told you there was something immense out there. I've been saying it for years. The Bermuda Triangle may have strange weather patterns that knock airplanes out of the sky, but those weather patterns do not always explain why seagoing vessels disappear off the face of the Earth. There has to be another explanation."

The other man remained silent. He didn't like what he was hearing.

The second man cleared his throat. "If I was you, I'd keep all vessels out of the new triangle."

"New triangle?"

"Don't you get it? The territory is changing. It could be any number of reasons why. New food source. Old food source no longer viable to sustain predator community. New predator takes over old stomping ground forcing old predator to move. Predator wants to expand territory. Could be any combination as well."

"This is nuts. You're talking completely from conjecture."

"No, I'm speaking from experience. That's why you hired me. I'm one of the best at what I do."

"Fine. Enough with the sales pitch. What do you propose we do?"

"I'm not sure. That's your area of expertise. All I know is if this thing is proven to exist, the scientific world could be turned on its head."

The first man sighed. "I'm afraid we're past the point of no return on information about this creature being divulged. Too many news outlets have it now. If things continue on their present course, we will be exposed. It's only a matter of time."

"How do you know?"

The first person barked into the phone. "I just know. And if I am to make any decisions, I'll need some time to ascertain the best alternative. I don't want to blow this by making a rash assessment and have more untimely information plastered all over the news." The first man paused. "Let me know anything new as soon as you know it. I need you to press things on your end. Time is of the essence."

"Got it."

"Very good. Oh, and by the way, never question me about protocol again. Remember, you work for us."

The second man sighed. "Sure."

The first man slammed his cell phone shut, slipped it into his sport coat pocket, and pulled out a pack of cigarettes from the breast pocket. He hated how the situation in which he found himself had become so complex. The plan looked so easy on the drawing board. But plans never materialize like you concoct them. There are always others who step in and foul them up. There always has to be at least one naïve idealist who sees the world in black and white. Always feels compelled to help. And all they do is get in the way of the bigger picture.

He lit his cigarette and took a large drag before grabbing his cell phone once more. Flipping it open and scrolling down through a list of names entered only by their initials, he hit Send and sucked on his cigarette again.

"Hello, Doctor. Because you are calling me, I assume there is a problem."

"Well, Mr. Gilliam, there is. Dr. Sims, the marine biologist whose husband was killed in the attack on the yacht, is far more advanced in her understanding of evolutionary science and its so-called flaws than we suspected. She could be a real threat."

"Dr. Fontaine, you assured me and my partners that you could handle her. You even said you had someone watching her so she would not cause trouble. Are you telling me now that this isn't so?"

Fontaine took another drag from his cigarette. "No, she's under surveillance." He blew smoke up in the air. "So are some other people who have joined forces with her."

"Who are they?"

"There is an assistant at NMI, a John Spencer—a recent doctoral graduate from Scripps in San Diego. I'm not too worried about him. The one I am concerned about is a Captain Micah Gregson. He's a Coast Guard officer and former Navy captain with considerable experience in Naval Intelligence before his resignation."

Gilliam sighed. "He could be a problem. Do you have him under surveillance?"

"No, sir. That's the problem. He was being followed by an FBI agent, but he figured it out and nearly killed the agent. When he is at

NMI, I can have him watched along with the others, but when he isn't he has the ties to cause problems, real problems. I would venture a guess that he has ties in the government that could expose my role and position."

"You're probably right, but before we knock him off, let's see how much of a problem he becomes. He may not pose as much trouble as you expect."

Fontaine flicked his cigarette. "He has already visited Regina Fleming and asked questions about the creature. He now has evidence from his interview with her on what the animal looks like and what sounds it emitted."

"Words from a confused, psychologically disturbed woman who has no evidence to back her wild claims. Doctor, you have to be patient and play these things out. Reacting too fast will draw too much attention to you and us. Let the woman talk. The wilder the claims, the more psychotic she makes herself out to be, and that plays right into our hands."

Dr. Fontaine at once felt a flush. *How do I tell him this?* "Uh, Mr. Gilliam, you won't have to worry about that Fleming woman any longer."

"Why is that, Anthony?" Gilliam said. "Please tell me you didn't—?"

"Sir, we had to before she gave out too much information."

"You're a fool, Fontaine. How did you do it?"

"I found a nurse in that hospital who needed some additional cash. I told her I may never need her services, but if I did, she'd have to carry out whatever orders I prescribed to the letter, regardless of who might be around. She agreed."

"What did you do?"

"I gave the order for the nurse to give her some medication. A little too much medication."

"You are one hundred percent confident that this will not become an issue?"

"The FBI stepped in and took care of the rest. Once Fleming died, her body was labeled "Classified" and flown to the FBI medical facility. I hear an autopsy was performed to show cause of death as heart failure due to a psychological disorder. Lucky for us, she was already being treated for psychological issues, so the medication found in her system was consistent with what had been used since her arrival." Fontaine took in another quick draw of smoke.

"If this comes out as a cover-up or some kind of dirty pool, then your days will be numbered, Doctor. I cannot afford to have a scientist who is really not qualified to make such decisions on a plan of this magnitude. I suggest you get advice before you make any other decisions that could become exigent. Is that understood?"

"Fully, sir."

Fontaine heard a *click* on the other end and frowned. He closed his phone and took one last drag. Looking around to see if anyone overheard the conversation, he crushed his cigarette against the tree and dropped the butt on the ground.

CHAPTER EIGHTEEN

Thursday, 5:15 p.m.
NMI Main Laboratory
Miami, Florida

"I was working at the Birch Aquarium for the Scripps Institution of Oceanography. My job was to study climate change on sea life. You know, with all the hype about global warming, it was a hot topic area. I told them I wanted to make a difference when I interviewed. So, that's where they placed me." Evelyn sighed. "Studying climate change was all well and good, but that's not what I intended when I said I wanted to make a difference. However, God had other plans."

Micah twisted up his face. "God had other plans? You don't strike me as the religious type."

Evelyn frowned. *Great. Can't tell, huh?* "I wouldn't consider myself religious. I did call myself a Christian at one point. But now, I'm not sure. My faith's been a little rattled of late, and since you thought otherwise, my faith has obviously suffered more than I thought. I'm apparently not a very good representative for God these days."

"Evelyn, I didn't mean to bash your faith. You actually seem," Micah paused, searching for the right word, "genuine. You know you have faults. You know you've made mistakes. And you're willing to admit you're far from being some super Christian." Micah shifted in his seat. "That sounds a lot like the religion my wife tried to get me to accept during the later years of our marriage."

Evelyn beamed a smidgen. "Thank you. All I know is that before I moved here, God had led me to each and every place I'd been. I sometimes knew where He wanted me to go before I went. But in the times like going to Birch, I didn't know until well after. In each and every instance, though, He led me." Evelyn's smile disappeared. "Well, except here. I ran from God to Miami, and now I'm paying for it."

"How did you know the Birch Aquarium was the place for you?"

"I didn't at first. I was studying the rising temperatures in the ocean coupled with the ice melts in places like Greenland, not liking it at all. I must've been working on data for three or four weeks when I ran across an article that questioned the entire global warming theory. After reading it, I then started to piece together why God placed me at Birch studying something I didn't want to study.

"The article said that the cause of global warming was not due to holes in the ozone or increases in the carbon dioxide levels. The author said those were symptoms, not the cause. Instead, he believed the Earth's electromagnetic field was to blame."

When Micah's eyes squinted, Evelyn could tell she was losing him.

"Think of the Earth as a big top," Evelyn told Micah. "You know, the kind you wind up and watch spin on a table or a floor."

Micah nodded. "Okay."

"What happens when the top spins?"

Micah, puzzled by the question, knew he was missing the obvious. "It spins."

Evelyn looked at Micah and motioned with her hands.

". . . and spins some more?"

Evelyn kept motioning.

". . . and spins?"

Evelyn's gestures urged him on to the logical conclusion.

"Ohhh . . . and eventually it slows down and falls over."

"Yes, exactly. And as the top slows down, what happens to it?"

"It starts to wobble."

"In other words, the axis of the top begins to rotate like this." She motioned with her finger pointing straight up, drawing little circles in the air.

"Right."

"Do you see the correlation?"

Micah looked her straight in the eye, searching for the answer she wanted him to give. He then shook his head. "Sorry."

"Micah, you're thinking about this way too hard. Stop for a second and think it through." She held up her hands. "Now, a top spins on its axis, right?"

"Yes."

"And the Earth also spins on its axis, true?"

Micah glowered at Evelyn. "Yes."

"When the top slows down, does the axis remain the same, or does something happen to it?"

"It starts to wobble. We established that already."

"Sooo?"

Micah's face brightened. "Sooo, what you're saying is, the Earth is slowing down?"

"Yes. Science has already proven that. Now, here's the bigger part. As the Earth slows down, the electromagnetic field weakens. Think of it this way. The spinning holds everything together by electromagnetic cohesion. But if it slows down, the EMF weakens, and gaps in the field appear." She looked at Micah as if hoping a bell would ring in his head.

It did. "The hole in the ozone layer."

Evelyn pointed her finger at Micah and winked. "You're a man of the sea, Micah. Have you noticed that when you go outside you have to wear protective clothing or use good sunscreen to keep yourself from burning?"

"Of course."

"But thirty years ago, we used to put on suntan oil. We'd slather that stuff on, and then lay out in the sun for hours to get a good tan. Remember? No sunscreen. No SPF ratings. Nothin'. Instead, the oils were rated by how deep and bronze you could get."

"I remember my dad telling me stories about that. Hawaiian Tropic versus Australian Gold? Which one was better?"

Evelyn's eyebrows raised. "Why the change?"

Micah sat silent for a moment. "The electromagnetic field?"

"Well, people want to point at the holes in the ozone, to be more precise. One near each of the two poles might account for rises in temperature, glacier melts, and the rest, but they should not account for you and me getting roasted out here on Miami's South Beach. Right? We're nowhere near the North or South Pole."

"So, why do we?"

"If the EMF is weakening, then the shielding that protected us from the sun's ultraviolet rays is weakening all over the planet. Not just in two specific locations. That's why we can be so near the equator—the farthest point from the poles—and still get burned a lot quicker than we used to."

Micah's befuddled look concerned Evelyn. "But you didn't answer my question."

"Okay," she said. "Imagine you're holding a clear plastic, hollow top. One shaped like a sphere that looks like a see-through ball. Got it?"

"Got it."

"Now, if I put colored liquid in it—say, a bright blue liquid that's easy to see—and I spin the top, what happens?"

"The liquid would be forced to the center by centrifugal force."

"Exactly. It would be at the 'equator,' if you will. That's where you would find the thickest concentration of liquid. The top and bottom of the sphere would see the thinnest concentration of liquid. Right?"

"And that's why the holes in the ozone are occurring at the poles first."

"Bingo."

As Micah mulled her words, the expediency of what she was saying struck him. "Oh my."

"What is it?"

"Do you hear what you're saying? If the electromagnetic field is to blame, how do we fix it?"

Evelyn pursed her lips and tossed him a slight shrug. "That's just it, Micah. The way I see it, *we* can't. That's why the scientific community found my article in the *Journal of Marine Paleontology* so ridiculous. Scientists are of the belief that mankind can fix everything. Just one more breakthrough. One more advancement. And everything will be all better.

"But, people and companies can buy their carbon offsets. Everybody can stop driving SUVs and start riding bicycles. Mankind can become as green as Kermit the Frog until they're tickled pink with their efforts, but all those efforts won't stop global warming because it has nothing to do with all that. There isn't such a thing as 'the greenhouse effect.' Those are all symptoms. It's like putting a band aid over a bullet wound. The patient is still going to die."

"So, who can fix it? I'm not going to believe we're all doomed."

"Micah, there's only one person who can stop global warming at this point."

"Who?"

"The One who started the top spinning in the first place."

Micah snorted. "Oh, great. I get it. If we're waiting for God to step in, we all might as well live it up and enjoy life as best we can because we *are* all doomed."

Evelyn tilted her head. "Why do you say that?"

Micah grumbled something inaudible under his breath. "I really don't want to get into it right now."

Evelyn could see Micah's agitated state and knew pressing the issue would only make matters worse. "Okay, we can leave that discourse for another time." She patted his hand.

Micah sat still.

Evelyn paused before changing the subject. "Okay, then." She pulled her hand away, feeling a little foolish. "You said over the phone that you had something to show me. What was it?"

Micah stood without saying a word, reached into his pants pocket, and pulled out the large tooth he'd recovered from the boat. He handed it to Evelyn and sat back down.

Evelyn gasped. "Is this what I think it is?"

"I don't know. What do you think it is?"

"It's a tooth, silly. A *really* big tooth. Where did you get it?"

"From the bottom of your boat."

Evelyn turned her head and scowled at Micah out of the corner of her eye. "I thought you weren't supposed to take anything from the boat? You know Jackson will hang you out to dry for this."

"Not if he doesn't know."

"Who knows about this besides us?"

"My chief boatswain's mate."

"Can you trust him?"

"With my life. Besides, he was with me when I found it. So, if he squeals, he's going down with me."

"This is one big tooth, Micah." She held it up to the light. "It's the size of a banana."

Micah pulled out his notepad. "Get this. I went back to the boat today and took some measurements. There were some puncture marks on the opposite side of the hull from where I found this tooth. The distance between bite marks was twenty-seven feet."

"Twenty-sev—" Evelyn squinted and stared at Micah. She couldn't believe it. "Are you sure?"

"I double-checked to make sure. There was one set of marks

where the tooth was found and one set at an equal point on the other side of the hull." Micah showed her the sketch he made. "But there's no telling if that distance is with its mouth fully extended or not."

"Let's hope so for our sake, huh? An animal with a mouth that envelopes a periodontal area that extends to at least twenty-seven feet . . ." She calculated in her head. "It must have a head at least fourteen or fifteen feet long."

"It's not like a plesiosaurus, though."

Evelyn appeared surprised. "What do you know about plesiosauruses?"

Micah inhaled, positioning himself as if for a long discussion, flipping the pages of his notepad. "I've always been fascinated with sea creatures. Especially the larger ones. Predatory types. When I spoke with Regina Fleming, she said the head looked more like kronosaurus queenslandicus, but the neck was more like plesiosaurus, only bigger, thicker, and longer."

Evelyn chuckled, amused at Micah's surprising knowledge. "I'm afraid that's one I'm not familiar with, Micah."

"Got a computer handy?"

Evelyn pointed over to the corner of the lab. "I'll log us in."

Micah soon located the webpage of the picture he had shown Regina Fleming that morning.

Evelyn peered over his shoulder. "Kronosaurus queenslandicus, huh? That Fleming woman said the head shape in this picture was pretty accurate?"

"Yep, but bigger," he said.

"The neck was more like a plesiosaur, only thicker?"

"And longer."

"And we know that this creature can leap out of the water and attack ships with at least thirty-foot-high decks." Evelyn began to pace back and forth behind Micah. "And who knows if that jump was its maximum range? It could jump out of the water even higher than that for all we know."

"True." Micah spun around in the office chair. "So, what are you thinking?"

"Did you get to see that video of the attack on the cruise ship?"

"No." Micah swiveled back to the computer and punched some keys.

Soon, before their eyes, the video streamed over the Internet. Micah couldn't believe the frozen image at the end. It appeared to be a gigantic mouth. "That's exactly what Regina Fleming described. A big mouth."

Evelyn began to pace again. "Micah, we may have a new species of dinosaur here."

Micah chuckled. "Right."

"No, I'm serious." She turned to face him. "It wouldn't be the first time."

"First time? What are you talking about?"

It was Evelyn's turn to laugh. "Ever heard of the *coelacanth*?"

Micah shrugged. "Of course."

"Well then, you know the coelacanth was a prehistoric fish found only in the fossil record until a fisherman—back in 1938—caught one. Scientists have since found schools of them in various parts of the Indian Ocean. Scientists thought the coelacanth was extinct—for about eighty million years—until a live one was found."

"But that wasn't a new species. That was just one they thought was extinct."

"True," Evelyn said with her finger raised. "But I'm not finished. Ever heard of the Highland Mangabey Monkey in Tanzania?"

Micah shook his head. "Nope."

"That's understandable. Most of the world's population hasn't. That species of monkey was just discovered in 2003. It's been around for ages; the locals had a name for it—*kipunji*. They knew it existed, but scientists didn't. Thus, it had never been classified.

"Then there was the rodent found in Laos being sold in open food markets. I forget the name of it, but it was verified by scientists to be a new species of rodent never catalogued before.

"And more recently they found an entire new breed of leopard in the jungles of Borneo. New breeds of fish and frogs were found as well. It's really amazing what's out there."

Micah held up his hands. "Okay, so you're suggesting there are animals out there that scientists didn't know existed . . . even ones thought to be extinct. I can buy that. The world's a big place. I'm sure scientists and explorers haven't examined every nook and cranny of each continent and ocean."

"That's just it, Micah. The more we discover, the more it shows how little we really know. For example, there was a fossil found in Russia of a dinosaur never before known to exist. It now resides in the Iwaki City Coal and Fossil Museum in Tokyo, Japan. Because they classified the dinosaur fossil in the pliosaur family—due to its alligator-like head, body-type, and its flipper-like appendages—they labeled it as *pliosaur sp*."

"Okay, so your point would be?"

"My point is, we have found prehistoric fish alive that were thought to be extinct. We have found monkeys and rodents, frogs and leopards never catalogued or even known to exist at all. And we have found new dinosaur fossils that we never knew existed. So then, why not combine all of that? A new dinosaur that not only was never known to exist, but is also alive?"

"You're crazy," Micah said, studying her eyes, "but . . . I have to admit, based on our initial findings, it does make some bizarre kind of sense."

Evelyn's eyes sparkled with playfulness. "Then that makes you crazy, too, mister."

Micah grinned at her.

Evelyn handed Micah a flash-drive from her coat pocket. "Can you save that video for me? And send it to my home computer, too. No, wait. That won't work. They took my computer this afternoon. Send it to my work e-mail."

"Sure, what's the address?"

She gave it to him.

"They took your computer, huh?" Micah said, tapping at the keyboard. "What did Jackson have to say?"

Evelyn sat on the corner of the table next to the computer. "He first wanted to know how well I knew you, and if we had spoken to each other after meeting last night."

"What did you tell him?"

"I told him you did call me. And when he asked what it was about, I said you were asking me questions about the schooner."

"That had to make him suspicious."

"It did. I tried to cover it up. I told him you were asking questions about our boat because . . ." Evelyn grimaced, "you were in the market."

Micah closed his eyes and pinched them together like he was in pain. "On a Coast Guard salary?"

"Yeah. That's what he said."

Micah began to rub his forehead. "He knows we know something, and that's not good."

"Why do you say that?"

"He had Agent Lowery follow me. Probably made that decision after our little episode in the hospital."

"Episode?"

"Never mind. He was just being a jerk, and I let him know I agreed."

"And he sent Lowery after you?"

Micah nodded. "I didn't know it was him at first, but when I saw Lowery, I confronted him before I arrived in Miami. I told him to lie to Jackson about his findings."

"Do you think he will?"

"Hard to say. Depends on how loyal Lowery is to Jackson. I'm counting on his dislike for Jackson as our ally. But we'll see. What he does will tell us a lot."

"Why would they have you followed?"

"Like I said, Jackson thinks we know something. Or, he thinks we might uncover something before he gets to it."

"That may be true. He was questioning me pretty hard about my biosphere."

"Really? What did he ask?"

"He wanted to know what the purpose of it was and how it related to my work here at the institute."

Micah winced. "How much information did you disclose?"

"He said he had read my article. I merely elaborated on what was already in the article. Nothing more, nothing less."

"Good. No sense in giving that creep any more information than necessary."

"He grilled me pretty hard, though. I got the impression he knew I wasn't telling him everything."

"Like what? I read your article, and I've read others like it. I think I understand the hyperbaric biosphere concept. Pretty wild, actually. I see hospitals using it for healing purposes now. It seems more and more commonplace."

"It's actually very simple science. It's all about how oxygen heals, and that's what I told Jackson . . . then I referenced the Bible."

"The Bible?"

"'Life is in the blood.' Leviticus 17:11."

Micah's eyes instantly focused on the ground, and then he spoke almost in a whisper. "Oxygen."

"I'm sorry," Evelyn said. "What was that?"

Micah shook his head slightly. "I just remembered something I had forgotten until now. I was about ten years old, and I was sitting in a Vacation Bible School class at my grandmother's church. We were learning about how God created everything. The teacher was an older lady with gray hair and glasses. I forget her name. Mrs. Finkelstein or Blankenship or something like that. She was reading the story of Adam and Eve, and the part that just came back to me was the scene where God breathed into Adam the 'breath of life.'"

"Oxygen?" Evelyn said.

Micah nodded with a bit of confidence. "Yes. Oxygen. It makes sense."

"Well, my theological training makes me think there's more to it than just oxygen, but yes, in this case, considering what we've been talking about, oxygen does make sense. However, I don't think Agent Jackson cares about my hyperbaric theories right now. He acted a little too weird when I referenced the Bible. Like there was more to it."

"Agent Jackson is weird."

"I agree. Arrogant, too. But when I referred to Scripture, he acted . . . different. His demeanor changed immediately." She snapped her fingers.

"Not to make excuses for Agent Jackson, but some people, especially those of us who aren't churchgoers, get a little uncomfortable when God is brought into the mix. I can see Jackson doing that. He thinks he's as much a scientist as an FBI guy. So, that makes sense."

"That's true. At the end of his interview, he did ask me if I was trying to debunk evolution."

Micah's face scrunched. "Huh?"

"I know," Evelyn said. "I'm sure I had the same look on my face when he asked me that question. We were talking about the biosphere. Then he says, 'Some people would view this research as a means of discrediting Charles Darwin and his theory of evolution, but you wouldn't be doing that, would you?' I thought that was a strange conclusion considering what we had already discussed."

"What did you say that would make him think that?"

"I'm not sure. I was explaining the correlation between my biosphere research and how it applies to our research here at the institute."

"How does it apply exactly?"

Evelyn offered a shamefaced grin. "Well, a little different from what I told him."

"You lied to him?"

"No, not exactly."

Micah shifted his head.

Evelyn rocked her head from side to side. "I said the biosphere helps us understand the concept of atmospheric pressure, so forth and so on, blah, blah, blah, which is true. But what I didn't tell him was how we have concluded that at our present rate of atmospheric pressure, there is no way large animals, like the ones found in the fossil record, could have survived."

Micah gazed at her. His look of contrived disbelief had morphed into perplexity.

Evelyn sighed. "Let me back up." She began to pace once more. "Do you believe dinosaurs once roamed the Earth?"

"Yes, I do. The fossil record proves it."

"Okay, I agree. So, the question becomes, then, how did they survive?" Evelyn looked at Micah with eyes begging for an answer.

"I don't know. Like other animals, I guess. Some ate plants; others ate meat. Herbivores. Carnivores. Some probably ate both." Micah shrugged.

"I'll give you that, Micah. But how did the big dinosaurs like *Brontosaurus, Apatosaurus, Brachiosaurus,* and *Tyrannosaurus Rex* survive?"

"Where are you going with this, Evelyn?"

She smiled. "We know that *Brontosaurus, Apatosaurus,* and *Brachiosaurus,* for example, had hearts that were not very big. Same with *T-Rex*. Therefore, at our rate of atmospheric pressure—which is fourteen point seven pounds per square inch—their hearts would not be large enough to pump blood to the animals' extremities. In order to do the job, the heart would have needed to be substantially larger. So, I ask again, Mr. I-read-your-article-and-want-to-learn-more-about-biospheres, how did they survive?"

Micah's eyes reflected the intended sarcasm. "They wore oxygen masks? Or ran a lot and were in great shape?"

"Cute," Evelyn said. "In order for animals that big to have survived with hearts so disproportionately small, they would have needed more atmospheric pressure. They would have needed two point one-four atmospheres of pressure to survive."

Micah cocked his head. His face revealed a lack of understanding.

"Our research has concluded that two point one-four atmospheres of pressure is the ideal atmospheric pressure. As I was telling Agent

Jackson, at that level you could run a hundred miles and never get tired, plants would grow considerably larger, you would heal faster, and insect bites and snake bites would be beneficial instead of annoying or deadly."

Micah's dumbfounded expression softened. "And that's what a biosphere does? Increase the pressure?"

"A hyperbaric biosphere does."

"Yeah, I meant that."

"Good, because there's a difference between a hyperbaric biosphere and a normal biosphere."

"Right. I know. And you told Jackson all this?"

"Most of it. I excluded the details about dinosaurs."

"Why?"

"Because I didn't want him to think I was trying to discredit evolution."

Micah was puzzled again. "But you are, aren't you? Doesn't your research do that?"

"Yes, but I didn't want to admit it to his face. I'm not ready for him to start turning my professional life upside down like he has my personal life."

"Oh, okay, I get it now. But you really are trying to disprove evolution?"

Evelyn scrunched her face. "It's not like it's a mission for me. I like to think of it as divulging the truth in the midst of accepted fallacies."

"Interesting," Micah said, his voice distant.

Evelyn puckered her lip. Her eyes drooped like a lost little puppy's. "You're not going to rat me out now, are you?"

"Are you kidding? I'm the one who found the tooth, remember? I'm in this neck-deep, too."

Evelyn nodded and sat on the edge of a table next to Micah. "It's all David's fault. I still can't believe it. It all seems like a bad dream somehow. He was having an affair. But before I get a chance to confront him, he's gone. The last person with him wasn't me. Instead it was his bimbo lover. And now, the FBI is tearing *my* house apart, digging into *my* personal life, digging into *my* professional life. And now you're involved. If David would've kept his nose clean, we wouldn't be dealing with this at all."

Micah pointed at Evelyn. "You see, that's one of the things that doesn't make sense. Agent Lowery told Wellman and me last night that they always investigate what amounts to paranormal cases. He mentioned the Abominable Snowman and Bigfoot. Whenever there's a case that involves things like that, Jackson and his crew are the ones sent to investigate. If that's true, then why would he care about your husband's supposed dealings with people tied to terrorism? If what Lowery said is accurate, then this case does not fit their normal MO."

"You know, you're right, Micah. Jackson told me they had been following David, and David lost them in a shopping mall the day before the accident. Why would they be following him? And why would they stake out our house?" She held up the tooth. "It's not like David *knew* he was going to run into this creature."

"You see? It doesn't add up. I'm telling you, Evelyn, there's something else going on here. You may have felt bad about not telling Jackson everything, but he's not telling us everything either."

Evelyn's eyes began to mist. Her head dropped. She grew silent for several uncomfortable seconds. "I don't know how much of this I can take, Micah." She looked up at him after reciting his name.

He leaned in and gave her a hug. "We're in this together."

Beginning to weep, she wrapped her arms around his neck, and they embraced each other.

Then, without warning, a throat cleared from behind them.

They turned to see Bud Kensington standing in the doorway with his eyebrows arched high.

CHAPTER NINETEEN

Thursday, 5:47 p.m.
NMI Main Laboratory
Miami, Florida

With celerity, Evelyn Sims and Micah Gregson released each other. Feeling like a couple of teenagers caught by their parents while engaged in an embarrassing act, they peered down at the floor, ashamed to look Bud Kensington in the eye. Evelyn wiped her eyes with her hands and dried them on her lab coat. Micah jammed his hands into his pants pockets, wondering if Evelyn still had the tooth.

Bud leaned on his cane, his voice steady. "I must ask. What did I just witness?"

Evelyn marched toward Bud, wiping her eyes one last time. "Bud, it's not what you think. Trust me. It's been a long, hard, twenty-four hours for me. And I was telling Mic—I mean, Captain Gregson—about things. You know, I am a woman, Bud. I have to get things out, talk about them. I can't keep things bottled up inside like you can. Captain

Gregson merely came by to see how I was doing. That's all. Isn't that right, Captain?"

"And to see how your investigation was going."

"Were you now?" Bud said.

Evelyn's voice changed from shaky to stern. "Bud, don't you even dare."

"Evie, pardon me for being a bit cynical, but you have been an employee and a friend for several years now. You just get word that your husband has been killed and, suddenly, Captain Gregson arrives on the scene?" Bud shrugged. "I'm no Dr. Ruth or Ann Landers, but it doesn't take a Phi Beta Kappa to see the handwriting on this wall."

"Excuse me, Dr. Kensington." Micah maneuvered closer to Bud. "I know we only met last night, and we don't know each other very well. But before you start throwing accusations and innuendos around this laboratory, can we cut the sarcasm and discuss this like civil men and women?"

Bud eyed Micah. "I'm always civil, Captain Gregson. Just ask Evie. But I'm always sarcastic as well. Years out at sea, away from your family, away from friends, makes you a little sarcastic, a little hard. You should know, Captain Gregson."

"How should I know?" Micah said.

"You're in the Coast Guard, right?" Bud shrugged as if the answer should be obvious.

Micah managed a hesitant nod.

"I'd be willing to wager you had a previous life on the sea. I'll bet you were in the Navy," Bud said with a wink. "Intelligence would get my vote."

Micah snorted. "And where did you get that information?"

Bud's eyes grew bigger. "It was an educated guess, Captain. You seemed too refined, too rigid to be anything else. My bet is that you were an officer in the Navy for several years." Bud shuffled closer to Micah and lowered his voice. "I ran into plenty of you guys when I was in port here and there around the world."

"And why were you in port, Doctor? Supplies, perhaps?"

Bud belched a hearty laugh and slapped Micah on the shoulder. "Let's just say I needed to be supplied with something and leave it at that."

Evelyn could tell Micah needed to be enlightened. "Bud spent several years serving on the *Calypso*," she said.

"I'm impressed. So, Doctor, hanging around all those French guys probably didn't help you with common decency then, did it?"

Bud laughed. "No, sir, it did not. When they were in port, all they wanted to do was—"

"Heyyy," Evelyn said, interrupting before the air turned blue. "Bud, why are you here? You hardly ever come to the lab, so it must be important."

Bud hobbled over to the nearest chair and plunked down in it. "I needed to talk to you about your husband's . . ." He paused, as if not knowing how to phrase it.

"My husband's what, Bud?"

"The accident, Evie. The FBI wants to know what we thought of the wreckage. They're requesting a formal report."

"You and I talked about it on the way back from Fort Pierce. We both were puzzled. Besides, who produces a formal report within twenty-four hours of seeing the crime scene for the first time and submits it no less?"

"I know, Evie. I told them we needed time to analyze the data."

"What data?"

"You know what I mean. You have to utilize terminology that sounds official and political to pacify these folks."

Evelyn shook her head in disgust. "Politics. That was my husband out there, Bud. He and that woman in the hospital are the 'data' you're talking about, along with what's left of the boat."

"Evie, if this case is too personal, I can get Spencer to take it over. I know everyone would understand, considering the circumstances."

"Not on your life, Bud. If you want John to help, great. We could use his help. But I'm not leaving this case. Anyway, I think we may have some possible leads."

Bud's eyes perked up. "Such as?"

Evelyn glanced over at Captain Gregson, wondering how much she should tell. "Did you hear about the cruise ship incident that happened last night?"

Bud's grip on his cane tightened as he shifted on his stool. However, his expression remained solemn. "No. What happened?"

Evelyn drew a deep breath. "You haven't? I'm surprised. Was CNN not on today? You always are surfing the cable channels looking for oceanic news."

"I've been a little busy today, Evie. I didn't get to come to work in the afternoon like some people. Plus, we reopened today after closing yesterday. The news hounds have been merciless, wanting information about the attack on your boat. They know we were there last night investigating it. They want to speak with both of us, especially you, and I'm not sure how much longer I can keep them at bay."

Evelyn smiled. "Bud, I appreciate you running interference for me. You should have seen Agent Jackson earlier trying to get me into my car without being assaulted. There must've been thirty reporters clogging the street in front of my house."

"They camped out here, too. Must've followed you from your house because there are more now hovering around the main entrance along Bayshore."

"I saw them out there. Good thing we have an employee entrance in the back." She winked at Micah.

"I told Spencer to make sure they didn't get into the park at all, not even the parking lot. I also relayed a message that we would give a statement later in the week when we knew something worth reporting. Now, what about this cruise ship?"

Evie sat down next to Bud. "A cruise ship was attacked by a large sea creature last night near Great Abaco Island. There was a video shot by someone with a cell phone. We've got it pulled up on the computer if you want to see it."

"Absolutely."

Evelyn and Micah showed the video to Bud a total of eight times. Bud kept replaying the piece, pausing it in various spots. He then leaned back in the chair.

"You know," he said, "that video is awfully grainy. You can't see much except at the very end."

"We know. The camera had a hard time focusing, especially when the creature was down at sea level. But you've got to admit that when the thing jumps up, the image gets pretty clear."

Bud nodded. "But it's still unclear what the image is exactly."

"But Bud, if this is what we think it is," Evelyn said, "then we may have the find of a lifetime here."

Bud turned in his chair to get better eye contact. "And what do 'we' think it is?"

"The ocean's version of the Loch Ness Monster."

Bud rolled his eyes, dropping his head. He then lifted his head and peered at Captain Gregson. "She's got you sucked in, doesn't she?"

"Excuse me?" Micah said.

"She's told you about her theories, hasn't she?"

Micah wasn't sure how to respond. "I'm not sure I know what you're referring to, Doctor."

"Bud, don't start," Evelyn said.

"I'm not, Evie. It seems you already have."

Evelyn spun away and grumbled something under her breath.

"Am I missing something here?" Micah said.

Bud chuckled. "I doubt it. Has she told you about her biosphere?"

"Yes. So?"

"And her theories on how we all came into existence?"

"Uh, no. We've only discussed things related to the *Greenback* and this video."

"Really? Interesting."

Micah turned to look at Evelyn. She was sitting at a table on the far end of the laboratory, facing away from the two men, trying not to cry.

"I'm sorry, Dr. Kensington, but I'm afraid I'm not sure what you're talking about."

Bud chuckled again. "Evie has some interesting ideas about things. How the world came into existence, how animals populated the Earth, et cetera, et cetera."

Evelyn was still facing the other direction. "And so do you, Bud."

"But mine are more accepted, Evie." Bud winked at Captain Gregson.

Evelyn stood and turned. "Just because they are accepted doesn't make them right."

"True enough. Can't argue with ya there. But as I've told you in the past, Evie, if you ever want to get ahead in this business, you must not ruffle too many feathers. It's one thing to study the ocean. It's quite another to call into question other scientists and their life's work."

"Why? Isn't that what scientists are supposed to do when they make new discoveries? If that discovery brings to light a fallacy, then isn't it unethical to censor the new information so that the flawed science can persist and certain scientists can continue to feel good about themselves?"

"It's not that the discovery must be silenced, Evie. There are simply better ways to ease the scientific community into a new way of looking at a new discovery. Shock therapy has always been a bad practice."

"No, it's that certain systems of belief become entrenched to the point where anyone who questions them is labeled a heretic or a lunatic or both. In those cases, there is no amount of shock therapy—or prolonged therapy, for that matter—that will help them see the light."

Bud sat silent for a moment. He then turned to Micah. "You see what I mean?"

Micah shrugged. "I know that she's right . . . in this case anyway. When you two were talking, I immediately thought of the Church in the Middle Ages and how they knew for certain that the Earth was flat. Science came along and showed that belief to be wrong. How long did it take the Church to acquiesce to that idea? Talk about shock therapy."

Evelyn smiled at Micah. "That's a good point, Captain."

Bud pointed at Micah with his cane. "Yes, that is a good point, and it proves my point exactly. Had the findings and theories not been so shocking, it might not have taken decades for theologians to accept them."

"But," Micah said, "don't you think certain discoveries are going to be shocking no matter when or how they are divulged? And that they are only shocking because the old beliefs are so ingrained into society that any new way of thinking would be shocking? I mean, there are still people who believe that all the Apollo missions to the moon were staged in a movie studio in Hollywood."

Evelyn pointed her finger at Bud. "That's what I was going to say. You said Captain Gregson's point proved yours. Well, it proves mine as well. People—scientists included—can get so enamored with their own beliefs and theories that when someone else comes along and says, 'Hey, you're wrong. That's not how it is,' they get defensive, just like the theologians Micah referenced. So, it really doesn't matter what you are—scientist, theologian, politician, historian, local yokel, you name it—when you have a belief system that is challenged, it threatens your comfort zone, and the first thing you do is defend your zone without even listening to see if your zone should change."

Bud exhaled an exasperated breath. "Here we go."

"What's that supposed to mean, Bud?" Evelyn said.

"Evie, we've had this discussion before. Many times. And I'm sure Captain Gregson doesn't want to hear it."

"How do you know?"

"Because it's boring."

"It's not boring. You only say that because you're a close-minded old man."

"Watch it, Evie."

Captain Gregson raised his hands. "Whoa, whoa, whoa."

Bud and Evelyn frowned at each other.

"I can see you two have had healthy conversations about this before. But an old debate is not going to help us figure out what happened to Evelyn's husband or their boat . . . or the cruise ship, for that matter."

Evelyn grunted. "Captain, Bud will never change his views. He believes in Panspermia, for Pete's sake. Nothing out there in the ocean is going to change that."

Micah's eyebrows crumpled together. "Pan-what?"

Evelyn chuckled. "Panspermia. Never heard of it, have you?"

Micah shook his head.

"Why don't you explain it to him, Bud?"

Bud Kensington shifted in his seat. "Evie, I think Captain Gregson is correct. Now is neither the time nor the place."

"Oh, now that we're going to scrutinize your beliefs, we don't have the time, but we sure had the time to dissect mine earlier. Well, guess what, Bud? I have the time." She turned to Micah. "Ever heard of people believing that we came from outer space?"

Micah glanced at Bud, then back at Evelyn. He nodded, not knowing what to say.

"People who believe in Panspermia think that some aliens came to Earth and deposited on it all the forms of life we have today."

"They think we are descendants of aliens?"

"Yes."

"Which aliens? Where do they think the aliens came from?"

"Bud, you want to field that question?"

Bud's voice blended into a subtle growl. "Evie, now's not the time."

"Of course it is. The answer to your question, Captain Gregson, is—"

The main laboratory doors burst open as John Spencer bolted inside, breathing heavy. "There you are. I've been looking all over the compound for you two. You could answer your cell phones, you know."

Evelyn snatched her phone from her coat pocket. "Sorry, John. Sound's turned off."

"Mine's in my office," Bud said. "What's so pressing, John?"

John Spencer, standing between Bud and Evelyn and wearing a lab coat with a surfer t-shirt underneath took a couple of deep breaths before answering. "The FBI is searching for both of you. They want you to examine the cruise ship that was hit last night near the Bahamas. It's supposed to be back in Port Canaveral by eleven p.m."

Bud looked at Evelyn. "Better get the Explorer ready. We'll leave as soon as the park is closed. I'll call Agent Jackson and let him know we'll be there as soon as possible." He shook his head. "It's gonna be another late night. John, I'll need to get with you about opening the park tomorrow because I doubt we'll be back in time, and we can't afford to close again."

A thought struck Evelyn. "Bud, why don't you send John with me instead? It would be good practice for him, and that way, you're here for tomorrow's opening."

Bud stood, groaning as he pushed himself up out of the chair. He peered at John.

John straightened like he was being inspected before roll call.

"Okay, that's a good idea, Evie. Put him through the drills. Show him how to get the Explorer prepared, how to handle an investigation, so forth and so on. I'll be up in my office."

Evelyn smiled at John. "Will do."

"Uh, guys, there was something else that just came across the wires that I thought you might want to know," John said.

Bud frowned, weary of the dramatics. "What is it, John?"

"Regina Fleming just passed away in the hospital."

Evelyn shot a look at Micah.

"Do they know how she died?" Micah said.

"The news report didn't say, but it did say she died around eleven thirty a.m."

"That's interesting," Micah said.

"Evelyn, are you sure you want to continue with this investigation?" Bud said. "I could go with John, and you could stay here."

Evelyn shook her head. "Not on your life, Bud."

Bud eyed Evelyn and Micah for a few clumsy moments. "All right, then. I'm going back to my office, kiddos. I'm assuming it's safe to leave you two alone down here by yourselves?"

Evelyn slapped Bud on the shoulder. "Bud, don't start now. Go close the park and go home."

"I think I will," Bud said.

John, standing off to the side, ran over to lend Bud aid.

Bud held his cane out like a sword, stopping John in his tracks. "I may be old, but I'm not feeble."

John stepped aside with his hands raised in surrender as Bud ambled out the laboratory door. He watched Bud until he disappeared, then turned to face Evelyn. His expression looked pained. "What was that about being alone?"

Evelyn rolled her eyes. "Never mind. It was just one of Bud's crude jokes."

"Ahh," John said.

"John, I do need to talk to Micah for a minute. If you'll go get the Explorer gassed up and meet me outside the research lab's main doors in fifteen minutes, I'll show you how to load up what we're gonna need."

John gave her a thumbs-up sign. "See ya in fifteen."

While Evelyn and John were talking, Micah had shifted over to the computer and was tapping on keys.

"Hey, what are you looking at?" Evelyn said.

"I'm trying to see if there is anything on the Internet yet about Regina Fleming's death."

Evelyn bristled. The mention of Regina Fleming's death should've alarmed her more than it did. A human being had died—one who seemed rather healthy according to Micah, despite the enormous trauma of the last twenty-four hours. Nonetheless, when faced with the news of this woman's death, a sense of relief washed over Evelyn.

Relief that this woman would not be allowed to wreck another marriage. Relief that she could not be cheated on by this woman anymore. Relief that although her husband would no longer enjoy the pleasure of Regina's company, neither would any other man.

Yet, Evelyn became overwhelmed with frustration, too. She would never know the details of the illicit affair which invaded her very soul. She would never get any of the questions of her heart answered now. Nagging interrogations of her psyche would be linked in a devilish, inexorable fashion to her daily life every time she saw a photo of Dave, heard his name, or thought of him.

How could Dave lie about his trips? Evelyn thought. *What was so attractive about Regina Fleming that Dave would risk it all? How could he have an affair knowing she was married? Why would she be willing to ruin her own marriage for another man? Did she find David attractive, or was she a gold-digger? How could she do it knowing there was another woman in the picture?*

Nevertheless, the worst aggravation of all for Evelyn was the repugnance of feeling relief and guilt at the same time—a feeling of simultaneous reprieve and remorse she knew was normal, yet wrong, with no answers for her sorrow. There was an acquittal from her so-called marriage, a release from an ever-increasing marital prison, but a guilt about feeling that way . . . about not feeling more sorrow for two lost souls. It was a combination of emotions so diabolical, so heinous, no person should ever have to deal with such cruelty.

Now, the two people who possessed all the answers were gone.

"That bothers you, doesn't it?" Micah shattered Evelyn's thoughts.

"What?"

"The fact that I'm checking on her?"

"No. I know you're trying to help."

"Then, what is it? I can tell something's wrong. You get rigid every time someone mentions her name."

"Of course. She was the one who was . . ." She couldn't bring herself to say it.

Micah gently grasped Evelyn's arm. "Yes, I know."

Evelyn closed her eyes before she started to cry.

"Hey, check this out." He grabbed the monitor and turned it toward Evelyn. "Read this section right here."

Evelyn bent over and read the section Micah had highlighted.

Hospital officials are withholding comment at this time. However, initial reports are indicating Regina Fleming suffered a massive heart attack precipitated by a sudden onslaught of hysteria induced by the trauma of the last hours of her life. Records also indicate that Regina Fleming had been under a previous doctor's care for no less than two psychological conditions.

"I don't get it," Evelyn said when she finished. "Was she drugged when you went to see her?"

"That's just it. She was a bit groggy. I saw the word 'clozapine' on the bag hanging from the rack next to her bed, but it was empty. The other bag was just a normal electrolyte bag. There wasn't anything else hanging from the rack. Besides, when she spoke, she seemed coherent and cognizant of her dilemma and surroundings."

"So, do you buy the heart attack story?"

"No. But what else do we have to go on right now?"

Evelyn smiled. "A cruise ship."

"Right." Micah held a finger up as he yanked out his cell phone and dialed. "And one other thing."

"Hello?" the voice on the other end said.

"Richard, this is Micah."

"Hey, Captain, am I glad you called. Have you been following this story? Did you know that Fleming woman is dead?"

Micah exhaled. "That's precisely what I wanted to talk to you about, Richard. I need to ask a favor of you."

"Shoot."

"I need to know everything you can find out about her death."

Micah heard a sigh on the other end.

"When do you need to know by?"

"ASAP."

"You know it's still my day off."

"Richard, I know I can't ask you to do this as an officer, but I'm not asking as a captain to his second-in-command. I'm asking as a friend to a friend."

"Well, since you put it that way . . . that Evelyn Sims chick is standing right next to you, isn't she?"

Micah peered up at Evelyn. "Actually, yes."

"And you've got the hots for her, don't you?"

Micah blushed, turning his face away from Evelyn. "That will be all, Wellman."

"Uh-huh. Got the hots for the marine biologist chick. ASAP. Of course, ASAP for the SWF with the BMW."

"Thanks, Richard. I'll be awaiting your call."

Wellman stared at his phone when he heard it click on the other end. "Yep. He's got it bad."

CHAPTER TWENTY

Thursday, 6:21 p.m.
Office of the Secretary of State
Washington, DC

A light knocking originated at the door of a large office at 2201 C Street NW. It had nearly anything and everything an office could ever need—from the latest equipment to a large antique oak desk with three supple leather chairs fanned out in front as if paying homage. Pictures of former secretaries of state lined one wall, and an oval-shaped Persian rug adorned the middle of the room. The office, which had been hopping with activity, was experiencing a lull for the first time today.

The secretary of state, sitting behind her desk and reclining in her leather captain's chair, looked up toward the door. "Come in."

The door opened, and an older, grandmotherly-type woman peeked inside. "Madame Secretary, you have an urgent call on line two."

The secretary of state inhaled, holding it in for a prolonged moment before exhaling in a melodramatic manner. "Urgent call from whom?"

The messenger slipped through the door, shut it without a sound, and peeked behind her in a nervous fashion. "The Russian ambassador. He seems extremely agitated. He said he needed to talk to you immediately, and something about me getting the hotline to the president's office fixed?" She shrugged.

"Okay, thank you, Mrs. Penderghast. That'll be all."

The woman slipped back through the door, and it closed with the slightest of sounds. The secretary of state took another deep breath and grabbed a manila folder off the corner of her desk. The sealed folder was marked "Confidential." It had been hand-delivered by the president himself with strict instructions not to open it until she heard from him. She snatched her phone from its cradle.

"Mr. President, I think it's time I was quickly debriefed on the contents of this folder you gave me this morning. I've got the Russian ambassador on hold."

"I was afraid of this," came a voice that was on a speaker-phone.

"Afraid of what?"

"That he would call before I could explain things to you."

"I don't even know why he's calling. I don't want to sound incompetent or out of the loop. So, talk to me fast."

The president grumbled. "The Russians lost a sub in the Atlantic. The sub sent a picture to the Russian high command right before it lost contact. The picture is in that folder along with a copy of a detailed report from the Russian government. They are wondering if we had something to do with the disappearance of their submarine."

"That's preposterous."

"Agreed. But they're not so convinced. It's your job to convince them."

The secretary grabbed her forehead with her left hand and squeezed. "Wonderful. Do we have any information I can use in my persuasion?"

"Information is limited. We've got top people working in the field to ascertain what we believe is the cause. However, we're not ready to float those theories out just yet. The Pentagon feels that would only exacerbate the situation."

"So I'm supposed to diplomatically tell him something that will abate his fears of an American offensive against his beloved homeland long enough for us to get some answers that can be proven?"

"See, you can read my mind. That's why I made you my SOS. Let me know how it turns out. Oh, and by the way, everything you accomplish or don't accomplish could have serious ramifications on future relations with Russia and her allies."

"Yes, sir," she said as the phone on the other end clicked.

The secretary held the phone handset for a couple of seconds. She wanted very much to read the contents of the file first. However, she had already kept the ambassador from Russia on hold too long. So, with a dexterous handling of the phone coupled with the opening of the folder with a letter opener, she tapped the button for line two.

"Ambassador Vrilinko, this is Sandra Brown, Secretary of State. It's so good to speak with you again. What can I do for you?"

"I have been trying," the ambassador said with no attempt at being cordial, "to speak with President Walker for over two hours, Miss Brown. His direct line has been ringing busy all morning. I am getting very frustrated."

"Don't be frustrated, Ambassador Vrilinko. This has been one of those days, you know? Lots of things happening. Everybody wanting to speak with the president all at once. That's why I'm taking your call. I'm trying to help him out. What's your concern, Ambassador?"

There was a pause. "Has he apprised you of our situation with our submarine? The *Kirov*?"

"I have the report you faxed him right here in front of me." She scanned its contents in an attempt to get up to speed. "What's this deal with the 'flipper'?"

The ambassador sighed. "We do not know. That is what the captain of the *Kirov* said they thought it was. They were ultimately unclear and uncertain. But shortly after we received the photograph and the subsequent transmission, we lost contact with the *Kirov*. We have not heard from her since."

"When this report was sent to President Walker, no locator beacon had been detected. Has that status changed?"

"No, and that is why I am calling. I have been attempting to get your government to assist us in a joint effort while there may still be survivors. If we could just locate the beacon, we could send dive teams down. We have two battle cruisers accompanying a scientific vessel to the last-known coordinates of the *Kirov* as we speak, but their arrival to the area will take time. Your cooperation would be greatly appreciated and would be viewed as a great act of good will."

"Ambassador Vrilinko, we would love to help. I can get in contact with the Pentagon and see if we can send any ships and personnel to that region of the Atlantic. Of course, I'm sure you're aware that we have a situation of our own brewing that we are trying to ascertain. So, I will see what I can do."

"What are you dealing with, if I may be so bold to ask? Maybe we could help you as well? Return the favor, so to speak."

"I wish I knew exactly, Ambassador Vrilinko. Have you been watching any of the news?"

"Yes, I have. Something about a sea monster?"

"It seems you know about as much as I do."

"My people said they saw a flipper. Could we be looking for one and the same thing?"

"Ahh, now, Ambassador Vrilinko, we are trekking outside my area of expertise."

"Once we find our lost comrades, we would love to help you in any way we can," the ambassador said. "So, Miss Secretary, do I have the help of your country?"

"I do not see why not, but let me contact the Pentagon first. They'll know more about our Atlantic contingent than I do."

"You are not going to put me on hold again, are you, Madame Secretary?"

The secretary laughed. "No, no, no. I wouldn't do that to you. I will call you back as soon as I have some concrete details to relay to you. Fair enough?"

"I would really like to hear from President Walker, Miss Brown. No offense. I just need to talk to him. If I do not, then our prime minister will be riding my back, no?"

The secretary nodded. "I understand. We'll be in touch."

CHAPTER TWENTY-ONE

Thursday, 8:02 p.m.
I-95 Northbound Lane
Near I-395 Merger

Evelyn Sims rode in the passenger seat while John Spencer took the wheel for the first leg of what was going to be a three-hour trip to Port Canaveral. The green Ford Explorer with the National Marine Institute's insignia emblazoned on the doors raced up I-95 at seventy-five mph. Micah Gregson rode in the back, sitting in the middle so he could talk to both of them.

For the first several miles, John and Micah created small talk, getting to know one another. Questions about jobs and family were the topics of choice at first before the conversation morphed into a discussion of sports.

Evelyn sat in silence for several miles, appearing to sleep. Her mind, though, had jumped from one subject to the next in a frenetic pattern as the words of John and Micah faded in and out of her daydreams.

Her thoughts drifted through the day's events, one by one. Then, they turned to her family. How she missed them right now. How she missed seeing them at holidays. How she longed for simpler times. Like when she was a little girl. How she wished she was back in college amongst the confines of books and classrooms. How she—

"Have you guys ever wondered how marine fossils ever got deposited in Kansas?" Evelyn said, interrupting John and Micah's conversation about the Dolphins' upcoming season.

"Well, hello, Evelyn," Micah said. "I thought you had dozed off up there."

"Not a chance. I'm wide awake. The mocha cappuccino has kicked in. My mind is scattered in a thousand directions."

"I wish caffeine affected me like that," John said. "I can drink caffeinated drinks and go right to sleep. I have to stay moving at night, or I'm done. If I sit down and get comfortable, especially at night, after an exhausting day, it's over. Then I wake up in my recliner at two in the morning stiff and sore, and go to bed."

"I hear ya," Micah said.

"But it doesn't really matter what time of day it is," John continued. "If I'm tired and I stop to sit down, or worse lay down, it's naptime."

Evelyn turned in her seat, raising her left knee and leaning back against the door. "Did you guys hear my question?"

"What was it again, Evelyn?" Micah said. "We were talking, and I didn't get all of it. Something about fossils and Kansas was all I heard."

"Have you guys ever wondered how marine fossils got deposited in Kansas?"

John glanced over at Evelyn, trying to keep his attention on the road. "Where did that come from?"

Evelyn gave a half-shrug. "I was daydreaming. Recalling an article I had packed in my suitcase the last year I had vacationed at our family cabin before heading off to college. The article was written by a modern paleontologist at the time—I can't remember his name now. But what I do remember was how the author spoke of marine fossils excavated in Kansas in the 1860s. I was captivated by the idea of marine fossils being found in Kansas of all places. A place that was a thousand miles away from the nearest ocean in either direction, east or west. That tidbit of information fascinated me, fueling my desire to become a marine biologist and learn more about the sea, both past and present."

"Interesting," Micah said.

"I was sitting here thinking about all that's going on right now and remembered that article. So, my question to you two is, have you ever wondered how fossils of *marine* animals ever got to Kansas?"

Micah wrinkled his brow and looked at John.

John's eyes were on the road, but Evelyn could tell the wheels of his mind were turning as well.

"Looks like John has thought about it," Evelyn said.

"What do you think, John?" Micah said.

"It was called the Western Interior Sea."

"That's right. The article mentioned that," Evelyn said.

"Okay, so apparently, I'm at a disadvantage here," Micah said.

John glanced at Evelyn. "The water that used to cover the middle of North America has been named by paleontologists. They call it the Western Interior Sea. It's believed by most paleontologists that the majority of the Earth was covered by water at one time. Some believe that it could have been as much as seventy-five percent of the Earth's surface. They also believe that the Earth was primarily a tropical, humid place before the Ice Age set in and formed the polar ice caps. So, if this understanding of the fossil record is true, then marine fossils in Kansas would not be all that surprising."

"I never knew you were into paleontology, John," Evelyn said.

"You never asked. My PhD is in marine biology, but I minored throughout my bachelor's and master's work in paleontology."

"Wow. You think you know a guy." Evelyn realized that John was a better fit for NMI than she'd first thought. "How do scientists know the Earth was tropical before the Ice Age?"

"Fossil evidence. Recent finds corroborate that theory. Did you read about the study done by a Danish researcher from the University of Copenhagen?"

"Uhh, afraid not."

"He drilled three holes. One extracted the contents from the southern part of Greenland. The second hole was drilled in the middle of the Greenlandic ice sheet, and the third one targeted the John Evans Glacier in Canada. The Canadian sample was just to test the method used, but at the bottom of the two ice cores from Greenland, the researchers found the DNA presence of alder, pine, and yew trees along with genetic traces of butterflies, regular flies, beetles, and moths. The evidence suggests that there was an actual tropical forest in southern Greenland at one time."

"Fascinating," Evelyn said.

"Plus," John continued, "there's been animal evidence, like mammoths found frozen in Siberia, for example, with undigested vegetation still in their stomachs."

"So, what, they just up and died one day? Ate lunch and then keeled over from a massive heart attack or something?" Micah said.

John chuckled and checked his rearview mirror. "Not exactly."

"Then what was it?" Micah said.

"Are you sure you want to go down this road, Captain?"

"What road? I'm not sure I understand what you mean."

John glanced over at Evelyn, assiduous and sitting in the same position.

"It's okay, John," she said.

Micah noticed John's inquisitive look and raised eyebrows as well as Evelyn's playful smile. "Okay, you two. Is there something going on between the two of you that I should know about?"

John and Evelyn burst out in uproarious laughter.

Micah's face became more perplexed. "What? What did I say that was so funny?"

"Captain, there is nothing going on between Evelyn and me other than a close working relationship, I assure you. Remember, she was married, and I am seriously involved with someone. Not to mention the fact that I'm considerably younger than her."

Evelyn blurted out a stern chuckle. "Watch it, Assistant Boy. It's not like I'm old enough to be your mother."

"True. It's more like 'older sister.' Much older."

Evelyn reached across the seat and smacked John on the arm.

John grabbed his arm, feigning extreme pain. "You're gonna cause an accident."

"You're gonna be drinking your lunches through a straw if you make another comment about my age."

"Okay, then." John paused and fixed his eyes on the road again before glancing into the rearview mirror. "Anyway, what we were referring to, Captain—before I was beaten for telling the truth—was the topic of Evolution versus Creationism."

Micah's demeanor changed from mystified to remorseful. "Oh, I'm sorry I brought it up."

"No, don't be, Captain." John glimpsed in his rearview mirror once more to see Micah's face. "I know you don't know me. If anything, I am a scientist, but I also believe in the Bible. I am what you call a 'conundrum.'"

Micah's eyes narrowed a bit. "A conundrum?"

"That's what Dr. Harry Landover, my faculty advisor for my doctoral dissertation, called me. Of course, he called himself that as well. We were two peas from the same pod, I think."

"How so?" Evelyn said.

"We had a lot of the same beliefs. We were both Christians, but we were both not anti-science, either. Instead, we both saw science as man's proving ground for biblical truth. As Dr. Landover put it, 'God created the heavens and the earth, and now man, blind to spiritual things, has to analyze it all under a microscope to see his Creator once again.'"

"I never was much of one for the Bible, church, all that stuff,"

Micah said. "I know my wife wanted me to be, especially once we found out we couldn't have children, but I couldn't get into it. There were never two people who wanted to have children more than us. So, if there is a God out there, why would God keep us from having kids? Especially when there were kids being born every day to people who don't want children?"

John glanced at Evelyn with his eyebrows raised. "Captain," John said, "I wish I knew the answer to that one."

Micah snorted. "You're the first person to say that."

"To say what?"

"That you don't have an answer for me. I had people tell me that God didn't want us to have kids because there were too many people in the world already."

"You're kidding, right?" Evelyn said.

"No," Micah said. "They said we were supposed to adopt."

Evelyn shook her head in dismay. "Micah, I'm sorry."

"Why? You didn't say it. I just chalked it up to arrogant stupidity on their part. But they weren't the only ones. I also had someone tell me we must have done something really bad to be cursed like that."

Evelyn was growing more frustrated by the minute. "Micah, whatever you do, please don't hold God accountable for imbeciles who parade themselves as being His representatives but act like anything but that. I mean, look at me. You couldn't even tell I was a Christian when we met. I would feel horrible if you thought less of God because of my actions.

"Now, that's not to say my actions don't matter, because they do. I'm responsible for my actions. You should be able to see God in me, but when you can't, understand that it is not God's fault. It's mine. There are a lot of things I can live with, but impugning God's honor and holiness with my own sinful actions is not one of them."

Micah smiled at Evelyn. "Evelyn, I find you to be one of the most genuine people I've met in a long time."

Evelyn winced. "Genuine? There's that word again."

Micah placed his hand on her shoulder. "I meant that as a compliment."

Evelyn chortled. "I know. I just want to be genuine in a godly way, that's all. Obviously, there's vast room for improvement."

"Let me clarify then," Micah said. "What I meant to say was that of all the people who call themselves Christians, you're the most real person I've met in quite some time."

"Thank you."

John cleared his throat. "Hey, I hate to break up the little love fest here, but I have an idea."

Evelyn grabbed Micah by the arm and squeezed before turning her attention to John. "And what would that be, John?"

"How about I call Dr. Landover and set up a teleconference with him? We could sit down and discuss this case and see what he has to say. I think you'll find him extremely interesting. He's neither your average scientist nor creationist."

Evelyn looked at Micah and shrugged. "Sure. When can you set it up?"

John opened his cell phone. "Let me see."

CHAPTER TWENTY-TWO

Thursday, 11:42 p.m.
World Cruise Lines
Florida Region
Port Canaveral, Florida

Passengers of the cruise ship *Titan* were unloading when the trio from the National Marine Institute arrived. Some passengers were scampering down the platform, wheelie luggage in tow, not saying anything to anyone. Their frightened expressions indicated they just wanted to be back on *terra firma*. Others exited the ship very animated, still energized by the events of the last few hours. With their arms flailing and their voices raised, it wasn't hard to make out the topic of their discussion. Words like "huge" and "teeth" and "monster" intertwined with superlatives and expletives. Still others, standing along the railing of the ship, were refusing to get off the ship until they received a refund. Soon port authority officers escorted those folks off the boat, much to their chagrin, with promises of certain legal action spewing toward the officers who were just doing their jobs.

It was amazing to watch, Evelyn thought, as she and her two cohorts stood behind the police barricade witnessing the episode unfold. An entire ocean liner, equipped to carry hundreds of passengers for multiple days, was sent limping home by one animal. *That's two-for-two. My boat and now this one.*

It was also remarkable to see many of the same FBI, ATF, and FDLE agents who were, the day before, swarming around her boat. Except this time, there were at least three times as many, and they seemed more frantic, more anxious, even impatient.

Evelyn grabbed Micah by the arm to get his attention. "Micah, recognize any of these agents?"

Micah nodded. "You noticed that, too, huh?"

"Yes."

Micah motioned with his head. "Did you see Jackson over there?"

"No. Where?" Evelyn turned her head to search. Her expression of marvel at once transformed into one of disdain. "He doesn't miss a trick, does he?"

"Don't you find it interesting that he's here?" Micah said. "I thought he was interested in tracking down your husband and his terrorist associates? What does the attack on this cruise ship have to do with that?"

John, who had been taking in the scene with awe and listening to Evelyn and Micah's conversation, pivoted to face his two comrades. "Terrorists? Did I miss something?"

Evelyn started laughing and grasped John's shoulder. "John, I forgot. You've probably not heard all the details, have you?"

"No. Is there something I should know about before we go any further?"

Micah joined Evelyn in laughter.

"John, let me give you the short version for now, and I'll fill you in on any details you need on the way back to Miami. Deal?"

John glanced over at Micah, who was still laughing a little with his eyes closed and his hand over his face, rubbing his tired eyes.

"I suppose," John said.

About twenty minutes passed before the three were granted clearance and began the trek up the loading platform when they heard a voice call Evelyn by name. "Dr. Sims!"

Evelyn, John, and Micah all turned to see Agent Archibald Jackson hotfoot from a group of agents toward the boat.

"Oh, here we go," Evelyn said under her breath.

She stepped back down the platform and met the agent at the bottom. "Agent Jackson, what a surprise." She held out her hand.

"Shall we bypass the pleasantries, Dr. Sims, and get right to it?" Agent Jackson didn't return the handshake and walked right past her. "Where is Dr. Kensington?"

Evelyn rubbed her hand on her pant leg, wiping off the imaginary filth she would have received had they shook hands. "He chose to stay at the institute so Dr. Spencer could come along and get some experience out in the field. Now, get right to what, Agent Jackson?"

Agent Jackson spun and studied her face. "Come now. You must know what's happened to this vessel, thus you must know why I asked you to come. I need information, and I need it fast." He started up the ramp once more.

"Agent Jackson, let's get one thing perfectly clear before we go a step farther," Evelyn said, loud enough for John, Micah, and anyone within a forty-foot earshot to hear. "Neither I, nor the National Marine Institute, work for you. We will work in concert with you. We will assist you. We will help in any way we can. But we do not work for you, and we definitely do not take orders from you. Is that understood?"

Micah and John were standing at the top of the platform, watching the action. Micah leaned over to John and said in a whisper, "You go, girl."

"Who is this guy?" John said.

"A pain in our backside. He's also the guy who searched Evelyn's house this afternoon."

John nodded. "Ahh, now the picture comes into focus."

Agent Jackson stood before Evelyn with a smirk on his face. "So, what you're telling me is you'll pass up this opportunity and allow someone else from another facility to take your place?"

Evelyn exhaled a chuckle. "Good luck on getting someone here within forty-eight hours, and they'll tell you the same thing. We will not be pawns of the government, Agent Jackson. So, if you can live with us doing our job the way we need to in order to get it done properly, and at the same time stay out of our way, then we can have a civil and maybe even a cordial and productive relationship."

Agent Jackson started nodding as if he had just understood something. He pointed at her. "You're still upset because I came and searched your house, aren't you?"

"No. I'm not."

"You know, I was only doing my job."

Evelyn rolled her eyes. "That's not why I'm upset. You don't get it, do you?"

"Get what?"

Man, this guy is dense. "You're an arrogant man, Agent Jackson. An arrogant and pushy man."

With those words, Agent Jackson's tenor turned tenacious. He stepped closer, invading Evelyn's personal space.

John started down the ramp like the protective brother, but as he leaned into his first step, Micah grabbed him by the arm.

"Don't," Micah said.

"Dr. Sims," Agent Jackson said, "let me fill you in on a little newsflash, okay?"

Evelyn was cold, not moving away. "Sure."

"With running the risk of sounding too archaic or cliché-ish, there is more to this case than meets the eye."

"Really, now," Evelyn said. "Somehow, I already knew that."

Agent Jackson's eyes narrowed, accompanying a stern gaze.

Evelyn didn't flinch. "You're here, aren't you? Unless my husband owned this ocean liner or was on it, I'm not sure what the attack on this boat has to do with the case against my husband you are supposedly investigating. The only correlation between the attack on my boat and this ocean liner is the thing in that cell phone video." Evelyn gave a nod. "And whatever that thing is out there, it has nothing to do with my husband, now does it, Agent Jackson?"

Agent Jackson remained silent.

"And since we are having this little heart-to-heart, let's be honest now, shall we?" Evelyn continued. "You never were investigating my husband, were you? All that talk about cars at malls and terrorists and money being siphoned through the business was all a bunch of lies, wasn't it?"

"No, it wasn't 'a bunch of lies,' Dr. Sims. Your husband was into something either wittingly or unwittingly. But this event," he said, motioning to the cruise ship, "has taken on a different significance that is unrelated to your husband and your boat."

"That was clear as mud."

"Dr. Sims, I cannot be more specific. I wish I could, and then maybe you would cut me some slack. But I can't. Just know that this event and the one involving your boat are possibly tied to a matter of national security. That's why time is of the essence."

"Man, you are being cliché-ish, aren't you? A matter of national security . . . time is of the essence . . . more than meets the eye . . ." Evelyn chuckled. "You're not going to tell me now that in order to gain access to this vessel, the code is 'The swallows fly at midnight,' are you?"

Agent Jackson rolled his eyes and pointed up the ramp. "Shall we?"

"We'll call you when we have something."

Irritated by Evelyn's implication, Agent Jackson was stern. "There is something I need to show you first."

Evelyn gave a halfhearted wave and motioned for him to lead the way. Agent Jackson darted up the ramp.

Jackson whisked past the two men at the top of the ramp. "Hello, Captain Gregson. I'm not really surprised to see you here, although I am surprised Dr. Spencer is here. Can't believe Dr. Kensington would miss this."

Micah looked at John. "And it's good to see you, too, Agent Jackson."

John's eyebrows rose. He scratched the back of his head but didn't mutter a word.

The three followed Agent Jackson to the starboard side of the boat's main deck. Leaning over the gunwale, Agent Jackson pointed down. "See that whole area from the water up to here?"

"You mean the freeboard?" Micah said.

Agent Jackson glared at Captain Gregson. "How silly of me. We have a nautical know-it-all right here. Is that what you call it, Captain?"

Micah's teeth clenched. He thought briefly of grabbing Jackson and tossing him over the side but instead grabbed the railing. "The area from the surface of the water to the top of the boat is called the freeboard, yes."

Evelyn and John were already looking over the side, searching back and forth past the point below them.

"Do you see it?" Agent Jackson said.

"No, afraid not," Evelyn said. "What are we looking for exactly?"

Agent Jackson groaned and looked back over the side. "Oh great, the light's gone," he said, grabbing his phone. He punched buttons with a forceful sigh before lifting it to his ear. "Agent Lowery, call for that tug to get back over here with the spotlight. We need to be able to see the starboard side of this vessel."

Several minutes passed before the tugboat *Olivia* positioned herself, shining a flood lamp at the midsection of the freeboard. In the interim, Agent Jackson, Evelyn, Micah, and John had little to say. The four minutes they waited before the tugboat rounded the corner of the ship seemed like four decades.

Annoyed by being in such close proximity to Agent Jackson, Micah eased away from the gunwale, trying to see the ship as it was in the video. He remembered the railing having a distinctive nautical pattern embedded in its metal framing when the video tried to focus on the creature in the water. However, when the creature lurched at the ship, the railing had no pattern.

Micah looked toward the bow. The unique railing ran all the way to the bow on both sides of the boat. He then looked toward the stern and noticed that the pattern ran from the stern to a point near the middle of the boat. The railing from there for about thirty to forty feet was a normal railing until it met ladders that went over the edge.

It was then the tugboat rounded the corner and began shining its floodlight at the *Titan*.

"Do you see it now?" Agent Jackson said.

"Oh, yes," Evelyn said. "Look at that, John. See the dent?"

John's eyes said it all.

Micah, who was standing toward the center of the boat, darted back to the gunwale to get a look. His strange movements caught Evelyn's eye.

"What is it, Micah?" she said.

Micah studied the damage for several more seconds before responding, looking in both directions. "That damage was not made by the creature in the video."

"What? Are you crazy?" Agent Jackson said.

Micah peered up and down the length of the boat once more. "No, let me rephrase that. It may have been the same animal," he said, pointing to the dent, "but the creature we saw in the video did not do *this* damage at *that* time."

Agent Jackson snorted and rolled his eyes.

Micah stood erect and turned toward Jackson. "You don't believe me, do you?"

Agent Jackson blinked. "I didn't say a word, Captain."

Micah grinned. "You didn't have to. But that's okay," Micah said, looking at Evelyn. "I don't have to answer to you, either."

Evelyn grabbed Micah by the arm and pulled him away from Agent Jackson. "Micah, explain what you mean."

Micah took one last look at Agent Jackson. "At the end of the video, the railing was like this." Micah pointed at the plain, standard-issue metal railing next to them. He then moved toward the bow until the railing changed to a pattern reminiscent of the Greek gods for whom the vessel was named. "The person who took the video was originally standing up here because the railing at the beginning of the video was like this."

Micah held out his hand pretending to hold a cell phone. "I'm the person taking the video. The creature was down there swimming alongside the ship before it hightailed it to a point up ahead of the ship as the video shows." Micah then started moving backwards. "The person must have been moving backwards like this when the animal moved toward the ship."

"Why?" John said.

"To get a better angle, maybe? Better lighting, better focus . . . to follow the animal as it moved back toward the boat? Who knows? But what we do know is the person slid back to somewhere in this area because when the animal jumps up, this plain-looking railing is what's in view."

John leaned over the gunwale and examined the ship where Micah was standing. "Hey, is there any way we can get the tug to move that floodlight over to here?"

Agent Jackson nodded and grabbed his phone. Moments later, the area in question was bathed in light.

"You see that?" Evelyn pointed to a spot some twelve to fifteen feet below the gunwale.

The three men all leaned over the railing and examined it.

John strained his eyes while shielding them from the floodlight. "I see something, but it's hard to make it out. What about you, Micah?"

"Nope. Agent Jackson, do you have any rappelling gear available?"

Agent Jackson stood in a musing pose. "Let me check." He raced across the deck toward the ramp.

"What do you have in mind, Micah?" Evelyn said.

"To rappel down the side and see what that is?"

"Why don't we get a boat with a ladder or a cherry-picker on it?" John said. "That would be safer, and if you drop any evidence, it won't fall into the water as easily."

"Whatever," Micah said. "I'm not trying to impress anyone here, trust me. It was just the first thing that came to mind."

"I'd feel better if we waited for a boat," Evelyn said.

"And what if it takes a day or two to get one here? Then what?" Micah said.

Evelyn shook her head and shrugged. "I could wait, but I'm not sure Jackson would go for it. He said he needed us to get information about the attack ASAP. He said it had something to do with national security."

Micah looked over the railing again. "Amazing."

"What's amazing?" she said.

"National security? He actually said that?"

"Yeah."

Micah faced Evelyn. "I'll have to dig into that one. I can get to the bottom of it. I have a few friends in Naval Intelligence that owe me some favors. Sounds like it's time to cash 'em in."

"Well, that's what he said." Evelyn turned her head in time to see Agent Jackson and two other agents hauling rappelling equipment across the deck.

Evelyn watched, incredulous. "You had that in your car?"

"Yes, actually. It's not our car, though. I guess it's standard issue here."

"Standard issue, huh?" Micah said. "They do a lot of rock climbing in Florida?"

Jackson shrugged.

"Or is it for hunting Bigfoot or Abominable Snowmen?"

Agent Jackson's face became troubled. "Why do you ask?"

"Lowery. He said you guys investigate all those weird kinds of cases."

Agent Jackson closed his eyes. "I'm going to kill him."

"Let's see that gear." Micah snatched some ropes from one of the other agents and inspected them. "Top of the line. I wouldn't expect anything less."

Agent Jackson sneered. "Can we get on with it?"

"Sure." Micah started putting the equipment together. He instructed the others on what to assemble and where to tie things.

Soon he was straddling the railing and ready to rappel down the side. He swung his right leg over and stood on the gunwale. "Wish me luck."

"Be careful," Evelyn said. "You know you don't have to do this, Micah. We can get a boat."

"Uh, no, we can't," Agent Jackson said. "I already checked. The closest boat with an extendable ladder high enough to reach what we need to reach is two days away. Sorry, but I don't have two days, Doctor."

With that, Micah flipped on the switch to his headlamp and gave the others a salute before sliding down the side. He started out slow at first. It had been several years since he had rappelled with his brother in Yosemite. Mountains had things to grab like rocks, ledges, and holes. This ship, however, was slick as a whistle with only rows of well-ordered windows and lines of regimented rivets to interrupt an otherwise smooth surface.

When he reached the mark, he was astonished at what he saw, for stuck on the edge of a band of metal that had been creased by a great deal of force, was a piece of flesh.

"Hey, guys, you're not going to believe this," he said.

"What is it?" Evelyn said.

"It looks like a piece of meat."

Agent Jackson, Evelyn, and John all looked at each other.

Evelyn leaned back over the side. "Micah, put it in a bag and come back up here so we can see it in the light."

"Roger that." Micah pulled an oversized plastic zipper bag from his vest pouch and a pair of stainless steel tongs Evelyn had given him from her examination kit.

Micah examined the find to decide the best way to extract it. It appeared to him pulling the fragment up first would dislodge it. He poked it with the tongs. It reacted like a tough cut of beef. He pinched from the top and began to pull when the tongs slipped off. "Ohhh!" Micah said, almost dropping the tongs, pinning them against the boat.

"Hey, are you okay down there?" Evelyn said.

Micah grabbed the tongs and took a deep breath. "Everything's peachy."

"Doesn't sound peachy," she said.

Micah attempted again to extricate the fragment from the ship. This time, he slipped the tongs back into his vest pouch and put on a pair of rubber gloves. Grabbing the flesh with his right hand, he noticed the slimy texture of the back side of the specimen that had been against the ship. The front part must have dried out after being exposed to the sun and air, he thought.

Once he slid the specimen into the bag and secured it in his vest, he yelled up the rope, "All right, boys, I'm ready."

Agent Jackson and the other two agents, along with John, all started pulling on the rope. In a matter of minutes, Micah Gregson was standing on the deck, holding the bag up so everyone could see it.

"John," Evelyn said, "we need to get this back to the institute immediately."

"Evelyn, I've got a better idea."

"And that would be?"

"Send this to Dr. Landover. He has some of the best equipment in the world. We'd never be able to examine this like he could."

Evelyn had heard great things about Dr. Landover but didn't know him personally. To entrust arguably the most colossal find in centuries to a person she had never met felt wrong. "John, let's examine it first, then we'll talk about sending it to him. Deal?"

"How long are we talking about?" Agent Jackson said.

"It'll take us a day or two to examine it, then if we need to send it to Dr. Landover, it'll take a day to send it to California, then there's no telling how long he'll need."

"Dr. Landover would be able to tell you everything you want to know in two days," John said. "I could even fly out and help him."

"You seem pretty certain," Agent Jackson said. "How do you know this Dr. Landover?"

"I worked with him for four years as an intern and then as an assistant. He was my mentor. He's good. Really good."

"I see." Agent Jackson turned to Evelyn. "I want you to examine the other dent in the hull before you head back to Miami. We'll keep searching the ship as well for any other evidence. If we find anything else, we'll let you know."

Evelyn nodded.

"Oh, and one more thing, Dr. Sims."

Evelyn shifted her head.

"I want a report from your initial findings within twelve hours of your arrival at NMI and an updated report once you're ready to send it to California. I can't wait four days until this Dr. Landover gets finished. Understood?"

"Got it."

"Also, Dr. Sims, I'm still waiting on your report from the examination of the *Greenback*."

"Bud, I mean, Dr. Kensington was supposed to be getting that together."

"Ah, well, I'll have to call him then."

As Agent Jackson and the other two agents walked away, Evelyn motioned for Micah and John to come close. She held up the bag. "Guys, I'm telling you, this is huge. Micah, you're the man."

Micah smiled, embarrassed by the attention. "Evelyn, while I was down there, I noticed that the other dent was much lower than this one. I think they may be two different attacks."

"Really?"

"Think about it for a minute. The creature swims forward, gets ahead of the boat, and then stops. It rears its head like it's trying to scare the ship, but the ship doesn't run away. So the creature jumps up and attacks the only things moving on it."

"The people," John said.

"Right," Micah continued. "Then, as it attacks, it jumps up and scrapes its side against the boat, cutting itself pretty good. I mean, that piece of flesh must weight ten or fifteen pounds at least. Maybe more."

"Now the animal is mad," John said.

"Exactly. That's when he attacks the other part of the boat. From where I was, that other dent looked smaller but deeper. And it's right at the water line."

"Straight-on, blunt-force impact?" John said.

Micah nodded. "A blow severe enough could have caused a breach. That would be the only reason I could think of to get a boat this size to turn around and come back to port. These cruise lines just don't do that unless something catastrophic happens."

"A breach would definitely do that," Evelyn said.

"Especially if it was thought to affect any of the vital systems, like the engines, or somehow jeopardize the sanitation of the food and water supply."

"I've seen great whites attack like that. Head-on collision with a boat. Bam," John said, slamming his fist into his hand. "It's either a territorial move or an attack on prey."

Micah squinted his eyes. "Would great whites attack something as big as this ship?"

"No, not great whites. They're way too small. But this creature is easily large enough," Evelyn said. "So, I'm thinking it would have to be a territorial attack. Animals generally don't attack prey larger than they are unless they are pack hunters."

"Has there been any evidence that there is more than just one of these things out there?" John said.

"No, but it stands to reason. Unless this is the last of its species." Evelyn shook her head. "One thing is certain, guys. Whether we have one or several, we have a monster out there that will attack anything. Animals usually don't attack things bigger than themselves unless they feel threatened in some way. The fact that it attacked an ocean liner is incredible. That means nothing is safe."

"Either way, it's one bad mamma-jamma," John said.

"You know, this is really extraordinary, if you think about it," Micah said. "The first attack was about fifteen miles off the coast of Fort Pierce in forty meters of water. The second attack was hundreds of miles away in nine hundred meters of water. That's one whale of a territory."

Evelyn held up the bag again, thinking. "So, that means we don't know if the line between the first and second attacks is a northern boundary or a southern boundary."

"Or the eastern or western boundary," Micah said.

"Or the freakin' diameter, for that matter," John said.

"Right," Evelyn said. "But there are a couple of things we do know: this animal can swim fast, and its territory is going to be gigantic."

"No kiddin'," John said. "Four hundred-plus miles in a day? That's nearly twenty knots an hour. Make a territorial circle out of that, and you're looking at approximately a hundred and fifty thousand square miles. That's one big chunk of ocean."

"And it swam that distance from point A to point B without a break?" Micah said.

Evelyn's eyes grew larger. "Do you know how big an animal would have to be to swim that fast for that long without stopping?"

"No," Micah said, "but I'm afraid we're going to find out sooner or later."

"Micah, we're going to have to notify the proper authorities and create a 'no-fly' zone. Is that what you call it?"

"Well, no, but I understand what you mean. But where would we set the boundaries?"

"I don't know. But obviously, the area from Fort Pierce to the Bahamas is off limits. You just use your best judgment from there. But we can't afford not to warn people planning on boating in those areas."

"I can take care of it."

CHAPTER TWENTY-THREE

Friday, 12:43 a.m.
Location: CLASSIFIED

"Hello?" The man's voice was groggy.

"Why are you not where you are supposed to be?" the second man said. His voice transformed into a robotic tone.

"Where am I supposed to be? It's," the first man said, pausing, "twelve forty-three in the morning."

The second man's irritation grew by the minute. "I don't care what time it is, because while you were getting your beauty sleep, I was working."

"Good for you. Whatever floats your boat, mate."

The second man's voice evolved into a snarl. He turned away from a small crowd of people and walked to a more secure location. "Listen, you scum. I've about had it with you. As a matter of fact, maybe your usefulness has run its course. Maybe it's time to give the Feds a call . . . fill them in on your sordid past. I'm sure they'd be more than interested in your dealings with Fidel Castro, eh?"

"How did you know about that?"

"You forget, *mate,* I have connections in high places. They get me the information I need when I need it." The second man chuckled. "You didn't think I was the type of person who would go into business with someone without first checking out my business partner, did you?"

"What's so important that it can't wait until morning?"

"That's better," the second man said. "We have two serious issues we need to address. First, how well do you know the current Russian prime minister?"

The first man grunted. "Not at all. I've heard about him, but I never had the pleasure of getting to know him like his predecessors. I retired from that old line of work about three prime ministers ago."

"What have you heard about him?"

"Congenial unless you cross him. If you do, you'll wish you hadn't. Also loves to flex his muscles as he tries to make Russia a major player on the world scene again."

The second man let out a huge breath in frustration. "That's what I was afraid of."

"What's going on?"

"The Russians still cannot find the locator beacon on the missing sub. Certain U.S. government officials are starting to think the Russians believe the Americans had something to do with it. Everyone's getting anxious and rightfully so. The State Department has been on the phone with the Russian ambassador listening to demands. I just received a text message from an informant of mine stating a phone call was placed from the Russian prime minister to our president less than an hour ago. The stakes have been raised. The prime minister said if we don't help them find their sub, America will be inextricably linked to its disappearance. They want us to send ships to meet their rescue team at the last known coordinates of the *Kirov*. President Walker wants answers, and he wants them yesterday."

"Okay, so tell them what's going on. Be honest with them. We have nothing to hide, do we?"

"You're kidding, right?"

"No. Didn't your mother tell you that honesty was always the best policy?"

The second man sneered. "So, what do you propose we tell them? 'Hey, uh, we think your submarine got attacked by a sea monster.' Yeah, that should do it. I'm sure if we told them that, they'd understand and back off."

The first man sighed. "That's not what I meant, and you know it."

"What *did* you mean then?" The second man's blood pressure climbed another rung.

"Tell them that we're dealing with an incident of our own, and how we, too, have had some vessels attacked and damaged. Tell them that the two incidents may be related. Mention the ocean liner. I'm sure they've seen it on the news. That way, they'd know you're not making all this up."

"Gee, why didn't I think of that?"

"Hey, if you have more information about all this that you're not revealing, then don't ask me dumb questions and waste my time."

The second man strolled farther away from the crowds. "The plot does indeed thicken. Had you done your job instead of going to bed, you'd know that."

"They found something, didn't they?" The first man sniffed. "So what did they find? Davy Jones's Locker?"

"They found evidence that my team didn't find first."

The first man displayed a hint of jocularity in his voice. "Oh, my. Is that what all this is about? They showed up your team?"

"We're not in middle school anymore, Henry. They found a hunk of flesh from the creature. It was stuck to the side of the ship. Apparently, when the creature jumped and collided with the ocean liner, it caught its side on a part of the ship, and one of the metal panels somehow ripped a hunk of flesh from the thing."

The first man's voice became excited. "They found a real piece of flesh? From the creature?"

"Yes. Now, here's where it gets dicey. They're talking about contacting Dr. Harry Landover to examine the specimen."

The first man paused. "Please say you're joking."

The second man fumed. "I wish I was. That's the primary reason I called you. They must not be able to send that specimen to Landover. If they do, it's all over."

The first man sighed again. "Where are they taking the specimen?"

"NMI, as far as I know."

"Okay. I'll take care of it."

"Be discreet. If it comes up missing haphazardly, we're ruined. They'll figure it out."

"If they do, then we have ways of dealing with that, don't we?"

"As a last resort, yes. But keep in mind that if people involved in this case simply start showing up dead or disappear, it won't take long for everyone to put two and two together. We've already had to eliminate one, and I had to tell Gilliam about it. He wasn't happy. I've been instructed not to expand upon that number."

"Understood. Prison was never my forte."

"Yes, I know. One of Castro's men told me."

The second man slammed his cell phone shut and scanned his surroundings. He was afraid his elevated blood pressure had translated into a few decibels in the volume of his voice.

Kensington can be so grating, he thought, *and careless, too.* It was no wonder Cousteau kicked him off the team after the Europa incident. They wouldn't have lost any equipment if Kensington had been more vigilant in his duties.

The man inhaled. *Kensington had better do his job now and not drop the ball, or he'll pay with more than his livelihood.*

Several minutes later, confident the nearby crowds had not overheard his sensitive conversation and were still oblivious to his actions, the second man opened his phone once more and dialed while taking a couple steps even farther away from the masses.

A puzzled, wary female answered. "Hello?"

"Madame Secretary, my name is Dr. Anthony Fontaine. I'm sorry for calling you at such a late hour, but it's urgent that I speak with you."

"Who? How did you get this number?"

"I am using the phone the Bureau gave me. I was assured it was untraceable, and the director also assured me that all the numbers were accurate and cleared for me to use."

"The Bureau? You mean FBI?"

"Yes, ma'am."

"What was your name again?"

"Dr. Anthony Fontaine. I am an American. I am also an evolutionary biologist who has served on the faculty of such noted institutions as University College in Dublin and Cambridge University. Currently, I am the director of the NatSel Foundation in Paris."

"And how would you have ties to the Bureau? That's if you really are a doctor, Doctor."

"Madame Secretary, I can fully understand your dubious responses. Please feel free to check the FBI databases. My personnel file is all there, and besides, I did call your personal cell and give you my real name. That should account for something."

Sandra Brown paused briefly. "Very well, then, Dr. Fontaine. I'll play along for now and check your file later. But don't expect me to do anything before I have verified everything you tell me. Understood?"

"Very good, Madame Secretary."

"So, what is the purpose of this call, Doctor?"

"I do appreciate your cooperation, Madame Secretary. Rest assured I wouldn't have called you unless the situation warranted such an action."

"I'm sure you must have important news for me, Doctor, or you would not have called me at such an ungodly hour."

"I do. I'm afraid the circumstances have just taken a turn for the worse."

She sighed. "Doctor, it's late, and I'm tired. Could you cut to the chase, please? Just give me the highlights."

"Okay. But I must give you some background first, or everything I have to tell you will not make any sense whatsoever."

"Go on."

"I was enlisted by the FBI—because of my expertise in the field of evolutionary biology—to be on call to investigate any sightings of a . . . cryptozoological nature."

"Whoa, hold on, Doctor. Crypto-what?"

Fontaine blurted a wary chuckle. "Cryptozoology. It's the study of things like Bigfoot, the Abominable Snowman, Loch Ness Monster, and the like."

"O-kaaay," Brown said. "Proceed."

"My first assignment involved an investigation of an incident concerning a sighting by a fisherman off the coast of Walker Cay in the Bahamian Chain. Do you remember that incident?"

"Sorry."

"You see, I was sanctioned by the National Oceanic and Atmospheric Administration as part of the Aquatic Nuisance Species Task Force to investigate what was being reported as a sea-monster sighting."

"Go on."

"My team didn't find much at the Walker Cay site, other than several disturbed locals. But it's a different story here in Fort Pierce and Port Canaveral."

"You're in Florida? Where that yacht was attacked?"

"Yes, Madame Secretary. I'm in Port Canaveral right now. The incident with the ocean liner *Titan* has created a situation that, well, shall we say, is beyond the authority of the Aquatic Nuisance Species Task Force."

"So, what are you saying, Doctor? That whatever has attacked two American vessels is not a nuisance?"

"No, Madame Secretary. I'm saying we're not merely dealing with zebra mussels in the Great Lakes or lampreys sucking the life out of the commercial fishing market. What I am saying is it appears we have a bona-fide, true-blue, real-life sea monster on the loose in the Atlantic Ocean."

The silence on the other end of the line caused Dr. Fontaine concern.

"Madame Secretary, are you still there?"

"Oh, yes, Doctor. I'm still here. I'm jotting down some notes, even though I thought I just heard you say you believed we have a real sea monster on the loose."

"That's what I said, Madame Secretary. And here's where it gets ugly—"

"What? That's not why you called me?"

"No, Madame Secretary. The reason I called you is because I felt this situation fell under the jurisdiction of the Department of State now, more so than the FBI."

"Why don't you let me be the judge of that, Doctor."

"Fair enough." Fontaine switched the cell phone to his other ear. "The animal left a specimen behind after the last attack on the ocean liner. In its attack, the animal ran up against the ship and ripped off about a twenty-pound piece of flesh. This sample is being taken back to the National Marine Institute in Miami at my urging to be examined."

"Okay, so give me the bad news."

"The bad news is that the researchers at NMI want to send the specimen to Dr. Harry Landover at the Scripps Institute in San Diego."

"And why is that bad?"

Dr. Fontaine sighed and tried to control the fury mounting inside. "Dr. Landover is, for want of a better term, a nemesis of mine. If he acquires that specimen, he will send decades of research in the field of evolutionary biology back to the Dark Ages. The scientific world will be turned on its head."

Secretary Brown cleared her throat. "Look, Dr. Fontaine, I appreciate your passion, but I do not see the urgency you see, and I really don't have time for petty squabbles between scientists who have had bad blood in the past. If you don't want the specimen in the hands of this Dr. Landover, then don't send it to him. The Bureau gave you all this power, so use it. I don't see where this falls under my department's jurisdiction."

Frustration was evident in Dr. Fontaine's tone. "It's not that simple, Madame Secretary. I was told to keep this investigation from hitting the papers. As you can imagine, that's hard to do when a millionaire playboy makes front page headlines; the same playboy, mind you, who just so happens to be married to the very marine biologist who is now on her way back to the National Marine Institute to examine the aforementioned specimen.

"Then the ocean liner incident makes its way onto the Internet, courtesy of some amateur video-taking idiot, and every news station around the world has it now.

"This investigation has been a major obstacle from the outset, and I hate slipshod operations, Madame Secretary. All the publicity and the involvement of so many people makes me even more crazy."

"I'm sorry, Doctor, but I have bigger fish to fry right now. Your insignificant tiff with a colleague and your subsequent obstacles with the press are things you and your colleagues will have to figure out. Personally, I don't see what the big deal would be if this sea monster swam up to New York City for a *Time* magazine photo op."

Fontaine paused. He employed breathing techniques to keep from exploding. "By the way, Madame Secretary, how are the Russians these days? Is everything okay in Moscow?"

There was an awkward silence before Sandra Brown answered. "Dr. Fontaine, what do you know about the Russians?"

"Let's just say I am well-informed where it revolves around my work. I'm investigating this animal, and the Russians lost a sub mentioning a flipper. Now, unless Flipper the dolphin has become much more ferocious than I recall from the TV show, it stands to reason that the Russian sub had an encounter with that sea monster as well."

"But that information is classified, Doctor. The disappearance of the Russian submarine has not been leaked to the press."

"You're right. But don't forget, Madame Secretary, I am part of the government, too."

"What do you want, Doctor?"

"Madame Secretary, I'm merely trying to get you to see how dangerous this Dr. Landover can be."

"What could he possibly do that could be so catastrophic?"

"In the beginning, I was sent to investigate a sighting of a sea monster. The incident at Walker Cay. Then, the yacht was capsized, and the only remaining survivor on board told a story of a giant sea monster attacking their vessel. It supposedly killed the owner of the boat. A man whose body has not been recovered yet, I might add.

"Madame Secretary, do you know why *I* was chosen to be part of this task force and not Dr. Landover, or anybody else, for that matter?"

"No."

"Because not only am I an excellent scientist in my field, but I am one of the best supporters, if not the most ardent, of evolution you will find in the scientific community. I have made it my mission in life to prove Darwin's theory and silence all those who challenge his work."

"So, this Dr. Landover . . . he's not a *believer* like you are?"

"Dr. Landover is the antithesis of me. If he can prove that a sea monster exists, he may be able to prove other things as well, or at least damage Evolution's credibility. Madame Secretary, do you understand how devastating that would be to the understanding of science? Think about it. How would that affect science as a whole? What ramifications would a drastic change in scientific philosophy create? How would it ultimately affect science? Scientific funding? Education? Politics? Commerce? Sociology? Philosophy? Religion? How would it affect relations between countries? Institutions?

"Don't you see, Madame Secretary? Our entire existence has been built upon the argument that we and all other life forms on Earth are direct descendants of a lesser version—that we have mutated over the millennia to overcome various obstacles along the way . . . to better ourselves . . . to make life more efficient and more apt to survive. If that premise was changed, and I mean, stood on its head—because that's what would happen—the effects would be disastrous. I'm not sure anyone would be able to predict all the fallout. But I do know this. We would revert back to the Dark Ages where superstition reigns, and science would be looked upon with great cynicism. I mean, think about it for a second. If Evolution is viewed by the low-information masses out there as a farce, then all scientists would be lumped together. Every time we said the words 'studies show' or 'the data indicates,' people would simply laugh in our faces and say, 'Are these findings as reliable as Darwin's?' As a result, people would die. Diseases would run rampant. Political decisions would be made, impacting every facet of society from education to food production. Mankind would be doomed to a subhuman existence merely because of ignorance."

"So, Dr. Fontaine, let me get this straight." Secretary Brown huffed into the receiver. "You want to silence scientific discovery if that discovery disproves your theory of evolution?"

"No, that's not it at all. Scientific discovery can only *enhance* evolutionary biology. Only faulty science can 'disprove' Evolution, as you put it. That faulty science can be packaged very well and be quite convincing to those who do not understand all the nuances and complexities of Evolution. Therefore, I have made it my mission in life to squelch any misinformation that will hinder or stall our work. Besides, evolutionary biology has become so much a part of our daily existence, there are governments, agencies, companies, and even some religious organizations who feel the same way. The entire educational system is so convinced that evolution is the answer to all of mankind's ills, that defusing it would create a chain reaction. Everything that we know about the universe, from the Big Bang to life on Earth at this very moment, would be brought into serious question. It would literally topple institutions that have devoted their existences to it.

"Let's face it, Madame Secretary, even our country is against this sea monster destroying a hundred and fifty years of scientific progress. Our country is the one that came up with the idea for my elaborate cover. Their purpose was to get me to where the action was first. It wasn't France's idea, or Germany's or England's idea to devise my cover."

Fontaine stopped and took a deep breath. "I was overseas, in the region of the Red Sea and the Indian Ocean to be exact, studying the Lithothamnion pathway, when our very own U.S. government approached me with the plan, for Pete's sake. *They* called *me*."

Dr. Fontaine paused, waiting for the secretary of state to ask about his most recent study. But she didn't.

"Do you know what the Lithothamnion pathway is, Madame Secretary?"

"Never heard of it."

"It's an underwater seashore, for want of a better term. It marks what evolutionists believe was the actual sea level during the Ice Age. It's three hundred and fifty feet below our present-day sea level. It proves that oceans were once much lower than they are now. It proves global warming theories. It is just one piece of evidence in a long line of evidence that supports evolutionary theory. So, now what? Are we going to let one animal propel us a thousand years into the past and create another Dark Age?" Dr. Fontaine paused once more, allowing his words to penetrate. "Then, of course," he continued, "if our sea monster did so, it would open up science to the possibility of creationism. And you know what would happen if that occurred."

"Dr. Fontaine," Sandra Brown said, "I'm not a scientist, nor am I a theologian. So, before we get too far out of my realm of expertise, I do have some issues to consider. For example, how would other countries handle the news if Evolution was exposed to be false or in error?"

Fontaine broke his silence. "Madame Secretary, the United States would be viewed as a radical nation of right-wing extremists. We'd be seen as a bunch of fundamentalists trying to impose Judeo-Christian beliefs on the rest of the world."

Sandra Brown sighed. "If that's the case, it definitely would heighten hostilities between us and the Arab world . . . and heaven knows we don't need any more of that right now."

Fontaine formed a wry smile. "That's my point, Madame Secretary. We cannot run that risk."

"Dr. Fontaine, do we have any confirmation that this sea monster had anything to do with the missing Russian submarine?"

"Nothing yet, but the reports I've received via the Bureau had the last known coordinates squarely in the vicinity of the animal's range. Therefore, I cannot confirm it, but I surely wouldn't rule it out either."

"I'll need to research this more, Doctor. In the meantime, stay on top of the specimen. No official findings are to be released to any news outlet until they are cleared through my department. I'll notify NOAA, the FBI, and the president and let them know of that decision as well." She paused. "Oh, do you have anyone who can keep an eye on the specimen at NMI?"

"Already got it covered, Madame Secretary."

"Good. Dr. Fontaine, if you find out anything new on the specimen I want to know. Call me directly with any new information, if needed. Understood?"

"Absolutely, Madame Secretary."

CHAPTER TWENTY-FOUR

Friday, 6:39 a.m.
National Marine Institute Main Laboratory
Miami, Florida

Evelyn sat bleary-eyed, hunched over a microtome. She massaged her temples to relieve the enormous amount of stress and pain pounding inside. Several times she had to pull her head away from the device and rub her eyes. She'd roll her head clockwise and counter-clockwise on occasion. Her venti-size coffee with extra cream and sugar had run dry, and because the employee canteen hadn't opened yet, she didn't have the nerve to send Micah Gregson on a coffee run for fear he'd never be able to get back into the complex. John, who was her normal "gopher," had acquired a new significance with his knowledge in the field of paleontology. That left her with no options but to muddle through caffeine-deprived.

The mission was clear, she thought. She and her cohorts could be on the precipice of one of the greatest discoveries in scientific history.

They could be on the verge of a colossal polemic, the kind that creates tenured positions at prestigious institutions or implodes into a career killer. Scientific discovery was without a doubt a double-edged sword. It often depended on which side of the battlefield one stood, and Evelyn knew on which side she resided. Hence, the pitfalls were regnant in her mind. The "force" was about to be disturbed, and the shockwaves of this fracas might propel her into the most volatile spotlight of her life, dwarfing anything the death of her husband might generate.

A game plan had been drawn up on the way back from Port Canaveral. The preparation had to take into account all the situational dynamics: time deficiencies; lack of proper lab equipment; scourge of opposition against what they may find; Agent Jackson's need for speed and quick answers; their own lack of experience in this field of study; and their nagging lack of sleep. Evelyn and John knew all of these factors would hurt the research. It might even call into question any findings they uncover. That meant the game plan had to be the best plan they could muster.

When they arrived, Evelyn was in charge of slicing a portion of the specimen from both ends and placing the samples in the drying chamber while marking each sample. This process removed the water from the samples so Evelyn could attach them to slides with paraffin and begin a series of detailed tests. However, that technique, though better in the long run, took at least sixteen hours just to get the samples ready to examine. So, while those samples were on their journey in the critical point dryer, John took two additional samples from the same general areas of the specimen and placed them in the refrigerated centrifuge for the purpose of freezing the samples in a matter of minutes. This allowed them to begin testing the specimen much quicker. What they discovered would determine their next move.

Evelyn had already cut the frozen specimen into two equal halves. Having battened down the sample with epoxy resin, she slid the first half into the cutting bed of the microtome and adjusted the glass knives of the unit to carve several solid slices. With each pass, she adjusted the knives so that varying widths, ranging from fifty to one hundred micrometers could be used.

Each cut was done with precision. The sound of the blades slicing the specimen and the hum of the motor caused Evelyn's heart to race a little faster. This was the type of moment for which she had lived. All those hours reading books and writing papers could now pay off beyond her wildest dreams. What were they going to find? What would each test reveal? Was this the one, great moment in her life when Dr. Evelyn Sims would burst onto the scene as a leading scientist in her field?

And how would her findings jive with her beliefs? A creature possibly eighty, ninety, or even one hundred feet long . . . that would make it one of the longest, biggest animals to have ever existed, ever. Rivaling the blue whale—but much deadlier. *A bigger animal needs more oxygen,* she thought, *but it would have a larger lung capacity . . . and what about the heart? Would the heart be big enough to pump blood to its extremities?* She chastised herself.

Well, duh, Evelyn. It's alive, isn't it?

But, she continued as she sliced another section. *Bigger animals are hard to miss, though. Especially when they are the kind no one has ever seen before. If people see a whale, they might film it for themselves and tell their friends, but it's not news.*

She twisted the knob and started another cut.

Her mind jumped from one thought to another, one question to another, one issue to another, one problem to another. Each slice—fifty micrometers . . . fifty-five micrometers . . . sixty . . . sixty-five . . . seventy—caused her hands to shake just a little more. She almost stopped and asked John to complete the assignment, but then thought better of it. *I want to do this. I can do this.*

John Spencer readied the stereozoom microscope, grumbling under his breath about how he wished he was still in Dr. Landover's laboratory so he could have access to the TEM, Transmission Electron Microscope. Landover's research laboratory was one of the best-equipped labs in the world. There was nothing his lab could not analyze. Oh, how John wanted to be there right now. State-of-the-art scientific equipment meeting cutting-edge scientific discovery. That's how it was meant to take place. *After you drive a brand-new Cadillac,* he thought, *a run-down Chevy just doesn't cut it.*

"Hey, Evelyn," John said, "you know this microscope only goes up to 100x, right? And that polarizing scope over on the counter only goes up to 45x?"

"I know. I've been after Bud to get new ones. Better ones. I told him if he wants this lab to be top notch, he needs top notch equipment. He always gives me the same old song and dance about dwindling crowds and skyrocketing operating costs. I do have to give credit where credit is due, though. He did go out and spend seven thousand dollars on that centrifuge last year. That's a start, I guess."

"At this rate, we'll be top notch in about twenty years with old equipment that is no longer top notch or relevant," John said.

"I know, I know," Evelyn said. "You're preachin' to the choir, John."

Having cut eleven slices from fifty to one hundred micrometers in width, Evelyn then cut each sample into ten equal widths for multiple tests. Isolating the first sliver from each measurement grouping, she brought them over to the polarizing microscope, sliding the first sample in place. She rubbed her eyes once more and took a deep breath.

"Here goes nothing," she said as she peered into the oculars. Adjusting the focusing knobs, a sudden, brilliant mass of tissue sprang into view. The tissue, having become pliable now that it had thawed, revealed a stratum of fibers she was not expecting. "John, come take a look at this."

John strolled over, plucked his eyeglasses out of his lab coat pocket, put them on, and gazed into the microscope. "Wow," he said in a whisper. "What thickness is this?"

"Fifty micrometers."

"Let's look at the seventy."

John extricated the thinner sample from the microscope and set it down on the table. He took the sample cut at seventy micrometers from Evelyn, slid it under the scope, and looked into the oculars. "Amazing."

"What are you thinking?"

John nodded. "It's not mammalian. The epidermal layers bear that out. It's got to be—" A blank look crept onto his face. "Reptilian or amphibious? I really can't tell. I wish we had the technology here to run a DNA test. Let me see the fifty again," he said, swapping the samples once more. He took another look into the microscope. Twisting the knobs, he magnified the sample to 45x. "Man, this microscope is the pits. It doesn't come close to revealing anything else. I can't see any membranes," he said, standing erect with a scowl. "There's no sense in staining these right now. We'll need an EM to see the organelles."

"What are organelles?" Micah said.

John turned to look at Micah, who had maneuvered himself closer to the action. John cleared his throat. "An organelle is a distinct subcompartment of a eukaryotic cell specializing in carrying out a particular function. Some examples of organelles include mitochondria and the Golgi apparatus or complex."

Micah stared at John; the definition sailing well over his head. "Huh? You sounded like a scientific dictionary."

John began to chuckle.

Evelyn slapped John on the back. "John Spencer, that wasn't necessary."

Micah started to pace but then stopped. "This isn't a game, John. If we're to win this battle, we've got to stay focused."

Evelyn chortled. "Who said we were in a battle?"

"Agent Jackson."

"He didn't say that."

"Not in so many words, Evelyn, but you have to be able to read between the lines. And if you've never been in battle before, then you don't know what to look for."

Evelyn's blank stare caused Micah to smile.

"Micah, I'm tired," Evelyn said. "My psyche isn't in the mood for games. And besides, I think you're being a little overdramatic, don't you think?"

Micah leaned against the table. "There's something brewing, Evelyn. Something none of us knows about."

John squinted. "Can you be more specific and less . . . esoteric?"

Micah hopped up on the counter. "Evelyn, you said on the ride back that Jackson said something about national security?"

"Yeah."

"That can mean anything. Years ago, it meant there was something happening with Nazis or Communists. Those were our enemies." Micah turned his palms upward. "But today, it could mean your general, run-of-the-mill terrorists, radical Islamic extremists, communists, neo-fascists, neo-Nazis, anti-American sympathizers, and even drug cartels. It could even be members of our own government, trying to fulfill some political agenda. In this day and age, the enemies are much more prevalent but much less defined. So, let's think this through from Agent Jackson's perspective."

Evelyn and John both sat down on stools.

Micah jumped down off the counter and paced again. "Agent Jackson examines your boat, Evelyn, violating multiple examination procedures by removing and cleaning a supposed crime scene in the process. His excuse for being there was that your husband was involved with terrorists. Correct?"

"Uh-huh," Evelyn said.

"At that time, Jackson seemed normal, not anxious, and bothered by my presence with Officer Wellman. Then, this morning, he seemed much more animated, cooperative with us, and more pressed for time. Said he needed information about this latest attack ASAP, right?"

Evelyn and John both nodded.

"While you two were working this sample over, I stepped outside and made a couple of phone calls. One was to a friend in Naval Intelligence. He said the info I was requesting was Top Security. But he did say this, and I quote, 'The Ruskies have us running scared.'"

Evelyn wrinkled her face. "I still don't get it. What would this have to do with the Russians?"

"Good question. Get the answer to that, and you have the cause of Agent Jackson's angst."

Evelyn shook her head and stood up, moseying over to the microscope. She pointed at the samples. "Could the Russians be interested in this?"

"I don't see how," John said. "Except for news reports, they may know about the creature, but they wouldn't be aware of this specimen."

"That may be true, but maybe they encountered the creature first and kept it under wraps." Evelyn paused. "Maybe they want 'first rights' or something. Put their country and their scientists on the map."

"No, that doesn't explain Jackson's desire to get the information ASAP," Micah said, still strolling back and forth. "That wouldn't cause us to 'run scared.'"

"So, what would?" John said.

Micah remained silent for a few more steps before answering. "A threat of retaliation."

"Retaliation for what?" Evelyn said.

Micah stopped, clenching his teeth. The muscles of his jaws bulged. "We know there are a handful of countries in the world that are militarily equal to us. In other words, we don't want to fight them because it would cause worldwide destruction by the end of the confrontation. Also, many of those countries are our allies. That narrows the number down considerably of possible enemy attacks.

"Now, each of these countries knows the same thing. Start something with us, and it's over for everybody eventually. Diplomacy is always the way differences are settled. If one country does something to the other, the victim country will demand restitution in some form or fashion. If the restitution demands aren't met, then there's usually a promise of retaliation.

"None of these countries would just make a selfish demand or threat for no good reason. So, if we're running scared, then we've done something to them, or at least, that's the perception on the part of the Russians."

"So," John said, "what would that scenario have to do with the attack on the *Titan*?"

Evelyn pointed her finger at John. "Maybe it doesn't have to do with the *Titan*. Maybe it has to do with the creature."

"That would make sense," Micah said. "Jackson was there after your boat was attacked. He was there after the *Titan* was attacked. And there doesn't appear to be any connection between the two occurrences—"

"Except the creature," Evelyn said.

Micah continued. "And in this last instance, he seemed more adamant about getting answers than anything else. There's something about that creature. Somehow it's tied to the Russian thing. I feel it."

John guffawed. "You don't think we created some type of Godzilla creature that the Russians are upset about, do ya?"

Evelyn looked at John and raised her eyebrows. "Reptilian, huh?"

John shrugged. "It's hard to say with this equipment. But doesn't that strike you as odd?"

"What?" Evelyn said.

"All marine reptiles, including dinosaurs, have been classified as air breathers. Since all those found in the fossil record thus far have not had gills, paleontologists have believed that all marine reptiles lived in the first fifty feet of water. They would've needed to be near the surface to acquire oxygen."

"So, what's your point?"

"Evelyn, we're dealing with an extremely large animal here."

Micah, standing next to the two marine biologists, was squinting, trying to follow the conversation. "One at least the size of my cutter, we're guessing."

"And how big is your boat, Captain?" John said.

"Eighty-seven feet."

John shook his head. "That's one big animal, Evelyn. Eighty-seven feet? Maybe bigger? So, how in the world has a creature that big stayed undetected for so long?"

"You know, there are several ancient legends of sea monsters," Micah said. "I'm sure you've heard of some of them."

John pursed his lips. "Some."

There are actually stories dating back as far as the sixteenth century, and one as recent at 2009."

"Really?" Evelyn said.

"Stinson Beach, off the coast of San Francisco, was the longest-running series of occurrences. There had been a supposed sighting there back in 1885, too. There's a *New York Times* piece written about it. You can look it up online. The latest sighting there was in 1983."

"So, almost a hundred years," Evelyn said.

"But there have been multiple reports throughout history. Here, I'll show you." Micah sat down at the computer and began pounding the keyboard. "Here we go. See this? A priest by the name of Olaus Magnus wrote of a seventy-five-foot sea serpent way back in 1522. That was off the coast of Scandinavia.

"The first American sighting occurred in Cape Ann, Massachusetts in 1639. It was described to be ninety feet in length."

John peered over Micah's shoulders, reading along.

Evelyn straightened her stance. "That was just nineteen years after the Mayflower Compact."

"Yeah," Micah said. "And Plymouth Rock is only eighty-two miles from Cape Ann, by land. Even shorter by boat."

Evelyn leaned in for a closer look. "Wow. To think there could have been creatures like this circumventing the waters at the same time as the pilgrims is pretty remarkable."

Micah pointed at the screen. "There were other sightings in 1729,

1746, and 1818 describing sea serpents in various sizes and lengths. All of those were in and around Scandinavia.

"Then there's the one in Halifax in 1825. Again, not too far from Cape Ann. But probably the most reliable account in that era was written down by the captain of the HMS *Daedalus* in 1848 while on a trip near the Cape of Good Hope. It was the first time a *plesiosaurus* was described as the possible creature."

"You do realize that's practically everywhere on the map," John said. "Atlantic, Pacific, tip of Africa, splitting the Atlantic and the Indian Ocean."

"There's also one near Alaska. Check this out." Micah retrieved a video about a reported sighting in Cadboro Bay in Greater Victoria, British Columbia. "They named it the *Cadborosaurus willsi*, or 'Caddy' for short. 'They' being the local newspaper. They held a contest to name the creature in 1933. *Cadborosaurus* won. The '*willsi*' part came from the newspaper's editor, Archie Wills. But this video was taken by fisherman in 2009."

They watched the video.

"They reference the plesiosaur there, too," Evelyn said, motioning at the screen.

"Yes. And what Regina Fleming described sounded like a massive version of a plesiosaur." Micah leaned back in his chair. "The earliest recorded sighting I could find was the one in 1529 by Olaus Magnus. He said the beast was two hundred feet long."

Evelyn's eyebrow pinched together. "Two hundred feet?"

"Yeah. That's what others thought, too. They finally questioned his sighting and one person went so far as to say what Olaus really saw was a 'giant calamari.'"

"Imagine that as an appetizer," John said.

Micah laughed. "Right? Even a half order would feed an army."

"You know, guys, there are the pirate tales of the *Kraken*. That's a giant calamari."

"True," John said, "but are you saying all these sightings we've been reading about are giant squid? That the references to a plesiosaur-like creature are all made up?"

"No, I'm just saying we don't know what we have out there."

Micah lifted a finger. "But there's *something* out there. And an eyewitness who had nothing to gain by describing what she saw told me it looked like a giant sea serpent."

"Micah, you said you couldn't find any references older than the sixteenth century, right?" John said.

"Right."

"There are a couple of references mentioned in scripture that have intrigued me over the years."

Micah wriggled his fingers, ready to attack the computer. "Shoot."

"Psalm 74:13 is one of them."

Micah typed in the reference and waited for it to pop up on the screen.

"It mentions 'dragons,'" John continued, "using the Hebrew word *tannin*. It's the same word used in Malachi 1:3 to refer to 'land dragons.' Many Bible scholars believe the word is a reference to dinosaurs, because the Psalm 74 reference mentions 'dragons in the water' while the Malachi reference mentions 'dragons on land.'"

"Got it," Micah said, reading the verse from Psalm 74. "This talks about how God split the waters, causing the 'monster of the waters' and *leviathan* to become food for the creatures of the desert." Micah turned away from the monitor and peered at John. "Could that be a reference to that Western Interior Sea thing you were talking about?"

John shot Micah a surprised look. "You know, I've never caught that before. Here, let me see that."

John began to read out loud: "*It was you who split open the sea by your power; you broke the heads of the monster in the waters. It was you who crushed the heads of Leviathan and gave him as food to the creatures of the desert.*" John stood up straight. "It is believed that when God ended the flood, that's when the Western Interior Sea would have also ended. Any marine reptiles living in the region would have been caught between what we now know as the Rocky Mountains and the Ozarks."

"And much of that is now desert-like." Micah lifted his eyebrows.

John turned to Evelyn. She'd become extremely quiet. "What are you thinking, Evelyn?" John said.

She shrugged. "I was just thinking."

"About what?"

"We've got a monster that's probably never been seen before, attacking ships in a four hundred-mile area. By all indications, it's supposed to be an air breather. All known marine reptiles are. Which means it is supposed to hang near the surface. Therefore, sheer biology should've enhanced its chances of being detected long before now."

"And yet it hasn't," John said.

Evelyn thrust her hands in the air. "Right. So, how do we explain a reptile that big going undetected for so long? I mean, we've seen albino killer whales. They're rare enough. We've even spotted frilled sharks and goblin sharks. They're much smaller than this thing," she said, motioning to the microscope again, "and they're not even air breathers."

"This creature could be a deep-sea diver," John said. "Sperm whales are known to dive deep and remain submerged for hours. Alligators can stay submerged for hours as well."

"Turtles, too, right?" Micah said.

"Correct," John said. "So, to say that this animal could dive deep and stay underwater for long periods of time is not a stretch. And considering the size of the animal and the fact that we have not been able to study one in detail, this particular animal could have some advanced lung capacity that is not present in other species." John stopped and pointed his finger at Evelyn in an inquisitive manner. "Are you familiar with the work of William Buckland?"

She shrugged. "Afraid not."

"Buckland was a professor of geology at Oxford way back in the 1830s. He believed that sea dragons, ichthyosaurs to be specific, could stay underwater for extended periods of time because of the design of their rib cages. The ribs on the right and left sides were joined together by intermediate bones he called sterno-costal arcs. He believed this design enabled the animal to breathe in large quantities of air for the purpose of staying submerged for long periods of time."

"Interesting," Evelyn admitted, "but if all this is true, then my theory, John, is going to be false."

"What theory?" Micah said.

"Her theory in the *Journal of Marine Paleontology*."

"Oh," Micah said. "And how would that be proven false?"

Evelyn tucked her hair behind her ears. "Part of my theory deduced that marine reptiles would've been able to stay down longer because of the increased density of oxygen in the atmosphere."

"Oh, yeah, the two-point-whatever atmospheres of pressure, right?" Micah said.

"Precisely."

"But I'm still not clear on how that would disprove your premise."

"If the oxygen levels decreased over time after the flood, that would coincide with my theory. That would explain why sightings of the really big sea monsters have become less and less prevalent over time. Less oxygen would make it harder for bigger animals to live. But if we do have a huge dinosaur out there, it will prove my theory to be false, and—"

"Not exactly," John said. "Think about it. If an animal that big drew in air to fill a lung capacity similar to what Buckland was talking about at higher oxygen levels, then going down to great depths would not be that big of a deal. Thus, the animal could stay down for long periods of time. Now, if the animal was more nocturnal by nature, then coming to get air at night would lessen the sightings considerably, even if the creature had to make more trips to the surface because of the decreased atmospheric pressure."

"Right," Micah said, "and both of our attacks thus far have been when?"

"At night," John said. "So, what we could have is an animal that stays down during the day, still comes to the surface at night but has to do so more frequently because of the lower oxygen levels, and has suddenly, for unknown reasons, started attacking ships."

Quiet, Evelyn nodded, feeling somewhat vindicated, but still sensing holes in her theory that needed to be plugged. "Or, what if this is a new species?"

"I thought we had pretty much decided that." John said.

"No, I mean, not reptilian, not mammalian, but some kind of hybrid reptile-fish that can breathe underwater?"

"If it has gills of some sort," John said, "then maybe. If not, then there's no way oxygen could be extracted from the water."

Micah raised a finger. "Well, that's not entirely accurate. We know that if there's enough oxygen forced into a liquid, a human can breathe in water and live. The Navy's been working on GLV and liquid breathing for decades now."

"GLV?" Evelyn said.

"Gas/liquid ventilation. You see, it's not that we can't breathe underwater. It's that we cannot get enough oxygen out of the water and expel the carbon dioxide fast enough. The viscosity of the water is too thick for human lungs, but maybe we have an animal that already has that figured out."

"If it does have it figured out, then we're dealing with some kind of fish," John said. "That's the only type of animal that has GLV 'figured out,' to my knowledge."

"Right," Evelyn said.

"Well, it's got to have something special figured out to travel twenty knots and four hundred miles nonstop from where Evelyn's boat was attacked to where the ocean liner was attacked," Micah said.

"You know, you're right, Micah. That would have to be one heck of an animal to travel that far that fast without stopping." She paused, turning to John. "We've got to be dealing with more than one?

"There has to be at least two at a time, right, for reproduction, unless this animal somehow can reproduce on its own."

"And even if it did, there should be more than one at a time," John said.

"My point exactly."

"It could be the last of its kind, too. Either way, where has it been hiding all this time?" Micah said. "I keep my ear to the sea, so to speak, watching for anything like this. I've never heard of any reports about large sea monsters in my lifetime until now."

"That is a problem," Evelyn said. "But there is a lot about the oceans we don't know. We're discovering new species all the time, especially ones in the extreme deep."

Micah lifted his chin. "Methane vents, right?"

Evelyn was surprised again at Micah's knowledge. "Yes, methane vents do heat the water and create environments that sustain all forms of marine life, albeit it's mostly microorganisms and various types of worms. But there are also fish that exist in those conditions."

"And we're talking about some serious depths, too," Micah said.

John strolled over to the series of bookshelves along the back wall next to the computer and pulled a three-ring binder from one of the bottom shelves. Opening the notebook and rifling through the pages, he stopped at an article earmarked with a yellow sticky note.

"Listen to this, guys. I pulled this article off the Internet a few months ago. There are two basic kinds of, well, they call them *oases* here, but I like to call them *hydrothermal vents*. There are hot vents and cold vents. Hot vents are seafloor geysers that vent seawater that is heated up to four hundred degrees Celsius and is socked with nutrient-rich chemicals. Then there are cold vents, also called *cold seeps*. These vents come from bacteria in the mud. The bacteria digest the organic matter and create methane as a waste product. The methane then builds up under the surface and seeps out. These vents are usually located in colder ocean areas."

Evelyn stood up straight. "John, that's all fascinating and everything, but aren't we getting a little off topic here?"

"Getting off what topic?" came a voice from across the room.

They turned to see Bud Kensington, who had entered the lab undetected and was hobbling over to the two scientists.

"Bud," Evelyn said, "you're here a little early this morning."

"It's seven forty, Evie. That's my usual time."

Evelyn turned and looked at the clock. "Wow. It's seven forty already?"

"Yep." Bud limped over to a chair and sat down. "Hey, I got a call from Agent Jackson this morning telling me you guys found something interesting. So, I thought I'd come by and check it out."

"Why would Jackson call you?" Micah said from his corner spot.

Bud turned, caught off guard. "Oh, Captain Gregson, I didn't see you there. You startled me."

"Sorry."

Bud nodded. "I'm still the director of NMI, you know. Agent Jackson was calling me to fill me in on what has transpired since last night because I didn't go on the trip. He also wanted our report from the examination of your boat, Evie."

"I told him you were handling that report," Evelyn said.

"That's what he said. I just sent it to him via e-mail. CCed you a copy as well."

"Thanks. So, what did Jackson have to say about what we found?" Evelyn said.

"He said something about you found a specimen? One I might find interesting?"

She walked over to the table and pointed at the samples that had been cut and examined under the microscope. "He's right, Bud. This is the specimen of a lifetime. This will put our park not just on the map, Bud. It will make us an elite institution, if we handle it properly." She raised her arms out beside her. "We're all looking at promotions, conferences, speaking engagements, you name it. This is bigger than all of us."

Bud tilted his head. "How so?"

"The creature is probably either reptilian or amphibian. Well, as far as we can tell, although we haven't ruled out the possibility that it could be a fish of some sort."

"Yes," John said. "When we get the DNA tests back, we'll know for sure."

"DNA tests? What DNA tests?"

John's face revealed a sudden concern. "We were told to get as much information as quickly as possible. We were going to order DNA tests this morning."

"At whose expense?" Bud said.

"Ours, I guess. At least initially anyway."

Bud began shaking his head. "No, no, no. Not ours. If Jackson wants this piece of meat analyzed, he had better fork over the dough to do it, or the whole thing's off."

"You're not serious?" Evelyn said.

Bud snatched his cell phone off his belt. "Watch me."

"Bud, please, this is a once-in-a-lifetime opportunity. You can't just cut us out like that. You know, good and well, that if we bow out, Jackson will just go find another place to examine the specimen. Is that what you want? Some place like Scripps or Rosentheil to get all the publicity? Come on, Bud, let's proceed with the testing, and in the meantime, you can negotiate with Jackson about who's gonna pay for what. I'm sure he'll help us out. He asked us to do it. Besides, our investors should be ecstatic when they hear the news. They may fork over the money themselves."

Bud was holding his cell phone. His thumb poised to hit the Send button. He curled his lip, closed his phone, and snapped it back in its holder. "All right. How much is this going to cost us?"

A quirky smile materialized on Evelyn's face. "That's just it, Bud. We could use some stronger equipment."

"Out of the question."

"But we have tests to run. I can't even research this muscle tissue like I need to."

"I'm sorry, Evie, but we're broke. We still haven't recovered from that centrifuge over there," he said.

"We could rent the equipment then."

"Renting is more expensive than buying the stuff. Why spend a thousand dollars renting a bunch of equipment for a couple of days when I can buy one piece each year and own it?"

"Bud, if you rent the equipment we'll have more money than we know what to do with once this hits the periodicals and journals."

"I've got an idea." John stepped forward to accentuate his interruption.

"What?" Bud said.

"We can set up that conference call with Dr. Landover. I tried calling him earlier, but he wasn't answering his phone. I know he'd love to see these samples, and I know he has all the equipment needed."

"But that doesn't solve our microscope problem, John," Evelyn said, "or our light emitter problem, or any of the other deficiencies this lab has."

"That's true, but it will help us get these samples analyzed."

Evelyn glowered at Bud, fuming at his fatuous attitude. She felt as if her hands were tied by an old, misinformed, slavish lackey who had been promoted for no other reason than being a "yes" man . . . a spineless worm.

The atmosphere in the room grew wire tight.

At last Bud gave in. "Okay, we can send the samples and the specimen to that Doctor whatever his name is."

"Landover," John said. "Dr. Harry Landover. Scripps Institution of Oceanography, San Diego."

"I know where Scripps is, Spencer," Bud said. "How do I get a hold of Dr. Landover?"

"I will. I want to talk to him anyway. Then I'll give him your numbers and have him call you. You okay with that?"

Bud nodded. "Where are the samples you've already examined?"

Evelyn softened a little. "Bud, if you are going to send this to Landover, then you should probably take this as well." She stepped over to the cooler and pulled out the remaining portion of the specimen.

Bud's eyes broadened. "There's more?"

Evelyn handed the remaining eighteen point three lbs. of specimen to her supervisor.

Bud acted as if it was a great deal heavier than it was. "Wow, I thought all you had was what was on the slides."

"Bud," Evelyn said, "you're holding about twenty pounds of scientific history there. Sending it to Scripps could spell the end of NMI just as easily as it could elevate us to the top. If other rival institutions find out we have this and sent it to Scripps, then we could get a lot of heat from them to 'share the wealth.' It could get really ugly. People in this field have died mysterious deaths for less."

Bud sniffed. "Not happenin'. Either we get all or most of the credit, or nobody gets any. I've already been annoyed by Agent Jackson enough, too much, in fact, to allow others to horn in on our territory."

Evelyn held out her hand. "Well, then, can we have the specimen back and examine it ourselves as much as possible until you're ready to send it off?"

Bud looked down at the specimen enveloped in a sterile plastic bag. "Okay, but it won't take me long to get things ready. I'll call you when I'm ready to ship. Agreed?"

Evelyn and John both nodded.

"Just give us the rest of today, Bud," Evelyn said. "We'll probably have all the data we can muster with this equipment by midafternoon."

Bud frowned at Evelyn's backhanded comment and relinquished the specimen. "Fair enough."

CHAPTER TWENTY-FIVE

Friday, 7:51 a.m.
Office of the Secretary of State
Washington, DC

"Mr. President, I hate to bother you at such an early hour, but this cannot wait until later."

President Walker, holding his morning paper, set it down on top of a stack of debriefing files from the last twelve hours. He looked at the phone with concern. "Sandra, please don't tell me you've been in your office all night."

"Okay, I won't."

"You're going to run yourself into the ground. I know you feel the need to get everything done in a timely manner, but there's nothing in that office that's worth your health or possibly your life. Not that I don't care for my country, mind you, but what good am I to it if I'm incapacitated or dead? As my favorite character Jason Bourne says, 'Rest can be a weapon, too.'"

"Mr. President, you know I normally don't work after midnight, but there are several things coming to a head that I thought you'd like to be apprised of."

The president closed his eyes for a moment and nodded. "What's so pressing that you have to stay away from your family all night?"

"Two things at present. First off, Ambassador Vrilinko insists you call him this morning—"

"I spoke with the prime minister last night. Spent an hour assuring him we had nothing to do with the disappearance of his precious submarine. So, you can tell Vrilinko we spoke, and I assured his superior I would contact him just as soon as I received something worth calling him about."

"Sir, the reason why Vrilinko has called me twice since four o'clock is because he's getting reports now that rumors are cranking up in North Korea and Iran, stating we were behind a terrorist plot against the Russian sub. They are claiming we're angry because we disapproved of the missile testing being conducted on the Kamchatka Peninsula. The story I'm getting is Moscow is being fed substantiated intelligence naming one of our ships in the Atlantic as the culprit."

"That's absurd. I spoke to the joint chiefs myself right before I talked to the prime minister. They all assured me we had absolutely nothing to do with that submarine, and that is what I told the prime minister yesterday."

"With all due respect, sir, how many times have presidents in the past been fed those lines only to find that the converse was true?"

The president muttered in disbelief before answering. "I'd find it hard to believe they would lie to me so openly."

"Sir, we're both relatively new at this, only having been in office for a little less than a year. That makes your presidency even more vulnerable. That's why it's so important that you call Vrilinko and put his mind at ease. He thinks you're dodging him which, in turn, fuels the fire of the rumors."

"Okay, if you think it will help matters, I'll call him as soon as I get to the Oval Office."

"I do, sir."

"Okay, so what was the other issue?"

President Walker could hear her flip the page of her legal pad.

"This involves a scientist by the name of Dr. Anthony Fontaine. Do you know of him, sir?"

"Fontaine . . . Fontaine . . . afraid I don't."

"Dr. Fontaine is an American scientist who has spent the majority of his career overseas."

"Doing what?"

"That's just it, sir. He's one of the leading experts in evolutionary biology."

"Okay, so what?"

"I've been doing some checking. That's why I've been here all night. He was enlisted by the FBI several years ago to examine a badly decomposed body up in the Pacific Northwest. The body was thought to be human at first, but after further speculation, many experts concluded it was some sort of animal. Some even suggested it was Bigfoot. The report claims that Fontaine's examination confirmed it was an animal—a malnourished brown bear, to be exact."

"Why would the FBI bring in an evolutionary biologist to examine something like that? Wouldn't they want to bring in a paleontologist or a veterinarian? Or a park ranger, for crying out loud?"

"I know, sir, but it gets crazier. Fontaine's been called in on several occasions for similar expertise and not only by our government. And now, the latest is the examination of the two boats that were attacked in the Atlantic."

The president's voice emitted concern. "Something's not right."

"Ahh, but it gets even crazier, Mr. President."

"Please tell me you're joking?"

"I wish I was, sir. In each of these instances, Dr. Fontaine has been given a cover by the FBI so he can go in under their auspices. He goes by the name of Archibald Jackson. It seems he even has a great deal of clout when it comes to making executive decisions related to the investigations of which he is a part."

"What kind of clout?"

"Things like conducting investigations into people's lives, the dealings of businesses, and the like. Just about anything a normal agent would do as far as I can tell."

"Not alone, I hope."

"Not that I can see. There's always at least one FBI agent with him at all times according to records. But I found out he did visit the woman who was the lone survivor of the yacht that was attacked two days ago. She was undergoing treatment at an area hospital. I called the hospital myself earlier. According to the hospital's records, an Agent Archibald Jackson entered the room of Regina Fleming at approximately ten fifty a.m. Thursday morning to interrogate her—"

"I don't like this, Sandra."

"It gets worse, sir."

The president didn't say anything. He just sighed.

"Another agent was outside the door before Jackson arrived, but that agent left shortly before Agent Jackson entered the room. At that point, Jackson was in the room by himself with the patient. Then, about ten minutes later, a nurse entered the room to administer some medication—"

"You got all this from a hospital log?"

"No, sir, I got it from the police report. Regina Fleming died around eleven thirty a.m., according to the report. About thirty minutes after Agent Jackson and the nurse entered the room. Don't you find that a little odd?"

"Yes, and a bit too coincidental, don't you think? I need to call the director."

"Yes, sir, but before you do, there's more."

"Good grief."

"Dr. Fontaine called me . . . on my cell phone this morning urging me not to—"

"Hold on, Sandra," the president said. "How did he get your cell phone number?"

"I don't know, sir. He claims Director Belkin gave it to him, but I haven't confirmed that yet. I have been unable to reach Belkin."

"All right. Go ahead. What did this Fontaine have to say?"

"Remember the ocean liner that was attacked?"

"Yes."

"Apparently, there was a specimen found on the ocean liner. Dr. Fontaine claims it's the remains of a portion of the animal that attacked the ship. He urged me not to allow it to be shipped to a Dr. Harry Landover at the Scripps Institute of Oceanography in San Diego. He claimed that sending the specimen to San Diego would possibly create a scientific meltdown of some sort. I took it that this Dr. Landover was some kind of enemy or competitor."

The president couldn't believe his ears. "Huh?"

"He said that too many systems have been built upon evolutionary theory and to have evidence to the contrary would throw the world into chaos. He said scientific discovery would come to a standstill."

"Is this guy a lunatic or something?"

"Actually, he sounded quite convincing to me. Maybe because it was one o'clock in the morning. At first, I thought it sounded like a bona-fide threat. But now, with this additional information, I'm becoming extremely skeptical."

The president was exasperated. "Okay, Sandra, let me contact Belkin and see if I can get to the bottom of Dr. Fontaine's involvement. I'll get back with you later this morning once I know something."

"And don't forget to call Vrilinko."

"It will be the first thing I do. I promise."

CHAPTER TWENTY-SIX

Friday, 8:46 a.m.
National Marine Institute
Miami, Florida

Evelyn watched Micah vacate the laboratory after asking John for directions outside. He was gone for about fifteen minutes before she started to get concerned.

She found him sitting on a barstool with his arms crossed and his head down on the counter of the Tiki Hut near the entrance to the seal exhibit. Evelyn chuckled to herself as she watched through the branches of some adjacent greenery. NMI employees passed on occasion, inspecting Micah as they did, wondering who he was and why he was planted at a bar that didn't open until the afternoon.

She finally strolled up, leaning over to see his face. "Are you asleep?"

"Not yet," he said. "Give me five more minutes."

Evelyn grinned and sat down. "I know how you feel. I haven't stayed up all night in years."

"Well, I have, but as we get older, the nights seem longer somehow." Micah sat up, interlaced his fingers behind his head, and stretched with a groan before rubbing his neck with his thumbs. "I could never be a scientist. Too much inside work, stuck in a lab, squinting through some microscope to examine some bacteria or microbes. I know it's important, but it's not for me. I've got to be where the wind and the salt spray can hit me in the face."

"Wow, you make my work sound so mundane."

"To me, it is. But for you and John, I bet you two get the same exhilaration as I do when I'm cruising at fifteen knots across the ocean."

"Probably so." Evelyn stretched. "I told John I needed ten minutes or so. I thought I'd run to the canteen and get some coffee. Want to come along?"

"Sure. I could use some. Then I need to call Richard and see if he was able to find out anything."

"Richard?"

"You know, Wellman—the guy you met with me that first night in Fort Pierce?"

"Oh, yeah. Yeah."

"I also need to go to my car and get my sunglasses."

"I'm glad we pulled it around back. If it had sat out in the parking lot after hours, the security guards would've had it towed away."

"Glad I know somebody on the inside, then," Micah said with a wink.

Micah's eyes adjusted from the dark recesses of the lab better with his sunglasses on. Sitting again at the Tiki Hut, Micah sipped his coffee and watched Evelyn walk across the stretch of concrete which separated him from the building housing the lab until she disappeared inside. *I could get used to this.*

Taking a second to scan the smallish crowds as they trekked from one exhibit to the next, Micah finally grabbed his cell phone and called his second-in-command.

"Hey, Skip, where are you? You know you're late, right?"

"No, I'm not late if I'm not coming in, Wellman. That's why I called you. You're in charge today."

Wellman snickered. "Still after that Evelyn doctor chick, eh?"

"Wellman, grow up, will you?"

"Is she there?"

"No, and you need to stop. She's a sweet lady, and she's been through a lot."

"You like her, don't you?"

"Wellman, there are times when I'd love to ring your neck."

"I guess I'm wrong, huh? So, why are we playing hooky?"

"Did you hear about the attack on the cruise ship yesterday?"

"How could I not? It's been all over the news."

"I've been assisting Evelyn and the crew here at NMI. We examined the ship last night and found something very interesting."

"But you can't tell me, right?"

"I can't say over the phone. But suffice it to say, it will be in the news sometime soon."

"Okay. So, how long are you planning on being gone?"

"As long as it takes. Probably three or four days. I'll put the leave form in when I get back. Sector Miami is already apprised of the situation and has granted me approval to assist. Also, I've made a request for a quarantine zone to be put into effect from Fort Pierce to the Bahamas extending two hundred miles north and south of that line. Emergency and military personnel only are allowed in those waters. They will be contacting you and the other stations on the details. Just follow protocol, Richard, and you'll be okay."

"Roger that."

"Now, what did you find out for me about Regina Fleming?"

Wellman cleared his throat. "Not a lot. I kept getting stonewalled. Naval Intelligence wouldn't tell me anything. Even when I told them I was calling for you and gave them your old access code like you told me to, they just thought I was some weirdo hacker or something. They probably have Homeland Security staking out my house as we speak."

"I probably shouldn't have done that. Did you call the hospital yesterday evening?"

"Better yet, I went there. Man, did I get some juicy stuff."

"How in the world did you get access to anything?"

"I told them I was conducting an investigation for the Coast Guard in relationship to the attacked vessel and Regina Fleming. I just flashed my credentials and was in."

"You know you could be court-martialed for that?"

"I thought about that, but I was willing to take the risk," Wellman said. "If our superiors from Sector Miami decide to bust me, I'll plead for my job by stating that you and I sensed something sinister and wanted to help."

"Good luck with that."

"Oh, you're going down with me, Skip."

Micah shifted the phone to his other ear and grabbed his coffee cup. "Who are you, and why are you calling me?"

"Nice. Good luck with trying to disown me, oh, keeper of the tooth. Kind of hard to deny knowing me, don't you think?"

Micah smiled. *Wellman's getting braver. I'll give him that.* "So, what did you find out, Sherlock?"

"Our old friend Jackson went back into Regina Fleming's room right after you left yesterday morning. He was in her room for about fifteen to twenty minutes before a nurse entered. According to one of the other nurses, Fleming was supposedly freaking out and hallucinating uncontrollably. They tried to restrain her but couldn't. The weird part, though, was that there is nothing in Fleming's chart about the incident. When I confronted the hospital administrator about it, he stuttered and told me it must have been a clerical error."

"Right. Tell that to Fleming's attorneys."

"Hey, that's what I said."

"You actually said that to the hospital administrator?"

"Sure did. I also asked him if it was hospital procedure to have nurses from other floors show up and help restrain patients. The nurse I interviewed witnessed another nurse named Elysie Pruitt enter the room and then leave with Jackson. Nurse Pruitt was working two floors down, Skip. She had never looked at Fleming's chart, had never worked with Fleming, had never even worked on Fleming's floor. The administrator said it was uncommon but not out of the realm of possibility. He said it was a possibility that Pruitt knew Fleming and went there as a friend to try and help calm her down."

"Bull . . . loney," Micah said.

"Captain, I'm convinced Jackson had something to do with Fleming's death."

"Oh, so am I, Wellman. So am I. We just can't prove it, and that's the problem. Who was the nurse you interviewed?"

"Her name is Jodi Marek. I've got her address and phone number if you need it. She's hot, too."

"Good grief, Wellman. You need to find yourself a girlfriend."

"I have, Chief, but they get mad when you look at other women."

"Well, yeah, Sherlock. Doesn't it bother you when your girlfriend looks at another guy?"

"She can look all she wants so long as she doesn't touch."

Micah took another sip of his coffee and set the cup down. "But Einstein, don't you get it? It starts with looking. Then, looking leads to staring, staring leads to talking, and talking leads to touching."

"Got it, Master Yoda. And I assume to the dark side touching leads, hmmm?" Wellman said.

"No. Touching one woman while dating another might earn you a dirt nap in an underground condominium."

"Hasn't happened yet."

Micah scratched his cheek. "Well, Casanova, let me talk to this Jodi Marek before you make your move, okay? I want her to cooperate."

"Oh, I see how you are. You think my smooth moves and voluptuous appeal will have an adverse effect?"

"No comment. Just call me before you make an attempt to call her. I need to speak with her first."

"You're not going to beat me to the punch, are you? Steal my woman?"

Micah chuckled. "Trust me. You're safe."

CHAPTER TWENTY-SEVEN

Friday, 9:39 a.m.
White House—Oval Office
Washington, DC

President Walker peered out his Oval Office window, looking across the White House lawn. Deep in thought, he didn't turn around when he heard the buzzer on his intercom sound.

"Sir, Director Belkin is here to see you," the secretary said.

President Walker continued to gaze at the lush scenery and blue sky, wishing he was in the middle of it. "Send him in, Ingrid."

FBI Director Robert Belkin opened the door and stepped inside. A stout man with an ever-increasing beer belly, Belkin was now serving as the FBI director for his third administration. Viewed by most inside the Beltway as a solid, no-nonsense kind of guy, few people had ever questioned his credentials or ethics.

"Bob Belkin, come in. Come in. Have a seat." President Walker pointed to the sitting area in the middle of the room. "How's the family?"

"Good," Belkin said. "Kids are growin' up too fast. Haley's engaged, you know."

"No, I hadn't heard. She was going to college, right?"

"University of Virginia. That's where she met him."

The two men shook hands before sitting down. Belkin chose the sofa, and the president sat in the leather wing-backed chair facing toward the door.

"So, what does Dad think?" the President said.

Belkin bobbed his head back and forth. "He seems like a nice guy. Political science major. I was kinda hoping for somethin' outside of politics for my kids, you know?"

The president scrunched his eyes together. "You could do a background check on the kid, whole family, the works. Send a couple of agents over to his dormitory, or better yet, wait until he gets back home and then send them to his parents' house one evening to do a real interview. Give him a taste of the real world we live in. That might turn him away."

"From politics or my daughter?"

"Possibly both."

They both laughed.

"You'd let me do that, Mr. President? Let me use government resources to perform private investigations?"

"Of course not, Bob. It was a joke."

Belkin snapped his fingers. "Rats. I was hoping you would."

"You know me, Bob. I ran on the political platform of cleaning up the government, remember? That's just what I need. Knowing my luck, the boy's parents would turn out to be state attorneys, or worse yet, supporters of the man I beat in the last election."

Belkin smiled. "Mr. President, I came as soon as I got your message. What can I do for you?"

"I appreciate your promptness. Hopefully, what I have to discuss will not take up too much of your time. I have some questions, and I'm hoping you're the man with the answers."

Belkin grimaced in a joking way. "I'll try, sir."

"I know you will," the president said. "How much do you know about the current situation with the Russians and their lost submarine?"

Belkin straightened a smidgen, caught off guard by the inquiry. "Word is they lost contact with a Dolphin-class sub called the *Kirov* in the mid-Atlantic approximately," he said, glancing at his watch, "twenty hours ago. The last transmission they received was a communiqué about a picture taken by one of their external cameras of what appeared to be a flipper. That was the last the Russians heard from her."

"Anything else?"

"No, sir. Nothing except they're pressuring you for assistance. My department is in the final stages of preparing an official threat assessment for the joint chiefs as we speak."

The president sat forward in his chair, interlacing his fingers with his elbows resting on the armrests. His thumbs pressed against his lips. "What's your assessment of the situation?"

Belkin's eyebrows shot upward. "Not good. Three ships, a science vessel—equipped with a diving bell and a small one-man mini-sub—and two battleships set sail from Baltiysk this morning. They were given orders to locate the submarine and make every effort to salvage the crew and sub. Sir, one of the battleships is the *Peter the Great*."

President Walker's eyes grew large. "I see."

"We also just learned that if anyone tries to deter them from their mission, they have permission to fire upon the attackers."

"I was afraid of that. I just got off the phone with the Russian defense minister about an hour ago. I assured him we didn't have anything to do with the disappearance of the sub and would help in any way we could. I also told him I was waiting on a report from the joint chiefs before I made any calls about deployment of American ships for assistance."

"What did he say to that?"

The president exhaled. "Some of it was in Russian, but I know an expletive when I hear it. Suffice it to say, we will have to assist soon. The longer we wait, the guiltier we look."

"Sir, I'm no military man. As you know, I was an analyst and then a field man before becoming a deputy director during the Cold War. In all my years of dealing with Russia, they have been fairly consistent in their reasoning and planning of military operations. That submarine was not just heading to Venezuela for some sun and fun. That submarine was part of a ballistic missile test."

"Kamchatka?"

"Yes, sir. The *Kirov* was the one that performed that test. Sir, that sub was in the Kara Sea when it conducted those tests. Venezuela is a long way from the Kara Sea. And they were going to Venezuela, the entire crew, to simply vacation there? It sounds fishy to me, sir."

"Bob, you and I both know there was more to this submarine than what the Russians are telling us. The unfortunate timing of this . . . creature, monster, whatever you want to call it, is the kicker in all this. Had that creature not surfaced, we could be asking the hard questions of the Russians: Why were you there? What were you doing?"

"Why can't we ask them anyway?"

"We could, but this creature has given them the opportunity to play the victim card. 'We were just going to Venezuela for some R and R,' they would say. If we made a big stink about their presence in that part of the world, the media would demonize us. 'Oh, look at the big, bad United States trying to hit a comrade when he's down. Taking over Iraq and Afghanistan isn't enough. Now they have to pick on Russia.'"

Belkin grunted. "That's why I hate politics. It keeps us from getting real answers and results in so many cases. Criminals and thugs get off because 'good' people want to try and keep their noses squeaky clean to maintain an image."

"Gee, Bob, don't pull any punches. Tell me what you really think." The president laughed.

"I'm sorry, Mr. President. I get a little testy when it comes to stuff like that."

"I understand. We all have our soapboxes. So, while you're in a testy mood, tell me what you know about an agent Archibald Jackson."

Belkin squirmed in his seat, attempting to reposition himself. He grabbed his tie and slid it back over the buttons of his shirt. "Archibald Jackson. He's an interesting fellow."

"That I already know, Bob. How did he get to be an FBI agent without going through Quantico?"

Belkin cleared his throat as his face flushed red. "Well, Mr. President, it's a bit of a long story."

President Walker raised his finger in a pausing gesture while standing. Strolling over to his desk, he punched a button on his phone.

"Yes, Mr. President," came the voice of long-standing presidential secretary Ingrid Montes.

"Ingrid, could Director Belkin and I get some coffee and Danish pastries, please? Cream cheese this time?"

"Will that be all, sir?"

"Yes, Ingrid. If we can get that in ten minutes, I'll dance at your next wedding."

"At sixty-seven, sir, I'm too old to train another one. But thanks nevertheless."

The president laughed. "Thank you, Ingrid," he said, punching the button once more. "Presidents and members of Congress can come and go, but she's indispensable."

With coffee and pastries spread out on a silver platter, President Walker filled Director Belkin's cup and slid him the cream and sugar.

"So, Bob, tell me what you know about Agent Jackson."

Belkin had dodged the question for the better part of ten minutes, waiting for the food to arrive. He knew he was postponing the inevitable and now his time was up. He loosened his tie, took a quick bite of his pastry, and set it down on the coffee table.

"Approximately four years ago, your predecessor's administration directed me to seek out an American scientist—who had been teaching overseas for several years—to be a part of a clandestine group of scientists whose sole purpose would be to investigate any paranormal or cryptozoological incidents in North, Central, and South America. In cooperation with several other countries around the world, these scientists, thirty-two in all, were enlisted to be on call. When they were contacted, they would investigate the incident, giving their expert advice."

"Where was this Agent Jackson when you first contacted him?"

"He was briefly a professor of evolutionary biology at Cambridge. But by the time we found him, Cambridge had severed ties with him, stating ideological differences as the reason. Jackson then struck out on his own, starting his own research foundation. He was getting that off the ground when we first contacted him."

"And why was he so sought after and not somebody else?"

"I'm not sure. We were given a list of scientists and told to contact them."

"You're not making sense, Bob."

"Sir, we were directed to contact and enlist these scientists. Our job was to make contact, inform them of the job, and if they agreed, create a cover that could get them into any investigative forum needed. So, the easiest way was to give him and the others agent status."

"You gave all thirty-two scientists agent status?"

"No, sir. We were responsible for enlisting six of the thirty-two. The remaining scientists were enlisted by other countries but with the same orders. Of the six, we have three scientists remaining on our accountability list. Two scientists retired. One has since passed away. Of the remaining three, Jackson is the most prominent by far and has requested that he handle all the cases in the Americas. Because of his ability to drop everything and assist, he usually is the one we call. The other two scientists are university professors who seem bothered when we request their assistance and always have an excuse as to why they can't leave when we need them."

"Were you ever ordered to replace the other scientists?"

"No, sir."

"What is Jackson's job?"

"Whenever we have a case that falls under the heading of paranormal or requires a cryptozoologist, then we call him, and he comes and investigates it."

"Give me a for-instance."

Belkin grabbed his cup and saucer. "A couple of years ago, we got a report that a Louisiana fisherman hunting for crawfish in the bayous near Honey Island saw a thing that was described as a bigfoot."

"The Honey Island Swamp Monster?"

Belkin cocked his head. "Yes."

"Bob, you're looking at an old Louisiana boy at heart. I grew up in New York, but I visited my granddaddy every summer in Baton Rouge."

Belkin repositioned himself in his seat. "Jackson was sent to investigate it. His team never found anything except tracks in the mud. They concluded that the tracks were either fake or created by a crippled bear."

"Jackson has a team?"

"A team of real FBI agents, yes. One of the mandates of the previous administration was that the scientists had to be accompanied at all times by an authentic FBI agent. The easiest way to accomplish that was to create a team."

"Kind of like *X-Files*, huh?"

"Yeah, but don't say that around Jackson. He hates it that we think of him that way."

"I couldn't really care less what Agent Jackson thinks right now. I have evidence that he entered the hospital room of that Fleming woman—you know, the one who was attacked on the yacht off the coast of Florida—and entered the room alone. The police report says the other agent stood outside the room until Agent Jackson arrived. That agent eventually left, leaving Jackson alone in the room. Then, during this approximate ten-to-fifteen-minute window, a nurse entered the hospital room." The president paused to see Belkin's reaction. "Agent Jackson and the nurse were then seen leaving the room together. Thirty minutes later, Regina Fleming was found dead in her room—the autopsy said she died of heart failure."

Belkin's breathing had escalated. A slight glimmer of sweat formed on his face. "I will check into it, Mr. President. That is against protocol. Jackson should know better."

"As should the other agents assigned to accompany Jackson based on what you told me."

"That's correct, Mr. President," Belkin said, watching his career flash before his eyes.

"I also did a little checking into the autopsy, Bob."

Great, Belkin thought.

"The body was transported to an FBI facility, and the autopsy was performed there. Heart failure? That's the best Jackson could muster?"

"Sir, I will get to the bottom of this as soon as I leave here," Belkin said, positioning himself to leave.

The president shifted in his seat. "Director, one more thing. What is the real name of Agent Jackson?"

"Dr. Anthony Fontaine."

President Walker nodded. "Well, Director Belkin, I think it's time to reign in the good doctor and decommission him. There's a new sheriff in town."

CHAPTER TWENTY-EIGHT

Friday, 10:02 a.m.
I-95 North
En Route to Fort Pierce, Florida

Micah left NMI after his phone conversation with Wellman, assuring Evelyn he would try and be back before dark. He needed to travel back to Fort Pierce and interview Jodi Marek, a twenty-seven-year-old single mother of two who worked the day shift at the St. Lucie Regional Medical Center. She was the nurse interviewed by Wellman who seemed to be the only one who saw the entire Regina Fleming death from a different perspective.

On his way, he decided to call his buddy in naval intelligence, Jason Greene, and see if there was any information he could proffer, but he knew if he tried to call Greene on a direct line, they'd never let him get access that deep into NI. There were too many new people who had never heard of Micah Gregson. He'd been out of Naval Intelligence long enough to be forgotten by many. Call the hotline or some direct secure number for a department, and he wouldn't get past the first hello. He had to come up with a way to get the information he needed.

Then an idea hit him. He grabbed his cell phone and started browsing.

"Here we go," he said, copying and pasting the number and pressing Send. *Maybe the simplest route is the best way.*

"Office of Naval Intelligence. How may I direct your call?" said a female voice.

"May I have Military Personnel, please?"

"Please hold," the operator said.

Micah waited but a moment before another voice answered.

"Military Personnel."

"Yes, my name is Captain Micah Gregson, USN Retired. I was calling to see if Commander Rick Atkins was available. I believe he's still working in the Hopper Information Services Center."

"Can you hold?"

"Sure can."

The line started playing a continual advertisement for the Citizen Intelligence Personnel Office. Micah had to listen to the one-minute ad three-and-a-half times, wondering if he'd hit a brick wall.

Then, mid-advertisement, the phone rang.

"This is Commander Atkins."

"Well, you could start by calling a guy once in a while to see how he's doing, especially one you used to call a friend."

There was a short silence. "Micah, is that you?"

"Yes, sir. Reporting for duty, sir."

"I'll be . . . what makes you call me out of the clear blue? How ya doin', buddy?"

"Rick, I'm doin' well. I'm lovin' the CG lifestyle down here. I'd be hard-pressed to trade it in for anything else."

"So, I can't interest you in a second career in naval intelligence, huh?"

"Already been down that road, my friend. Loved it while it lasted, but I'm getting too old for it. I was thinking about that the other day. If I got into hand-to-hand combat with some young buck, he'd probably whip my butt."

"Too old? What are you now, forty, forty-one?"

"Just turned forty."

"And that's old?"

"For field work? For me? Yes."

"So, out of shape, are we? CG life too cushy?"

"I've been in better shape, but I was a lot younger then, too."

They both laughed and shared updates on their lives, filling each other in on the latest before Micah got to the heart of his call.

"Rick, I need a favor."

"What's that?"

"I'm sure you've heard about the attacks on the *Greenback* and the *Titan* down here?"

"Are you kidding? Top brass has been buzzing since the first attack occurred. It's the talk of the entire building."

"Well, I'm in the middle of it."

Commander Atkins snorted. "Can't stay out of the loop, can ya?"

"I didn't volunteer. Trust me. I got sucked in this time, Rick."

"Sure you did."

"No, really, I just happened to be on duty at my station, Station Fort Pierce, the morning the *Greenback* was attacked. It was my boat that responded to the mayday."

"Wow. That's awesome. Right place at the right time, huh? Must be pretty cool to see things like that up close, instead of being tied down in a Washington office pushin' pencils."

"Well, I'll let you know. For right now, I need some information."

Atkins drew in a deep breath. "It'll depend on the info, Micah."

"I know. That's why I need to speak to Jason Greene. He would have access to what I need, and he knows what he can't divulge."

"You know he's working as a liaison between NI and the other agencies? His position opened when Homeland Security came into existence."

"I know, Rick. Jason and I keep in touch, even if others don't."

"Ouch."

"Hey, last time I checked, phone lines run in both directions, right?"

"I couldn't have said it better myself."

"I knew, because of his position, that if I called Jason directly, no one would give me the time of day."

"Oh, I get it. Use the commander that you haven't spoken to since you left NI to circumvent protocol."

"It does pay to know how things work."

Atkins chuckled. "I can patch you through, Micah, but there is only so much Lieutenant Greene will be able to do."

"Look, Rick, anything will be helpful."

"So, what have you gotten yourself into?"

"It's complicated."

"Let me give you my cell number. If you need anything, you can call me directly. You know I'll help you as much as I can."

"I really appreciate it. I may take you up on that soon."

"Please do," Atkins said, giving Micah his number.

Commander Atkins transferred Micah, and he was on hold once more.

Micah plugged his phone into its carjack before it started to die when a voice came on.

"I can't believe it. The infamous Micah Gregson. How are you doin', man?"

"Jason Greene, what's up?"

"Commander Atkins told me who was on hold and why you were callin'. So, what's it like being in the national limelight?"

"Right now, I'm in the dark about way too much, and I was wondering if you could help me shed some light on a few areas."

"Whatcha need?"

"Let me fill you in first, and then my requests may seem more plausible."

"Okay, shoot."

"There is an FBI agent down here investigating the attacks on the *Greenback* and the *Titan*. I'm assuming that he'll investigate any other attacks that surface as well. He claims to be FBI and has all the credentials to back that up, but there's something fishy about his whole team. They cleaned up the *Greenback* before the investigation was completed. They claimed the owner of the boat was involved in some sort of terrorist activity, but then they showed up at the *Titan* to investigate that, too. The owner of the previous boat had nothing to do with the *Titan*. And then there was—"

"Whoa, whoa, Micah. I'm losin' ya, buddy. What is the agent's name?"

"Archibald Jackson."

"Hold on. Let me access their database. I can check out anyone from any agency now, thanks to Homeland Security. Isn't that great?"

"That must be nice."

"It's a double-edged sword. All those things usually are, you know."

"Uh-huh." Micah could hear Jason Greene tap on computer keys.

"Okay," Greene said, "Agent Archibald A. Jackson, a.k.a., Dr. Anthony A. Fontaine, Dr. A. A. Fontaine, Dr. A. Fontaine."

"Hold on, Jason. Which one is his real name? Fontaine or Jackson?"

"The way this is written, it could be taken either way really. Usually, the real name appears first, aliases second. But they usually do not use 'a.k.a.' for the other names. At least, in all the files I've accessed since I got this job, this is the first one written like this."

Another abnormality for Agent Jackson, Micah thought. "Continue."

"Age fifty-one. Born in Nantucket Island, Massachusetts. Graduated from Princeton with a PhD in Evolutionary Biology. Taught at Harvard for twelve years before moving to Ireland where he taught at University College in Dublin. Then, three years ago, he moved to England where he became a professor at Cambridge. Was there briefly before being dismissed. Started the NatSel Foundation two years ago. Joined the FBI at the age of forty-seven?" There was a pause. "That's weird."

"What's weird?"

"At forty-seven, he was way too old to be joining the FBI, for starters, and there's no mention of attending Quantico, either."

"Huh. That is strange. What else does it say?"

"He's designated as lead investigator for a special unit affiliated with the Aquatic Nuisance Species Task Force of National Oceanic and Atmospheric Administration."

A rush of adrenaline flushed Micah's face. "So he lied."

"Lied about what?"

"He told us he was investigating Evelyn Sims's husband because he was possibly a terrorist."

"Unless she married a merman with a grenade launcher, being the lead investigator for a special unit of the Aquatic Nuisance Species Task Force would not qualify him to chase terrorists. Especially if he hasn't been through Quantico."

"Right. That's my point, Jason. He's hiding something. Is there anything else in his file?"

"Nope. That's where it ends."

"All right, Jason. I've got one more favor."

"Let me hear it."

"Is there anything else I need to know about these two ships that have been attacked?"

"Were you aware there's a deal brewing between us and the Russians?"

"A source told me the Russians have us running scared. That's all I know."

"The Russians lost contact with one of their subs. It was in the middle of the Atlantic, sent a transmission about what was described as a flipper, and then fell off the face of the Earth. The Russians think we had something to do with it, so they're demanding our help. Some think it's truly to get us to help in case there are any survivors. Nothing more than a rescue operation. Others think it's a ploy to get the U.S. military to exonerate itself from any wrongdoing by helping out."

"They think we had something to do with it?"

"That's what Iranian and North Korean sources are telling the Russians."

Micah held the cell phone against his ear, but his mind was racing. "Jason, when did this occur?"

"No one is sure, but the last transmission was received by Moscow around twenty hundred hours, Moscow time, Thursday."

"That would be about noon, one o'clock in the mid-Atlantic. That adds up, Jason. Jackson made a comment that his investigation was a matter of national security. That's what he was referring to. The Russian sub."

"To let you know, Micah, the Russians sent three ships to the Atlantic to look for the sub. A science ship and two battleships."

"Whoa. Expecting trouble, are they?"

"Right now, they feel they can't trust us."

"And why was a Russian sub running submerged in the middle of the Atlantic, Jason?"

"That's what our government wants to know. The Ruskies said they were on their way to Venezuela."

"Venezuela, huh? Wonder why they were heading there?"

"I'm not sure, buddy, but I bet whatever it was can't be bought and delivered over the Internet."

CHAPTER TWENTY-NINE

Friday, 10:10 a.m.
Approximately 87 Nautical Miles East of Titusville, Florida

A sixty-six-foot fishing boat named *Sea-Saw*, manned by a complement of ten men, meandered its way in a zigzag pattern in twenty-five hundred feet of water. Dragging a net over seventy feet in length and some fifty feet in width, the vessel seemed like a flea on the dog's back of the ocean.

The boat itself was somewhat of an eyesore. The hull was rusty from its years of fighting the salt. Chipped and flaking paint dotted the ship's exterior, giving it a diseased, mangy appearance. Long steel arms jetting out on both sides seemed to cry for mercy as they helped to hold the net in place. Tools of the trade were pinned to the walls of the cabin—both inside and out—their handles gouged and scratched from rough usage. Life on the sea was treacherous, and the *Sea-Saw* had seen its fair share of life.

The crew of the vessel maneuvered above and below deck, from side to side, from bow to stern and vice versa. Each man had a job to do—a responsibility that would without a doubt keep him and the other nine men alive and well—so they could return home to their spouses . . . and their "spices," with a couple of the men having both.

They were a haggard bunch, logging their last leg of a four-week jaunt that brought them down the coast from Cape Hatteras to Miami for two weeks, and then they were to spend another two weeks drag-netting up the coast and back home. The beards of all the men had already become grizzled and scraggily. Their clothes, soiled with the spray of salt water, fish guts, blood from various self-inflicted nicks and cuts, and wave after wave of perspiration, screamed for a washing machine and a mountain of soap.

The captain of the *Sea-Saw* was not the owner/proprietor of the boat, but instead a hired hand of the owner. His job was based on two very important things: bring the boat back in one piece—in essence, in the same shape in which it left port—and bring it back full of fish. In this case, Atlantic Mackerel and anything else they could catch and take back to the man for profit. The more weight they had, the more money they would earn. The more money they earned, the more beer and whiskey they could buy. It was a simple case of supply and demand.

Trolling as the sun blazed down upon them, the captain, a wily soul, perched himself on the small bridge behind the wheel. Relaxed as he could be and joyous over the calm seas, he steered the vessel while whistling an old pirate's song.

His first mate watched another sailor at the stern of the boat. He was leaning over the side in a precarious way. Then, in a frantic manner, the other sailor looked up at the wheelhouse and motioned at the water with his right hand while tugging at a rope with his left.

"Captain, I think we have a problem."

The captain stood and peered out the window, grunting at the thought of having to stand. He jerked the throttle back to a mere sputter. "What is it now?"

A crewman suddenly bolted up the stairs. "Captain, the stern is taking on water. We've got something huge snagged in the nets."

The captain's eyes became concerned. "Start the pumps. Keep us afloat. Let me come down there and have a look."

"Aye, Captain," the man said, disappearing in an instant.

"Take the wheel, Bobby," the captain said to his first mate. "Keep us straight and true at idle speed."

The captain slapped on his weathered ball cap with a big North Carolina Tarheels insignia plastered on the front and moseyed down the steps, moaning and whining to himself, his knees and hips protesting every step's jolt.

What met his eyes, however, was nothing like what he expected. All his crewmen were either helping pump water overboard or trying to ascertain the condition of the nets. Their collective actions made even the veteran captain nervous. The stern of the boat, being only six to twelve inches above sea level, didn't help matters, either.

"What in Neptune's fury is going on?" the captain said.

"We don't know, Captain," crewman Peter La Belle said. "We've snagged something, and it's heavy. We're trying to decide if we can pull it up or not to get a better look."

"We've been pulled down over three feet, gentlemen," the captain said. "We've only got half a foot left and then it doesn't matter now, does it?"

"That's the problem, Captain. Something's in the nets; that much we know. But what? We don't know. Permission to send a dive team?"

"Have we sunk any further since we slowed?"

"No, sir. We actually came up a little."

The captain's cockeyed frown showed his disgust. *I don't get paid enough to decide such things.* "Go ahead. Two men. Get down and get up. I want an answer within five minutes of hittin' the water."

Another crewman, Steve Richmond, nodded and motioned for the two usual divers to get ready. The two men, Jack Wiggins and Marlon Stanford, bolted for the diving equipment and began stripping down to their skivvies. The other men prepared the tanks and other needed gear while the divers struggled into their wetsuits. The captain barked out orders, making sure each man had a job to do before, during, and after the divers were in the water.

Soon the divers sat on the edge of the boat, giving each man on deck a thumbs-up sign before flopping over backwards into the ocean. The bubbles, first hitting the surface in large, bulky masses, dissipated into smaller, finite ripples until they vanished altogether. The crew stood, nervous and feeling powerless, watching the waves for any sign of their comrades.

"Richmond, get a man up in the crow's nest and keep a lookout for sharks. If we've got a carcass in the nets, we might have company."

"Aye, sir." Richmond pointed to another man named Kinnard, then gestured to two other men. "Grab a rifle and scan the horizon both bow and stern and listen for Kinnard. If he yells 'shark,' find it and take it out."

Both men nodded and raced to their tasks.

The divers' descent was methodical at first, staying within sight of one another. They gripped the net and followed it down, peering inside to see the cause of the chaos. There was nothing for the first thirty feet except blue water and an occasional fish darting around the boundaries of the net in search of an exit.

As the two men slid further down the net, the water became murkier and darker. A thermocline was moving in and obscuring visibility. They had to hurry or soon, especially if they ventured too far down, their tank gauges would be invisible to them unless they held them against the glass of their masks. Wiggins motioned to the second diver, Stanford, that they would travel about twenty more feet, but if they encountered too much resistance, they would go back to the surface. Stanford shot Wiggins a thumbs-up sign and continued down the net.

Ten more feet down and to the right of where the two men clung to the net, a dark mass emerged from the shadows. Wiggins held up his fist, motioning for them to stop, and pointed in the direction of the mass. The two divers pulled themselves sideways around the net toward the object. It was then the water cleared for a moment, revealing a jagged mass of raw flesh. Its frayed edges dangled to the rhythm of the ocean current.

The gruesome sight caused Stanford to almost spit out his regulator before shooting upward toward the surface. He clawed at the net, trying to move as fast as he could. Bubbles erupted as he flailed like a madman toward the surface.

Wiggins, watching his companion act like he had seen a ghost, started to shake. He spun around, fearing a stealth shark attack from behind, but there was nothing behind him but blue water.

He turned and leaned forward, straining to see inside the net which by now had become engulfed in silt. *I can't see a thing,* he thought as he pulled himself around to where his fellow crewman had been seconds prior.

Then he saw it.

Amongst the shadows and spears of sunlight that managed to penetrate the depths, a mass appeared. Goosebumps shot all over his body. His breathing became erratic. He shivered. His arms, though bracing him against the net, quivered. The water suddenly felt twenty degrees colder.

Another cloud of silt passed.

Then he saw it again.

This time it was very discernible, even if only for an instant.

Flesh.

Torn.

Mangled.

Bloody.

Its tattered edges swaying back and forth at the will of the current. He tried to establish what kind it was, but the silt masked his vision once more. He reached into the net and felt around until he found it.

The carrion was slimy.

That makes sense. It's underwater. Of course it would be. He felt for anything that might lend him a clue. A wall of flesh. A mass that must have weighed thousands of pounds.

Something big.

Something enormous.

It was then he latched onto a mass around which he could barely wrap his hand. A wave of current pushed the mass toward him, giving the feel that whatever he grabbed was still alive. He dropped it and pulled his arm back through the net in time to see suction cups smash against the net. "Squid," he said, almost dropping the regulator out of his mouth.

Giant one.

I've got to get back to the surface.

Topside, the captain was helping Marlon Stanford back into the boat along with another sailor. "You idiot! You left him down there?"

Stanford, short of breath and feeling faint, had trouble speaking as blood trickled from his lips. "Sorry . . . panicked . . . light-head—" Then he passed out.

"Stupid fool's got the bends," the captain said. "Remind me that he never dives again. Get him below and on some oxygen before I throw him overboard and use him as trolling bait. And wrap him tight. No doubt his body temperature has dropped as well."

"Aye, Captain," two men said in unison.

"Any sign of Wiggins?" The captain peered back out over the water. "I hate it that he's down there alone. If he was to get snagged, he'd drown."

"No sign of him yet," Richmond said. "Want me to send another diver down?"

The captain of the *Sea-Saw* placed his hands on the railing and studied the water. "Not yet. He's still got some time left on his tank. If he doesn't come back up in ten minutes, then send two more down to retrieve him."

Jack Wiggins scaled the net, trying not to snag his equipment. With each movement upward, he would peer into the net for signs of how big the squid might be. The silt from the disruption of the thermocline was now rising. More and more of the net's contents were being swallowed in darkness. An occasional burst of icy cold water engulfed Wiggins, causing him to shiver.

Wiggins had covered about twenty feet of net in a diagonal path, heading over to where he thought the rope was located that would lead him back to the stern of the boat. As he maneuvered himself up and sideways, he took one last look down into the net. Those same fish he and Stanford had seen earlier were still imprisoned, swimming around in a larger school now, having found comrades in a similar condition.

Then something beyond the school caught his eye. It was a tentacle, fifteen feet or so in length, and it appeared to protrude from a cave. Wiggins slid back down the net, keeping his eyes fixed on the tentacle's base. Moving ever so slowly, he focused on the target, trying to ascertain where the body of the animal was. Then, in a gust of warm water, the area cleared.

Wiggins gasped. He saw it now.

Letting go of the net, he ascended to the surface and soon appeared about thirty feet off the port side.

"Diver! Port side!" the lookout shouted.

The crew turned to see Jack Wiggins swimming over to the boat. A crewman grabbed the life preserver and tossed it out. Soon Jack Wiggins was being hoisted on deck.

"Did you see anything, Jack?" the captain said.

Wiggins pulled his mask off and squinted, trying to get his eyes to adjust to the bright sunshine. "Captain, you're not going to believe this."

CHAPTER THIRTY

Friday, 11:40 a.m. (EST)
The M23
Two Kilometers North of Crawley, England

A brand-new silver Bentley Continental Flying Spur zipped past a decaying delivery truck en route to Sussex, racing down the highway at a comfortable hundred and ten kph. Eric Gilliam decided by noon that a healthy dose of fresh air, compliments of his sprawling estate, was a needed vaccine against the viruses of city life . . . and dimwitted people.

Indignant and in disbelief, Gilliam replayed the phone conversation. With each rerun, he gripped the steering wheel a little tighter. The car's speed increased a couple of notches each time.

He yelled, smacking the wheel with his hand. "Called the secretary of state! Incredible. Twenty years. He's going to destroy twenty years of planning." He slammed the steering wheel again. "Twenty years of dreaming!"

With his cell phone plugged into its cradle, he scrolled down to the Bs and punched Send.

"Belkin," came the voice on the other end.

"Director Belkin, this is Eric Gilliam. Are you private?"

"For the moment. I have some people on their way to see me, so if I end it quickly, you'll know why."

"Very well. Have you heard the news?"

"Depends on what you're referring to."

"I am referring to Fontaine."

"There seems to be a great deal of interest in him these days."

"What's that supposed to mean?"

"I was called into President Walker's office this morning. He grilled me about Fontaine. He already knew a great deal about him and was fishin' for information. He knew things about Fontaine I didn't even know. That's what my meeting in a few minutes is all about. I've been instructed to gain any and all information about him and deliver it to the president immediately. I am then to pull Fontaine into my office and terminate his position."

Gilliam spewed a tirade of expletives. "I'm going to kill him. He'll wreck the entire plan. Years of work ruined in a matter of days because a moronic scientist gets an ego."

"That's nothing new, you know."

"I don't have time for scientists and their egos, Director. They want their name in lights. They want the fame and fortune. They make me ill."

"Mr. Gilliam, are you aware he called the secretary of state early this morning?"

"Yes, that is why I called you. I did not get any information about the nature of the call, however. Do you know why he called?"

"I'll have more information after my meeting. But I did find out from the president that Fontaine called Secretary Brown because he was afraid a specimen recovered from one of the boats attacked in the Atlantic was going to be handed over to a Dr. Harry Landover. This Landover character must be some rival or competitor of Fontaine's because he told Brown if Landover got the specimen he would turn the scientific world on its head."

Gilliam white-knuckled the steering wheel with both hands. The Bentley was soaring at a hundred forty-two kph. He couldn't believe what he was hearing. His worst nightmare was coming true. His grand plan was now in great peril. Some rogue scientist was allowing a personal battle with a fellow scientist to lure him into breaching his contract. If that happened, Fontaine's actions would be catastrophic. A government takeover of all the businesses involved in his plan would be imminent; the beginning of World War III would ensue once the Middle Eastern and Asian worlds heard of the plan; the West would be in great danger before the armies were ready. *It would lead to the possible destruction of the Western world as we know it,* Gilliam thought. The consequences could possibly bring the world to a catastrophic conclusion.

Gilliam attempted to constrain his anger. "Who is this Landover fellow?"

"He's a marine biologist at the Scripps Institute in San Diego. I have a file here on him. According to our sources, he and Fontaine taught together at University College in Dublin, Ireland. They also were keynote speakers at the thirty-ninth and fortieth European Marine Biology Symposiums in Genoa, Italy, and Vienna, Austria, respectively."

"So they must have had a falling out," Gilliam said.

"It would appear that way. I don't have anything describing the nature of the disagreement, but I'm hoping my meeting will shed some light on it."

"Very well." Gilliam sighed. "Director, I cannot stress enough how important it is that we get Fontaine under control. Since he is acting under your sponsorship, I am counting on you to take care of him. May I remind you that the welfare of your family depends on it?"

"Don't threaten me, Gilliam. I got into this mess because I believe in your cause. You don't have to bully me to get me motivated."

"Very well, then."

"How do you propose getting rid of Fontaine? If I pull him off the case and strip him of his agent status, he's going to talk. You know that, right?"

"Simply taking his agent status away was not what I had in mind."

"What are you saying exactly?"

"You know what I'm saying, Director. Your government has always been good at making people disappear. And I am not speaking of the witness protection program. I'm sure you can find a way."

Director Belkin sat silent. He hated it when things did not go according to plan, especially when it meant someone had to die. "When and where?"

"If you want, I'll set it up. That way, you have fewer ties to the event. Does that ease your conscience, Director?"

"No, but I guess it'll have to do. I never wanted to enlist the arrogant idiot to begin with. I knew he'd be trouble."

"After today, he will be out of your hair."

"Good."

"Very well. Until then." Gilliam lowered his speed for fear of drawing the attention of a motorcycle cop hiding over the next hill. He was anxious but uncertain of what to do next. In his rage, he had promised Dr. Fontaine's demise. However, he'd never been to Florida, let alone Fort Pierce or Port Canaveral. Arranging the hit was going to be difficult.

Then it occurred to him. One of his twelve partners, William Forster, owner and proprietor of the largest medical supplier in North America, vacationed on the west coast of Florida all the time.

Gilliam peeked at his watch. *It's noon there.* Grabbing his briefcase and arranging the numbers on the locking mechanism, the case popped open. He reached inside and grabbed a notepad and pen while trying to keep his hundred-thousand-pound car on the road.

He punched a number on his cell. "William, this is Eric Gilliam from across the pond, as they say. How are you doing?"

"Speak of the devil, Eric. I was just thinking about you."

"Were you, now?"

"Sure was. Imagine you calling on the day my company's stock just split and made me even richer. It must be a sign." Forster spewed a rich, hearty laugh. "I probably should shoot down to the jiffy store and buy a bunch of lottery tickets."

"I love it when stocks split, William, so I can understand your jubilation, but I doubt you really need lottery tickets."

"Money's money, old boy. It's like friends at a party. The more the merrier." Forster's Southern, Georgia accent was in full bloom.

"I cannot argue with you there."

"How's everything goin', my friend? Is the plan still on track?"

"That's what I wanted to call you about."

"Uh-oh, that doesn't sound good."

"It seems we have a rogue scientist on the verge of exposing our plan. So, before he does, I would like to . . . make it happen, if you catch my drift?"

"I hear ya. Tell me, what's happened exactly?"

Gilliam enlightened Forster about Dr. Fontaine's call to the secretary of state and his phone conversation with the FBI director minutes prior.

"Oh, is that all?" Forster said. "I know Sandra Brown personally. Helped her get elected to our state senate here in Georgia many moons ago. She tapped me as a personal liaison to her department when she was chosen by the president to be the SOS. I'll call her and convince her that Fontaine's crazy, and that she doesn't have anything to worry about."

"Do you think you can convince her, William?"

"Sure. It won't be a problem."

"I hope you're right."

"I am. Fontaine's days as an FBI agent have got to be numbered. I'll bet the president made that a top priority. He ran on the platform of cleaning up Washington. God bless him."

"Clean up Washington, eh? Is that possible, William?"

"Of course it is. When Hades drops below thirty-two degrees Fahrenheit. In the meantime, there will be dirty politicians who love to have their stocks split like I do, and I make sure they have plenty."

Gilliam chortled in a lighthearted manner. "I knew I could count on you. So, where's a good place to . . . make it happen? You know the west coast of Florida better than I do, obviously."

Forster paused. "It doesn't make any sense for you to try and arrange something like this from across the Atlantic. Let me handle it, Eric. Fontaine will be gator food by morning."

Gilliam sighed. "Very good. I'll call Belkin and keep him advised."

"Belkin? You mean Director Belkin? The director of the FBI?"

"Yes. What about him?"

"You have him enlisted, too?"

"Yes, William. You don't know the half of it, and it's better that way. Plausible deniability and all that jazz."

CHAPTER THIRTY-ONE

Friday, 12:45 p.m.
The Home of Jodi Marek
Fort Pierce, Florida

Micah Gregson was in a fog. Jackson had strung them along like a dumb bass, feeding them information, until he had them hooked. Although Micah sensed an abnormality with Jackson's persona, he never could put his finger on it and chalked it up to the agent's arrogant attitude.

Micah also had to admit that other distractions to his mental faculties were knocking him off his game. These interferences, if he was honest with himself, caught him off guard and made him a little vulnerable. Yet, to his surprise, he didn't mind at all. In fact, if he allowed himself enough time to analyze them—which he did on the ride up I-95 to Jodi Marek's home—he realized they weren't simply mild interruptions which could be shunned at a moment's notice.

They actually engrossed him

Her giggly laugh.

The cute dimple in her cheek when she smiled.

The way her unique hazel eyes sparkled when she got excited.

Her hair, and how it lilted against her cheeks.

He kept replaying scenes of their personal discussions over and over as the billboards whisked by one after another. He didn't recognize it just yet, but Micah Gregson was falling for her. The plans he had of becoming a beach bum bachelor after his stint with the Coast Guard were in serious jeopardy.

Now, with this new information about Agent Jackson swimming in his head, it had become apparent his days away from Naval Intelligence had dulled his abilities more than he wanted to admit.

And that bit of information made him angry.

Adding the two together made him fearful for Evelyn now. If this "Agent Jackson" wasn't a real agent, then what was he doing acting like one with governmental approval? His agent status was an obvious cover, but for what? And would Jackson's directives from whoever had inserted him into the FBI supersede a person's life?

Having turned onto North 16th Street and checking the addresses, he found the home of Jodi Marek and parked along the curb. Before he could get out of the car, the front door opened, and a tall, spindly woman with long brunette hair and brown eyes stepped into the doorway. Wearing a nurse's uniform, she appeared anxious as Micah closed his car door and made his way up the walkway.

"Hello. Miss Marek?"

"Yes."

"I'm Captain Micah Gregson." He showed her his credentials.

"Please, come in." She allowed Micah to enter first. She then looked to the right and left before closing the door.

"Were you expecting someone else?" Micah said.

"My ex."

"Well, if I need to come back later, Miss Marek, I—"

"No, no. That's not it. He often spies on me." She stepped to the window and peeked through the blinds. "If he saw you pull up and walk in, he'd flip out."

Oh, great. Jealous ex-husband. That's all I need right now. "Miss Marek, I can make this brief. I know you're missing work."

"Oh, don't worry about that. I needed to get out of there today anyway. It's been crazy since that Fleming woman died." She pointed to a chair. "Please, sit down."

Micah sat on the edge of a worn recliner. "How so?"

Jodi Marek plopped down at one end of the couch. "Reporters, police, government types, you name it. They've been hounding everybody from hospital administration right down to us common workin' folk. I was thinkin' about takin' a mental health day several days ago before all this happened. Now, with all this, I just had to get away from it all."

"Who exactly has been at the hospital investigating?"

"I remembered seeing that FBI guy and Elysie go into the room and leave together. I was the one who walked into the room and found the Fleming woman dead. I thought it was strange, you know? Her dying so soon after they left? I called the police, which isn't necessarily protocol in a hospital. But since I don't trust our administration, I felt I couldn't call anybody in-house. So I made an anonymous call to 911. Since then, the FBI came back to obtain some records, the police sent an investigator to ask some questions, your Coast Guard was doin' their investigation, and we've had scads of reporters nosin' around the hospital, camped outside along the entrance, askin' questions."

"What records did the FBI obtain?"

"I don't know. I just heard they wanted the records of Regina Fleming."

To alter them, no doubt. "Is there anything else you can tell me?"

"You know, there was somethin' I was thinkin' about this morning. I knew you were comin', so I thought I'd check it out."

"Go ahead."

Jodi Marek snatched a pack of cigarettes off the end table. She held the pack up to Micah.

"No, thank you."

"Do you mind?"

"It's your house."

Jodi lit up, tossing the cigarette pack onto the coffee table and flopping back in her seat. "When Nurse Pruitt entered Fleming's room, I happened to notice her holdin' a syringe, which she quickly slipped into her pocket. When she left, she didn't have anything in her hand. This morning, I went down to her floor and accessed the medication charts. At that time, four syringes of medication were prepared. Fluphenazine hydrochloride, thorazine, lithium, and haloperidol."

"I'm sorry, Miss Marek. I've heard of three of those, but I don't know what they do."

"They're all anti-psychotics." She blew a cloud of smoke into the air.

"Do you normally give a patient all four at once?"

Jodi shrugged. "At those dosages? Only if you want to kill 'em. But that's just it. The records showed those four medications were supposed to be for different patients."

"Could a nurse receive medication for a patient and not administer it?"

"Sure. I could have a syringe in my pocket I brought from the outside. All I'd have to do is put saline solution in it. Then, go get the real meds from the pharmacy. On my way to the patient's room, I switch the syringes and carry the fake one into the room. Log into the computer, notate that I've given the patient his haloperidol, shoot him up with the saline solution instead, and walk out. Do that three more times to three different patients, and I have my four anti-psychotics."

"But you said you only saw her with one syringe while four medications were doled out."

"That's right."

"What do you suppose happened to the other three syringes?"

"One of two things. Either the other three syringes were already in her pocket and I only saw one of the four, or she put the four medications into one syringe."

"Would any of the four syringes be big enough to hold all four doses?"

"No. She would have to acquire a bigger syringe or bring one in from outside."

"How big was the syringe you saw in her hand?"

"Pretty freakin' big. Bigger than what we normally use."

"So, of the two possible scenarios, you are leaning toward the latter one."

Jodi nodded and blew another puff of smoke toward the ceiling. "That's where I'd put my money. It would be nothin' to smuggle a syringe in from the outside."

Micah jotted down a couple of things. "Anything else?"

Jodi leaned over and flicked her cigarette ashes into the ash tray on the coffee table. "Yeah. I just remembered. That agent, the one who went into the room—"

"Agent Jackson."

She nodded. "Jackson. That's his name. Remember how you two argued in the hall before you left?"

"Sure do."

"When you left, I overheard him and the other agent talkin'. Agent Jackson was furious with you over somethin' you said or did. He said you were hinderin' his investigation and somethin' about an . . . um," Jodi said, closing her eyes and trying to remember, "an NI guy?"

Micah forced a slight smile. "NI stands for Naval Intelligence. I used to work for NI."

Jodi's eyes widened. "That must've been what he was referrin' to. He said if that NI guy gets in the way again, he was goin' to make sure you got arrested and out of the way."

Micah laughed. "As you can see, Miss Marek, I'm scared."

"He also said—and I heard this very clearly, Captain—that once the NI guy was arrested, he would see to it that he was used for trollin' bait to catch that monster."

Micah straightened. "You heard him say that?"

"Yes, sir. As surely as I'm hearin' you now."

Micah Gregson's face darkened two shades of red. It took all the composure he could muster to keep from telling Jodi Marek just what he thought of Agent Jackson, or Dr. Fontaine, or whatever his name was.

"Miss Marek, you've been a great help." Micah handed her his card. "If you think of anything else that might be helpful, call me. Will you?"

"Most definitely, Captain," she said, putting out her cigarette and taking the card. "Uh, Captain, I couldn't help but notice that you're married," she said, pointing to his finger. "Tell me this. Why is it that all the good ones are already taken?"

Micah blushed another shade of red and started for the front door. "Miss Marek, I know for a fact that your assumption is not true. There are a bunch of great guys out there."

"If you know of any like you, send them my way, will ya? I could use a man in uniform in my life . . . and so could my young-uns."

"I take it your ex-husband was not a military man?"

Jodi Marek guffawed. "Are you kiddin'? The only uniform he ever wore was his prison blues."

"Ahh, I understand."

"Don't forget, Captain." She threw Micah a wink. "You've got my number, too."

"Bye, now." Micah smiled and waved as he exited the house, but he didn't say any more. Leaving was all he wanted to do.

CHAPTER THIRTY-TWO

Friday, 1:42 p.m.
National Marine Institute
Miami, Florida

Evelyn stretched out on one of the laboratory tables with a lab coat wadded up for a pillow. She was in one bedraggled state. Never in her entire lifetime had she stayed up for more than twenty-four hours. Now, she was pushing thirty-six, felt like it had been ninety-six, and couldn't take it anymore. There were sleeping quarters in her office on the other side of the property, but she didn't want to leave the action. She thought that, even if she fell asleep, John would wake her if he discovered something inscrutable or prodigious.

John finished the last of the tests. "That does it, Evelyn." He stretched and turned when there wasn't an answer. "Ahh, she's asleep. Good for you, Doctor."

It took John another twenty minutes to put everything away and consolidate the findings on the computer. He then pulled up the teleconferencing software and readied it for their call to Dr. Landover.

"Evelyn?" John nudged her. "Evelyn? I'm done testing the specimen." He nudged her again. "Dr. Sims?"

Groggy and sluggish, Evelyn opened her eyes and shielded her face from the fluorescent lights above her head. "No, no. Please don't wake me up."

John smiled. "Dr. Sims, I'm ready to call Dr. Landover. Don't you want to be a part of that?"

"Yeah." She spoke like she was talking in her sleep.

"Do you want to get up and move around a bit before we get started?"

"Yeah."

"I'm gonna run to the canteen. You want anything?"

"Yeah."

John laughed. "Like what?"

Evelyn took a deep breath like it was strenuous. "Coffee. Really strong coffee."

"Okay, I'll be back in a few minutes, and then we'll be ready to call."

Evelyn didn't move a muscle. "Yeah."

When John returned from the canteen, Evelyn had managed to sit up on the edge of the table. She was still tired and wanting to go back to sleep; her head hung with her eyes closed.

John handed her a steaming cup of coffee. "You get whiny when you're awakened, don't you?"

"No. I get whiny when I've lost my husband, and when my house gets torn apart by the FBI, and when I haven't slept in a day and a half. I think I'm entitled, don't you?"

John offered a sympathetic pat on the shoulder. "I guess you are." He jumped up and sat on the table next to her. "You know, in all the excitement, I never did get to tell you how sorry I am about the loss of your husband. It must be horrible."

Evelyn took a sip of coffee. "To be perfectly honest, John, we've been so busy chasing this creature, I haven't had time to think about it much since I left the house yesterday afternoon." Evelyn faced John. "Is that bad?"

"Why are you asking me?"

"Shouldn't a woman who's recently become a widow be more distraught?"

"Everybody handles it in different ways, I'm sure. It'll all probably hit home once this investigation settles down." John took a swig of his coffee. "You're lookin' at a bachelor, though, so I'm probably not the one to ask."

"I guess I try not to think about it. This creature has been a good distraction. It's kept my mind off things for now. I figure once this ordeal is over, I'll have plenty of time to grieve."

John wrapped his arm around Evelyn and gave her a friendly hug. "Just know that I'll be here for you. I'll help in any way I can."

She wrapped her arm around him. "I appreciate that." She patted him on the back. "Let's go call Dr. Landover."

John hopped down off the table while Evelyn slithered off, grabbing the edge for balance; the effects of her slumber not altogether dissipated.

John was excited. "I called Dr. Landover earlier. I told him I'd be calling him sometime after lunch. He said he'd be by his computer waiting."

Evelyn said nothing. She just plopped into the chair John had slid over from the other desk.

John punched some keys, and moments later, a gray-haired man with a tightly trimmed beard and moustache appeared. His wire-rimmed bifocals reflected the glow of the computer screen.

"Johnny," said the man with an Irish accent. "You finally made it. Good to see you. You look well."

"Hi, Dr. Landover. How's everything at Scripps?"

"Things have been buzzing of late, as you can quite well imagine. We are envious, though, what with being on the coast of the wrong ocean and all."

"You don't know how I wish I had your lab right now, Doc."

"Ahh, missing the equipment now, are we? You would not be the first, trust me."

"Yes, sir. I remember what you said when I left for Miami. 'Johnny,'" John said, attempting his best Irish brogue, "'all the promises in the world will not help one whit if you cannot examine anything.' I'm afraid those words may have proven prophetic."

"Got something to examine, do you?"

"I guess you could say that." John smiled at Evelyn.

"And who do you have with you there, Johnny?"

"This is Dr. Evelyn Sims. She's the assistant director here at NMI. She was at the Birch Aquarium before you arrived at Scripps, Doctor."

"It's a pleasure to meet you, Dr. Sims. I presume you are the same Dr. Evelyn Sims that wrote the article in the *Journal of Marine Paleontology* entitled 'Biospheres and Bios-Fears: Keeping an Open Mind in a World and Time of Scientific Discovery'? I think that was the title."

Evelyn looked at John, astonished that Dr. Landover knew the title of her work.

John muttered to Evelyn under his breath. "He's got a mind like a steel trap. Remembers everything."

Evelyn leaned forward and smiled as John backed away. "Yes, Doctor. That was me, I'm afraid."

"Afraid? Don't be, dear. Despite the rancor from the banal scientific community, I thought the article was a breath of fresh air in what is usually a tedious tome."

Evelyn straightened. "Really?"

Dr. Landover frowned. "Oh, you poor dear, you were dismantled by the erudite scientific elite, weren't you?"

"I guess you could say that."

"Do not take their impertinence to heart, Doctor. If God Himself walked into their laboratories and proclaimed evolution was a farce, they would deride Him, too, claiming that He should mind his own business and stay in the halls of the religion and philosophy departments on campus. The way I look at it, my dear, we are in good company."

Evelyn grinned. "Thank you."

"Oh, don't mention it. You've been through a great deal, what with the loss of your husband. My condolences, Doctor."

Evelyn shot a puzzled look at John. "Did you—"

John shook his head.

Dr. Landover smiled. "No, dear, Johnny did not tell me. I read the papers. I watch the telly. I can do the simple math. Two plus two, A-squared plus B-squared equals C-squared, and so on. A man named Sims on a boat. A female Dr. Sims as a marine biologist. The good doctor investigating these strange occurrences. Both resided in Miami." Landover gave a half-hearted shrug. "No need for a rocket scientist here."

Evelyn smiled. *I like him.*

"Dr. Landover," John said, "I contacted you because we do have a specimen we'd like your lab to analyze. We've done about all we can here."

"What kind of specimen, Johnny?"

"From the creature."

Dr. Landover repositioned himself in his seat. "Really? Well, now, I'm all ears."

John told Dr. Landover about the two attacks on the *Greenback* and the *Titan* and their subsequent investigations, including Agent Jackson's desire to have the specimen examined by NMI staff pronto.

"Johnny, why would an FBI agent be so enamored with scientific specimens?"

"He has been an enigma, Doc. I've got to admit that. Not to mention a pain in the backside."

"Who is this Agent Jackson anyway?"

"He claims he was assigned by our government to catch Evelyn's husband because Mr. Sims was supposedly working with terrorists."

Dr. Landover furrowed his brow. "What does that have to do with this creature?"

"That's just it, Doc. It doesn't. That's why we don't believe his story. We know he's up to something else, and that it has to do with the creature. But we don't know what yet."

"Do you have a picture of this Agent Jackson? I would like to see what he looks like."

"No, but he was in a brief MSNBC piece. You should be able to pull it up on the Web."

John punched more keys, found the Web address, and relayed it to Dr. Landover. Dr. Landover opened his browser and in seconds was watching the video.

Out of the blue, Dr. Landover became animated, snatching off his glasses. "What? John, are you sure you gave me the right Web page?"

"I think so." John rattled off the URL address.

"Aye, it appears I have the correct video." Dr. Landover began to laugh, putting on his glasses. "That good-for-nothing scoundrel."

"Excuse me, Doc?" John said.

"Johnny, your 'Agent Jackson' is no agent at all. That is Dr. Anthony Fontaine, former associate professor of Evolutionary Biology at the University of Cambridge."

"Former *professor*?" John said.

"Yes. It seems Anthony's adversarial approach to science coupled with his predilection for altering data when it suits him made Cambridge uneasy, and rightfully so. A big, prestigious institution like Cambridge has too much to lose than to join at the hip with the likes of Anthony Fontaine. Had they known about his character flaws prior to hiring him, I'm sure they never would have." Landover sighed. "I hear Anthony's started his own research foundation, situated somewhere outside of Paris."

John looked at Evelyn and then back at the screen. "Are you sure that's who you think it is?"

"Johnny," Dr. Landover said, leaning toward the camera and leveling his eyes, "I think I know the face of the man who got me defrocked from University College."

CHAPTER THIRTY-THREE

Friday, 1:55 p.m.
National Marine Institute
Miami, Florida

"Nooo," John said. His eyes grew in disbelief. "He's the one?"

Dr. Landover nodded. "That is Anthony, all right—arrogant, irritating voice and all. Everything makes sense now. It all makes sense."

"What do you mean, Doctor?" Evelyn said.

"Well, dear, your 'Agent Jackson' and I go way back. We used to teach together at University College in Dublin. We coauthored several papers and spoke at symposiums and conferences around the world.

"Then, one day, I sat down to read a published study we had done on the Burgess Shale in the Canadian Rockies. As I read the article, I noticed that the numbers did not add up, and several segments of information had been inserted into the text of which I was previously unaware. That information with its accompanying data turned out to be completely fabricated.

"As a result, I confronted Anthony, and we argued at length. He asserted I had added the erroneous information to gain notoriety for myself. Of course, that was an unmitigated lie; the last thing I needed was notoriety. I was working on my fourteenth book and writing regular articles for no less than three periodicals and journals at any given time. Trust me, *more* notoriety? I did not have enough time for the notoriety I already had accumulated.

"But Anthony insisted I had falsified the data and finally took the article and the actual study with the correct information to our college president. I argued my case, but Anthony had covered his tracks far too well. In short, he set me up to get me out of the way, almost ruining my reputation in the process."

"What caused him to do such a thing?" Evelyn said.

"He never said, but my conversion to Christianity coincides with the timing of the demise of our friendship. I started questioning some of the things we had studied in the past and how the studies were conducted. When I started asking questions, that is when Anthony became choleric. I had heard he could be that way, but I had never witnessed it directed toward me until then."

"You never did tell me what exactly caused your falling out, Doc," John said.

Dr. Landover sighed. "Ironically, John, it was the cumulative data."

"The *cumulative* data?"

"All the studies we had conducted, Johnny, showed me that the focus of all the research and papers and conferences was not the point. Oh, we made it important with all our work, but it lacked something.

"The data made me realize that regardless of how we try to synthesize evolution with the world around us—whether it be anthropology, psychiatry, sociology, theology, or any other subject you wish to discuss—what we were *doing* was not the point.

"Mankind attempting to get evolution to answer all the questions of life was not the point, either.

"We were so hell bent on trying to keep evolution at the forefront of the scientific world.

"Our opponents tried feverishly to keep it out of the public-school system.

"We told the religious activists to be quiet, getting a judge, in essence, to ban them from bringing their religious arguments into the hallowed halls of the campus science building. We told them to go to the religion and philosophy departments and vent there.

"Yet, all that strife, trying to prove we were right and they were wrong wasn't the point, either."

"So what was the point, Doctor?" Evelyn said.

Dr. Landover smiled. "Sorry, dear. My wife, God rest her soul, always told me I could ramble on so. The point became a question for me; a question which haunted me for weeks. Turned out to be quite the dagger to my soul." He smiled again. "*Why are we here?*"

"I've been wrestling with that question lately myself," Evelyn said kind of under her breath.

"Well, dear, I wrestled it for about twelve years until one night when I was reading Darwin's *Origin of Species*. I had highlighted practically fifty percent of the book over the years and was re-reading the marked-up sections in preparation for one of those articles I told you about. It was during the reading of a paragraph from chapter four that got me to thinking." Dr. Landover left the screen for a moment and returned holding a book. "Listen to this," he said, and then began reading.

> *Natural selection will modify the structure of the young in relation to the parent, and of the parent in relation to the young. In social animals it will adapt the structure of each individual for the benefit of the whole community; if the community profits by the selected change. What natural selection cannot do, is to modify the structure of one species, without giving it any advantage, for the good of another species; and though statements to this effect may be found in works of natural history, I cannot find one case which will bear investigation.*

"Darwin goes on to use the example of a bird needing a strong beak to break out of its shell upon hatching. If the beak is weak, then the weak-beaked birds would all perish in their shells because they can't get out, while the strong-beaked birds would not only get out, but eventually strengthen the entire species of bird because eventually only the strong-beaked birds would survive."

"It does make a certain kind of sense," Evelyn said.

"That's true, but this entire process got me thinking, *Why would nature do that?* Think about it. If weak-billed birds were to become the bane of that particular species, causing them to be weaker by design, then why were they ever allowed to live? Why did they exist at all? Or maybe the better question is: *How* did they ever come into existence?"

"Darwin argued," John said, "that it's all about the betterment of the species. The weaker members of a species would eventually die off in favor of the stronger members. That nature, by the force of sheer living on this Earth, would weed out the weaker members while allowing those who've adapted to the subtle changes to live."

"Exactly," Evelyn said. "And if those stronger members find it difficult to adapt later in life or the species as a whole finds it harder to adapt later—however many years that is in the future—then they may become the casualties of natural selection, whether it be in favor of a modified version of themselves or by extinction."

"I see you two are well-versed in the realm of evolutionary biology. Good show. But wrestle with this question with me," Dr. Landover said. "If we are members of the *weaker* species, then *why* are we here? What's our *purpose*? And if we are members of the *stronger* species—albeit stronger for now, for as you said, we may be the weaker group in the future—*why* are we here? Why are we allowed to *remain* while our brothers and sisters *perish*?"

Evelyn chimed in. "Darwin would say Natural Selection doesn't play favorites. Nature selects the survivors based on the period of evolutionary change. What proved to be a very adaptable species this year may prove to be unable to adapt to the climate change, societal change, structural change experienced years later."

"But Dr. Sims," Landover said, "if we are the surviving species—and in this case, I'm referring to humans—is my perpetuation, your perpetuation, Johnny's perpetuation in this life so we can say we were better? Call ourselves the most advanced form of life to date? Was the purpose of our being here solely to get rich, grow old, and leave all our precious belongings to our offspring? Is that it? Is that why we are here occupying space on planet Earth? Hundreds of millions of years of evolution culminating in the grandest species of them all, mankind? Trying to hoard as much as he can, sometimes at the expense of his fellow man and other less fortunate species, so that he can have fun, die, and leave it to his offspring? Is that the purpose of it all, or was there going to be an even grander species that would evolve from mankind? And if so, what would that species's legacy be? Why would they exist?"

"Darwin would have to say *yes*," Evelyn said.

"But," Landover said, glancing at the book again, "I thought he said, 'In social animals it will adapt the structure of each individual for the benefit of the whole community; if the community profits by the selected change.' So, how does the child in West Africa benefit from your purchase of a diamond at the local jewelry store when we know that child is being used and abused to mine that gem from the earth?"

Evelyn squirmed. "That's a good question, Doctor."

"You see, Dr. Sims? I'm not trying to play the devil's advocate here. Nor was I trying to be one the night I was lying there rereading these passages from this book." He held *Origin of Species* up so she and John could see it on the monitor. "I wrestled with this conundrum for weeks afterwards.

"I wanted to synthesize evolution with this question. I wanted to believe." Landover allowed a smirk to escape. "But the more I tried to justify my own existence at this point in my species's evolutionary timeline, the more I realized my existence—however short my blip on the radar screen of history was—was really for nothing. It had no real merit. No real reason. No purpose.

"The only real reason I was on planet Earth was to survive."

CHAPTER THIRTY-FOUR

Friday, 2:22 p.m.
National Marine Institute
Miami, Florida

"That became my purpose, Johnny. Survival. To survive in this vicious world of scientific discovery. To race to publication before my competitor beat me to the punch. To make discoveries no one else had so I could have my fifteen minutes of fame. To create a lifestyle I could live with."

Landover set the book down and slipped his glasses off his face. He rubbed his eyes, like he was exhausted. "Then, another question posited itself in my self-evaluation while conducting a study in Montana. A disturbing question, I might add.

"If that was the case, I wondered—if all there was to this life as a human was to survive, then die, and leave all our goodies to our kids —then there were several subgroups of the species we call 'mankind' who were definitely *inferior*. You could say they were 'weak-billed.'

They couldn't seem to get out of their own shells. They were destitute, ignorant, less-educated, and seemingly unable to reverse their fortune. They lived in perpetual poverty. They fought incessantly with one another. And they had become a huge economic drain on the surrounding societies.

"So, evolution taught me that I, a European white male, was superior to the black males of Ethiopia, for example, and to the brown males of many South American regions. Why? Because I was rich and able to exact my will upon much of the world while they seemed to languish in a never-ending cycle of poverty and war.

"Natural Selection's mantra of survival of the fittest thus dictated that it would be perfectly acceptable—and may I add, beneficial for the community we call 'Europeans'—for my superior species to wipe out any and all human species that are inferior to me. First, we would accomplish this by producing more offspring than our inferior competitors. In this step, it becomes a numbers game. There are more people like me than people like them.

"Second, I would then eventually assimilate the weaker species and force them to become like me, or simply destroy them. By doing so, white males could and therefore should take over the world, thus benefitting the overall species known as 'European,' and ultimately, mankind."

Dr. Landover paused and peered into the computer camera. "As you can see, dear ones, I was traveling down a very dubious and devilish road—one that Hitler and Mussolini and Stalin had already traveled. And for true evolutionists—if they are completely honest with themselves—they would have to conclude that rulers such as Hitler, Mussolini, Stalin, the Pharaohs of Egypt, the rulers of Babylon, Assyria, the kings of Medo-Persia, the emperors of China and Rome, the kings of Britain and France, Napoleon, Idi Amin, Pol Pot, Saddam Hussein, and every other ruler and king like them throughout all of human history, were actually *correct* in their ambitions. Thus, any group of people who overpower and dominate another people group are merely applying simple evolutionary principles to life and thus *cannot* be denounced. Survival of the fittest *demands* that they act on these ambitions. For the survival of their species."

"And that's why you began to have problems with Fontaine," John said.

"Well, it wasn't that quick. As I said before, I wrestled with these questions for weeks. No, actually months. I read and reread books and articles, trying to find evidence that would calm my fears. Answer my questions in a definitive manner. But the more I read and reread the more troubled I became." Landover paused, thinking. "I actually left Anthony in Montana and took a short sabbatical. While I was on that break, I found God. From that moment, everything I was doing, everything I had done, was scrutinized."

"So," John said, "that's when the rift between you and Fontaine began."

Landover nodded. "When I began to look at Darwinism through this new lens, I became extremely bothered by what I had believed all these years. I realized I had been irony impaired. Suddenly, the truths I had once held so dear didn't make as much sense as they once did. Not even to those who espoused them, I might add.

"For example, the road men like Hitler, Mussolini, and Stalin had traveled is one that has been condemned by every feeling human being on the planet, many of which were probably devout evolutionists themselves.

"This dilemma—of trying to put a happier and more compassionate spin on the realities of evolutionary thinking—has even caused many evolutionists to make their theory *evolve*. They say various species can still mutate and change for the betterment of their environment. This, they say, removes the unfeeling, animalistic, barbaric aspects of evolution out of the equation, making the theory a kinder, gentler theory."

Landover sniffed. "They use a particular plant called the Acacia Plant as an example. As you know, plants have two dangers out there: disease and predators. The Acacia Plant biochemically produces a substance that makes it immune from other pathogens and microorganisms which could infest its roots, stems, and leaves. So, that takes care of the disease problem.

"It also creates a very specific food source called *extrafloral nectar*, or *EFN*. This nectar draws an ant called *Pseudomyrmex*. These ants colonize on the plant and eat the nectar while protecting the plant from other insects and certain other animals like small rodents in a kind of symbiotic circle of life.

"This example and others like it have become the proof evolutionists use to demonstrate their evolved sense of evolutionary theory. The Acacia Plant has become the flagship of all the feeling evolutionists around the world."

"Isn't it interesting that even evolutionists see a major problem in their theory, Doc?" John said.

Landover nodded. "But if they stand by it unequivocally and wholeheartedly, aglow in all of Darwin's glory, Johnny, then they have to admit that the likes of the Adolf Hitlers of the world become their standard bearers. Pretty damning, don't you think? I mean, who in their right mind wants to agree with Hitler?

"I understand why evolutionists are changing their tune. A kinder, gentler evolutionary theory sounds good, but it still doesn't account for the cheetah in the bush that chases down the slower wildebeest of the herd. It doesn't account for the great white shark that out-swims the seal. No matter how much the wildebeest adapts, the cheetah is still programmed to hunt, and hunt it will. So, too, the great white.

"Therefore, they can try to transform Darwin's theory into a kinder, gentler theory, but the fact still remains: the theory of Natural Selection is just that—a theory that says nature will do whatever it takes to survive. The fittest, the smartest, the most adaptable will ultimately win.

"When you think about it, even the Acacia Plant has unwittingly fallen in line with true Darwinism, in a passive, albeit self-serving way because of its inability to fight back."

Dr. Landover lifted his hands up in the air and let them fall with a thud on his armrests. "So, there I was, wrestling with the question,

Why am I here? That question was coupled with the enormity and complexity of Darwinian philosophy taken to its logical conclusions, teaching me that the Anglo-Saxon population of the planet should rise up and take over the world."

"That is a dilemma," Evelyn said.

"Ahh, but my musings didn't stop there, dear. Another question that came to mind was this: If mankind through evolution is forced to explain his existence—and no doubt philosophical discussions will demand this explanation and answer the *Why am I here?* inquiry—then what is the end game? What is the goal?

"If evolution believes that organisms assimilate and dominate for the purpose of bettering themselves and their environment, then there must be something beyond the accumulation of goodies for the kiddos, right?

"Then it occurred to me." Dr. Landover peered into the camera. "What status is viewed by mankind as being a higher existence? A grander state of being?"

Evelyn drew in a breath. "God."

Dr. Landover pointed at the monitor. "Precisely. For those who wish to speculate about—and even manipulate—evolutionary theory's next step, the next stage they see in evolution is to become divine. And what have you heard bantered about over the last thirty or so years?"

"To find the divine in all of us," Evelyn said.

"A *spark* of the divine, not to put too fine a point on it, Doctor. But yes, to find the divine in all of us. This is the next step in evolutionary theory. So, you can understand why people like Anthony get a little agitated when that philosophy is questioned or endangered. People like him are mentioned in the Book of Romans: 'They exchanged the truth of God for a lie and have worshipped and served created things rather than the Creator, who is forever praised. Amen.'

"The most ironic part of all, Dr. Sims, is we now have the clay telling the potter to go away while it surmises how to form itself into a pot. Humans still recognize the need for the divine, and they look everywhere for it, but want to find it *apart from God.*"

Landover reached over and grabbed the book again. He thumbed the pages and held it open. "Listen to this and tell me it doesn't sound like a man who used to be a theology major, giving a nod to an old belief system, believing something grander is on the horizon."

> *Thus, from the war on nature, from famine to death, the most* exalted *object which we are capable of conceiving, namely, the production of higher animals, directly follows. There is* grandeur *in this view of life,* with its several powers, having been originally breathed into a few forms, or into one; *and that, whilst this planet has gone cycling on according to the fixed law of gravity, from so simple a beginning endless forms* most beautiful *and* most wonderful *have been, and are being, evolved.*

"The production of higher animals, huh?" John said. "Has mankind evolved all that much over recorded history?"

Evelyn shook her head. "Some would say we've devolved."

"Aye, lassie," Landover said, "but what will become the 'most exalted' form? A form that had 'life breathed into it'?"

"Sounds very biblical."

"Yes, it does. But why?"

John scratched his head. "Because you can't have divinity without God."

"Absolutely. Divinity has to have a reference point. Otherwise, no one will know they've attained that 'grander view of life' when they get there."

"So, he used theological terms and religious references to pave a familiar road for those who followed him."

"Well, Johnny, I'm not sure Darwin was being sinister or planning some diabolical conspiracy theory when he wrote down his findings while on the *Beagle*. But I do know he had found God's view of things wanting. And when people try God on for size and walk away dissatisfied, the Bible calls that 'blaspheming the Holy Spirit.'

"In other words, you were given the cure for eternal cancer and rejected it, only to choose another alternative cure you believe will ultimately heal you. But all it will do is leave you spiritually dead and apart from the One who was the cure."

"By His wounds, we are healed," Evelyn said.

"Amen." Landover peered into the camera and continued. "Well, after months of soul searching, it occurred to me: The grand paradox in the entire framework of evolution is that the missing link they search for—to prove their theory of moving mankind from a savage species to a higher form of animal—is actually God. And in order for mankind to reach that pinnacle, they must find the divine in everything, including themselves. But they never will because there is only one true source of anything divine, and that's God."

"That's pretty profound, Dr. Landover," Evelyn said.

Landover flashed his eyes and thinned his lips. "Just the musings of an old duffer, dear."

"So," John said, "it isn't that the link is missing. They can't find it because they've rejected it."

"I guess you could say that," Landover said.

"I take it Agent Ja—I mean, Dr. Fontaine—didn't agree with you at that point in your relationship?"

"My change in beliefs caused some problems as time went on, yes. At first, I kept my thoughts to myself, but as I slowly walked away from evolution and embraced Christianity, I started to question many of the experiments we had performed in the past. I still wanted the truth, mind you, but I had a different set of lenses to look through.

"In addition to that, I felt Anthony was willing to distort the truth when it was convenient to do so. I had caught him manipulating data to 'fix' certain mathematical anomalies which existed in the real data we were producing.

"Things got quite contentious at times, and we started to do more and more on our own until one morning when we were contacted by the Royal Canadian Government and asked to conduct a detailed study of the Burgess Shale. I thought the study went well despite our increasing philosophical differences. Obviously, I was wrong."

"When was the last time you spoke with him, Dr. Landover?" Evelyn said.

"Not since I left Dublin, although I did call a couple of times to tell him I no longer had any hard feelings. I had to leave voice mails, though, and I never heard back from him."

"Why do you think our government would place him in an FBI position?" John said.

Dr. Landover exhaled. "I haven't the foggiest, John. Obviously, they wanted something covered up. Why give him a false name if they have nothing to hide?"

"That's a good point. Maybe our specimen will shed some light on that question," John said.

Dr. Landover moved his computer and centered himself. "What do you have exactly?"

"We have approximately twenty pounds of meat, Doc," John said. "When the animal attacked the ocean liner, it must have scraped itself on the side of the boat, because when it did, it ripped off a hunk of flesh."

"And what kind of analysis have you done thus far?"

"Not much. We sliced up some samples and have examined them under our pitiful microscopes in varying conditions, thawed and frozen."

"Have you used a TEM yet?"

John scoffed. "Are you kidding?"

Dr. Landover grunted. "I had heard the rumors. I guess they were not entirely fictitious, huh?"

"What rumors?"

"That NMI was on her last leg."

"I wouldn't say that." Evelyn frowned. "Well, last leg may be exaggerated a little, but she has fallen on hard times, yes."

"I'm sorry to hear that. I remember when NMI was a first-class facility. Of course, that was when the Navy operated it."

"Yes, they subsidized us for a while, but grants have been cut drastically, and I'm afraid although my article may have garnered a lot more support from the private sector, it also may have been the kiss of death for future government grants."

Dr. Landover formed a comforting smile. A slight glint in his eye appeared. "Welcome to my world, Dr. Sims. Fortunately, I have a very open-minded group of colleagues who believe my personal beliefs are merely the ramblings of an old man.

"They do still respect my work and my ability to study marine life, while at the same time producing a study that is not full of fraudulent data. So, my advice to you, dear, and to you, Johnny, is to remain true to who you are, even in the midst of adversarial assaults. As Dr. Sims said in her article, 'Time is on the side of truth.' And in this day and age when scientific data is seemingly falsified more than it is truthful, being a trusted scientist who will not fall prey to the almighty dollar or one's ego can and will be your saving grace."

"Good advice," Bud Kensington said.

Evelyn jerked around with a start. "Oh, Bud, you scared me."

"Sorry." Bud hobbled up from the corner of the room.

"And who may this be, Johnny?" Dr. Landover said.

"Dr. Harry Landover, this is Dr. Henry Kensington, but everybody calls him 'Bud.' Bud's the director here at NMI."

Bud stepped closer and stood in front of the internet camera. "Dr. Landover, I've heard a great deal about you from John. It's nice to finally meet you."

"Oh, Dr. Kensington, the pleasure is all mine, although I do not envy your position there in Miami, what with all the media coverage."

"Tell me about it. If there was ever a time when I felt like committing homicide, these last few days have been that time. I believe you're about to enter the realm of annoyance as well, if I am not mistaken. Did John and Evelyn tell you about their desire to send the specimen to you for examination?"

"Yes, they did, and my laboratory will be more than happy to assist. And, of course, we will do this *pro solvo, non ut pecuniae*. I am glad to assist one of my former students." Dr. Landover flashed a big grin.

"That's very generous, Doctor. As a matter of fact, I came here to pick up the specimen and get it ready to ship to you. I was going to send it immediately, but where should I send it?"

"Send it to Scripps to my attention. I will let the mailroom know to contact me the moment it arrives. Do you think it will get out today?"

"If I can get these two to part with it, yes."

Evelyn stood, strolled over to the refrigerator, and grabbed the specimen bag. "It's all yours, Bud. Now, hurry. We need those results."

"Well, Dr. Landover," Bud said, "it's been nice meeting you, but I guess I have to go now."

Dr. Landover chuckled. "Likewise, Doctor. I'll be awaiting your special delivery."

"Fair enough." Bud exited the room with the specimen.

Something caught Dr. Landover's attention. He stood and disappeared for a moment from the monitor before returning. "Are you seeing this, Johnny?" he said, pointing to something off camera. Turn on your telly to the news."

"We don't have one down here," John said.

"Let me try this then," Dr. Landover said. He turned the internet camera and faced it toward his television. "Can you see that, John?"

"Just a little more to the left."

"Now?"

"Perfect." John and Evelyn watched as Dr. Landover turned the volume up.

"So, Wanda," the news anchor said, "what can you tell us?"

"Well, Rachel, we are told that the Coast Guard received a radio transmission from a fishing boat off the coast of Florida that claims it had snagged something enormous in its nets. Now, the nature of what was snagged is yet to be determined. But according to authorities, the captain of the fishing boat had to have his crew cut the nets to release whatever they had snagged because the weight was pulling the boat down, and dangerously close to sinking it."

"We don't know yet what they caught in their nets?"

"No, we don't. We don't know if the authorities were told and are being tight-lipped at this juncture, or if their transmission simply didn't disclose that information. And with all the news in the Atlantic these days, we have to wonder if this fishing boat actually caught the creature that has been attacking boats in the region."

"Where is the boat now, Wanda?"

"They are heading for Port Canaveral. They are expected to make port anytime now. We will definitely keep you posted as new information arises, Rachel. This is Wanda Wright, CNN, Port Canaveral, Florida."

"What do you make of that, Dr. Landover?" John said.

Dr. Landover repositioned the camera on top of his computer monitor. "Hard to say, really. Snagged something in the nets that almost sank the boat." He winced a little. "You are probably looking at a fifty- to seventy-five-foot vessel. Whatever it snagged would need to be pretty big to drag down a boat that big far enough to spook a seasoned captain."

"But if they snagged the creature, it would've sunk the boat, dragged it right down."

Dr. Landover nodded. "Aye. It must have been something else then."

"I wonder if they'll want us to investigate?" Evelyn said.

"Well, dear," Dr. Landover said, "just remember, your Agent Jackson will probably be there. If I were you, I would not let him know we talked. That will only make matters worse for you both. There's no sense in creating issues for yourselves based on my past with Anthony."

"That's easier said than done, Doc," John said. "He seems to have ears all over the place."

"Who said it was going to be easy, Johnny?"

CHAPTER THIRTY-FIVE

Friday, 2:39 p.m.
Location: CLASSIFIED

The first man got into his car and slammed the door shut. He felt like a heel. The complexity of the job had becoming overwhelming. He yanked his cell phone out of his coat pocket and dialed.

A male voice answered. "Have you got the sample yet?"

"Yes. I have it right now."

"Good. And what are your plans?"

"To get *rid* of it. What else would I be doing with it?"

The second man sniffed. "I know that. But how?"

"I plan on feeding it to the sharks after hours."

"And what happens if they don't eat it? Then you'll have a large piece of meat floating around your shark tank. Don't you think that will draw a little attention in the morning when your people come and tend to the tanks?"

"Got any better ideas?"

"Of course. Box it up and ship it just like you were supposed to. Except, instead of sending it to San Diego, send it to me in Paris. If you send it in a refrigerated container, they'll just place it in a cooler until I return. Then I can examine it at my leisure."

"If that's what you want."

The second man paused. "What's goin' on? You don't seem like your heart is in this anymore."

"I'm not sure it is."

"You know, that could be a very precarious position to be in at this point in the game."

The first man cranked the engine. "Things have become more complicated, I'm afraid."

"How so?"

The first man grunted. "I met Dr. Harry Landover today."

"You what? How? He's not here, is he?"

"No. Over the Internet. John and Evelyn were having a meeting with him, and I walked in on it when I went to pick up the specimen. I had no idea that's who it was since I've never met the man before."

The second man exhaled in exasperation. "So, they went ahead and contacted him. That does complicate matters. I'm sure they told him about the specimen, so he'll be expecting it."

"Yes, they did, and yes, he is," the first man said nervously. "But that's not all."

"What now?"

"When I walked in on their conversation, I overheard Landover say something about University College in Dublin and the FBI, wondering how someone could've been appointed to a government position with the agency. Got any ideas about *who* they were talking about?"

The second man cursed. "You know as well as I do who." Bud could hear things banging around. "I was afraid of this. They know, Henry. The gig's up. He's blown my cover. Somehow, he's been able to identify me. Somehow, he's—" The second man interrupted himself. "I'll bet it was that persistent reporter from MSNBC. She hounded me and hounded me. Gilliam said, 'Go ahead. Do the interview. Just don't say anything worth hearing.' But he forgot one very important thing."

"Your face would be plastered all over the Internet."

The second man cursed Gilliam. "We've got to end this now, Henry. Before it blows up in our faces."

Bud Kensington looked at the specimen in the front seat. "Maybe not. Maybe they were talking about another person who was working for the FBI."

"Don't you get it, Henry? Landover told your two scientists the whole story. Why would he even mention Dublin or University College unless he was telling them about our . . . falling out? And the fact that John Spencer used to work for Landover as a graduate assistant means they have a familiarity that would lend to this type of conversation. The fact that they know of my FBI appointment means Landover somehow identified me." He cursed again. "I told you he was going to cause trouble."

"For you maybe, Anthony, but not for me. I'm not afraid of Landover like you are."

"I'm not afraid of Harry," the second man said, almost growling.

"Well, he was also giving them advice when I walked up . . . something about staying true to who they were, not giving 'fictitious data,' and 'time being on the side of truth.'" The first man paused. "I didn't catch it all."

"This is not good. Your two scientists' days are numbered, my friend."

"Now hold on, Anthony," the first man said, tagging his friend's name with some choice expletives. "When I signed on, I did it with the understanding that no one would get hurt. That has already been a lie. The Fleming woman is dead, and I'd bet my bottom dollar you had something to do with it. But you're not going to lay a finger on my people, or you'll have me to deal with. And I know a lot more than they do. I could have you locked up for years. But I've worked with you because we believe in the same things when it comes to science. So, don't push me to the other side, Anthony."

"Finally, the tough sea dog bares his teeth. I promise, Henry. I will not hurt them. They are so far down the food chain right now, and so long as they stay there, they're safe. But I cannot afford for them to cause any more trouble. I have to put them on the sidelines until this is over."

"Meaning what?"

"Meaning they will be safe but out of the picture."

Just then, the second man's phone rang with another call. "Henry, I've got another call coming in. I'll talk to you later."

"But wait. What do you mean 'out of the picture'?" The first man sat in his car, looking at his phone.

There was silence on the other end.

"Hello?"

"Dr. Fontaine, are you where you can talk?"

"Who is this?"

"This is William Forster. I'm an associate of Mr. Eric Gilliam. I live here in the States, so Mr. Gilliam has asked me to meet with you in person for the purpose of getting some issues under control."

"What issues?"

"Dr. Fontaine, I'm sure you can put two and two together. Mr. Gilliam is concerned, as am I, about the stability of our plan. We realize that there have been many circumstances that were beyond anyone's ability to forecast—or control, for that matter—and thus have created a series of exceptional situations that no one person could possibly manage alone. So, that's where I come in. I just want to meet with you and see if we can come up with a blueprint that can salvage our plan and see it through to completion."

"What did you have in mind exactly?"

"I don't want to meet anywhere where we could be seen together. That would not be good for the anonymity of the plan and its constituents, and since you have been in the news concerning the creature in the Atlantic, that makes it even more paramount that we meet secretly."

"What are you proposing?"

"Somewhere clandestine. Where are you right now?"

"I'm on my way to Port Canaveral again. We've got another incident to investigate."

"Oh, yes, the fishing boat. It's all over the news."

Great, Fontaine thought.

"Dr. Fontaine, before you get to Port Canaveral, can we meet somewhere? It's important that we get this ball rolling."

"I'm sorry, but whatever it is will have to wait. The boat is due to arrive any minute."

"Okay, so what about afterward? There's a road off Highway 528 that winds back into the scrub. That would be a great meeting place. Very private, yet very accessible."

Fontaine paused. "Okay, I'll call you when I'm done. Text me the directions and GPS coordinates."

"Will do. Now, do you have any idea when you'll be ready for our meeting?"

"Sorry, Mr. Forster. It will all depend on what I find. I'll call you when I'm ready. I promise."

"All right then. I'll be awaiting your call."

CHAPTER THIRTY-SIX

Friday, 5:41 p.m.
I-95 Northbound
One Hour North of NMI

The National Marine Institute's Ford Explorer sped north on I-95 toward Port Canaveral. Evelyn and John had been instructed by Agent Jackson to meet up with him upon their arrival and assist in the interviewing of the crew members as well as with the examination of the fishing boat.

Evelyn had attempted to call Bud and apprise him of the request and see if he wanted to accompany them, but all she got was his voice mail.

Hesitantly, they agreed to help, but Evelyn knew it was going to be difficult. They were going to have to act ignorant of their new knowledge about Agent Jackson. They agreed to keep their conversations short and sweet, strictly on the business at hand, and Evelyn knew it would take every ounce of goodwill she could possess to keep from blurting out what she really thought of the FBI fraud.

"I wish we had called Dr. Landover earlier. It would have been nice to know about Jackson, or Fontaine, or whoever that man is, before now," Evelyn said.

John gripped the steering wheel a little tighter. "He definitely had us fooled. And it seems he's been fooling a lot of people. Had we found out about him sooner, though, there's no telling what ramifications that would've created for us."

"I wouldn't have felt so stupid, for one," she said.

"Have you heard from Micah lately? He needs to know about Jackson, too."

"That's a good point." Evelyn picked up her phone.

"Hello?"

"Micah, where are you?"

"I'm back at my house. Since I was so close, I thought I'd come back and get cleaned up a little, grab a bite to eat, get a little rest."

"Guess what? You're not going to believe this."

"Believe what?" Micah said.

"We met with Dr. Landover. John set up the video conference with him."

"I'm sorry I missed that. I'd have liked to have been there."

"He told us who Agent Jackson really is, Micah. Dr. Landover knows him."

Micah sat up on the edge of the couch. Snatching the TV remote from the coffee table, he turned down the volume. "What did he say?"

"The two of them used to work together in Dublin, Ireland, at University College. Then, one day, they had a disagreement," she said, explaining in detail what Harry Landover had disclosed.

"Interesting."

"That's it?" Evelyn was befuddled. "That's all you've got to say? 'Interesting'?"

"Evelyn, I already knew about Jackson. Dr. Landover's testimony just confirms what I already knew. So, that's great."

"You . . . what? When did you know?"

"I got in touch with one of my buddies in Naval Intelligence. He read me Jackson's FBI file. He was placed in the FBI against every known protocol including never attending the FBI Academy. He is listed as a member of the Aquatic Nuisance Species Task Force, which is a branch of NOAA. That's his cover, anyway."

"You mean you knew all this and didn't call to let *anyone* know?"

"I wasn't sure what to make of it, yet. I wasn't even sure which name was his real name, although I assumed Anthony Fontaine was his real name. I'm still trying to find out why he was placed in that position. You don't create an elaborate cover for someone unless they have something to hide or protect, or both."

Evelyn huffed. "Well, maybe if you had called us, we could've filled you in and answered all your questions."

"You already know why?"

"I think so."

Micah feigned anger. "And you didn't call *me* until now? How long have *you* known?"

Evelyn managed a slight chuckle. "I did call first."

"Yes, you did." Micah leaned back into the couch. "So, what do you know?"

"We know Dr. Anthony Fontaine is Agent Jackson. We think he is here to keep any and all information that may shed doubt on evolutionary theory suppressed, or if he has to deal with any information, he will distort the data and make it say what he needs it to say."

Micah sat up straight. "Or destroy any of that evidence."

"Possibly."

"No, Evelyn, there is no 'possibly' about it. That's exactly what he did with your boat. You'll never be able to recover any of those items he pulled from the cabin of your boat. Trust me."

"You know, Micah, I was hoping some of those things might help me get some closure and figure out what Dave was doing."

"I'm sorry, Evelyn, but they're long gone by now. I'm positive of that."

"You're probably right. That means any evidence collected from any of the . . . oh, no."

Micah could hear her mumble under her breath. "What is it?"

"The specimen from the *Titan*."

Micah shot up off the couch. "Where is it, Evelyn?"

"Bud has it. He was supposed to overnight it to Dr. Landover this afternoon."

Micah headed for the bedroom. "Evelyn, where is Bud right now?"

"We haven't seen him since he left the lab with the specimen over two hours ago."

"Evelyn, call him. I'm going to get ready. Let me know what you find out. If you can't get a hold of him, let me know, and we'll figure out our next move. Hopefully, he sent it before Fontaine got to him."

"You think Bud's in danger?"

"Jackson killed Regina Fleming. I have enough proof to substantiate that. So, yes, if Bud gets in his way—" Micah stopped, not completing the obvious.

"All right. I'll call you as soon as I find out."

"Hurry, Evelyn."

Evelyn hung up and dialed Bud's cell number.

"Hey, Evie. How are you holding up?"

"Bud? Are you okay?"

Bud was puzzled by the inquiry. "Uh, yeah, as far as I know. Why the dire tone?"

"Where are you?"

"I'm back at NMI. Where are you? Somebody told me that you and John were seen leaving in the Explorer."

"That's right. Agent Jackson called us and requested our help with the fishing boat that was in the news. It's already made port in Port Canaveral."

Knowing Jackson was on the lookout for his two associates, Bud opened his mouth, almost informing Evelyn and John to watch their backs. Then, afraid of retaliation from both sides, he stopped.

"Bud, are you still there?"

"Yeah, Evie. I was just wondering why Jackson didn't call me first."

"Maybe he did. We tried calling you several times and kept getting your voice mail."

"Oh, you're probably right. I never think to check my voice mail."

"Bud, where's the specimen we gave you? Have you shipped it to Dr. Landover yet?"

"Already done. Should reach its destination by this time tomorrow."

"Are you sure, Bud?"

"Yes, Evie. I just got back from mailing it. What's the problem?"

"Bud, I don't know if I should tell you this right now."

"Tell me what?"

"We have reason to believe Agent Jackson is not who he says he is."

"What are you talking about?"

"That name is an alias. Agent Jackson is really Dr. Anthony Fontaine."

"What? You're talking nonsense, Evie."

"Bud, he can't be trusted."

"How do you know that?"

"I'm not at liberty to say right now, but trust me. He's up to no good."

"Evie, are you sure the trauma of the last few days hasn't finally caught up to you? I mean, making accusations like that about someone, especially a federal agent, is serious stuff."

"I'm not traumatized, and I'm not hallucinating. Jackson's not an agent. Dr. Landover recognized him, and Captain Gregson has read his FBI file. This whole 'Agent Jackson' routine is a cover."

"Oooh, I get it," Bud said with a laugh. "A conspiracy theory. It sounds plausible, Evie, but why would this man go to all that trouble? Why would our own government go to all that trouble? For what?"

"To suppress or destroy evidence."

"What evidence?"

"Evidence like that sample you shipped. Are you sure it got shipped?"

"It got sent to where it was supposed to get sent. No conspiracy theory here." He laughed again. "Wow, Evie. You really need to go home and get some rest."

"Bud, I've got to go."

"Get some rest, Evie, or I'll place you on administrative leave."

Bud Kensington listened as his last comment was lost in the sound of a busy signal.

CHAPTER THIRTY-SEVEN

Friday, 6:02 p.m.
Rasmussen's Commercial Marina
Port Canaveral, Florida

Standing next to the fishing boat *Sea-Saw*, Agent Archibald Jackson supervised his unit working to interview every member of the crew and begin hauling out boxes of evidence. It was routine now. He didn't have to explain protocol or go over procedures. His team knew what to do.

Pleased with the initial examination of the vessel, the only evidence that lent any credence to the captain's account were the trolling nets. The one diver's report corroborated the evidence, but now that the nets were lost at sea, the diver's story would be nothing more than that—a story.

Nothing to cause much trouble.

His report would say the *Sea-Saw* could have snagged anything.

The carcass of a whale. The remains of a squid. A massive school of dead fish caused by global warming or man-made pollution.

Easy money, he thought.

He could breathe a little easier.

Now, he could make his calls.

"Mr. Forster, this is Dr. Fontaine, how does nine p.m. sound for our meeting?"

"Nine o'clock will work. You still have those directions I gave you?"

"Yes."

"Okay, good. Just make sure you come alone. Our two cars will be plenty. Any more and it might arouse suspicion. And I don't have to remind you how nervous Mr. Gilliam gets concerning such topics."

"Copy that," Jackson said. He punched the End button. "Of course, Mr. Forster," Jackson said to himself, "you never said anything about associates on foot."

Jackson learned many years ago to follow his gut and trust very few people. He also learned from his paternal grandmother the value of reading between the lines, like during his sophomore year of high school when he predicted his parents were destined to separate. He was correct, of course. He knew his father would move out before the summer, and his mother would eventually commit suicide as a result of being left for an incredibly younger woman. He knew it would happen, and he owed it all to his grammy. She taught him how to read the signs, read between the lines, hear what people weren't saying.

She also taught him how to save himself. If it wasn't for his grammy, he too may have driven off the cliff of life long ago like his mother.

So, standing still with his gut screaming, he began planning how the meeting with Forster would go down. Agent Jackson scrolled down the address book of his cell and then placed another call.

"Yes."

"It would appear I am going to need your services after all," Jackson said.

"How many?"

"Hard to say. Plan on twelve, just in case. More than likely, you'll encounter four to six."

"Do you have the coordinates?"

"I just sent them to you."

"Very good, sir. When should we be in place?"

"By seven thirty, but the meeting isn't until nine."

"As soon as it gets dark, we'll get into position."

"Very well."

CHAPTER THIRTY-EIGHT

Friday, 6:10 p.m.
I-95 Northbound
En Route to Port Canaveral

Evelyn Sims ended the call and dropped her hands into her lap. She was completely puzzled.

"What did Bud say?" John said.

"He thought I was losing my mind. Said if I didn't go home and get some rest, he'd place me on AL."

"What? Did he say anything about Jackson?"

"Yeah," she said, grabbing her phone again. "He said I was hallucinating. I've got to call Micah." She pressed the phone to her ear and listened to it dial his number.

"Hey, Evelyn. What did you find out?"

"Micah, Bud was acting really weird."

"In what way?"

"I told him about Agent Jackson. He kept saying I was being paranoid and wondered if I was hallucinating. He just brushed it off. Is that the right behavior for someone who finds out that a major player in a major investigation is not who he says he is and apparently has been using you and your institution for who knows what?"

"No, it isn't. Bud knows something he's not telling you. What did he say about the specimen?"

"He said it had already been shipped."

"Shipped where?"

Evelyn blinked. "You know, he never said. He said it was shipped to where it was supposed to be shipped, but he never said San Diego or Scripps or Dr. Landover."

"Look, Evelyn, I'm leaving my place right now. I'm on my way to Port Canaveral. I'll probably beat you there by thirty minutes to an hour. Call me when you get close, and I'll get you in. We need to find evidence on this boat, if it hasn't been removed already. And this time, we will need to keep it in our possession."

"You still have the . . . other specimen, right?" Evelyn said.

"Yeah. But for now, let's keep that to ourselves. Don't even tell John. If he doesn't know about it, it can't get him into trouble."

Evelyn looked at John.

John glanced over at Evelyn and smiled. "Everything okay?"

"No, John. I'll fill you in when I'm off the phone."

John's face scrunched. "What other specimen?"

Evelyn put her finger to her lips and pointed to the phone.

"Evelyn, did you hear me?" Micah said.

"Yes. And I agree."

"Look, you need to be careful. At this point, there's no telling what Fontaine will do. Now that his cover is blown, he will resort to some drastic measures until he believes his mission is completed."

"We will, Micah. And you be careful, too."

"I'm always careful, Evelyn."

John and Evelyn were an hour away from Port Canaveral, becoming antsier and antsier as they approached their destination.

"How do you look a man in the eye," Evelyn said, "whom you know to be a killer and play along like he's merely another governmental Joe?"

"This is where my spy training would have come in handy . . . if I'd have taken it," John said to lighten the mood.

"This is the part I don't get, though," Evelyn said, not acknowledging John's comment. "How could our government allow a kook like Jackson to be in this position? I mean, how much longer will he be allowed to masquerade as an FBI agent before someone blows the whistle and ends this madness?"

"It sounds like Micah's hot on his trail."

"Yes, but are we all walking into a hornet's nest? Should we drop everything and move on? Is this simply bigger than all of us? And if we keep pursuing this, will *we* be able survive it?"

John shrugged. "I'm not sure anyone knows the answers to those questions. But I do know this. When you see an injustice and do nothing about it, then you're just as guilty, if not more so, than the perpetrator. I said that to say this—we see the injustice; it's Jackson. Now, what are we going to do about it?"

"Nothing like living on the edge."

"So long as you don't jump off one, we're good."

Evelyn frowned. "Someone sure doesn't want this creature found, I know that much. Somebody put Jackson in that position. Someone bigger than Jackson." Evelyn shook her head and began rubbing it. "Makes me wonder if our evidence will ever be made public, or will it get squashed?"

"Man, you are all over the map tonight. Maybe Bud was right. Maybe you do need some R and R."

Evelyn shot John an agitated glance. "Just shut up and drive."

All these questions and more whirled in Evelyn's mind. She felt her mental acuity starting to deteriorate from a lack of sleep when flashing lights appeared a hundred yards behind them.

As the lights dashed closer, John kept glimpsing back and forth between his rearview mirror and the road.

Evelyn noticed John's sudden activity. "What's wrong, John?"

"Nothing as far as I know. Some police lights just turned on back there, and they're heading this way."

"You weren't speeding, were you?"

John shook his head. "I've had the cruise set below seventy miles per hour for almost the entire trip."

"Oh, he's probably after some other car or got a call."

As they talked, the lights got closer and then pulled up right behind them. The police car rode John's bumper like it was drafting for a NASCAR race.

"What's goin' on?" John slowed down and steered the vehicle onto the shoulder.

"John, I've got a bad feeling about this."

"Keep the doors locked."

Evelyn turned around in her seat in time to see two additional cruisers come screaming down the interstate. One parked behind the first car while the other, a Florida state trooper, pulled past the NMI vehicle and parked in front of it, boxing in the Ford Explorer.

"I've got a really bad feeling about this, John. I need to call Micah."

"No, wait. If they see you calling anyone, it might escalate things. We haven't done anything wrong, Evelyn. Let's not make matters worse for ourselves."

"If you haven't noticed, there are three state troopers surrounding our car. Things are already worse."

The first officer got out of his cruiser and walked up to the Explorer with his flashlight shining into the windows and finally focused on the driver's window. "Can you roll your window down, please?"

John did. "Good evening, Officer. What can I do for you?"

"I need to see your license and registration, please. I'll also need to see her license or some form of identification as well."

John looked at Evelyn and shrugged, reaching for his wallet. She grabbed her purse.

They handed the requested credentials through the half-opened window.

The officer took the items and went back to his cruiser. One officer, who had been standing off the back corner of the Explorer, met up with him. As they spoke, they kept looking back at Evelyn and John. The first officer then went to his cruiser and got inside. The third officer, from the cruiser in front of the Explorer, stood beside his car. His hand resting on his weapon. His eyes peering holes into the front windshield.

A few minutes later, the first officer returned to the window. "Mr. Spencer, Mrs. Sims, I'm going to have to ask you to step out of the vehicle."

"Officer," John said, "can I ask what the purpose of this stop is all about?"

"Please step out of the car."

"No, wait a minute." Evelyn leaned over so she could see the officer. "Before we get out, we demand some answers. What have we done?"

The first officer's eyes shifted up, glancing at the other two men.

The second officer moved up the other side of the car to have a clear view of the front passenger window.

The third officer drew his weapon and used his cruiser as a shield.

The first officer then placed his hand on his holster. "Please step out of the car."

John looked at Evelyn and sighed. "Now it's worse."

Evelyn rolled her eyes and clutched the door handle. "What else can we do?"

They both opened their doors and stepped out together.

At once, the other two officers lurched forward, barking orders and grabbing John and Evelyn, forcing them to turn and face the Explorer while placing their hands on top of the SUV.

John was frisked for weapons. "Hey, what's goin' on?"

"I demand to know the meaning of this," Evelyn said. She was still talking when handcuffs were affixed to her wrists.

The first officer stood in front of John. "There is a warrant out for your arrest."

"What?" Evelyn said. "What are the charges?"

"Impeding a government investigation. Conspiracy. And tampering with evidence."

Evelyn pulled against the grip of the officer. "You've got to be kidding. We were called *by* the FBI to help with an investigation. We work for NMI. See the name of the institution on the side of our vehicle?"

The first officer pulled out a sheet of paper from his pocket. "You are Dr. Evelyn Sims, Director of Operations at the National Marine Institute of Miami, Florida? Correct?"

"Yes, but—"

The first officer turned to John. "And you are Dr. John Spencer, Assistant Director of Operations at the National Marine Institute of Miami, Florida? Correct?"

"Yes," John said in a deflated tone, "but there has to be some mistake."

"There's no mistake, sir."

With her breathing labored, Evelyn turned to the officer gripping her arm. "Please let go of me. You're hurting my arm. I'm not going to run very far or fast in handcuffs."

The officer complied, but Evelyn could tell he was ready to pounce if she so much as twitched.

"Who put out the warrant for our arrest?" Evelyn said.

"FBI," the first officer said.

"Jackson," Evelyn said. "Was it Agent Archibald Jackson?"

"It doesn't say, ma'am, but when we get a BOLO from the FBI, we take it seriously."

"Well, Officerrr," Evelyn said, squinting to read his name tag.

"I am Officer Remington, ma'am."

"Officer Remington, you are being used as a pawn in a huge chess game. I hope you're happy with that."

"Ma'am, we're only doing our jobs. It's not our job to decide on the innocence or guilt of people we arrest. It's our job to arrest and place into custody. The other stuff falls under the purview of the investigators, the lawyers, and the judges."

Perturbed, Evelyn rolled her eyes. "How convenient."

"You both have the right to remain silent," the first officer began. "Anything you say can and will be used against you in a court of law . . ."

CHAPTER THIRTY-NINE

Friday, 7:35 p.m.
Rasmussen's Commercial Marina
Port Canaveral, Florida

Micah arrived in Port Canaveral, wearing his Coast Guard garb and flashing his new Naval Intelligence provisional credentials at all the checkpoints. He was back in the game, sort of. After calling Jason Greene and uncovering Fontaine's file, some calls were made at the hastening of Greene's superiors, and Micah was asked to investigate Agent Jackson in a little more detail to find out his real agenda.

"How am I supposed to do that?" Micah asked Jason Greene when he called back about thirty minutes later.

"I've been instructed to give you whatever you need, Micah. Special requests will have to be cleared, of course."

"Well, for starters, I'll need credentials that can get me into any area needed, a clean cell phone with all necessary numbers programmed, a PDA, a weapon, and possibly an expense account."

"Done."

"And how am I supposed to get these items? I'm in Fort Pierce, Florida."

"We will have everything you need delivered to your door within two hours. We will have someone from Patrick Air Force Base deliver them. Please stay home until they arrive."

No problem, Micah thought, thinking that a two-hour rendezvous with his couch would be wonderful.

"Captain Gregson, I didn't know you were still part of Naval Intelligence," Agent Jackson said as he approached the last checkpoint. "My sources told me you were decommissioned when you left the Navy."

"I've been reinstated."

"Really now? And what would cause the U.S. Navy to reinstate an old hand like you?"

To keep a wary eye on you, Doctor, Micah thought. Oh, how he wanted to tell Jackson what he did know. "Not sure, actually. Navy contacted me. They knew my boat was the one that responded to the *Greenback* incident, and they also knew I'd investigated the *Titan,* so they asked me to investigate this fishing boat. So, here I am."

Agent Jackson was silent for a moment. Micah could see the wheels turning.

"So, Captain, what do you need to see?"

"The boat first. Then I need to interview the crew."

"No sense in holding you up. You know the drill by now, right? Anything that's found, see Agent Lowery."

Micah gave Jackson a thumbs-up sign. "Gotcha."

When Micah stepped aboard the *Sea-Saw,* he scanned the boat, knowing what a fishing boat was supposed to look like. He had searched a myriad of them in both the Navy and while with the Coast Guard, and they all had the same look about them. Items used to pursue commercial fishing were universal. The trade had become so competitive; efficiency was the name of the game. So, like any other trade, whether it be installing ceramic tile in a bathroom or installing the offensive line of a football team, the intense competition forced the templates and subsequent tools of the trade to look very similar as everyone borrowed techniques from proven winners to increase productivity.

In addition, Micah had noticed the "swept clean" look of the vessel, despite the fact it was a fishing boat that had been on the ocean for days. An unlikely situation considering the look of the crew. He had seen them sitting together earlier, sipping coffee and looking beleaguered. They didn't look swept clean. As he suspected, Agent Jackson must have already examined the boat just like he did the *Greenback*.

After fifteen minutes of searching and finding nothing, he moved to the back and focused on the stern. Looking up, he saw the captain of the boat sitting cross-legged on a curb, smoking a cigarette and rubbing his knees. Micah let out a loud whistle to get his attention.

"Captain," Micah waved his arm.

The captain looked up.

"Captain, I need to see you."

The skipper stood with a little help from one of his crew members and moseyed down the steps and onto the boat. "Yeah?"

"Captain, I'm Captain Micah Gregson, Naval Intelligence." He showed the man his credentials. "I've got a couple of questions about your nets and what happened."

The captain shrugged. "Okay."

"I see these nets were severed with something pretty sharp."

"Yeah." The captain strolled over to the doorway of the cabin and, reaching around the corner, produced a *machete*. "We cut 'em at sea."

"Why did you cut them?"

"We weren't gonna make it back to shore if we didn't."

"What was in the nets?"

"Something big. One of our crewmen saw what it was."

"How close was your boat to taking on water?"

The captain placed the machete back in its place and then went straight to the stern. Leaning over, he surveyed the side of the boat before placing his hand about six inches away from the edge. "The water came up to here. I had to reposition some of my crew to the bow to try and compensate. The others had the pumps going."

"How far out were you?"

"Hundred miles or so. Too deep to snag any reef. I couldn't believe it when that FBI guy over there even asked the question. Snag a reef in three thousand feet of water? C'mon."

"Remember, he's FBI, not Navy, or an old sea dog like yourself." Micah winked.

The captain laughed. "You got that right."

"Who saw what was in the nets?"

"Wiggins." The captain turned and yelled in a scratchy voice, "Wiggins! Front and center!"

Without delay, a younger man jumped up, snuffed out a cigarette on the ground under his foot, and jogged down to the boat.

"Captain Gregson, this is Jack Wiggins. He saw what was in the nets. Tell him, Jack, what you saw."

Micah reached out and shook Jack Wiggins's hand. "Good to meet you, Mr. Wiggins. I'm Captain Micah Gregson, Naval Intelligence. What did you see exactly?"

"I saw a giant octopus-lookin' thing. It was hard to see at first because the bottom was all churned up. Silt everywhere. But every now and then, a gush of warm water would clear the view."

"You think the thing your nets snagged was a giant squid?"

"What was left of him."

"It was dead?"

"Yeah. It looked like it had been eaten by somethin' else."

Micah's tenor turned from disappointed to energized. "Really? What do you mean exactly?"

"Well, these long tentacles were floatin' and stickin' out of what looked like a cave or a large hole. The hole looked ragged, just like the edges of the squid."

"So you think the squid was inside of something else?"

Wiggins nodded. "That's what it looked like. It looked like somethin' had eaten the squid, then somethin' ate whatever ate the squid. Darnedest thing I've ever seen."

"You know there are sperm whales out there that eat giant squid, right?"

"Yeah," the captain said. "We run into 'em from time to time. They've never bothered us, though."

"But," Wiggins said, "what could eat half a whale that grows seventy feet long? The whole front of the whale was gone."

Micah Gregson sighed. "That's why I'm here, Mr. Wiggins. That's why I'm here."

CHAPTER FORTY

Friday, 8:56 p.m.
Dirt Road off Highway 528
Approximately Four Miles West of I-95

Agent Archibald Jackson sat in a dark SUV, parked in the darkest spot he could find—off the road, out of sight—for nearly an hour. He hadn't seen any other car lights yet, so he knew William Forster could not have sneaked in ahead of him. He watched for any movement, thinking Forster might have parked down the road a bit and walked to the meeting location. But there was nothing.

In his hands, updating every few seconds, was a PDA, showing heat signatures of the area using infrared satellite. Per Agent Jackson's meticulous directions, seven of his agents had placed themselves in a semicircle around the clearing where the meeting was to take place. There, they sat incognito, red dots on a screen, like anxious deer hunters in tree stands waiting for the prize buck to clear the brush.

Thirty minutes before nine p.m., another grouping of red dots, four heat signatures to be exact, snaked their way from a half-mile down the road into the woods on the west side. The red spots on the screen fanned out and formed a line on the far end the clearing.

"Just as I thought," Jackson said, muttering mild expletives as he watched four red dots approach from the south and spread out. "Let's be fair now, shall we? Maybe William only wants to make sure he's protected against any foul play."

Nine o'clock came and went. Jackson's angst descended into an ever-increasing malevolent degree of anger every time he glanced at his watch.

"He sent his goons in to take me out. Gilliam had Forster do his dirty work for him." He paused, attempting to gain some composure. "Let's give Mr. Forster a call, shall we?"

Jackson dialed.

Busy signal.

Jackson dialed again.

Still busy.

Jackson sat motionless, staring at the PDA. All the red dots remained still. *One more chance, William,* he thought as he dialed again.

It rang.

"Hello?" came a man's voice.

"Is this Mr. Forster?"

"Who?"

"William Forster? Is this 404-555-7823?"

"Yes, it is, but there's nobody by that name that lives here. You must have the wrong number, chief," the man said in a distinct Bostonian accent.

Jackson slammed his cell phone shut. "Who does he think he's messin' with?"

Jackson checked his PDA once more. The positions of the men were unchanged. He reached up and pressed the button on his earpiece.

"All teams, do you copy?"

Each man called in his position.

"There are four hostiles who have entered the perimeter. Assume they are armed and dangerous. They are positioned in a line at your two o'clock position. They are approximately ten to fifteen yards apart. All hostiles are to be eliminated. I repeat. All hostiles are to be eliminated. Do you copy?"

All the men replied in the affirmative.

Jackson watched as seven red dots moved in on the other four. He rolled down his window and heard several spits of gunfire

In a matter of minutes, the team leader responded. "Red Leader, this is Number One. All four hostiles have been neutralized. What do you want us to do with the bodies?"

"Leave them," Jackson said. "We'll let Mr. Forster take care of the funeral arrangements. I've got a boat to catch."

CHAPTER FORTY-ONE

Friday, 9:09 p.m.
Brevard County Jail
Cocoa, Florida

Evelyn Sims stood in a holding cell at the Brevard County Jail, yelling down the corridor, "I want my one phone call!"

"I doubt you'll get it," John said. Sitting in the cell next to her on a small concrete bench, he eyed the other "criminals" down the hall. "Our circumstance is not your normal circumstance. We didn't rob a convenience store, you know."

"It doesn't matter. They can't deny me my rights."

"Uh, yes, they can."

Evelyn stood against the cold steel bars, gripping them, wondering how she had landed in jail of all places. Her husband was dead, her marriage was over, her job was in peril, and now her very freedom was questionable. Her life was in a shambles.

She stared across the hallway. "I was supposed to be at the movies tonight," she said.

"Huh?" John said.

"I had plans tonight with a friend of mine. Plans we made over a week ago. We were goin' out to eat and to a movie. She's probably called my house tonight, wondering why I'm not answering."

"She doesn't watch the news, I take it?"

"You know, that's true. You'd think she would have seen something on the television or heard something on the radio and called as soon as she heard," she said with a sniff. "She probably works for Jackson, too."

"Don't be so cynical, Evelyn. I'm sure there's a legitimate reason you haven't heard from her."

"Sure." She plopped down on a similar bench in her cell and, in one overwhelming flood of emotion, started to cry.

John sat in silence. His friend in the next cell had experienced a hellish two days. He felt so sorry for her and even more powerless to help. Almost breaking down himself, he bowed his head and prayed.

Evelyn spoke after several minutes of silence. "You know, John, this is what you call extremely ironic."

"What is?"

"Our entire situation. Think about it. Centuries ago, scientists were thrown into prison by religious zealots because they believed things like the Earth being round instead of flat, or the Earth revolving around the sun instead of vice-versa. Now, here we are, sitting in jail —thrown in here by a scientific zealot, I might add—because we believe in something other than evolution." Evelyn sighed. "How the tables have turned. It's exactly the opposite now."

"You know, Evelyn, some say Darwin said people had made a religion out of his work. Evolutionary scientists argue vehemently that he never said it. But whether he did or didn't, isn't the point. The point is, he did create one, whether he intended to or not."

"How do you create a religion?"

"Let me put it to you this way. It takes just as much faith, if not more, to believe that we, and everything we see, touch, taste, feel, and hear, evolved from a slimy pit of goo than to believe in a God who created the heavens and the earth. It takes more faith to believe that we are the descendants of Lucy and Ida than to believe we are the creative masterpieces of God. Yet, each position tries to find evidence to prove the validity of its belief system while at the same time disproving the other."

Evelyn leaned back against the wall. "True. It would seem, however, that not everyone is in search of the truth."

"But that's the problem, Evelyn. What is truth? And what truth matters the most? Obviously, there are truths that are accepted and believed by all, like gravity, for example. We all know that if a person falls from a thirty-story building, the result will be the same. The rate of speed by which the person falls will vary based on weight, how they fall, gravitational pull, wind speed, et cetera. But that sudden stop at the end will likely produce the same effect."

"That's the truth."

John chortled. "Very punny. But seriously, in the grand scheme of things, what relevance does that particular truth play? Other than keeping us from floating into space, it really doesn't have too many other significant relevancies, per se."

"I would say that's pretty important. Wouldn't you?"

"Yes, I'm very grateful for gravity, but the truth we seek as Christians is different. It's spiritual. The truth we seek has eternal ramifications.

"Jesus said it himself when He stood before Pilate. Pilate asked Him if He was a king. Jesus said that Pilate was correct in calling Him a king. Then Jesus said that was the reason He was born. That was the reason He came into the world. He came to testify to the truth. Then He said, 'Everyone on the side of truth listens to Me.' That's pretty definitive, Evelyn. If we are on the side of truth, we listen to Jesus; we do what He says."

"Yet, as scientists," Evelyn said, "you and I want to collect scientific evidence to prove that God was right. Prove that He exists, and that everything in the Bible is true, so we can say, 'See, the Bible is correct and believable.'"

"If you want to talk about irony, the ultimate irony is that God doesn't need us to do that. He just needs us to listen to His Son. I mean, we can work as scientists to reveal the world as the hard evidence it is—the master plan of a Master Creator. But when it comes to living, God wants us to live by faith, not by sight. In other words, live by faith, not by science."

Evelyn stared at the woman sitting across the hallway in the neighboring cell. The woman was studying her, hanging on their conversation, as if waiting for Evelyn to answer. Evelyn looked back at the woman. One soul to another.

Evelyn's world had come crashing down into a small, dirty jail cell with no windows. So, that was where God had to take her to open her eyes again, huh? "So, this is what persecution feels like?"

John frowned. "Nooo. We haven't been thrown into a mass of hungry lions yet or been lit up as human torches in a maniac's garden."

"Thank God for that." Evelyn heard a door open from down the hall and stood to see.

A deputy strolled up the hall and stopped in front of Evelyn's cell. "I hear you want to make a phone call?"

"Yes, I do, Officer."

The officer opened the flap. "Place your hands through the hole to be handcuffed."

Evelyn gave a skittish chuckle. "This is all new for me." She stuck her hands through the hole.

The deputy slapped on a pair of cuffs and opened the door. "First time for everything. This way." He pointed in the direction from which he came.

John stepped to the front of his cell. "Evelyn, it'll be all right."

CHAPTER FORTY-TWO

Friday, 9:58 p.m. (EST)
Patrick Air Force Base
Satellite Beach, Florida

Dr. Anthony Fontaine stood on the tarmac at Patrick Air Force Base, waiting for a chopper. He needed it to deliver him eighty miles out over the Atlantic to rendezvous with the *USS Gettysburg*. From there, the naval vessel would be on a covert mission to the mid-Atlantic of which only a handful of top officers and government officials knew the details.

In the meantime, he assessed his situation. The plan was like playing chess. The key to winning at the game of chess was to always be two to four moves ahead of your opponent. Those moves always left you with multiple options and often suckered the foe into making a move thought to be advantageous. Little did the rival know that, more times than not, a trap lay hidden, like a hole in the ground covered with brush. Costing them dearly.

This was how Dr. Anthony Fontaine always played. Whether it be the game of chess or the game of life, the rules of engagement, in his mind, were always the same.

Play to win.

Fontaine glanced at his watch, pulled out his cell phone, and dialed.

A groggy voice answered.

"Mr. Gilliam, sorry to wake you, but there is an urgent matter we need to address right now. Where are you?"

"Fontaine? Is that you?"

"Yes. Where are you?"

"I'm in Sussex. Do you have any idea what time it is here?"

"By my calculations, three fifty-eight a.m., in London, of course."

"That is four in the morning, Fontaine. This had better be good."

"Oh, it is. Trust me."

"I will be the judge of that."

Fontaine raised his eyebrows. *No, I'll be the judge.* "Mr. Gilliam, it seems we have a problem. Do you know William Forster?"

Eric Gilliam coughed. "Yes, what about him?"

"It seems ol' William had been given a job to do?" Fontaine paused for effect.

"And?"

"Unfortunately, he was unable to carry out that assignment. Instead, he has four dead men lying in some woods about twenty or so miles from here. Now, Mr. Gilliam, you wouldn't happen to know anything about that situation, would you?"

"Uh, no. Did Mr. Forster contact you?"

"Yes, he did." Fontaine's ire rose. "Can we just cut the bull? I know you had something to do with it. I believe you actually ordered the hit on me, and I'll bet Belkin was in on it, too. But I'll tell you what. I can let bygones be bygones." Fontaine paused again. "If you cut me in this time."

Gilliam's voice increased in volume. "Cut you in? On what?"

"Your little plan, Mr. Gilliam. You know? The whole 'cloning an army to defeat the enemies of the West?'"

"I . . . don't know what you are talking about."

Fontaine flashed a devilish smile.

Check.

"Surely you do, Mr. Gilliam, or should I call you Eric since we'll be getting to know each other better?"

Gilliam was silent.

"You see, Eric, I know all about your little reproductive twinning plan. I also know of your enlistment of Cesare Antonella, Forster, Schmitt, and all the others. I was the one who did the initial research upon which you have based your entire plan. So, all I am asking is that you cut me in. I believe half would be a fair amount."

"Half of what?"

"Half of whatever it is you stand to make out of all this. I'll start with half of your initial investment into this grandiose plan of yours for starters. You must have a great deal of money already invested, huh?"

"You're not going to blackmail me, Anthony. All I have to do is call the proper authorities and tell them you murdered that woman in the States. And what about that man in South America two years ago? And that family in Western Canada last summer? The fact that I know all about those incidents will do more than pique their interest."

Fontaine chuckled, looking up into the night sky. "You feel rather proud of yourself right now, don't you, Eric? Empowered, even? You think you have me backed into a corner with no way out."

"I believe those who deliver blackmail often have too many skeletons in the closet. It's only a matter of time before the door pops open."

"You see, Eric? That has always been your Achilles heel. You were always too proud of your plan. Too proud of your accomplishments. You simply couldn't be satisfied with millions of dollars and a lifestyle every human being on this planet would envy."

"You have no idea what's at stake here."

Fontaine hesitated to answer and instead drew in a deep breath to calm himself. He shifted the phone to his other ear. "No, I believe I do. You wanted to play God. I simply took advantage of your haughtiness, Eric. Used it to *my* advantage. Saved it for a rainy day, so to speak."

"What could you possibly do to me that presidents and prime ministers have yet to accomplish?"

"The information I gave you? About reproductive twinning? Well, it was inconspicuously incomplete."

"Meaning?"

"Meaning the crucial data—the data needed to connect the dots, if you will—was omitted and replaced with other data that was not so—how shall we say it?—accurate."

"Fontaine, what have you done?"

"What I had to. What I always do. People are always trying to *prove* their points, *force* their wills, *make* others march to the beat of someone else's drum. So, I skew data back into *my* favor. It's like planting a computer virus. No one knows it's there until it's too late." Fontaine bellowed a confident laugh. "It's served me well over the years. And when you're really good at it, there's almost no limit as to how far you can go."

"Do you realize what you've done?"

"I do. But before you pull the hair off that British head of yours, we can right the ship almost instantly."

"Why would I want to do business with a madman?"

"Come now, Eric. Who's the one making a secret army?"

"How do you know I can't just hire a good scientist and fix the damage you've done?"

"Oh, I'm sure you could. Eventually. But it would probably take the top scientists in several fields at least a year, maybe more, to determine what data has been altered. Then, another six months to figure out what the right data may look like. Then, another six to test it. Do you have that long to wait, Eric? Your grand plans of making an army being placed in a two-year holding pattern? It doesn't have to be that way. I have the pertinent data that you need to make it happen, and you don't. I can make it happen in a week. My fee? Half."

Gilliam's voice growled. "Fontaine, I will have your head on a platter when I am through with you!"

Fontaine laughed again. "And all I have to do is give Cesare Antonella a call and relay to him the URL address of a website that contains all the erroneous information I've fed you and the others. That won't bode well for your plan, now, will it, Eric? I know Cesare has had second thoughts about this plan all along. Giving him this information would make him back out in a heartbeat. So, I suggest you let me in, give me half, and when the time is right, I'll supply you with the correct data. Your plan would still be in play, and you'd be able to amass your army and invade whichever country your little heart desires. I, on the other hand, would disappear to some exotic island and try my hand at dating a few island beauties."

"You are not getting a dime, Anthony. I swear, before the day is over, I will have you hanging from the rafters."

Fontaine sighed. "Is that your final answer, Eric?"

"Anthony, if you don't stop this madness, I'm going to kill you. I promise."

"Are you sure that's your final answer? Are you sure you don't want to phone a frien—Oh, wait, you already used that lifeline, didn't you, Eric."

"You're dead."

Fontaine sighed once more. "Well, actually, no. I'm not. Despite your best efforts."

"You're going to live to regret this, Fontaine."

"Wrong answer, ol' chap." He pulled two small black items out of his coat pocket. They resembled garage-door openers. Both items had a word written on the back with a silver permanent marker. On one, the word *Estate*; on the other, *Office*.

Slipping the latter back into his pocket, he held the former device up in the air. Lifting a protective cover, he pressed the red button. The device made the sound of a phone dialing a number.

"Anthony, did you hear me? I'm going to—"

Over the cell phone, Eric Gilliam's voice disappeared and twisted into grating static . . . then into a quick-paced busy signal . . . then silence.

Anthony Fontaine slipped the detonator into his coat pocket. "No, Eric, you won't, ol' chum."

Fontaine closed and opened his cell phone once more, dialing a long series of numbers.

"Dresdner Bank Aktiengesellschaft, Zweigniederlassung Singapore. How may I direct your call?" said a female voice in German.

Fontaine took a deep breath. It had been a long time since he had used his rusty German. "Extension 10087, please?"

Fontaine heard canned music played through some awful synthesizer, waiting for the person at Extension 10087 to answer. *You'd think they'd be playing Beethoven or Mozart instead of this shallow Muzak,* he thought.

Another German voice. This time, a man's. "This is Niklas Krüger."

"My name is Eric Gilliam. My access code is XY7, 546, 854, Z9B, 2JX."

Fontaine heard the man tap on computer keys.

"Very good, sir. Now, what is your security question?"

"What is the maiden name of my father's mother's aunt?"

"Very good, sir. And the answer?"

"Graham. G-R-A-H-A-M."

More keys were punched on the computer. "Now, sir, if you will submit your thumbprint."

Fontaine, who already had plugged a small fingerprint device into his phone, slipped a nicotine patch-looking square out of his jacket pocket and peeled one side off. Positioning his right thumb so the center of his thumb lined up with a small red line, he pressed his thumb against what was a copy of Eric Gilliam's fingerprint, securing it to his own. He then pressed his thumb down on the fingerprinting device and pressed the number nine on his keypad.

"It is uploading now, Niklas."

Niklas Krüger tapped a few more computer keys. "Yes, Mr. Gilliam, how may I help you?"

"The money in my business account entitled 'Brennine Pharmaceuticals—Valdosta' can now be transferred to this account number," Fontaine said. He supplied Niklas Krüger another account number within the same bank set up by Eric Gilliam some months prior which gave Fontaine full access without Eric's knowledge.

"The full amount, sir?"

"Yes, Niklas. All six million pounds, please."

"Please hold, Mr. Gilliam."

Fontaine waited, knowing they were checking validity, et cetera, et cetera. *William Forster will love me for this,* he thought. *Actually, he'll think Eric did it.*

"Mr. Gilliam?"

"Yes, Niklas."

"Your funds are being transferred. They will show up on the account balance for tomorrow and be available for use within ten business days. Is there anything else I can do for you?"

"No, Niklas. That will be all. Thank you so much."

"You have a good day, Mr. Gilliam."

Evelyn stood next to what appeared to be a pay phone, clutching the receiver with both hands. *I've never been so humiliated in all my life,* she thought, dialing the phone with handcuffs wrapped around her wrists. They'd been on for a mere few minutes and were already recreating the painful red marks that were imprinted earlier.

"Hello?"

"Micah, it's Evelyn."

"Hey, why are you calling me from this number? I didn't recognize it and almost didn't answer."

"John and I got arrested."

"What? Arrested? By whom?"

"State troopers. They stopped us about twenty miles south of the Port Canaveral exit."

"What for? Who ordered it?"

"They said the FBI put out a warrant for our arrest. They said it was for conspiracy and impeding an investigation and tampering with evidence."

"Okay, whoa, whoa, whoa. The FBI ordered it?"

"That's what they said."

"We know who's behind that, don't we?"

"Jackson. We figured that out. But how do we get out of here?"

"Leave that to me. Where are you being held?"

"Brevard County Jail."

"Sit tight. I'll have you out in no time."

CHAPTER FORTY-THREE

Friday, 10:17 p.m.
The Oval Office
Washington, DC

President Walker leaned back in his high-backed leather captain's chair with his eyes shut. It was the first moment of peace he had experienced all day. Phone calls on secure lines sandwiched between security briefings and other assorted meetings with everybody who's anybody in his administration, overlapped each other in importance, all trying to get a handle on what should happen next while, at the same time, preventing World War III.

For the majority of the day, he had been putting out brushfires. Brushfires with the media. Brushfires with different heads of state. Brushfires with members of Congress and his own administration. All these fires ignited due to one reason.

A creature in the Atlantic.

And its actions had flushed out some other animals, too.

Rats.

Rats who had chewed their way into key areas of the government for purposes yet unknown.

Now, while trying to ease his mind and determine which rat needed to be exterminated first, his phone's intercom buzzed.

"Mr. President, I have the Russian ambassador on Line One," the switchboard operator said.

President Walker sighed with his eyes still closed. *Six minutes of silence,* he thought. *That's all I'm going to get today. Six minutes.*

"Put it through." President Walker listened as his phone rang three times before picking it up. *Just because I've managed to grab six minutes of rest doesn't mean I'm not busy.*

"Ambassador Vrilinko, working late I see."

"President Walker, you know as well as I do that we never have time off, yes? Even when we are on vacation, we are only a phone call away."

"Very true, comrade. Can you imagine how it was in the days before cell phones and television media coverage?"

"Yes. We were living under Stalin's reign of terror, and you were trying to survive an economic depression with people jumping out of thirty-story windows, if my history is correct. 'The good ol' days,' I think you call them. Is it not funny how we always think our present situation is the most difficult?"

President Walker yawned quietly. "You make a great point. So, what can I do for you?"

"I am calling to get your final response to my government's request for assistance concerning our lost submarine. Our ships are less than three hours away from the *Kirov*'s last known coordinates. If your ships have not left port yet, then any assistance they can lend will be relatively useless, for by the time they get there, we will have already done most of the work."

President Walker leaned forward and thumbed through the stack of file folders on his desk before grabbing the one marked "Operation Comrade."

He rifled through the pages of the document loud enough so that the Russian diplomat could hear. "Ambassador Vrilinko, I have before me a comprehensive plan set out by our defense department. We have two ships en route to that location as well. They might get there before yours do, but they are scheduled to arrive simultaneously and assist. Tell your vessels to be on the lookout for the *USS Carney* and the *USS Philippine Sea*. They are the two that have been commissioned for this operation. I understand you already have a science vessel en route, correct?"

"Yes, accompanied by two battle cruisers. It is equipped with a diving bell, a small one-man submarine, and an unmanned submarine."

Reading one of the pages describing the area where the Russian sub was thought to be, President Walker frowned. "Ambassador, you are aware that the last known coordinates of your missing submarine are in at least three thousand meters of water."

"Yes, we know. We also know that the possibility of finding any survivors is extremely doubtful."

"But, you have to try, right?'

"Precisely, Mr. President," Vrilinko said. "And let me say, Mr. President, that despite the delay, our government is appreciative of your help. We are hopeful that this gesture of comradeship will help strengthen relations between our two nations. One can never have too many friends in these perilous times."

"You're right, comrade. Building and maintaining trust *is* the first step."

CHAPTER FORTY-FOUR

Friday, 10:45 p.m.
Brevard County Jail
Cocoa, Florida

Micah Gregson arrived at the Brevard County Jail furious. The locals had "gone governmental." *Mindless drones,* he thought. He knew they were just doing their jobs, but even at the most elementary levels of law enforcement, the syndrome affected everyone, even state troopers and deputy sheriffs.

He flew through the front doors of the complex and flashed his Naval Intelligence credentials. "I need Evelyn Sims and John Spencer released immediately," he said to the deputy manning the front desk.

"Can I help you, sir?"

"Officer," Micah said, looking at his name tag, "Johnstone, my name is Captain Micah Gregson, Naval Intelligence." He held up his credentials again. "You have two people in custody who were wrongly arrested on a falsified report. The person who authorized the warrant was Doctor Anthony Fontaine. He is posing as an FBI agent by the name of Archibald Jackson. Therefore, I need these two people released immediately. They are crucial to carrying out a vital investigation that has serious implications on national security."

The officer's eyes grew to the size of Buick hubcaps by the time Micah had finished explaining the situation. "Can you hold on a minute, Captain?"

"Sure, but make it quick."

The officer snatched the phone from its cradle and pressed a couple of buttons. "Hey, Sarge, come up here to the front. You've got to hear this one."

Evelyn Sims had been trying to reach Bud Kensington by phone for over ten minutes. His number kept ringing and ringing with no answer, not even voice mail. She kept rubbing her wrists, imagining the handcuffs still attached.

It had been an appalling feeling being locked up, sitting in a cell used numerous times to house everything from drunken drivers and women of the night to stone-cold killers. Just the thought sent shivers all over her body. She felt dirty. Her clothes felt soiled. She wanted to bathe, but she knew that option would not present itself for a while.

Instead, Micah, John, and she were heading to Patrick Air Force Base. Micah had made arrangements for Wellman to send a Coast Guard chopper up the coast, refuel, pick them up, and head out to rendezvous with the *USS Carney*. It would be upon that vessel that they would then be carried out to meet the Russian ships.

Micah had gone to all this trouble because of a classified report he had received just prior to arriving at the jail. A U.S. Air Force helicopter had been used by an FBI agent. The mission orders stated to transport the agent from Patrick Air Force Base to a ship in the Atlantic. But the two sanctioned ships of Operation Comrade had received no such orders.

That meant only one thing.

There was a third vessel in the Atlantic.

And she was sailing dark.

Bud Kensington had been trying to reach Fontaine for over two hours but to no avail. The events of the last few days had been frenetic. The plan, one he and Anthony Fontaine had concocted, went terribly awry. And he knew Anthony well enough to know that when things went south, his colleagues suffered so he could skate.

Now, sitting in his drab office, he was recapitulating. Had he done the right thing? His intentions were good, but when do good intentions mixed with bad affiliations cancel themselves out? Or do they? Do the good intentions outweigh the means by which they are reached? Can a person feel good about good intentions when he knows those same intentions cost people their lives and livelihood? Could he live with himself, knowing his beliefs and subsequent alliances had hurt people for whom he cared?

He picked up his cell phone and started to call Anthony Fontaine again when it rang.

Bud looked at the number but didn't recognize it. "Hello?"

"Where have you been?" Evelyn said.

"Evelyn? Where are you?"

"I just got out of *jail*. That's where I've been. That lunatic Jackson had me and John arrested."

Bud winced. *Good intentions,* he thought. *All I had were good intentions.* "Where are you now?"

"We're with Micah. We're heading out to sea. Micah believes Jackson is going to try and kill the creature."

Bud's head dropped. *Destroy all the evidence. Even if the thing exists. We have to destroy all the evidence. That's what Fontaine kept chanting. Man, have I been an idiot.*

"Bud," Evelyn said, "did you hear me?"

Bud gripped the phone tighter. "Evelyn, uh, I have something to tell you."

"What is it?"

Bud managed a deep breath. "Evie, I've been working with Agent Jackson."

Evelyn sat stone still. She reached out and grabbed Micah, digging her nails into his shoulder.

"What's wrong?" Micah said.

Evelyn just started shaking her head. "Unbelievable. *Un-be-lieve-able*. How could you, Bud?"

"What's happened?" Micah said.

She shouted into the phone, "Bud's been working with Agent Jackson all along! What about the specimen, Bud? Did you really send it to Dr. Landover like you said? Huh? Huh, Bud? Did you?"

Bud's silence gave her his answer.

She screamed into the phone. "I can't believe this is happening! You didn't send the specimen to Landover, did you? What did you do with it, Bud?"

"I, uh, sent it to . . ." Bud sighed into the phone. "Paris, France. To Fontaine's foundation headquarters."

Evelyn dropped the phone in her lap.

"Where did he send it?" John said.

"Paris," Evelyn said in almost a whisper.

"What's Paris got to do with all this?" Micah said.

John groaned. "That's where Fontaine's research foundation is located."

Micah held out his hand. "Can I talk to Bud, please?"

Evelyn slapped the phone into Micah's hand.

"Bud, this is Micah Gregson. I assume you are saying you have been working covertly with Agent Jackson all along then?"

"Yes."

"Did you know he murdered Regina Fleming?"

Bud paused. "I think I need to get my lawyer."

"You'll need more than a lawyer, Bud. Trust me. Were you aware of who Anthony Fontaine was and what he was capable of doing?"

"I guess not completely."

"Real smart, Bud. So, when was the last time you heard from Fontaine?"

"Early this afternoon, just before I sent the specimen to Paris."

"You have no idea where he is right now?"

"No."

"Do you have any way to reach him?"

"Yes. I have his cell number. Want it?"

"No. If he knows we talked, your life will be in jeopardy. This is what I want you to do. If you help us, I can go to bat for you. Maybe get your sentence reduced."

Bud huffed an exasperated sigh into the phone. "What do you need?"

"I need you to call Fontaine and find out where he is and what he's up to. I'd like to get one step ahead of him for a change."

"I'll see what I can do."

Dr. Anthony Fontaine watched as the HH-60 helicopter made its approach. The *USS Gettysburg* had stopped to allow the chopper to land on the pad at the stern of the vessel. The waters were choppy, and it was nearing midnight, making it a little trickier than usual. Fontaine sat motionless except for an occasional turn of the head to see the maneuver take place.

The chopper landed, and Fontaine unbuckled his safety harness. As he opened his door, Fontaine's cell phone rang. He looked at the number. *Henry Kensington,* he thought, rolling his eyes. *Tonight, of all nights, you're not asleep at midnight. You just can't seem to get it right, can you, Kensington?*

"What is it, Henry? I'm extremely busy at the moment."

"Sounds like you're on a chopper, Anthony. Where are you?"

"My location at present is classified, Henry. There are only a few people in the world who know where I am. Let's keep it that way, shall we?"

"Did you hear about Dr. Sims and Dr. Spencer?"

"No." Fontaine feigned interest. "What happened?"

"They were arrested by state troopers before they got to Port Canaveral. Did you have anything to do with that, Anthony?"

Fontaine paused to descend a ladder off the platform before the chopper lifted off the helipad. "Henry, I've already covered this with you. They were getting too close. They had already put two and two together about me. I didn't want them in the way any longer. I'm going to have them released once this mission is over. Their arrest was just a temporary setback. Nothing more."

"I hate to be the messenger, Anthony, but they're already out of jail."

"What? That's not possible. The orders were specific. They were to remain in custody until I released them myself. How did they get out?"

"Captain Gregson."

"How did he—never mind. Where are they now?"

Bud paused. "I don't know. They didn't say. What are you going to do, Anthony? I think I have a right to know since I'm in this thing neck deep."

Fontaine snorted. "Henry, you're in this a lot deeper than the neck. And like I already told you, I cannot tell you where I am or what I'm doing. This is top secret. Suffice it to say that when I'm finished, our job will be done."

"But they know about Regina Fleming. They know you killed her, and it will only be a matter of time before they link me to you."

"Fleming's death is insignificant at this point. I'm not worried about that at all."

"But what about me, Anthony?"

"What about you, Henry?"

"If all this hits the fan, what's going to be my defense?"

"Henry, that was and is your business. How you prepare for war is just as important, if not more so, than how you fight."

"What's that supposed to mean?"

"I've been putting my affairs in order, Henry. That's what it means. So, when things 'hit the fan,' as you so eloquently put it, I'll be okay. They'll never be able to make anything stick, and that's if they can find me."

Bud Kensington now felt like a runner in an Olympic marathon that just heard the report of the starting pistol. The same report the other runners heard two hours earlier. The race was about over, and he had not even left the stadium yet. "You set me up."

"No, Henry. I did no such thing. I only used you. That's the bad thing about alliances. Each party has their own agenda and purpose for the alliance. It's kind of like musical chairs. In an alliance, you never want to be the one standing."

Bud hunched over in his chair, clutching the phone like it was his last conversation. *What do I do now?*

Fontaine was ready to enter the bridge of the *USS Gettysburg*. "Henry, I've got to go. Take care of yourself."

Fontaine hung up.

Bud, still holding his cell phone, lowered his head down onto the desk, resting it in the cradle of his arms. He was a mere shell of the roughhewn man who had run NMI all these years. Now, it was all crashing in on him. Evelyn and John would never let him walk. The stockholders, once they found out about his involvement, would have his hide. He'd spend the rest of his life in prison.

Leaning back in his chair, he opened the bottom drawer of his desk. He reached in and flipped a lever which loosened a false bottom to the drawer. Pulling the piece of wood out, he exposed a semi-automatic hand gun. He pulled the gun out and set it on the desk. He then opened a deeper drawer which held his trusty bottle of whiskey and a shot glass. Pulling them out and setting them on the desk, he opened the lap drawer and snatched a pad of paper and a pen.

He poured himself a drink and threw it back before pouring another. He repeated the process three times, staring at the pad of paper in between shots, before picking up the pen.

Scribbling in a shaky hand, he wrote a letter to his children, expressing all the love he had left in him.

CHAPTER FORTY-FIVE

Saturday, 12:03 a.m.
En Route to the USS Carney
Atlantic Ocean

Evelyn Sims, Micah Gregson, and John Spencer, aboard an MH-60T Coast Guard helicopter, sat three across. Strapped in and wearing helmets and headsets, they tried to make sense of the last couple of days. They realized what Agent Jackson's game plan had been all along —destroy any and all evidence of the creature. Make it so no one can study it, examine it, or investigate it. That was his goal.

Evelyn understood now why Agent Jackson had asked the questions he did when he visited her home. They discerned why Evelyn's boat and the fishing boat were cleaned up so well. Micah joked, saying if Jackson had seen the dents in the side of the *Titan* in time, he would've had someone pull them out before the team from NMI arrived.

But where is Jackson now? she thought. *And how far is he willing to go to complete his mission?*

"We have to assume," Micah said, "that Jackson will not rest until he is assured the creature is destroyed. If his goal is to wipe out any and all evidence, the biggest piece of evidence is still out here somewhere."

Evelyn nodded. "Assuming you're right, how would Jackson get out here?"

Micah paused with a strained look on his face. *Should I tell them?* He finally shrugged. "You two might as well know now. This is classified information, but it will become evident sooner or later. Jackson requested the use of an Air Force chopper for transport a few hours ago. That one was transporting one person to a classified location in the Atlantic."

"A classified location . . . ?" John appeared perplexed. "In the middle of the ocean?"

"Got to be a ship." Suddenly, a look of understanding spread across Micah's face. "And that chopper pilot has got to know by now where he dropped off that person." Micah looked forward. "Lieutenant, can you raise the pilot of the other chopper that left Patrick before you did?"

"I can try, sir. We ought to be passing him any minute."

"Get him on the horn. I need to talk to him."

"Aye, sir." The pilot flipped a couple of switches. "Air Force Rescue Patrick, this is CG6077. Requesting location. Over."

"This is Air Force Rescue Patrick. Location is classified. Over."

"Air Force Rescue Patrick, I have Navy brass on board. Wants to talk directly to you. Do you copy?"

"Copy that."

"You're on, sir," the pilot told Micah.

"This is Captain Micah Gregson of Naval Intelligence." He relayed his Department of Defense identification number. "Do you copy?"

"Yes, sir."

"I'll wait while you run my number. But hurry. Time's ticking, soldier."

"Copy that."

The line went dead for over a minute before the Air Force pilot returned. "Identity and Coast Guard flight path confirmed, Captain. Go ahead."

"Who am I speaking to?"

"Lieutenant Reginald Rivers, sir."

"Lieutenant Rivers, I am in pursuit of a man who goes by his real name, Dr. Anthony Fontaine, and his alias, FBI Agent Archibald Jackson. Did you transport a man by either of those names to a ship within the last hour?"

"Captain, I would like to help you out, but my orders are explicit. I am not allowed to say anything about my mission."

"Lieutenant, I understand your orders and respect your willingness to follow them, but there is a situation brewing out here in the Atlantic that may be the precursor to World War III. The man you delivered to that ship could very well be the catalyst. Now, is there anything you can tell me about your mission?"

"No, sir."

"Who gave you these orders, Lieutenant? The orders not to talk, I mean?"

"They were part of the mission orders, sir. I was to fly dark until I dropped off the cargo. Once I rendezvoused with the target, then I was to return to base and tell no one of the mission. As you can see, I've already violated that directive."

"Lieutenant, you know the phrase 'I was just following orders' has gotten many a military man in trouble and saved very few of them."

The pilot of the returning HH-60 was silent.

"Not to mention the fact, Lieutenant, that you have already said more than you were supposed to. And more than likely, those orders to remain silent probably came from Dr. Fontaine himself. He *is* the one who originated those orders via FBI channels. I do know that much. And you can verify that as well, if you like."

"Okay," the pilot said. "I can tell you this much, but you didn't hear it from me. The ship was a destroyer. Arleigh Burke Class. The *USS Gettysburg*. The person I transported was an FBI agent. Last name Jackson." He sighed heavily into the mic. "And now I'm in hot water."

"No you're not, Lieutenant Rivers. That man you transported is being hunted by me, the FBI, and probably some other people we don't even know about. Trust me, those orders you are following came from him. That's his style. So if you break them, he's the only one that will be angry. And he has no authority in this matter."

"I hope you're right, sir."

"Lieutenant, trust me. Tell your superiors what you've just learned as soon as you land. Tell them Captain Micah Gregson of Naval Intelligence told you to do so. That is an order, Lieutenant. Do that, and you'll be covered. I will vouch for you."

"Yes, sir. I will."

Micah looked at Evelyn and John. "He's on a destroyer. He picked just the right boat to go hunting."

"Really?" Evelyn said.

"It's got everything he needs. A couple of shots from the five-inch guns, and your creature won't know what hit it."

"Micah, we've got to prevent him from killing it."

"We've got one thing going for us," John said. "The Atlantic is a big ocean, and the creature seems to have an expansive territory. So the odds of Jackson just running across it are in our favor."

Micah frowned. "I'm not as worried about that as I am Jackson running into the Russians."

Puzzled, Evelyn looked over at John. "Russians?"

John shrugged and raised his hands. "Don't look at me."

"You two might as well know this since you're on board with me," Micah said, turning to the pilot. "Lieutenant, what I am about to disclose is highly classified. You listen in at your own risk."

The pilot gave Micah a thumbs-up sign and switched off his headset.

Micah smiled. *I would have done the same thing.*

"The Russians lost a submarine out here about a day and a half ago," Micah began. "It was on its way to Venezuela after performing some missile tests in the Kara Sea, according to the Russians. While on its way, it sent a photograph taken by one of its outside cameras of what was referred to as a flipper. According to reports, the picture was rather uncertain, but the communiqué from the sub just before the Russians lost contact said they thought it was a flipper. Ever since, the Russians have been in the process of sending a recovery team to the last-known coordinates, which were about a hundred miles northeast of Nassau."

"Okay," Evelyn said, "so they're looking for their sub. What's that got to do with us?"

"The Russians asked for our help, and our government stalled while they tried to ascertain information about the creature and why the Russians were in that region of the world. I mean, think about it. The Kara Sea *is* a long way away from the Bahamas."

Evelyn seemed bewildered. "The Russians thought we had something to do with the submarine's disappearance?"

"They asked for our help, and we kept vacillating," Micah said. "Now, the Russians are skeptical—and rightfully so. We made ourselves look guilty.

"So late last night, President Walker finally deployed two ships, one of which we're scheduled to meet in about ten minutes. These two ships are being sent to help the Russians find their lost sub."

John's eyes lit up like he'd made some grand connection. "I get it. The Russians are only expecting two ships, not three."

Micah pointed at John and winked. "And since we do not know where Jackson is, he could pop up at the most inopportune time."

"And spook the Russians, making it look like we set some kind of trap," John said.

"Exactly. Part of our mission, if we make it, is to inform the two American ships of the situation and somehow alert the Russians before Jackson's boat is seen."

Evelyn scowled. "What do you mean, 'if we make it'?"

Micah took in a deep breath. "Let me rephrase that. This helicopter has a range of about a hundred and eighty miles round trip. The ship we're going to rendezvous with said they could meet us ninety miles off the coast of Satellite Beach before turning and heading for their destination. So we'll make it to the ship okay, but we'll need to get off quickly."

Revulsion struck Evelyn as what Micah said became clear. She gestured toward the pilot. "You mean, he may not make it back?"

Micah pursed his lips. "It'll be really close. He'll be flyin' on fumes the last mile or so, but he knew that going in, Evelyn. They're trained for situations just like this one. They'll have personnel waiting back at Patrick if they should need to mount a rescue."

"Does Jackson know how many people he's placed in harm's way?"

Micah smirked. "I'm sure he does. And I'm sure he doesn't care."

Anthony Fontaine had informed the bridge crew of their orders once he arrived, and the *USS Gettysburg* was well on her way to the coordinates Fontaine provided—*Latitude: 27 degrees North, 58 minutes, 29.9926 seconds; Longitude: 77 degrees West, 41 minutes, 3.5742 seconds.* The orders were simple. It was a search-and-destroy mission. Find the animal and kill it. Send it back to the depths from which it came. It was the same order Fontaine gave for every mission he and his team ever mounted.

If a creature was found, it was to be destroyed. No remains. No evidence of the killing. No record of the confrontation. Nothing. The government didn't want to have to house any remnants in some warehouse in the middle of the desert. They didn't want to have to answer for some report filed deep within the recesses of Washington's bureaucracy. They just wanted the problem to go away. Calling people "nut jobs" and "treasure seekers" was a lot easier than having to admit to anything.

The *USS Gettysburg* started searching for the creature as soon as Fontaine gave the order. It was to continue searching while en route to the coordinates. Before Fontaine was shown his quarters, he turned to the skipper before leaving the bridge. "I'm going to clean up and get a little rest, Commander. If you see anything, I want to be notified immediately."

"Very well, Agent Jackson," the commander said. "But before you retire to your quarters, sir, I must speak with you. Privately."

Fontaine eyed the commander for a moment. "Very well."

The commander motioned for them to leave the bridge and step outside into the night air. "Agent Jackson, you are aware that we are running dark, correct?"

Fontaine sprinkled disdain into his voice. "Yes, Commander, I ordered it."

"And you are also aware that we already have two ships heading for similar coordinates?"

"Yes, I was aware of that as well. We will reach those coordinates approximately an hour before they do. If we do not find the creature before then, we will initiate a grid search that will take us away from where they're heading. By the time they get there, we'll be out of the area and have no need to return."

"And what about the Russians?"

Fontaine's face remained deadpan. "What about them?"

"They have sent three ships to those very same coordinates."

"Yes, to look for their lost sub. I know that." Fontaine exhaled. "Those men are dead, Commander. Crushed by the depths of the ocean. They can look all they want, but we'll be long gone before they arrive, too."

"And if we're not? What am I allowed to tell them?"

"Tell them we are on a rescue mission as well. That we are looking for an American vessel lost in these waters yesterday, the day before, whatever. Make something up. I don't care, really, so long as they leave us alone to do our job. Just make sure your story is plausible."

The commander peered at Fontaine. "Understood."

"Now, Commander, if you will excuse me. I haven't slept in three days. I'm sure the bags under my eyes tell the entire story."

CHAPTER FORTY-SIX

Saturday, 12:55 a.m.
Aboard the USS Carney
Approximately 90 Nautical Miles East/Southeast of Satellite Beach, Florida

The MH-60T touched down, and Evelyn Sims, Micah Gregson, and John Spencer departed as fast as they could, being helped by crew members of the *USS Carney*. As soon as they and their gear cleared the rotors, the chopper leapt off the pad and started its trek back to shore. Evelyn stood on the deck as the bird disappeared into the dark sky, leaving only blinking lights visible as it veered to the west.

She gripped Micah by the arm. "Are you sure they'll make it back okay?"

"They should so long as the headwinds don't pick up."

"You used to do this sort of thing, didn't you?" Evelyn's eyes searched Micah's. "Risk your life to stop madmen like Jackson?"

Micah nodded in the direction of the flashing specks of light. "I've done much more dangerous things than that."

A man with several insignias embroidered on his shirt approached the trio with another officer flanking him. The first man saluted Micah. "Captain Gregson, I'm Commander Brandon Wilson. This is Executive Officer Charles Jordan. We were not aware that you would have company, sir."

Micah saluted the commander and his men. "This is Dr. Evelyn Sims and Dr. John Spencer," he said, pointing at each. "These two dear people are the two best marine biologists I know, and I need their expertise on this mission. They are to be treated as top brass, Commander."

"Understood, sir. If you'll follow me, I'll show you your quarters."

"Commander, before we settle in, I need to brief your bridge crew on the latest developments. It would seem things have become a bit more complex over the last hour."

"Commander Wilson, as you are aware, there are three Russian Federation ships heading for these coordinates," Micah said. He handed the commander a folded-up sheet of paper he extracted from the breast pocket of his jacket. "These are to be our new orders and coordinates as well."

The commander read the coordinates to his crew and the operations specialist sitting in front of the radar screen plunked a few keys on the keyboard. "Plotted in, sir."

"Good. Now, Commander," Micah said, "are you also aware of another American ship heading for those same coordinates?"

"Besides us and the *Philippine Sea*?"

"Yes."

The commander shook his head. "No, sir."

"There is a destroyer somewhere out there heading to what we believe are the same coordinates. It's the *Gettysburg*. We believe she's running dark, and she's got at least an hour head start. We believe she has orders to pursue and kill the creature that has been wreaking havoc out here. And if we get in her way, we might have a firefight on our hands."

"Two U.S. ships firing on each other? Never happen."

"Commander, do you know FBI Agent Archibald Jackson?"

He shook his head.

"I do, Commander. Don't believe for one second that he will not fire on you or the Russians. He is a rogue agent following his own orders."

"You do know, Captain, that if he fires on the Russians, he could start a war."

"That's why we have to find him before the Russians do."

Fontaine had been asleep for less than an hour when his cabin door opened.

"Sir, the commander would like to see you on the bridge."

Fontaine rolled over and rubbed his eyes. "Did they find something?"

"Sir, I'll let the commander apprise you of the situation."

"Status report, Commander."

The commander swung around, mic in hand. He was annoyed that a civilian would enter his bridge and think he was in charge, even if this civilian was part of the intelligence community. But he knew the orders. Fontaine was in charge of the mission. He had *carte blanche*.

"The Russians have spotted us," the commander said. "We reached our destination about ten minutes ago and began plotting a grid search when we were hailed. They've been asking for us to identify ourselves. I told them why we were here as we discussed earlier, but I don't think they bought it."

"You didn't identify us, did you?"

"Negative."

Fontaine grabbed a pair of night vision binoculars and scanned the horizon. "So, what did you tell them?"

"Just what you said to tell them. They said they had not heard of any American vessels going down out here."

"I don't care what they've heard or not heard. It's not their business. Tell them we are simply on a search-and-rescue mission and will not interfere with them in any way. Tell them we will be moving out of the area very soon."

"You know they'll call it in."

"I figured as much. The longer we stay unidentified, the better." Jackson continued to scan the area. "I don't see them. How did they find us?"

"Our transponder signal is disabled, per mission orders. They must be using satellite to track us."

"All the more reason not to trust them, eh, Commander?" Jackson set the binoculars down. "Adjust your grid search to take us away from their ships. Head east first, then north. That should keep us out of their way and out of the path of the other two American ships as well."

The Russian captain of the lead warship, *Peter the Great*, was not pleased.

He spoke in Russian. "We were told that the Americans were sending two ships from the west and would not arrive until after we had started our search. So, what is this ship doing here?"

His first mate motioned for his superior to step to the side of the bridge for a semiprivate discussion. "Captain, it could be a trap. This ship was running dark. Its transponder signal is not operational. Our sensors would have picked it up if it was. If it was not for the satellite you ordered over this sector, we would have never known she was here."

The captain scratched his head. "You answered my question. Why would they be running dark if they are just performing a search-and-rescue mission?"

"Exactly, Captain. Remember, before we were sent out, the politburo said they believed the Americans had something to hide."

"Comrade, we no longer have a 'politburo.'" The captain chuckled. "We are a democratic society now." His eyebrows rose.

"Of course, Captain. And I am Boris Yeltsin. Call it what you want. It will be a politburo again."

The captain gazed out over the waters in the direction of the *USS Gettysburg*. "It will be visible soon. We will need to know what we are supposed to do before that happens."

"What?" Russian Defense Minister Nicolai Nikitin said, holding his cell phone.

"It is true." One of Nikitin's trusted colleagues relayed the message from the captain of the lead warship. "We have a log and a transcript of the discussion between the two ships, plus the satellite images."

Defense Minister Nikitin slammed his cell phone shut. "Leave me," he said to the underling standing inside the door before bellowing some expletives in Russian and grabbing the phone on his desk and dialing.

The Russian defense minister spoke in his native tongue. "Prime Minister Korshanenko, we have a situation."

Minister Nikitin sat in Prime Minister Korshanenko's office, a large pine desk separating the two men. Korshanenko was pacing.

"What do you make of all this, my friend?"

"We have been duped. The Americans set us up."

"For what purpose?"

"Is it not obvious, sir?"

Korshanenko shrugged. "Perception is not always reality."

"So what are you saying?"

"That what appears to be a set-up may not be at all. There could be another explanation."

"What other explanation can there be other than ambushing our largest and most dangerous warship?"

The prime minister stopped pacing long enough to turn and gaze at his old comrade. "So, why not call President Walker and ask him?"

"Good luck with that, sir. He has been evading me all day."

"With all due respect, Nicolai, my calls carry a little more clout . . . or at least I hope they do." He smiled and stepped to his desk, picking up the receiver of a special phone.

"I need to speak with the president immediately."

"I'm afraid he is unavailable, sir," said the low-level secretary covering the White House night shift.

"Let me put it to you this way." Korshanenko's voice lowered in pitch but increased in volume. "If I do not talk to President Walker in two minutes, he will wake up to World War III."

A Secret Service officer tapped on the president's bedroom door of the White House. "Sir, I hate to wake you, but there is an incident that needs your immediate attention."

After a few woozy moments, the president rolled out of bed and draped his robe around him, cinching it up with the belt. "What now, Atkins?"

The Russian prime minister is on the phone. He claims if we put him off until morning, you'll wake up to World War III."

President Walker rolled his eyes. "Korshanenko can be so dramatic sometimes. But if he's calling, it must be of some urgency. He usually has his staff handle things."

The Secret Service agent escorted him to the nearest phone.

President Walker motioned for Agent Atkins to exit the room.

"Prime Minister Korshanenko, how is your search proceeding? I hope everything is going well."

The prime minister skipped the pleasantries. "President Walker, why is there another American ship in the area where our sub went down? You told my people there would only be two ships, but instead, there are three, and the third is sailing dark. So, Mr. President, what is happening? It would appear that for some unknown reason—at least unknown to us—you have a covert plan in operation."

President Walker's jaw dropped open a little. "What are you talking about? I only sanctioned two boats. That's it. There shouldn't be any more of our ships out there."

"Well, Mr. President, there is a third ship out there. In fact, they have already arrived at the coordinates ahead of *our* search-and-rescue team and *your* other two ships. They told our lead captain they were on a search-and-rescue mission of their own. They said they were looking for an American vessel that had been lost at sea? Were you aware of any missing American ships in that region, Mr. President?"

The president seethed into the phone. "No. But give me ten minutes, and I'll have an answer for the both of us."

"Please be aware, Mr. President, that if I do not get a sufficient answer before our ships arrive and obtain a visual, they have been instructed to engage that vessel and board her. If they resist, they will be detained. If they become hostile, my lead captain has my authority to sink her."

Approaching from the west, running near full throttle, were the *USS Carney* and the *USS Philippine Sea*.

"How much longer, Commander?" Micah said.

"About an hour at present speed."

"What is our current speed?"

"Thirty knots."

"Pretty much maxed out, aren't we?"

Commander Wilson smiled, impressed that Micah knew the specs of his ship. "Yes, sir. I might be able to get a smidgen more out of her."

Micah's eyes perked. "The faster the better, Commander. This *is* a race."

Just then, a call came in.

"Commander," another petty officer said, "I have a call for you. It's Admiral Stevenson."

Commander Wilson's eyebrows shot up as he looked at Micah. "I wonder what he wants."

Micah said nothing. He just wanted to hear, picking up an extension.

"Yes, Admiral. This is Commander Wilson."

"Commander, I have just been informed by the president that we possibly have a rogue ship in your vicinity. Can you confirm this?"

The commander cleared his throat. "Yes, sir. I was made aware of that ship about two hours ago."

"You mean to tell me, Commander, that you've been aware of an unauthorized vessel in your vicinity and didn't notify anyone?"

The commander glared at Micah. An expression of frustration and desire for help filled his face.

"Admiral Stevenson, this is Captain Micah Gregson of Naval Intelligence. I am aboard the *Carney* right now. I was the one who informed Commander Wilson and his crew of the ship in question. I also told him not to report it for three reasons: first of all, because we do not know the location of the vessel in question yet; secondly, the other vessel could be monitoring our transmissions, and third, this other ship probably has been authorized to carry out its mission at all costs, so the crew of that third ship does not believe they are doing anything wrong or unauthorized."

"Who authorized that vessel?" the admiral said.

"We're not sure, sir," Micah said, "but I have reason to believe an FBI agent by the name of Archibald Jackson is aboard that ship and calling the shots. He probably issued the authorization himself."

"FBI? They have no—" The admiral cursed. "What was that agent's name again?"

"Archibald Jackson, sir," Micah said. He explained the situation, getting the agitated admiral up to speed on Jackson's role.

"I don't believe this," the admiral said. "Do we have any idea what Jackson's intentions are?"

"Well, sir, we believe he's out to destroy the creature that attacked the *Greenback* and the *Titan*. We also believe this creature could very well have been the cause of the Russian sub's disappearance."

"Give me the name of the ship, Captain, and I'll order her back immediately."

"It's the *Gettysburg*, Admiral, but they're running dark. They've disarmed their transponder signal and will not answer our hails."

"Captain, what is your purpose on the *Carney*?"

"To use this ship in stopping Agent Jackson before he does something all of us will regret, sir."

"How do you propose to accomplish this feat?"

"That is still undetermined, sir. We won't know until we confront them."

"That's not very consoling, Captain."

"Yes, sir. I agree, but under the circumstances, we cannot predict with any certainty Agent Jackson's intentions at this time."

The admiral sighed. "Let me call the president back. Keep this channel clear."

The Russian captain of *Peter the Great* hunched over the map of the Atlantic, studying it with his first mate. He was trying to put the finishing touches on their search-and-rescue mission for the *Kirov*.

"I wonder why we have not heard anything from the defense minister yet," the first mate said.

The captain stared at the same spot on the map. "I am sure he is trying to avoid Armageddon."

"But we would have the advantage, Captain. Our government was told by the Americans that they were only sending two ships. Now a third one materializes? And I bet they will tell us they did not know anything about it, no? So, who has got the right to act?"

The captain tossed the grease pencil down on the table. "We may have the right to act in our defense, but if World War III starts as a result, will there be any true winners?"

"Yes. We will win."

"At what cost, Alexei? We shoot, they shoot. We bomb, they bomb. We fire ballistic missiles, they shoot missiles. We drop *the* bomb, they drop one, too. Our allies join in; their allies join in. By the time it is over, the radiation alone would make life unbearable for decades. So, comrade, I ask you, who truly wins?"

The first mate mulled over his commander's words. "Your point is well taken. Nevertheless, if we do not act in a strong fashion, the world will perceive us as weak. That is all our enemies need—an excuse to invade."

The captain peered at his first mate with wrinkled brows. "You live too much in the past, my friend. You have too much communist blood still coursing through your veins."

The first mate beamed a huge grin. "Why thank you, Captain."

"I have spoken with our top military people, Prime Minister," President Walker said. "No one seems to know why that ship is out there or why it is running silent."

The prime minister wrapped his fingers on the desk. "So, Mr. President, you have a very capable warship in the middle of the Atlantic following its own orders. Is that what you are telling me?"

"For now, yes, but I am going to send orders to the other two ships to intercept that rogue vessel and take control of her."

"And if she does not comply?"

"They will have orders to sink her."

"How long will this take? Remember, Mr. President, we have a submarine to find. Time is crucial."

"I understand. Our two ships should be in the vicinity within the hour. Please inform your vessels to remain stationary until we can find this other ship."

"I can give you until our ships arrive. Once they do, they will commence with their search. And if any of your ships get in their way, Mr. President, or try to prevent them from conducting their search—"

"You don't have to threaten me, Victor. I know what's at stake."

CHAPTER FORTY-SEVEN

Saturday, 2:57 a.m.
Latitude: 27 degrees North, 58 minutes, 29.9926 seconds
Longitude: 77 degrees West, 41 minutes, 3.5742 seconds.
Approximately 80 Nautical Miles North of Cooperstown, Bahamas

Peter the Great arrived at the coordinates with the other two Russian vessels. Although its captain had requested a Russian satellite be moved over the designated area to aid in the search for the missing submarine, little did he know he would also use it to track the unidentified American ship. It made the Russian captain feel uneasy. *I don't like having my enemies scattered all around me,* he thought. Despite his edginess, his demeanor was one of someone fully in charge.

"Let us get the science team into position. I want them in the water at daylight."

"What about the American ships, Captain? They are almost here."

"Communicate with them that we will conduct the search

ourselves at first. We need them to be on standby in case we require their assistance."

"Aye, Captain," the first mate said. "Communications Officer, hail the American ships."

The officer switched some dials. "American vessels, *USS Carney* and *Philippine Sea*, this is the Russian warship, *Peter the Great*. Do you copy?"

"*Peter the Great*, we read you loud and clear. Over."

"Captain," the communications officer said, "I have them."

The captain stepped over to the officer's station and took the mic. "This is Captain Mikhail Siniakov. To whom am I speaking?"

"This is Commander Brandon Wilson of the *USS Carney*. We have you within visual range, Captain. We should be with you momentarily. Over."

"Commander Wilson, I believe the safest and most prudent way to handle this operation is for us to begin our search for the *Kirov* alone. If you will remain one kilometer away, that will give us a wide enough berth to conduct the search using our science team. If we need your assistance, we will contact you with specific directions. Over."

Commander Wilson peered over at Captain Gregson. "What about Jackson?"

"Inform the Russians," Micah said, "that we have new orders that just came down. Those orders are to assist them in their search by intercepting the *Gettysburg* and boarding her."

The commander did just that.

"I hope your missing ship will not pose a threat to the success of our rescue mission," the Russian captain said.

"So do we."

"Very well. Please inform us of any other changes. Over."

"We will, Captain Siniakov."

"Captain," the Russian first mate said, "why didn't you tell them that we already know where that vessel is based on our satellite imagery?"

"Ahh, Alexei, you have so much to learn. Although we are supposed to be one big, happy, democratic family now, we never show our hand unless it is necessary. I do not want them to know we have a satellite watching."

"I was always terrible at poker," the first mate said.

The captain placed his hand on his first mate's shoulder. "You have got to know when to hold them, know when to fold them," he said with a wink.

They both laughed.

Commander Wilson switched off the mic and turned to face the bridge crew. "Begin plotting a grid search for the *Gettysburg* and utilize radar as best we can."

"Commander, do we have access to any satellites in the area?" Micah said.

"No. I already checked. It will be another two hours to get one into position."

"May I?" Micah said, motioning toward the crew.

The commander nodded.

"When you plot that grid search, plot it starting north, then east. Agent Jackson is cunning but not experienced. More than likely, he started his search heading east because he knew we were coming from the west and the Russians were coming from the north. He then would head north, then west, circling around behind us. So, if we head north, then east, we should intercept him at some point."

The bridge crew nodded, understanding Micah's logic.

"All right, people, get to work," Commander Wilson said.

"Agent Jackson, we have something on sonar," the commander of the *Gettysburg* said. "It's faint, but it's there."

Jackson strolled over to the sonar station. Peering at the screen, he saw a mass moving underneath them, parallel to the ship. One second it was there; the next second, it disappeared.

"What's our position?" Jackson said.

"We have traveled three nautical miles since our turn to the north," the helmsman said. "We are twelve nautical miles from our beginning coordinates."

"Full stop, Commander," Jackson said. "Let's see what this blob does."

"Full stop," the commander said. He then listened to his crew bark the order down the ranks.

They watched as the sonar contact slid ahead of the ship, still phasing on and off the screen. It drifted ahead of the ship's position by one thousand yards before banking.

Jackson never took his eyes off the screen. "How deep is this thing?"

"Sonar contact at four hundred meters," the operation specialist said.

Agent Jackson shook his head in disbelief. "Can you determine the size of the contact from here?"

"No, sir. Not at this depth."

"What's it doing?" Jackson said.

The sonar contact, having turned a complete hundred and eighty degrees, was now growing larger. The contact on the screen had almost doubled in size.

"The contact is closing in on our position, sir . . . three hundred and fifty meters . . . three twenty-five . . . three hundred meters and still closing."

"Commander, if this is what I think it is, and we suffer a direct hit from below, it might split this ship in two," Jackson said.

The commander smiled while half of the bridge crew snickered. "You're kidding, right?"

"No, Commander, I'm not. This creature, if this is actually it, attacked a full-size passenger cruise ship. It put a six-foot crease in the hull. We assume it was from a direct hit."

"Agent Jackson, with all due respect to whatever it is you're hunting out here, we can manage a direct hit. Unless this thing shoots torpedoes, we're okay," the commander said with a nod.

"When we do confront this thing," Jackson said, "we will see how smug you are."

"Sonar contact has shifted direction, Commander," the operation specialist said. "New bearing two-seven-zero."

"What does that mean?" Jackson said.

"It's shifted its course and no longer heading in our direction."

"Then follow it, Commander."

"That takes us right back to the Russians. Not a good plan."

"Look, Commander, if you don't have the stomach for it, then I can get someone in here who does."

"Oh, I've got the stomach for it, Agent Jackson. No worries there. But starting World War III is not on my bucket list."

"I'll handle the Russians. Follow that contact until we can determine what it is."

The commander stared at Agent Jackson, wondering what kind of sociopathic maniac he'd been ordered to allow on his ship. Without moving his eyes away, he said, "Helmsman, follow the contact. But keep me updated on distance to the Russians."

CHAPTER FORTY-EIGHT

Saturday, 3:22 a.m.
Aboard the USS Carney

Evelyn Sims and John Spencer, refreshed from a shower and a quick meal, were escorted to the bridge of the *USS Carney* wearing naval jumpsuits in place of their dirty clothes. The two marine biologists stood in awe as they entered, watching the men and women of the bridge crew perform their tasks.

Micah noticed his two friends enter. "Evelyn, John, come on in. You're just in time."

Evelyn's eyes were wide. "I've never been on a ship like this before. So, this is what you do, Micah?"

"Well, not anymore. My boat's a lot smaller than this, but I used to command ships like this, yes."

Evelyn gazed into Micah's face. "What an awesome job."

Micah tilted his head. "Maybe you should refrain from those comments until this ordeal is over."

Evelyn scrunched her forehead.

"Trouble?" John said.

"There's been a change of plans since you went to your quarters," Micah said. "We've started looking for Jackson's ship. We left the Russians about fifteen minutes ago and are heading north. The *Philippine Sea* won't be staying to help the Russians either."

"What happens if we can't find Jackson?"

"That's just it. We have to. I have them searching for the creature while we search for Jackson's ship as well. If we find the creature first, it may lead us right to Jackson." Micah glanced around at the bridge crew. "Here's where it gets dicey."

"Oh, I'm not a big fan of *dicey*," John said.

Micah let out a small chuckle. "It's one thing to have one ship chase you, catch you, and demand that you stop and allow yourself to be boarded. When two ships enter the fray, you usually feel backed into a corner with only one way out."

John formed his hands into revolvers. "Butch and Sundance."

"Yeah, but the guns are torpedoes and cannons instead. And since the person running the show on the *Gettysburg* is Agent Jackson, you know they aren't going to go down without a fight."

"Is there a way you can contact the captain of that ship and talk some sense into him? Have him arrest Jackson?" Evelyn said.

"That's one of our plans. But we can't get them to respond to any of our hails."

Evelyn glanced around the bridge and then grasped Micah by the arm, pulling him aside. "Micah, let's say we find this creature before Jackson does. What are we going to do with it?"

"I'm glad you asked." Micah perked up as if prepared to hand over a gift to a beloved friend. He spun around on a pivot. "Commander, were you able to get fitted for the special harpoon before you left?"

The commander frowned. "No, sir, but we were able to secure the next best thing." He motioned for them to follow.

The commander led Evelyn, Micah, and John outside, up some stairs, and onto a special platform which sat on top of the bridge. It was rigged for a man to stand and act as either lookout or sniper. Commander Wilson placed his hand on a gun that was secured to the wall.

"This is a modified tranquilizer gun with a heavy duty, hollow, spear gun shaft and a steel cable attached for retrieval. It can be fitted with this spearhead that spreads to a width of one foot once it pierces the target. You first shoot the animal with the dart. The dart injects its contents and tranquilizes the animal. Then you attach the spearhead, which is already fastened to this braided cable, and you shoot the animal again. The spearhead is designed to ram through the target. Then the cable stays with the target until immobilization takes place. After that, it's only a matter of reelin' it in."

"You make it sound so simple, Commander," Evelyn said.

"It is, actually."

"Oh, really." Evelyn's eyebrows arched. "So, what pound test line do you have there, Commander? I hope it's a doozy."

The commander looked perplexed.

"You know how much the animal weighs?"

"No, Doctor, but we believe this cable can handle it."

"Okay. Let's say you're right. So, what's the heart rate of the animal? What is the metabolic rate? Which barbiturates should we use and not use to tranquilize it?"

The commander shrugged.

Evelyn turned toward Micah. "I understand what you're trying to do here. And it might very well work, but I seriously doubt it. What if the tranquilizer doses are too high? If they are, you'll kill it in a matter of minutes. You'll do the same thing if the animal has an allergic reaction to it. Animals react to medications just like we do—each to its own. Some work and some don't." She huffed a sigh. "Don't you see, Micah? There are too many variables. It's never been tried before. So none of us knows how it will play out."

"That's a risk we're gonna have to take, Doctor," the commander said.

"Okay, then, Commander. What if the animal dies? Can this ship stay afloat under the dead weight of an expired sea monster?"

Commander Wilson looked unsure. "I think we could handle it. Of course, we can always cut the line if we have to."

Micah held up his hands. "Evelyn, we get it."

"Do we?" Evelyn said. "Have you thought about what you plan on doing with it once it's caught? There isn't a tank built that is big enough to house an animal this size." She looked at all three men. "Where are you going to put it, gentlemen?"

"Evelyn, it's either this gun or those over there." Micah pointed to the five-inch, .54-caliber guns.

When Evelyn turned and saw the huge cannon-looking weaponry, she dropped her head slightly.

John patted the tranquilizer gun. "I vote for this one. I understand what you're saying, Evelyn, but at least this gun gives us a chance to save this creature from the likes of Jackson. You know which guns he's going to use."

Micah and the commander looked at each other. Being military-trained, they were on the same page.

"Evelyn," Micah said, "it's your call. We'll do whatever you decide. You're the expert here. But you need to decide before we come in contact with the creature. There can be no hesitation once we confront this animal."

Just then, a voice came over the ship intercom. "Commander Wilson, please report to the bridge. Commander Wilson, please report to the bridge."

The commander looked at Evelyn and Micah. "Doctor Sims, you might have to make that decision a little sooner than you thought."

Operations Specialist Second Class Richie Higgins, manning the sonar for the *USS Carney*, detected a mass heading in the ship's direction. "Commander, you've got to see this. Sonar contact, bearing two-seven-zero."

The commander stepped to the console and leaned in for a better look. "What is it, Higgins?"

"I'm not sure, sir. It comes and goes, but it is definitely heading this way. No, wait, it's heading south of us."

"Commander, that bearing will take whatever it is straight to the Russians," Micah said.

"Should we alert them?" John said.

"Alert them of what?" The commander swiveled his head. "'You have an unidentified mass of something heading straight for you. We don't know what it is, but be careful?' They'll think we've lost our minds."

"I wonder why it's heading for their ship?" Micah said.

"Higgins, contact the Russian captain," the commander said, "and ask him if they've started trying to find their submarine yet."

"Aye, Commander," Officer Higgins said. "Russian vessel, *Peter the Great*, this is the *USS Carney*. Do you copy?"

"*USS Carney*, this is *Peter the Great*. Go ahead."

"Have you started your search for the *Kirov* yet? Over."

"We have begun first sonar scans, yes. Over."

Evelyn grasped Micah's shoulder. "That's why this thing is heading straight for them."

"How do you know?" Commander Wilson said.

"This creature is a deep diver, Commander," Evelyn said. She turned toward crewman Higgins. "How deep is it right now?"

The commander motioned for the operations specialist to answer.

"Sonar contact still bearing two-seven-zero. Depth: three hundred meters and rising."

"That's nine hundred feet, gentlemen. At that depth, sonar is the only way to navigate. So, if the Russians are using sonar to search for their lost sub, they are sending those signals straight down. They'll draw that animal in like a shark to blood."

The commander eyed Micah and John, asking for their opinions.

"She's right," John said. "And if this thing is hungry, meeting it face to face will not be pleasant."

"Captain Siniakov, this is Commander Wilson. Do you copy?" the commander said, waiting for a response.

"This is Captain Siniakov. Go ahead."

"Captain, we have reason to believe that your sonar activity might be drawing in a bogey."

"A bogey? I am not sure I know that term, Commander."

"A hostile, Captain."

"What makes you think that, Commander?"

"Have your sonar officer verify with ours," Commander Wilson said, turning to crewman Higgins. "What's the latest bearing?"

"Sonar contact still bearing two-seven-zero. Distance: two nautical miles; Depth: two hundred and fifty meters and rising. Speed: twenty knots and slowing."

"Can your sonar station verify, Captain?" Commander Wilson said.

"Stand by, Commander," the Russian captain said.

Captain Siniakov stepped over to the console. "Sonar, can we verify?"

"Yes, Captain. There is a sonar contact bearing two-seven-zero. It's heading straight for us. Also, confirmed at two hundred and fifty meters and rising."

"Is it a torpedo?"

"No, sir, but it is on a collision course."

"Stop all sonar activity," the Russian captain said. "Let's see if it stops."

"Agent Jackson, the sonar contact has changed direction, sir."

"What's the new heading?"

"It is banking, sir."

"Depth?"

"Two hundred meters."

"Distance from the Russian ship?"

"Two nautical miles."

"What's our present speed?"

"Twenty-five knots."

Agent Jackson peered out into the night sky. "Amazing. We were doing twenty knots, and we lost ground? That thing was right under us before it took off."

The commander glowered at Agent Jackson. "Whatever it is, Agent Jackson, it can outmaneuver us and outrun us."

The Russian petty officer manning the sonar station started pressing buttons and grabbing his headset. "Captain, satellite imagery is showing the other American ship has turned. It was heading north at bearing zero-zero-five, but it has changed to bearing two-seven-zero. Speed: was twenty-five knots but has increased to thirty knots within the last few minutes. Distance: fourteen nautical miles."

The Russian captain had returned to his chair, awaiting news on the hostile's reaction to their temporary stoppage of sonar activity. *It would seem,* he thought, *that there may be two with which to contend. One of flesh. One of metal.* "What about the hostile?"

"Sonar contact has changed bearing and depth. It initially turned and was on bearing one-three-zero, but it has changed again, Captain. New bearing: zero-eight-five. Depth: two hundred meters."

"It is searching," the captain said in a whisper.

The first mate didn't hear the captain. "Sir?"

The captain jumped from his chair and walked to the sonar console. "It is searching for something, Lieutenant. It was heading straight for us until we stopped our sonar activity. Now, it has turned and headed back the other way and turned again. It is searching."

"Good heavens, Captain. What is it?" the first mate said.

"It would seem, Alexei, we may have found Leviathan."

"Helm, turn this ship around," Commander Wilson said. He slapped the back of his captain's chair in anger. "Head for the sonar contact."

"Commander, sonar contact has changed direction twice since the Russians shut down their sonar sweeps. It is now at bearing zero-eight-five."

The commander turned to Evelyn. "Interesting. Doctor Sims, what do you make of that?"

Evelyn lifted her shoulders a little. "You stopped the bleeding, so now, the shark goes into search mode, trying to pick up the scent again."

"Doctor, what if we start sending sonar pulses down to the bottom? That would draw it to us, correct?"

"More than likely."

"Captain Gregson, what's your opinion?"

"That's a good idea, Commander." Micah bobbed his head. "Draw that animal to us, and while doing so, we just might draw the *Gettysburg* as well."

"I have a question," John said. His hand was raised.

"Go ahead," the commander said.

"We are just assuming this thing swimming around down there is the creature. But we don't know that. It could be something else."

The commander was troubled that things might not be as black and white as he thought. "So, you're suggesting this could be some other sea creature?"

"No, it's true. John's right," Evelyn said. "It could be a giant squid. Could be a sperm whale. Could be something else."

"That may be true," Micah said, "but we need to proceed as if it is the creature. Until it surfaces, no one will know, including Jackson. By then, it will be too late for him."

"And what happens if Jackson starts shooting at the creature when it's close to us?"

"Evelyn, those are risks we'll have to take."

She shook her head. "I'd never make it in the military."

"Trust me. Just because we do things the way we do doesn't mean we like them all the time. Getting shot at by an American frigate while trying to battle some sea dragon is not my idea of an acceptable situation. But it may be the only option we get." Micah started to walk away. He then stopped. "If things get scary, you might want to get a life vest on."

"You're kidding, right?" Evelyn laughed. "Float around in the middle of the Atlantic while an eighty-foot sea monster lurks in the water? No, thanks."

"Beats treading water," John said.

Evelyn stared Micah right in the eyes. "I'll think about it."

The *USS Carney* had made its turn and was doubling back toward the sonar contact, launching indiscriminate pings, trying to draw the attention of the creature.

"Higgins, has the sonar contact changed its heading?"

"No, sir. Contact is still at bearing zero-eight-five."

"Why would it head that way?" the commander said.

"There's no telling, Commander," Evelyn said. "It could be simply searching for its next meal."

Just then, a lookout caught sight of a dim light in the distance off their port bow and called it over the radio.

"That's not the Russian ship, is it?" Commander Wilson said.

"Negative. Russian ship is dead ahead, sir."

"That must be the *Gettysburg*, Commander," Micah said. "Their heading straight for the Russians."

"Higgins, what's the location of the sonar contact?"

"Sonar contact still bearing zero-eight-five, sir. It is heading straight for that ship."

"What's its depth and speed?" Micah said.

"Depth: a hundred and fifty meters and rising. Speed: twenty knots."

"Wow," Commander Wilson said. "That thing is movin'."

"But why?" Micah turned to Evelyn. "That doesn't sound like a leisurely search for a meal to me. That sounds like an attack."

"Could the other ship be doing the same thing we are?" John said.

The commander stared at John. The sudden suggestion of something so simple made him blink before nodding.

"Pinging, I mean," John said.

"That's exactly what they're doing, John," Micah said. "They're drawing the creature in."

"Helm," the commander said, "get us to that ship ASAP. Communications, hail that vessel by name."

"Agent Jackson, we're being hailed. By name. They know who we are and that we're out here."

"By whom?"

"It's the *USS Carney*. They're telling us to stop all transmissions including our sonar activity and prepare to be boarded."

"Oh, they are, are they?" Jackson said. "Helm, increase speed. I want to get to the Russians before the *Carney* gets to us."

"Why?" the commander said. "We're just asking for trouble."

"No, Commander. We'll actually be saving ourselves and the others. If we use the Russians as a shield, it will buy us more time. The last thing Washington wants is to have one of their ships boarded by a 'friendly' in front of hundreds of Russian sailors."

Jackson snaked around to the sonar station. "Commander, tell the *Carney* to stay away. Tell them we are conducting a top-secret operation, and if they proceed with their plans, we have orders to shoot."

"I can relay most of that message, sir, but I will not tell a fellow Navy vessel that we will fire on them."

Jackson envisioned having the commander thrown into the brig. He thought better of it, realizing he might start a mutiny. "Very well, then."

The commander snatched the mic off its cradle and took a deep breath. "Commander, *USS Carney*, this is the commander of the *USS Gettysburg*. Do you copy?"

"Commander, *USS Gettysburg*, we copy. Go ahead."

"Who am I speaking with?"

"This is Commander Brandon Wilson. Who am I speaking with?"

"Commander Thomas Goodrich. Over."

"Commander Goodrich, we have orders from the President of the United States to stop your vessel and board her. Do you copy?"

Commander Goodrich glared at Agent Jackson. "What have you done?"

Jackson's expression was unbending, intransigent. "I haven't done anything, Commander. I have a job to do, and the president will have to wait until we're finished."

"Agent Jackson, with all due respect, the president's orders supersede anything you may have. I am stopping this vessel right now. Helmsman, full stop."

Jackson drew his weapon and pointed it at Commander Goodrich. "Belay that order, Helmsman. We will not stop until we have reached the Russian ships. Is that understood?"

"You're mad," the commander said.

"And you're getting on my nerves." Jackson pulled the trigger, sending the commander to the ground, holding his shoulder. "Cross me again, Commander, and the next shot will be between the eyes." Jackson punched a button on the communications console. "We need a medic on the bridge."

"Commander, they aren't stopping," Operations Specialist Richie Higgins of the *USS Carney* said.

Commander Wilson looked over at Captain Gregson. "You know this Agent Jackson better than I do. What do you think is going on over there?"

"He's probably arguing with Commander Goodrich right now."

Commander Wilson pressed the mic button once more. "Commander Goodrich, did you copy? You are to stop your vessel and cease all sonar activity. Over."

“Give me all your weapons,” Jackson said to the bridge crew, his gun aimed at the lieutenant. “One at a time.”

Reluctant yet stymied, the bridge crew of the *Gettysburg* conceded to the agent’s demands. Jackson collected the firearms, placing an extra pistol in his waistband before throwing the other weapons outside of the bridge.

Jackson motioned to the petty officer. “Lock the doors. No one gets in or out without permission.”

“What about the other ships?” the commander’s first mate said.

“You’re going to tell them, Lieutenant, we have our orders from the president as well and will not stop until we have completed our mission.”

“They won’t believe it.”

Jackson cocked his gun in one heartless motion. “I don’t care what they believe. Send the message.”

Operations Specialist Richie Higgins, aboard the *USS Carney*, grabbed his headset. “Commander, sonar contact has changed direction again.”

“What’s its new bearing?”

“Bearing two-nine-zero, sir. It’s heading straight for us.”

“Distance?”

“Six nautical miles.”

“Depth?”

“One hundred meters and rising.”

“Speed?”

“Twenty knots and slowing.”

Just then, the microphone beeped.

“This is the *Gettysburg*,” came a different voice. “We have our orders from the president as well and will not stop until we have completed our mission. Please respect a fellow American vessel. Over.”

Commander Wilson looked at Micah. “Is that Jackson’s voice?”

Micah shook his head. "I'm not sure, but regardless, he's not going to identify himself if he can help it."

"I wonder what happened to Commander Goodrich."

Micah's eyebrows lifted. "No tellin' with Jackson."

"Could what he said be true, Captain Gregson? Could they be operating off some old orders from the president?"

"No, Jackson's been issuing his own orders." Micah gave a brief explanation of Jackson's role in the events of the last couple of days.

The commander pressed the mic. "I want to speak with Commander Goodrich. Over."

"Commander Goodrich is unavailable at this time, sir. Over."

"Who is this?"

"Lieutenant Scott Windham, sir. I am Commander Goodrich's first lieutenant. Over."

"Where is Commander Goodrich, Lieutenant?"

"He . . . had an accident, sir. He'll be okay, but he is unfit at present to command this vessel. Over."

"So, Lieutenant Windham, that means you are in charge now," Commander Wilson said. "As your ranking officer, I command you to stop your vessel immediately, stop all sonar activity, and prepare to be boarded. Do you copy?"

Lieutenant Windham looked at Agent Jackson with raised shoulders. "He's right."

Jackson stood motionless, his gun still trained on the lieutenant's head.

"What do you want me to say?" Windham said.

"Stall. Tell them we will have to check with Washington or your superiors or whoever. Just stall them."

"You know, Agent Jackson," Windham said, "if we could send them a copy of our orders, that might do the trick. They would then be forced to contact Washington themselves to get clarification, which would buy you the time you need."

Jackson gripped his gun tighter. His mind was analyzing the move to decide if it conformed to the overall game plan. "Then what happens when they discover their orders are newer than ours, Lieutenant?"

"By the time they confirm it, we will have reached the Russian vessel."

Jackson inhaled, lowered his weapon, and pulled out an envelope from his jacket pocket. Looking back and forth between the envelope and Lieutenant Windham, he handed it to the lieutenant, lifting his weapon again as he did. "No funny business. Send them exactly what's on that page."

"Aye." Windham took the envelope from Jackson's hand, opened the envelope, and pulled the page out. Unfolding it, his eyes flared with disbelief as he read the words. Sitting down at the communications station, Lieutenant Windham began to tap out a message in Morse code.

> *Lieutenant of* USS Gettysburg *to Commander of* USS Carney. *Stop. Orders for this vessel confirmed. Stop. Following message is exact wording. Stop.* USS Gettysburg *is ordered to seek and destroy unknown creature that attacked civilian vessel* Greenback *and commercial vessel* Titan. *Stop.* USS Gettysburg *is to sail dark until mission is completed. Stop. End of transmission.*

As he sent the last letters of the communiqué, he added seven additional letters not in the original orders: C-O-D-E-R-E-D.

CHAPTER FORTY-NINE

Saturday, 4:14 a.m.
Approximately 80 Nautical Miles North of Cooperstown, Bahamas

"Uh-oh. Commander."

"What is it, Higgins?"

"We just received the orders from the *Gettysburg*. They look legitimate, sir, but listen to the end of the transmission." He read them back, word for word, including the final message: Code Red.

Micah shot a look at Commander Wilson. "Code Red."

Commander Wilson nodded.

"Code Red?" Evelyn looked confused. "It sounds bad, but what does it mean?"

"It means something's wrong over there," Micah said. "Knowing Jackson, he's probably taken out Commander Goodrich. That would explain why he's not responding anymore."

"This Agent Jackson of yours must be a double idiot if he thinks he can commandeer a destroyer and get away with it."

"Commander, you won't hear me argue the double idiot part. But one thing I've learned in the three or so days I've dealt with Agent Jackson and from what I read in his FBI file; he doesn't do anything 'off the cuff.' If he commandeered that ship, he has an exit strategy already planned. And he's not afraid to kill anyone who gets in his way. He's already killed one person we know of. I'm sure there are others."

The commander squinted his eyes in anger. "He wouldn't?"

"He will fire on this boat if he feels threatened, yes."

Commander Wilson ran his hand over his balding head and down the back of his neck. "Then we have no choice. We have to disable them before they can get a shot off at us."

"And how do you propose we do that, Commander?" Micah said.

"We remain silent and put ourselves between them and the Russians. Then, confront them one last time. If they comply, great. If they don't, then we send a coded message to Lieutenant Windham telling him of what we are going to do before we fire. That will give him time to get the crew ready."

"That's awfully risky, Commander. If they fire at us and miss, the Russians will be in the line of fire."

"We'll make sure if they miss us, the Russians will be far enough off our stern and to one side or the other."

"Commander, may I make another suggestion?" Micah said.

"If you've got a better idea, I'm all ears."

"Fire an MK-32 now while they're not expecting it. Detonate it just before contact. The blast might damage the ship enough to immobilize her without sinking her. Then, at the same time, send the *Philippine Sea* to flank the *Gettysburg* from the north. With two ships mounting an attack, Jackson will not be able to focus on the Russians or the creature."

"Then what?" Commander Wilson said. "If this Agent Jackson is as treacherous as you say he is, then who's to stop him from firing back?"

"We would alert Windham ahead of time like you suggested. When the blast hits, he should be able to jump Jackson and overpower him and take over the bridge."

Commander Wilson stared at Micah. "I don't like relying on one person I don't even know."

"Neither do I, Commander. I'm not even sure Windham can overpower Jackson, but what choice do we have?"

Commander Wilson turned and walked away from Micah. "Higgins, what's the status on the contact?"

"Bearing two-nine-zero. Depth: seventy meters and rising. Distance: three nautical miles. Speed: ten knots and slowing."

"Distance from the *Gettysburg*?"

"Seven nautical miles, sir."

"Are we still sending out sonar sweeps?"

"Yes, Commander."

"So, we might make contact with the creature before we get to the *Gettysburg*. That'll draw them to us."

Micah stepped closer. "Trust me, Commander. If Agent Jackson thinks you will do something to hinder his mission, he will fire on your vessel. Reaching the creature before he does would definitely accomplish that."

"But wasn't that our plan before? Draw the creature to us first? And then draw the *Gettysburg* in, too?"

"Yes, Commander. That was our plan when we were twenty miles away from them and a lot farther away from the Russians than we are now. And, it was our plan when we had a Naval commander in charge of that ship."

Commander Wilson spun around on a pivot. "Stop all sonar sweeps," he said, walking over to his first lieutenant. "Plot a solution for the MK-32. I want it blown up twenty yards off her starboard bow. Hopefully, the concussion of the blast will disorient them enough."

"But sir," the first lieutenant said, "twenty yards that close to the surface might tear a hole in the side, especially if it detonates closer than that."

"The bulkheads should prevent it from taking on too much water. Do it, Lieutenant. Quickly."

"Status on sonar contact?" Micah said.

"Bearing unchanged. Depth: sixty meters. Distance: two nautical miles. Speed has slowed considerably. Present Speed: five knots."

"Did the speed slow when our sonar sweeps ceased?"

"Yes, sir."

The *USS Gettysburg* sailed toward the Russian contingent at top speed. Anxious, Agent Jackson stood on the bridge, asking for reports and wondering why the other American ships had not been in contact. Even though their orders had been transmitted, the silence was now disturbing.

They were six nautical miles from the Russian ships and the same distance from the two American ships, forming a small triangle in a vast ocean. The sonar contact was heading straight for the *USS Carney* despite Jackson's efforts at drawing it toward them with sonar sweeps.

"This creature is a fickle animal," Jackson said to the bridge crew. "Very unpredictable. Therefore, when we confront it, we will need to zero in on it quickly and take it out before it causes any serious damage."

"Sir," the lieutenant said, "if the creature surfaces near us, we can utilize the CIWS."

Jackson threw his shoulders back a little, attempting to show off in front of the crew. "The Phalanx Close-In Weapons System? Very good."

"You know what that is, sir?"

"Yes, Lieutenant. That's why I chose this vessel. It was the closest one with that weapons system on it."

The Russian captain despised being in the dark. He was attempting to monitor radio transmissions between the Americans and watched the show on satellite but wasn't getting any answers. He had been given his orders: shoot on any foreign vessel that attacks you; and protect the other two Russian ships at all costs so that the *Kirov* can be located. Now, precious time was being wasted.

He grabbed the mic and depressed the button. "This is Captain Siniakov of the Russian warship *Peter the Great*. I want to know what is going on, Commander Wilson. Over."

Micah glanced at Commander Wilson. "Timing is everything."

Commander Wilson chuckled and grabbed the mic. "Captain Siniakov, this is Commander Wilson. We are attempting to intercept the American vessel heading straight for you. Over."

"May we be of any assistance, Commander? As you are well aware, precious time is ticking away."

"Captain Siniakov, you can be of assistance by putting some distance between your ships and the *USS Gettysburg*. The purpose of this move is to protect you, Captain."

"Protect us from what? We can surely take care of ourselves."

"I know you can, Captain, but we will be firing on the *Gettysburg* shortly. I do not want you to get in the way, get caught in possible crossfire, or be blamed for the attack. Over."

There was a pause, then the Russian captain said, as if disbelieving, "You are going to sink your own ship?"

"Not exactly, Captain. We are going to fire on her and detonate the torpedo before it gets to the ship. We are hoping the blast will enable an officer working covertly for us on the other vessel to seize control. Over."

"When is this operation scheduled to take place, Commander?"

"In approximately eight minutes, Captain," Commander Wilson said. "Therefore, it is imperative you back your ship out of the area as much as you can in eight minutes. Back it away, bearing two-five-zero. That should place you in the safest place in the time allotted. Over."

The Russian captain gave a simple nod to his first mate before the second-in-command started barking orders.

"I would like to have had more lead time, Commander."

"I understand, Captain. I would have desired the same. But the decision to fire was just made. There is no more time to have."

"And when will we know this operation has taken place, Commander?"

"Just look out your windows, Captain."

"Solution plotted, Commander," the petty officer said. "Firing of torpedo tube number one on your command, sir."

"Contact the *Gettysburg,*" the commander said, scribbling on a piece of paper. "Tell Lieutenant Windham of our plan and to be prepared to jump Jackson upon detonation." He ripped the sheet out of his memo pad and handed it to his petty officer.

"Aye, Commander." The petty officer slid his chair down to the next station and began tapping out the message.

"How do you know Jackson didn't hear that exchange, Commander?" John said. Don't they have the same radio frequencies?"

"They do," Commander Wilson said. "We are anticipating Lieutenant Windham has control of the radio communications now that Commander Goodrich is incapacitated. Windham may have heard it, if he was on the right frequency. If he's smart, though, he'll keep it to himself."

"Lieutenant Windham," the petty officer manning the communications station said, "incoming message from the president of the United States being received, sir. It is flagged as 'Top Brass,' sir."

"What does that mean?" Jackson said.

"'Top Brass' means only the ranking officer can see it. His eyes only."

"Since Commander Goodrich is not available, that means I am the commanding officer," Jackson said. "So let's see it."

"I'm sorry, sir. I can't let that happen."

"Why not?"

"You're not Navy, sir. 'Top Brass' means the highest-ranking officer of that ship and him only. Therefore, since I am the second-in-command, I am the one to read it."

Jackson clenched his teeth to the point that the muscles in his temples ached. He fumed, wearied by all the red tape and bureaucratic mumbo-jumbo. Too many people had muddied the waters of his overall plan. He was near the end of his mission now, and further delays were draining the last vestiges of his already shallow pool of patience. He raised his weapon and aimed it at Lieutenant Windham's head once more. "Make one false move, Lieutenant, and you're history."

Windham shook his head in disgust. "Understood." He turned to the petty officer. "Give it to me."

The officer handed Windham the sheet of paper.

> *Commander of* USS Carney *to Lieutenant of* USS Gettysburg. *Stop. Detonation of MK-32 in approximately six minutes. Stop. Upon explosion, take control of bridge. Stop. Tell Agent Jackson president commands full stop and to be boarded. Stop. Radio when successful. Stop. End of transmission.*

"So, Lieutenant, what does it say?" Jackson said.

"The president has ordered us to stop and be boarded, Agent Jackson." Windham folded the paper and slipped it in his pocket.

Jackson's gun remained aimed in Windham's direction. "If you want to live, Lieutenant, you will ignore that order."

Commander Wilson took in a deep breath and blew it out between his lips. "It's show time, ladies and gentlemen. This has to go off without a hitch. Is that clear?"

The bridge crew responded in the affirmative.

"Lieutenant, I want to know when that torpedo gets within thirty yards of the *Gettysburg*. I'd rather err on the side of more distance. Understood?"

"Aye, Commander."

Commander Wilson turned and faced Micah. "Captain Gregson, may all your plans be good ones."

Evelyn grabbed Micah by the arm, and he turned to look her in the eye.

He placed his hand on hers and squeezed.

Commander Wilson picked up a pair of binoculars and peered in the direction of the *Gettysburg*. "Lieutenant. Fire!"

The creature had closed to within forty meters of the *USS Carney*, zeroing in on the vibrations of the engine's propeller but uncertain of the message being received as propellers from other, more distant boats sent addling signals of their own. These pulses coalesced with the sonar sweeps of the *USS Gettysburg*, creating a perplexing predicament for the animal to decipher.

As the creature slowed and buoyed itself toward the surface, a sudden rush of sound rocketed past the animal in the opposite direction, clearing its head by a mere few meters.

The creature, curious and confused, turned and followed the new signal.

The operations specialist of the *USS Gettysburg* grabbed his headset. "Lieutenant! New sonar contact. Bearing: one-three-five. Distance: five nautical miles. Speed: twenty-five knots."

"What is it?" Jackson rushed over to the sonar station. "Is it another creature?"

"Negative. Sonar contact is a torpedo. And it was armed when it left the chute."

Jackson stood up straight and spun to face Windham. "They fired on us!"

"I know, I know," Lieutenant Windham replied but didn't look at Jackson. "Helmsman, launch counter measures off the stern on my command. Engine room, full speed ahead. I need every ounce of muscle we can get out of those engines."

The helmsman appeared bewildered. "But sir, the 25 mm guns could easily—"

Lieutenant Windham's eyes narrowed. "Officer, I don't have time to explain. Just do it."

"Aye, sir." The officer punched some buttons to enact the order, ready to release the counter measures.

"Don't have time to explain what?" Jackson said, holding his weapon ready at his side.

"The strategy."

"What is the strategy, Lieutenant?"

"We don't have time, Jackson," Windham said. "Status on new contact."

"Bearing unchanged. Speed unchanged. Distance: three nautical miles."

"What is the strategy, Lieutenant?" Jackson stepped closer to Windham. His face turning a new shade of red. The gun already drawn again.

Lieutenant Windham glowered at Jackson, trying to keep himself from exploding as well. "We had less than eight minutes from the time that torpedo left the *Carney* until it hits us. If we can speed up, we might have it sail past us and hit the counter measures." Windham paused. "If not, the counter measures won't help, and we'll take a direct hit."

"Then what?"

"If it misses us, it will try to acquire a new target once it clears the counter measures, but by then, we should be able to activate the CIWS and blow it out of the water before it reacquires."

"But why not activate the CIWS now, Commander? Blow it out of the water before it reaches us?"

"And just remain stationary? Like a sitting duck?"

"The CIWS can handle it."

"Since when did you become a weapons expert, Agent Jackson?"

"I just know what I read about this vessel."

"Well, book learnin' will only get ya so far. What if we miss the target? We won't have time to get out of the way."

"Okay, so there is some strategy to what you're doing. I like it. Proceed."

Oh, there's a strategy all right, Lieutenant Windham thought. "There is another possibility, Agent Jackson. If that torpedo misses us and hits the counter measures, it could reacquire the Russians as a new target. Then I'll make it my personal mission to ensure that you explain before a senate judiciary committee why you started World War III."

"Lieutenant, in your solution did you plot for the *Gettysburg* to pick up speed?" Commander Wilson said.

"Yes, sir."

"Did you also have the engineering room disable the tracker?"

"Yes, sir."

"Good. Helmsman, full speed ahead."

Evelyn Sims tugged at Micah's arm. "What was all that about?"

"Torpedoes have the ability to home in on a target. It works off a kind of sonar. When you disable it, the torpedo just runs true and straight and impacts on the first thing it hits if it isn't detonated manually or blown out of the water."

"Oh, so this whole exercise is a ruse?"

Micah nodded. "For Agent Jackson's benefit. He'll think we fired on their ship, and if the lieutenant over there is as sharp as we hope he is, he'll play it up and make the necessary maneuvers to look like he's trying not to get hit. Then, when the torpedo gets close enough, we'll blow it up, shake up their ship, and give the lieutenant a chance to knock Jackson out and take over command."

Evelyn nodded with a slight smile. "Smart move."

"We'll see. It isn't over yet."

"Commander," Officer Higgins said, "first sonar contact has changed bearing. New bearing: one-three-five. Distance: two nautical miles. Speed: twenty knots. Depth: twenty meters and rising."

Micah moved toward the sonar station. "It's chasing the torpedo."

Evelyn followed him, looking at the screen. "The animal must have picked up its signal."

"It has no signal," Commander Wilson said. "Lieutenant, you just said the tracker was disabled, right?"

"Yes, sir. I oversaw it myself. That torpedo's tracking device is inactive."

Commander Wilson turned to Micah and Evelyn. His palms faced upward.

"It doesn't have to be sonar, Commander," Evelyn said. "It can sense vibrations in the water, just like a shark."

"The torpedo's prop," Micah said. "That must be what it senses."

"That would do it," Evelyn said.

"And what happens if that thing gets to the torpedo before it reaches the *Gettysburg*?" Commander Wilson said.

Evelyn shrugged. "It could have a very nasty case of indigestion, I imagine. But I'm more concerned about it being really close to the torpedo when you detonate it."

"Would the blast kill it?"

"You better hope so."

CHAPTER FIFTY

Saturday, 4:27 a.m.
Approximately 80 Nautical Miles North of Cooperstown, Bahamas

Captain Siniakov stood on the outside deck with a pair of long-range night vision binoculars trained on the targeted American ship. He scanned back and forth between the *Gettysburg* and the *Carney*, trying to spot the torpedo. He pulled the binoculars away and glanced at his watch before raising them once more.

One minute left.

His first mate stood next to him monitoring the same areas with his own binoculars. "How much time is left, Captain?"

"Less than a minute. Do you have the guns trained on the stretch of ocean between us and the targeted American ship?"

"Yes, Captain."

"Good," Siniakov said. He continued to peer at the *Gettysburg*. "If that ship fires on us, I want to be able to blow it up."

"Yes, sir."

"Also, you have two of our missiles prepared to sink that ship if it does fire on us, yes?"

"Firing solutions are already plotted, sir. Awaiting your command," the first mate said. He, too, raised his binoculars once more.

"Let us pray we don't have to use them, Alexei."

"If we do, sir, it will be a justifiable action. The way other countries have been bashing the American government of late, it will be easy to sell the world on the idea of the Americans starting it."

Captain Siniakov drew in a deep breath and exhaled. "Alexei, do you have children? Grandchildren?"

"No, sir."

"Then I cannot ask you to understand the depth of my reservations."

Commander Wilson watched through high-resolution night vision binoculars. His operations specialist afforded him a countdown from the thirty-second mark. "One hundred yards. Ninety yards. Eighty yards. Seventy yards. Sixty yards. Fifty. Forty-five. Forty. Thirty-five. Thirty."

"Detonate!" Commander Wilson said.

With the push of a single button, a large flash of light illuminated the dark night sky. Water spewed upwards into a cascade over a hundred feet into the air. The concussion of the blast pounded the *Gettysburg*, knocking every person standing to the left with great force.

Lieutenant Windham had positioned himself to Agent Jackson's right, knowing where he would be driven when the fulmination erupted.

When the torpedo exploded, he lurched at Jackson, driving his forearm into the agent's right temple. The explosion sent both men onto the floor of the bridge. Windham landed on top of Jackson, grabbing his right arm, pinning the gun to the floor. The lieutenant then threw his right leg up into the air and rammed his right knee into Jackson's torso, knocking the air out of him. He then raised up and struck Agent Jackson in the jaw with a crunching right hook. The gun fell lifeless onto the floor as Agent Jackson's eyes closed. His mind drifting off into unconsciousness.

Lieutenant Windham grabbed the gun, stood, and snatched the other handgun stuck in Agent Jackson's waistband. "Helmsman, full stop!"

"Aye, Lieutenant."

With both guns trained on Jackson, Windham flirted with the idea of pumping the man full of lead. Just as he was about to pull the triggers, the operations specialist shouted, "Lieutenant! We have a problem!"

Windham turned and raced up the steps. "What is it?"

"Sonar contact is right next to us."

"What sonar contact?"

Before the operations specialist could respond, the creature's head came out of the water, as if being lifted heavenward by an invisible cable. The creature extended its neck until it was staring straight into the bridge.

"That contact, sir," the operation specialist said.

"Evelyn, do you see that?" Micah pointed toward the *USS Gettysburg*.

Evelyn's voice shrieked. "That's it! That's it!" She was like a little girl on Christmas morning who just saw all the presents under the tree for the first time.

Commander Wilson's eyes were like hubcaps. "Helm, best speed to the *Gettysburg*."

"Commander," the first lieutenant said, "shouldn't we try to shoot it?"

"And risk hitting the other ship? No. We've got to get closer."

"Target that thing and fire," Lieutenant Windham said. He rammed the handguns in his waistband, both front and back.

The turret began to pivot and raise the five-inch gun at the bow.

The monster roared, bearing its teeth. Water dripped from its head as it scanned the deck of the *Gettysburg*. Its teeth glistened as they reflected the glow of the bridge lights. Seeing movement inside the bridge, it moved closer. Its neck extended toward the bridge windows.

With a sudden lurch forward, it rammed the side of the ship with its body. Those personnel not sitting down were sent staggering to keep their balance. A couple of officers tumbled to the floor.

"Fire!"

The gun belched its mortar shell in the direction of the creature.

The animal ducked when it caught the flash of the gunshot out of the corner of its eye.

The shell grazed the animal's neck and ricocheted downward, striking the water and exploding. Shrapnel flew in all directions. Pieces of casing pierced the side of the hull, shattered one of the Plexiglas windows of the bridge, and punctured the animal's neck.

The creature, angered by the injuries, vociferated in defiance, and slithered down the length of the ship. It grabbed the gun with its teeth and began to pull upward, wrenching its head back and forth. With each motion, the turret turned, damaging the synchronization mechanism.

The monster then attacked the turret and bent it upwards enough to make it unusable.

Releasing the gun, it raised its head high into the air, roaring in contempt. Its head swooped down, its mouth opening wide. It clamped down on a section of the radar array and ripped it from its moorings with ease. Tossing the battered parts aside, the animal thrust its body at the ship, shoving it with force. The jolt sent everything not fastened down sailing through the air.

The operations specialist hunched over his screen, trying to use his chair as a means of protection. "Lieutenant, the round did not hit its target."

"You think?" Windham said. He was still hiding behind the bank of metal counters that lined the upper ring of the bridge. "Fire another one at that thing. But this time, kill it."

"Sir, the five-inch gun has been damaged."

"What about the close-in guns?"

"The radar has been damaged also."

The lieutenant, still crouching down, was at a loss. The two main weapons systems were useless. The gun was out of commission, and attempting to utilize the CIWS by trying some form of blind compensation would only create more chaos.

"Helmsman, full speed ahead. Get us out of here."

"Aye, Lieutenant."

A rumbling started, and the ship slid forward. The lieutenant stood and felt both guns in his waistband. Pulling them out, he gazed out the shattered window and saw the creature lower its head and submerge itself in the water.

"Send out a distress call. Ask the *Carney* and the *Philippine Sea* to lend us aid," the lieutenant said. Both guns were in his hands. "Turn this boat and head straight for the other two American ships. Strength in numbers, guys. Strength in numbers."

"Aye, Lieutenant."

The bridge crew of the *USS Carney* watched in awe as the battle unfolded between the *Gettysburg* and the creature.

Evelyn stood dumbfounded. Words seemed hard to find. "Micah, uh, how long . . . is that ship? The one the creature just attacked?"

"Over five hundred feet. You thinkin' what I'm thinkin'?"

Evelyn began to nod slowly. "It's a lot bigger than we thought."

"I don't get it. How can something grow to be so enormous?"

"I'll explain it to you later."

"How long before we intercept the *Gettysburg?*" Commander Wilson said.

"Five minutes, sir," the Lieutenant said. "The *Gettysburg* has changed course and is heading straight for us. They're also sending out a distress call, Commander."

"Micah, we've got to use the tranquilizer gun," Evelyn said.

"Evelyn, you saw what that thing did. Do you want to be the one standing out there pulling the trigger?"

A troubled look filled Evelyn's eyes. "Everyone's gonna want to kill it now. Look at how big that thing is."

Micah looked back and forth between Evelyn and John. "This is nuts."

"Evelyn," John said, "killing this thing might be the best option. It is obviously not going to go quietly. And if it's not afraid of five-hundred-foot ships, then anything is fair game."

"He's right, Evelyn. This thing may have been responsible for attacking and killing that sperm whale that got snagged in that fishing boat's nets. Half the whale was missing."

"But guys, this is the greatest find since . . . maybe ever. If you kill it, it'll sink to the bottom, and we'll never get a chance to study it. If we can somehow tranquilize it, immobilize it, then we might be able to snag it and drag it in. Just imagine the possibilities if we could study it?"

John snorted. "Study it where, Evelyn? You said it yourself. There's not a tank built that could hold it. We have to kill it. Then, maybe we could snag it, drag it in, and study it, *as a corpse.*"

Micah snapped his fingers and pointed at Commander Wilson. "Do you have a video recorder on board?"

"Yes, we do."

"Can we use it to record the animal? We might be able to get enough footage of the thing so we don't have to bring it back to port."

"Lieutenant," Commander Wilson said. "Make it happen." The

commander then turned back to face Micah. "Who's gonna be your 'on-the-scene reporter'?"

Micah looked at Evelyn and John. "We've got to decide who's gonna man the camera and who's gonna man the tranquilizer gun."

John raised his hand. A sheepish smile spread across his face. "I'll run the camera."

Evelyn gazed at John in disbelief. "You're so brave, John."

"No, I'm not. And you know it."

Evelyn shook her head and raised her hand in disgust. "Okay. I'll take the gun."

"No, no, no. I've got the gun, Evelyn," Micah said. "They'll need you in here in case they need information on the animal."

"But I'm a marine biologist, too," John said.

Micah placed his hand on John's shoulder. "And you're manning the video recorder, Braveheart. Remember?"

"Don't remind me."

"But they need you in here, too, Micah," Evelyn said. "If it wasn't for you, Jackson might still be running things over there."

"I'll be wired in. I'll still be able to communicate with the bridge."

"So, you're gonna stand on the platform?" Evelyn said.

"Better up there than down on the bow. If I'm going to be midnight snack, I at least want to make that thing work for it."

"Let me do it instead."

"Have you ever shot a gun like that before, Evelyn?"

Evelyn's face contorted. "I shot a BB gun . . . long time ago."

"A *BB gun*?"

"When I was twelve."

"Great. I'm sure you were hunting sea serpents, too. Right?"

"No. Annoying squirrels."

He lowered his head at Evelyn, as if he were peering over the top of some eyeglasses. "Well, then, that's just like it. Very little difference between the two."

Evelyn snorted a chuckle. "Okay. Point taken. You get the gun."

Micah hunkered down against the wall, facing the starboard side of the ship. The tranquilizer gun was loaded, secured to a line, and ready to be deployed. The gun rested in an upright position, strapped against the wall as Micah surveyed the landscape for movement. He knew his location was tenuous at best and wished he was strapped against the wall as well.

The metal railing outlining the platform would provide little protection against the animal. If anything, it would be the animal's girth that might save him. The creature might be too bulky to reach this high. *That,* Micah thought, *was not much comfort.*

John stood inside the bridge; the camera ready to record. He, too, scanned the water for any disturbances.

"John, you're gonna have to go outside and film. You know that, right?" Evelyn said.

"Why?"

"We need shots of the animal in the water, too. We need to see how it maneuvers, how big it is, how big it is in relationship to the ship, all that."

"I'm not sure I can do that, Evelyn."

"Look, John. If we aren't going to catch it, then we need as much footage of it as we can get, because you know what the naysayers will say: We doctored the video. We added the creature. We faked its existence. Just another Loch Ness Monster. That's what they'll say. Lots of stories. Lots of sightings. But no proof to back it up."

John scowled. "Okay. You know this is different than filming great whites, right?"

"Yeah, and you haven't done that, either."

"Commander," Operations Specialist Higgins said, "the *Gettysburg* is closing and slowing. The sonar contact is directly behind her."

"Open a channel."

The operations specialist punched some keys.

"This is Commander Wilson, *USS Carney. USS Gettysburg,* please respond. Over."

"This is First Lieutenant Scott Windham, sir. Over."

"Lieutenant, where's your commanding officer?"

"Commander Goodrich is in the infirmary, sir. He has a gunshot wound to the shoulder. Over."

"What? Who shot him?"

"Agent Jackson, sir. Over."

"Is Agent Jackson there?"

"Yes, sir, but he is incapacitated at the moment as planned. Over."

"Good. What's your status?"

"Our armaments took on heavy damage. Both our gun and our CIWS are inoperable. Over."

"So, all you have are missiles and torpedoes?"

"We do have one five-inch gun at the stern still available, but our radar has been damaged. We'd have to guess when firing. Over."

"Lieutenant, we need you to change course and pull up behind the *Philippine Sea.* We will then pull up behind you to form a line. We believe this will be our best defense against this animal. Since you are disabled, we will be able to protect you and attack the animal at the same time. Do you copy?"

"Copy that, sir."

"Also, Lieutenant, be advised that the animal is fifty meters astern and closing."

The *Gettysburg* pulled into position behind the *Philippine Sea* and throttled down. The two vessels became stationary and watched as the *USS Carney* maneuvered herself into position.

The creature had banked and was heading out to sea before turning again.

"Lieutenant. Status Report."

"Commander Goodrich, are you all right?"

Goodrich carried his arm in a sling. The bandages wrapped around his right shoulder were already starting to soak through with blood. "I've been better. Where's Jackson?"

Windham pointed to the other side of the bridge. Jackson was cuffed behind his back to a chair.

Goodrich nodded. "What's our status, Lieutenant?"

Lieutenant Windham informed the commander of the battle with the monster, the damage suffered, and the recent positioning of the vessel.

"Where did you get those?" The commander nodded toward the lieutenant's waistband.

"Jackson. The rest of the guns were out on the deck before the attack. They're gone now."

"Overboard?"

"More than likely, unless the monster took 'em."

"Judging by the way he bounced us around, I don't think he needs them," the commander said.

"Captain, sonar contact has turned and is heading straight for the Americans."

"Alexei, do you think we can move in closer without drawing that thing to us?"

"Not right now, sir. If we move, it will hear the props and might head this way."

"Yes, I know. I guess I was hoping for another answer I had not already thought of. Have everything ready. I want to be able to join in and help at the first sign of another attack on the Americans. Understood?"

"Aye, Captain."

"Get me the commander of the *Carney*. I need to let him know ahead of time so he doesn't think we are swooping in to take advantage of a comrade when he's down."

Alexei nodded. "Very good, sir."

"Commander Wilson, this is Captain Siniakov. Do you copy?"

"Go ahead, Captain."

"Commander, we are ready and waiting for the creature to attack again. Once it does, we will come to your aid. But we believe that making a move prior to another attack will cause the monster to head in our direction. Do you concur?"

Wilson looked at Evelyn Sims. "Is that right?"

Evelyn nodded.

"Captain, we concur. Remain at your position until another attack ensues. Then come to our aide from our stern or the bow of the *Philippine Sea*. We are forming a—"

"I see what you are doing, Commander," the Russian captain interrupted. "You are forming what amounts to an ocean version of the Lines of Torres Vedras. Very smart."

Commander Wilson peered at his first lieutenant and Evelyn Sims. He raised his left eyebrow.

"What are the Lines of Tor . . . whatever he said?" Evelyn said.

"I'll fill you in later," Commander Wilson said. He looked out the window toward the Russian vessels. "But one thing is for sure. Our Russian captain over there is well-schooled."

"Commander, sonar contact is heading straight for us."

"Status report."

"It's on a collision course, sir. Speed: thirty knots. Distance: sixty meters. Fifty meters. Forty."

"All hands, brace for impact!" the Commander shouted into the mic.

"Twenty meters. Ten. Five."

The monster struck the ship with such intensity Micah Gregson was just about knocked unconscious as his head slammed into the metal wall.

"Damage report!" Commander Wilson said.

"We have a hull breach in engineering, sir. They are taking on water."

"Have them find the leak and seal it off. We can't lose power."

The monster's head rose out of the water opposite Captain Gregson's position. The deafening creature's roar pierced Micah's ears.

Micah spun to see the creature traverse the length of the ship, looking for movement. He grabbed his radio. "Commander Wilson. This is Captain Gregson. Over."

"Captain, do you have a clear shot?"

"Negative. It came up on the wrong side. The bridge is shielding it now. It's heading toward the back of the boat."

"Is there any way you can make some noise, get its attention?"

Micah peeked over the edge. "That wouldn't be my first choice, no."

"Captain, we are taking on water in the engine room. If that beast decides to jump up on the helipad, it'll sink us for sure. We can't wait around. We've got to make the next move."

"Fire the five-inch, Commander. Draw the animal to the front. Aim it out into the ocean away from everybody. When the animal swims by, I'll nail it."

"Roger that. Lieutenant, fire the five-inch bow out into the Atlantic away from everybody. We need to draw this thing to the front of the boat and keep it away from the engines and the stern."

"Aye, sir." The lieutenant scrambled to help the petty officer. "Five-inch is ready, sir."

"Fire!"

The gun fired a shot that sailed out into the night sky.

The monster whirled and watched as the mortar shell sailed in an arc. It started to follow the weapon until it struck the surface of the water and exploded. The creature then turned on the ship and rammed it, almost as if angry for being deceived. It worked its way toward the front of the *Carney*, ramming it as it swam.

When it cleared the bridge, Micah had a small window in which to aim and fire before the beast was out of range.

The monster turned perpendicular to the ship and lunged forward, latching onto the five-inch gun.

Micah aimed and pulled the trigger, sending an overgrown cylindrical metal tube sailing. The tranquilizer struck the animal in the neck, about two feet below the jaw line. Micah pulled the gun in and squatted, attempting to reload for another tranquilizer shot but wanting to watch the animal at the same time.

The animal roared in anger, relinquishing its grasp of the gun while turning in the direction of Micah Gregson.

Evelyn shouted, seeing the eyes of the beast were fixed on something above the bridge. "Micah!"

The creature then looked down, twitched, and shook its head in a violent manner. The tranquilizer dart at once tumbled onto the deck of the ship as the beast bellowed a loud, piercing cry before submerging into the dark ocean waters.

CHAPTER FIFTY-ONE

Saturday, 4:39 a.m.
Approximately 80 Nautical Miles North of Cooperstown, Bahamas

The Russian vessel *Peter the Great* moved into position behind the *USS Carney* after watching the attack firsthand. When the animal disappeared, the Russian skipper commanded his crew to bring the ship to a full stop. Maneuvering a ship over eight hundred feet in length into position took time . . . time the captain of the Russian vessel didn't think they had.

The monster, stimulated by the new sound of propellers and a ship's hull cutting through water, slipped under the *Carney*. It swam straight down fifty meters before banking, turning, and aiming straight for the *Carney*'s underbelly.

Micah, having reloaded, leaned forward to take another shot and noticed his target was missing. He scanned all around him. Clutching his radio, he said, "Where is it?"

"It submerged itself, Captain," Commander Wilson said. "Sonar contact went under the ship and descended."

"Commander," Operations Specialist Higgins said, "contact has turned and is heading straight for us."

"Location?"

The operations specialist grabbed the console. "Brace for impact!"

The *Carney* lurched to the port side as the creature rammed the boat just right of the keel, glancing off like a cornerback trying to separate the football from the wide receiver. The thrust of the animal caused it to rocket from the water like a missile.

Micah, who had just started scanning the water on the starboard side, was knocked back off his haunches, smashing into the metal railing. The tranquilizer gun fell from his hands, smacked the ground next to his feet, and started to slide over the edge toward the bow. Micah reached out with his foot and pinned the nylon shoulder strap with the toe of his shoe before securing it with his hand.

Still on his knees, Micah spun around to see the beast splash back into the water like a killer whale at a theme park show. The sight inspired awe.

And concern.

Micah grabbed for his radio, but it wasn't there. He began looking around, scanning the platform.

Nothing.

He gazed over the side and began scanning the deck below. And there, caught precariously in-between the wall and a piece of the radar array about fifteen feet below, the radio rested.

Another vicious jolt and it's goin' in the water.

Micah scanned the ocean. No sign of the animal.

I need that radio.

Micah began climbing down the ladder, hurrying so he could get back on the platform. He grabbed the railings and slid the last four feet until he was even with the radio's position. He stepped out onto a metal box jutting out from the wall and reached out, straining to span the last two inches. Finally, he released the railing just long enough to lurch at the radio, grasp it, and get back to some semblance of a firm grip.

When he clipped the radio to his belt, the ship rocked sideways, toward the starboard side. The momentum sent the top of the boat in Micah's direction.

Micah heard a load roar on the other side of the ship. A piercing shrill of a sound unlike anything he'd heard before.

The ladder tilted toward him. The steps under his feet pulled away as the railing pushed him backward. Micah felt a vicious vibration through the metal in his hands as his feet slipped off the steps.

Micah hung in the air for a second or two before the ship righted itself, slamming him into the steps.

Scurrying to get a footing, Micah raced up the ladder, trying to get to higher ground and safety.

He reached the platform railing where he'd stood just minutes before, and hopped over it. With the gun still over his shoulder, he looked toward the port side of the ship, trying to see if the beast was still there.

Nothing.

He grabbed his radio. "Commander Wilson, status report on sonar contact?"

No response.

He checked the channel and tried again.

Still no response.

Great. The fall must have damaged it.

Micah knelt down, peeled the battery off the back of the radio, and began to examine it.

Another horrendous hit sent the radio battery out of Micah's hand. It slid across the platform like a hockey puck on ice. Micah lunged for it and seized it just as it reached the edge of the platform.

Crawling back to his knees, Micah felt something spray him on the back of the neck. Spinning around, he saw it.

The monster's head rose ominously, positioning itself only ten feet away. Its black eyes peering holes into its new targeted prey. Its teeth, large and jagged, lined its mouth, giving it a prehistoric flare.

Only the metal railing separated Micah from certain death.

The beast's neck, writhing like a snake's skin, had extended to its maximum length, making the railing a tough obstacle to scale.

The creature studied the platform, sizing up its options before sinking down into the water and lurching up into the air. As the monster's mouth opened, a loud roar emitted, causing Micah to wince in pain.

Micah lifted the gun up with his right hand and twisted his torso around, securing the forestock with his left hand. From the hip, he aimed it at the creature in one hopeless shot of desperation and pulled the trigger. The tranquilizer sailed into the beast's mouth and lodged itself in the back of its throat.

Micah jerked his left hand away just as the beast's mouth clamped shut on the end of the gun.

The gun strap, still wrapped around Micah's right arm, pulled him toward the animal. Frantically, he tried to unravel the strap with his free hand.

The behemoth's loud roar transformed into a grumbling, stifled growl as it crashed its jaw into the metal railing, collapsing it like a tinker toy.

Micah's arm began to ache as the weight of the animal pulling on the gun tightened the strap.

As the creature plunged toward the water, it yanked Micah over the edge.

Micah gripped the crumpled railing with his left hand, and maneuvered his arm, trying desperately to free it.

The damaged railing tore free from one area and became a metal lifeline of sorts.

Micah dangled closer to the monster, feeling like the rope in a tug of war.

A final turn of the arm outward allowed the strap to slip past his elbow and rip at the flesh of his forearm before pulling free completely.

Micah reached up with his right hand and gripped the damaged railing with both hands as the animal disappeared into the inky water below.

Agent Jackson, having awakened slumped over in a chair, realized at once he was handcuffed. He acted like he was still unconscious for a few moments, trying to ascertain his predicament. Seeing Commander Goodrich standing outside the bridge window with Lieutenant Windham, he rolled his right thumb under, pulled his pinkie finger in, and utilized his hyperflexibility to his advantage. Freeing his right hand from the cuffs, he then surveyed his surroundings, gripping the handcuffs in his left hand like a weapon.

When the animal struck the *Carney*, the bridge crew was completely engaged. Everyone inside was either peering at monitors with headsets covering their ears or was looking outside in the direction of the battle.

Jackson slinked from his chair and eased toward the bridge door. He bent down and felt for his ankle holster.

It's still there. Good.

When the commotion rose, he unsnapped the holster and retrieved his Glock 43. Snagging his cell phone and wallet off the console where the petty officers had left them, he slid over to the bridge door and opened it.

"Stop!" came a voice from the bridge. Jackson looked up in time to see a petty officer run toward the door. With one well-placed shot from his Glock, the crewman fell face first to the ground.

Jackson bolted out the door and made a beeline to the stern. Grabbing his cell phone, he speed-dialed as he ran down the railing on the port side.

"Come get me now!" he yelled.

"We've been monitoring your transmissions. Is it safe?"

"No. But you're gonna come get me now!"

"The cost just went up."

"We'll argue money later. Now, come get me before I withdraw the funds that have already been sent to your account."

"Which ship are you on?"

Jackson ran to the railing and looked in both directions. "It looks like the second ship of four. It's the *USS Gettysburg*. I'll be on the helipad."

"They won't shoot us down, will they?"

"I can't guarantee anything. Just get here."

One minute later, the animal surfaced fifty yards off the starboard bow of the *USS Carney*, appearing dazed. It started to thrash the water, slamming its head into the surface, acting like it was losing control of its physical abilities.

"What's it doing?" Commander Wilson said.

Evelyn's eyes pooled. "I think the tranquilizer is taking effect now."

"Good," Wilson said. He grabbed his radio. "Captain Gregson, stand down on the harpoon gu—"

Just then, a mortar shell blast fired from behind the *Carney*. The shot whizzed through the night sky like a laser.

The animal, stunned and losing its mobility, saw the flash of light and turned to face it. Just before the shell reached the creature, the beast ducked in a lackadaisical way, sending the shot sailing past and impacting on the surface near the creature's tail.

The monster bellowed in pain as the shell exploded. Shrapnel tore into its flesh, gashing its hind quarters.

"Where did that come from?" Evelyn said.

"The Russians. It was their salvo."

"Tell them to stop. And tell Micah to shoot it with that gun you showed me earlier."

Commander Wilson looked at Doctor Sims, understanding her concerns. "I don't think you want to do that, Doctor."

"Yes, I do. We have to try and capture it. Secure it before it dies. If they kill it out there, it will sink before we get to it."

"Doctor, with all due respect, I don't want to get any closer to that thing. It has already damaged two ships tonight. The last thing I want to do is be responsible for hauling that thing into port."

Micah Gregson, breathing heavily and holding his damaged right arm, sat on the platform and peered out at the creature. He wasn't sure how much of the animal's distress was caused by the tranquilizer gun and how much was caused by mortar shells. What he did know, though, was the creature was not well.

Feeling contrite, he looked down, contemplating his role in the beast's demise when he noticed something shiny on the ship's deck.

He leaned forward and examined the metal ladder reaching down to the deck. It had been damaged at the top, like someone had taken a large hammer and flattened it.

Compliments of the sea serpent, Micah thought.

He scaled down the ladder, keeping his eye on the ailing creature. He snatched the dart off the deck floor and examined it. The dart had malfunctioned. It never fired its injection. Micah then peered back at the monster, wondering now if the other dart had worked properly or not.

It was then Micah heard another sound in the distance. Cocking his head to one side, he tried to pinpoint the location of what sounded like the rotors of a helicopter.

Without warning, he saw the blinking lights of a chopper approaching from the south.

Reaching for his radio, he then realized his plight. *I can't warn them.*

"Commander?"

"What is it, Lieutenant?"

"Did you order a chopper?"

"Chopper? No. We were ordered to leave our chopper on shore, remember? So our landing pad would be free for Captain Gregson and company."

"Well, our radar is showing a chopper heading this way."

The helicopter sailed right over the Russian warship, banked around the *Carney*, and swooped down, rotating its position before plopping down on the landing pad of the *Gettysburg*.

The chopper pilot's eyes were bugging out of his head as he looked out across the water in the direction of the creature.

Anthony Fontaine, placing his feet on the railings and skipping the last eight steps of the ladder, bolted for the helicopter. He ran to the passenger side and opened the door.

"Hurry! Get in," the pilot shouted. "They're coming for you."

Fontaine glanced up, seeing three officers running down the left side of the ship, heading for the ladder. He climbed into the chopper. "Go, go, go!"

Without delay, the chopper leapt off the pad as the officers reached the bottom of the ladder and sprinted toward the machine. It lifted in a jerky motion as the pilot tried to manage his sudden rush of adrenaline.

All three officers stopped, drew handguns, and opened fire.

Bullets careened off the glass bubble, leaving small marks but causing little damage.

"Man, am I glad you had me install that bulletproof glass," the pilot said.

"Just get us out of here before they figure out the rest of this thing isn't bulletproof."

"Roger that."

The pilot backed the chopper away as long as he dared, keeping the front facing the onslaught of bullets before banking and accelerating, lifting out over the water.

Fontaine finished buckling himself into his seat and grabbed the helmet at his feet. Looking outside as he picked it up, he saw the creature start to pass underneath the chopper. A nervous tingling shot up his spine as he pushed the helmet on his head.

"Get us higher," Fontaine said nervously.

The creature, wobbling back and forth, saw the helicopter approach. As the noisy machine approached, the creature sank into the dark watery depths.

The helicopter sailed over the creature. Fontaine looked down, feeling pleased with his efforts. *Although it didn't go as planned,* he thought, *my mission ended well enough.* "Best speed to the boat," he said to the pilot. "Then it's on to Aru—"

The beast burst from the water and lunged at the helicopter. It latched onto the tail boom, encasing the tail rotor. When the animal plunged back into the water, it ripped the entire tail assembly off the chopper.

The helicopter started spinning in circles and losing altitude.

Fontaine shrieked in terror. "Get us out of here!"

"I can't control it!" The pilot's hands shook, trying to keep the aircraft from crashing.

The creature thrust upward, roaring as its head lifted out of the ocean, pieces of the aircraft falling from its mouth. As the chopper descended, it began to angle back toward the creature. The animal dodged it by submerging seconds before the main rotor struck the surface of the water. It shattered into lethal projectiles, spraying the surrounding boats like machine gun fire.

Anthony Fontaine and his pilot were both submerged within seconds as the chopper turned sideways and sank. Wrestling to unlatch themselves from their seatbelt prisons, Fontaine fumbled with the buckles for what seemed like an eternity to his aching lungs.

Releasing himself, he looked over at the pilot. He saw the man jerk on his strap with no luck, yelping in gurgled fear. Fontaine thought for a moment about helping the pilot but feeling the chopper sink deeper and deeper into the dark ocean, he shoved his door open and struggled against the chopper's momentum with feverish strokes.

With no point of reference and no sunlight, Fontaine swam in the opposite direction of the plunging chopper. His mental faculties, starving for oxygen, started to wane as he reached the surface. Gasping for air, he began treading water, scanning the surface, searching for the four ships in a line.

It was then he felt drips of water smacking him on the top of his head like heavy rain drops.

Looking up, he saw the creature baring its teeth, almost as if smiling. Fontaine yawped a shrill scream.

With one facile motion, the creature snagged Fontaine from the waves, stifling the sound of his sickening howl. It growled and ripped its head back and forth like an angry dog with a toy. It then threw his body up into the air and clamped down with little effort, like a blue heron making a meal out of a bluegill. Then, with a renewed vigor, the animal sank back into the ocean.

When the creature seized Fontaine, Evelyn Sims watched the entire event. She shivered in horror and turned her head away in nauseated revolt. Despite her anger and hatred for the man she knew as Agent Jackson, she would never wish such a death even on her worst enemies.

"Are you getting all this, John?" she said.

"Are you kidding? I sure am." An excitement was in his voice. "We just witnessed an evolutionary biologist get consumed by the very creature he was trying to kill. On the topic of survival of the fittest, natural selection, and all that, this should create some interesting dialogue about evolutionary irony, don't ya think?"

Evelyn placed her hand over her mouth. "Just remember, mister, which side of the fence we're on."

"Oh, yeah. They'll probably think we had some movie production company make this film for us."

Standing outside when the chopper was attacked, Micah knew what was going to happen and ran for cover before the rotor blades hit the water's surface and splintered into a hundred deadly missiles. He then got up and made his way to the bridge to see Evelyn.

He was almost in the bridge when Fontaine screamed. Micah swiveled toward the water just in time to see the monster jerk its head from side to side before tossing Fontaine's lifeless body into the air.

He spun back toward the bridge. He knew what was happening. His mind's eye was vivid enough without seeing the real thing.

He finally entered the bridge.

Evelyn saw him and his injured arm. "Micah? Are you okay?"

He walked over to Evelyn and John. "I'll live." *Better this than the alternative I was faced with.* "Are you okay?"

Evelyn nodded. "I am, but what about the animal?"

"Do we know where it is?"

Commander Wilson was studying the sonar screen. "Yeah. It's floating about ten feet below the surface. I assume it's . . ." He stopped, not wanting to state the obvious.

Micah waved at the commander. "We understand."

The animal resurfaced closer to the *Carney*, pushed in that direction by the current. Floating and gasping, its breath appeared labored. The animal's body movement began to merge with the waves.

"Commander," one of the petty officers said. "The creature has surfaced directly off our port side."

Micah, Evelyn, John, and Commander Wilson raced outside.

Seeing it, Evelyn gasped. She grabbed the railing. "Oh, no."

"What's wrong with it?" Commander Wilson said.

"The tranquilizer doses must have been too high. It's dying."

"Are you sure, Evelyn?" Micah pulled the first dart out of his pocket and held it up. "The first dart hit it in the neck. At first I thought it injected the tranquilizer before the creature shook it loose, but it never did discharge. It malfunctioned." He handed it to Evelyn.

"Did you get off any more shots?" Commander Wilson said.

"I did get off a second shot. That dart lodged in the back of the creature's throat. But it could have malfunctioned, too, for all we know."

"So if it's not the tranquilizer, then what could be causing the animal to act like that?" Commander Wilson said.

"Well, I'm not saying the second dart did malfunction," Micah said. "But even if it did function properly, we still don't know if that would be enough to immobilize a creature this big."

"Oxygen," Evelyn said in a whisper.

"What was that?" Micah said.

Evelyn gazed up at Micah. "Oxygen. It's gasping because it can't get enough oxygen."

"What are you talking about?" Commander Wilson said. "There's no lack of oxygen here."

"Not for us, Commander. But for it, there's not enough."

Commander Wilson formed a look of incredulity.

"The air pressure would not be strong enough to sustain an animal this big, Commander, if its heart is not big enough."

"You think its acting like this because it's *suffocating*?"

"In a manner of speaking, yes."

The commander's eyebrows pinched together even tighter. "No

way. It's acting like this because we shot it, the Russians shot it, and Captain Gregson was able to get enough of that tranquilizer into its bloodstream. That's why it's lying here, about to die."

"Do you see any blood, Commander?"

"I can't tell, Doctor. It's too dark. Besides, most of its body is underwater."

"Can we shine a light over here so we can see?"

"Sure," he said, turning back toward the bridge crew. "Let's get a spotlight on this thing, pronto."

Within seconds, a large beam of light shot down on the creature."

"Now, Commander," Evelyn said, "move the light around and see if you can see any blood. If an animal this big is bleeding out, there should be significant amounts of blood on the surface."

The commander called out to the operator to shine the light on every square foot of the beast and the immediate area surrounding it.

As it moved back and forth, there was little blood to be seen.

"Yes, Commander, it's been wounded, but it's not dying from blood loss."

"Sorry, but I still don't buy the suffocation theory," the commander said.

The light continued its thorough movement over the body of the massive beast as Evelyn Sims and Commander Wilson remained at odds, debating their cases in front of the small audience.

"Hey, what's that?" John said. He pointed at the animal while trying to focus the camera on the spot in question.

"What's what, John?" Evelyn said.

"Look, just below the jawline. About three feet down the neck. What is that?"

"Can we get the light to focus on that area, Commander?"

"Move that light back towards the head," Commander Wilson said into his radio. "Keep moving . . . keep moving . . . a little to the left . . . Stop. Right there. Don't move." He stopped transmitting. "What the—"

The light revealed the right side of the creature's neck and what appeared to be gashes. Gashes without blood, all parallel to one another with a negligible curve to each.

"Those must be injuries from when the shell exploded." Commander Wilson nodded, seeming pleased with his assessment. "Pierced its neck."

"Those aren't wounds," Evelyn said. "The flesh would be tattered, torn. These are too even. Plus, look at the skin. See how thin it is? And when the water pushes it back against the neck, the gashes disappear?"

"What are you thinking, Evelyn?" Micah said.

She watched as the current pushed the skin back, revealing the openings, then forced them closed. *They're arched in the direction of the creature's head. If the animal was swimming, they would . . .* "Gills. They're some type of underwater breathing system. See how they're arched. If the animal was swimming, they would be forced shut. But if the animal opened its mouth underwater while it was swimming, it would work much like the gills of a fish."

"That would explain a lot of things," John said, still taping.

The commander stood, still unconvinced. "Like what?"

"Like why we couldn't determine back at the lab whether this thing was reptilian or amphibian, for starters," John said.

Evelyn pointed at the creature. "Or, how an animal this big could have remained undetected for so many centuries?"

The commander conceded a nod.

"Or, how an animal this big could have survived diving the depths we know it can dive? Your sonar recorded depths of what? Three hundred meters?"

"When we first detected it, yes."

"And who's to say it couldn't go deeper than that?" Micah said.

Evelyn turned toward Micah. "Exactly. Which, if so, might explain why it's dying now."

"What do you mean?" the commander said.

"Commander, we've established this animal to be a deep diver. Agreed?"

"Agreed."

"And we also established that this creature stayed underwater for a long period of time, right?"

"Yes."

"While traveling long distances at high rates of speed, too," Micah said.

Evelyn pointed at Micah. "Good point. So, if it is an air breather, in order for it to dive that deep, it either had to have the ability to breathe in large quantities of air, like a sperm whale does before it goes hunting for giant squid, or this creature has to be able to breathe underwater.

"To breathe air like a normal reptile, it would have to surface often. Both day and night. Therefore, it stands to reason that we would have seen one of these things long before now.

"If it was able to breathe underwater, as those 'gashes' suggest, and still dive that deep, then it would more than likely have to keep moving like a shark does in order to survive. If it stops swimming for too long, it dies."

The commander turned to face Micah.

Micah shrugged.

The commander looked at Evelyn once again, appearing more mystified.

"Also, there's the issue of size. The oxygen levels at three hundred meters down would be at a considerably higher pressure than the oxygen levels it would experience near sea level."

"The whole fourteen point seven pounds per square inch thing we talked about earlier?" Micah said.

Evelyn acknowledged Micah's comment. "An animal this large would need to be able to dive deep in order to survive. Diving deep would get enough oxygen into its bloodstream and thus to its extremities. Diving at those depths and even deeper would also account for this creature's size. Gentleman, when this thing attacked the other ship, it was almost half its size in length. We can watch the video to confirm, but I was shocked when I saw its tail that far away from the head."

"The *Gettysburg* is a five-hundred-foot ship, right?"

"A little bigger than that, but close enough," Micah said.

"That puts this thing at roughly two hundred to two hundred and fifty feet long. There's nothing in the fossil record to suggest anything this big ever existed."

"And there wouldn't be if this is a deep diver," John said. "All the fossils would be at the bottom of the ocean, covered by silt in a matter of weeks."

"So, Evelyn, I asked you earlier how this creature could get so big, and you said you'd explain it later." Micah shrugged. "Now'd be a good time."

"We call it *bathymetric gigantism*."

The commander was still flummoxed.

Evelyn sighed, trying a different course. "Commander, you're a Navy man. If a naval pilot flies a plane up high into the air, does the air he breathes change at all?"

"Of course. It gets thinner as the plane flies higher."

"Okay. Now, if the pilot was engaged in combat at sea level, then started flying higher while remaining engaged in combat, would the pilot be able to remain at the same combat readiness, or would the pilot eventually become disoriented as the plane flew higher and higher?"

"Depends on how high we're talkin'."

"Well, I just read recently that the highest recorded altitude flown was sixty thousand feet by the *Concorde*," John said.

Evelyn nodded. "Okay, so for argument's sake, let's say the highest a plane can reach is sixty thousand feet. And let's say, Commander, that one of your pilots can fly at that altitude for ten minutes before feeling light-headed and fifteen minutes before he loses consciousness. Okay?"

"Okay."

"So, Commander, what happens when the pilot flies that high for sixteen minutes? Or seventeen? Or twenty?"

"He would become disoriented . . . would eventually pass out . . . and the plane crashes and burns."

Evelyn nodded, then pointed at the animal. "Commander, there's your pilot, and he's been flying at this altitude for nearly an hour."

The commander's expression changed at once from one of agitation to one of comprehension.

"You see, Commander, I'm sure the animal was injured, and those injuries may have altered the behavior of the animal. Had this animal gone back down to the depths, it may have survived."

"That would explain the duration of the other attacks," John said. "They didn't last very long before the creature disappeared."

Evelyn nodded.

The commander threw his hands out in question. "Then why didn't it go back down this time?"

Tears pooled in the corners of Evelyn's eyes. "I'm not sure. It may have felt too threatened. Maybe, too engaged? Like a fighter pilot not paying close attention to his surroundings." She blinked several times while straightening her stance. "Suddenly, it's too late. You're too ill. Too disoriented. And your body functions start to shut down because they're oxygen deprived."

Lifeless, the creature floated for only a few minutes more before disappearing below the waves. Like a leaf detaching itself from the tallest tree and drifting to earth in majestic flight, the behemoth drifted down to the icy depths of the ocean floor, falling in a graceful dance, taking with it the answers to the mysteries it produced.

CHAPTER FIFTY-TWO

Saturday, 6:51 a.m.
Aboard the USS Carney
Heading for Mayport Naval Station, Jacksonville, Florida

The *USS Philippine Sea,* the only undamaged American ship, remained behind to assist the Russian vessels in their search for the *Kirov*. The other two American boats limped back to Mayport Naval Station, grateful they were still in one piece. The *Carney* was still pumping water from its engineering section along the way.

Evelyn and John retired to their quarters to clean up and rest. Micah went to sick bay to have his arm bandaged before doing the same. The last several days had been a long stretch. Miles of travel, sleepless nights, and loads of stress had all taken their toll.

Micah found himself gazing up at the ceiling of his room. Despite the intrigue of discovering a new species—even one of such magnitude certain to create a firestorm of scientific discussion and controversy—something else struck him with a force as hard as anything the creature could muster.

He wasn't agonizing over his temporary stint in Naval Intelligence, although it felt good to be back in the saddle again. Nor was it over his career in the Coast Guard. He loved his real job too.

Instead, he'd been smitten with an ideal.

An ideal that evaded him for several years . . . or had he been evading it? Was he afraid of it? Even running from it? Did the thought of embracing it again frighten him?

Yes, he admitted. *It does*.

So much so, it had taken him all these years to be able to get to this point in his life when he could, with reverence and awe, embrace the ideal once more.

Micah sat up on the edge of his bed and glanced down at his ring finger. The gold band glistening in the lamplight. He removed the ring in a careful, loving manner and held it between his two index fingers and thumbs. Turning it, he read the inscription engraved inside: "Till death do us part, all my love is yours. RJG."

Micah closed his eyes and kissed the ring. "I'll always love you, Becca," he said in a whisper. For several moments, he held the ring with it pressed against his lips.

Then slowly, almost like his effort wasn't enough, he stood and placed the wedding band in his pants pocket.

Standing in front of a mirror, searching his own eyes and trying to suppress the guilty feelings he'd always felt, he walked out of his cabin and down the hallway.

On the bed, lying on her stomach, Evelyn Sims jotted down notes before they escaped her. She didn't want to stop. Not because she was afraid the images would be forgotten.

That'll never happen.

Instead, the events of the last few days became a convenient and powerful diversion. Maybe *escape* was the better term.

It's easier to dwell on a sea serpent than my snake of a husband, she thought as she pictured the pain waiting for her back in Miami.

Four gentle knocks arrived at her cabin door, but she never turned to look at the door. She wanted to remain focused, or else, the loss she'd experienced may overpower her. "Come in."

The door opened, and Micah peeked inside. "Am I interrupting something?"

Evelyn spun her head around and smiled. "No, no. You're fine."

Micah stepped through the doorway and closed the door. "You look busy. I could come back later."

"Don't be silly." She jammed the pen inside her notebook and sat up on the edge of the bed. "I was just writing down some thoughts about what happened tonight. That's all."

"You sure that's all? You look like you've been crying."

Evelyn rubbed her eyes. "I'm okay. Really."

Micah offered a comforting smile. "I don't know about you, but I think the images will remain fresh for a long while in my mind."

"Tell me about it. Wasn't that wild?"

"That's an understatement, not to mention a pun."

Evelyn grinned and then sat silent for a moment, staring at Micah. "You don't have to stand. You can sit down."

Micah looked around and saw only one small desk and a chair. He grabbed the chair and turned it so he could face Evelyn and sat down. "So, what's on your agenda once we get back to the mainland?"

She laughed. "After many hours of sleep or before?"

"Both."

"I'll have to get back to NMI first. We still have some of the specimen left that Bud didn't send to Paris. I'll examine it again and probably send it to Dr. Landover and let him take a look. Then I'm sure there will be a paper or two to write." She smiled again but in a more solemn way. "Of course, I have some other paperwork to deal with as well."

Micah dipped his head. "I imagine your life is going to get really busy once that video is released, huh?"

"All depends on how well I'm received by my peers."

"Well, you deserve it. Play your cards right, and you'll probably be runnin' NMI."

Evelyn squinted a little. "I'm not sure I want the job."

"So, where do you go from here if not the institute?"

"Who knows? I'll take it one day at a time. If there's two things I've learned through this whole ordeal, it's to not run from God, and to not try to run ahead of Him, either. Instead, I have to wait on Him. Trust Him. 'Trust in the Lord with all your heart, and lean not on your own understanding. In all your ways, acknowledge Him, and He will make your paths straight.' That's what I've got to get straight, Micah. I definitely have some soul searching to do. That's for sure." She inhaled and sighed. "Before I move forward with my career, I've got to get right with God first."

"If you find time, I'd like to get together. Maybe have some dinner? See a movie?"

Evelyn's smile grew bigger. "Are you asking me out, Captain Gregson?"

"When you're ready. It's an open invitation. I know you have some issues to deal with and closure to obtain. Trust me, I understand. But when you're ready, give me a call." He handed her a slip of paper.

She opened the folded paper and saw a phone number and address.

"That's my home phone and address. You already have my cell number."

She looked up, her eyes moist. "Thank you . . . for being a friend. That's what I need right now."

Micah nodded, stood, and slid the chair back to its original station.

Evelyn, watching him prepare to leave, jumped up and wrapped her arms around him, hugging him. She then leaned back and stared into his eyes, stroking the side of his head. "Thank you."

Micah wiped the tear which had trickled down her cheek. Then, he winked. "I'll be waiting. I've got some soul searching to do as well."

He gave her one more hug, took her by the hand, and let it slide out of his as he walked out of the cabin.

CHAPTER FIFTY-THREE

Sunday, 2:24 a.m.
Atlantic Ocean
Approximately 25 Nautical Miles North of West End, Grand Bahama Island

The sound of the ocean breeze flitted about on an invisible course, mixing with the lapping of the waves as they traversed their way across the great watery expanse.

The moon, full and unencumbered, shone magnificently upon the deep. Its reflective glow bounced off the surface in painting-like glory.

Amongst the quiet, in this distance, a sound emerged.

The sound of a whale surfacing.

BIBLIOGRAPHY

Achenbach, Joel. "Dino-Size: Why Were Dinosaurs So Humongous?" *National Geographic*. July 2005: p. 1.

Altman, Lawrence K., and William J. Broad. "Global Trend: More Science, More Fraud." 20 Dec 2005 *New York Times* 21 July 2008 <http://www.nytimes.com/2005/12/20/science/20rese.html>

American Physiological Society. "Giant Insects Might Reign If Only There Was More Oxygen In The Air." 12 Oct 2006 *Science Daily* 31 Dec 2007 <http://www.sciencedaily.com/releases/2006/10/061012093716.htm>

Andrews, Lori. *The Clone Age: Adventures in the New World of Reproductive Technology*. New York, NY: Henry Holt and Company, 1999.

Andrews, Lori, and Dorothy Nelkin. *Body Bazaar: The Market for Human Tissue in the Biotechnology Age*. New York, NY: Crown Publishers, 2001.

"Architeuthis dux – Giant Squid." (No Date). *MarineBio.org* 05 Jan 2007 <http://marinebio.org/species.asp?id=156>

Asimov, Isaac. *The Genetic Code*. New York, NY: Orion Press, 1962.

Associated Press. "Scientists Find 24 New Species in Suriname." 04 June 2007 *MSNBC.com* 01 March 2009 <http://www.msnbc.msn.com/id/19028712/>

Avise, John C. *The Genetic Gods: Evolution and Belief in Human Affairs*. Cambridge, Massachusetts: Harvard University Press, 1998.

Baker, Mace. "Sea Dragons." *Impact*. August 2003: pp. i-iv.

Bakker, Robert T. *The Dinosaur Heresies: New Theories Unlocking the Mystery of the Dinosaurs and Their Extinction*. New York, NY: William Morrow and Company, Inc., 1986.

Baugh, Carl E. *Panorama of Creation*. Oklahoma City, OK; Hearthstone Publishing Ltd., 1989.

Behe, Michael J. *Darwin's Black Box: The Biochemical Challenge to Evolution*. New York, NY; Free Press, 1996.

———————. *The Edge of Evolution: The Search for the Limits of Darwinism*. New York, NY; Free Press, 2007.

Bell, Robert. *Impure Science: Fraud, Compromise, and Political Influence in Scientific Research*. New York, NY; John Wiley & Sons, Inc., 1992.

Bergman, Jerry. "Why Abiogenesis Is Impossible." *Creation Research Society Quarterly*. 36. No. 4. March 2000. 05 Jan 2007 <http://www.creationresearch.org/crsq/articles/36/36_4/abiogenesis.html>

————. "Why Mammal Body Hair is an Evolutionary Enigma." *Creation Research Society Quarterly*. 40. No. 3. March 2004. pp. 240-243. 05 Jan 2007 <http://www.creationresearch.org/crsq/articles/40/40_4/Bergman.pdf>

Blick, Edward F. *A Scientific Analysis of Genesis*. Oklahoma City, OK; Hearthstone Publishing Ltd., 1991.

Bohlin, Ray. (1997). "Can Humans Be Cloned Like Sheep?" 11 June 2001 *Probe Ministries* 06 April 2006 <http://www.probe.org/docs/humclon2.html>

Brewin, Bob. "Navy develops two-way radio communication for submerged submarines." 05 March 2008 *GovernmentExecutive.com* 18 Oct 2010 <http://www.govexec.com/dailyfed/0308/030508bb1.htm>

Caldwell, Roy, Mark Erdmann, and Kirsten Lindstrom. (April 1999). "Sulawesi Coelacanth: The Discovery." 12 Nov 1999 *University of California Museum of Paleontology*. 9 Jan 2007 <www.ucmp.berkeley.edu/vertebrates/coelacanth/coelacanths.html>

"Carcharodon carcharias – Great White Shark." (No Date). *MarineBio.org*. 05 Jan 2007 <http://marinebio.org/species.asp?id=38>

Carroll, Robert Todd. "Loch Ness 'monster'." 14 Jan 2007 *The Skeptic's Dictionary*. 19 Jan 2007 <http://skepdic.com/nessie.html>

Cousteau, Jacques-Yves, and Philippe Diole'. *Life and Death in a Coral Sea*. Garden City, NY; Doubleday & Co., Inc., 1971.

Darwin, Charles. *The Origin of Species: By Means of Natural Selection or The Preservation of Favoured Races in the Struggle for Life*. New York, NY; Bantam Books (Reprint), 1859.

Department of the Navy – Frequently Asked Questions. “The Bermuda Triangle.” 11 April 2007 *Naval Historical Center*. 17 July 2008 <http://www.history.navy.mil/faqs/faq8-1.htm>

Department of the Navy – Dictionary of American Naval Fighting Ships. “History of USS *Cyclops*.” 08 Aug 2001 *Naval Historical Center*. 17 July 2008 <http://www.history.navy.mil/danfs/c/cyclops.htm>

Doughton, Sandi. “UW Biologists: New Fish Species is Psychedelica.” 28 Feb 2009 *The Seattle Times* 01 March 2009 <http://seattletimes.nwsource.com/html/localnews/2008796010_weirdfish28m.html>

Elias, Paul, and Malcolm Ritter. “Science Fraud Shakes Stem Cell Field.” 24 Dec 2005 *New York Times* 21 July 2008 <http://www.livescience.com/strangenews/ap_051224_stem_cells.html>

Everhart, Mike. *“Kronosaurus queenslandicus: Ancient Monarch of the Sea.”* 06 Oct 2005 *Oceans of Kansas* 24 July 2007 <http://www.oceansofkansas.com/kronosar.html>

————. *Sea Monsters: Prehistoric Creatures of the Deep*. Washington, D.C.; National Geographic, 2007.

Flock, Jeff, Rhonda Rowland, and The Associated Press. “Clinton Stresses Urgent Need for Human-Cloning Ban.” 10 Jan 1998 *CNN* 08 June 2001 <http://www.cnn.com/HEALTH/9801/10/Clinton.cloning/>

“Fossil DNA Illuminates the Life and Climate of the Past.” 05 July 2007 *University of Copenhagen*. 06 July 2007 <http://www.ku.dk/english/news/fossil_dna.htm>

Frankel, Richard B. and Dennis A. Bazylinski. “Magnetotaxis in Bacteria." (May 2005). *Cal Poly State University & Iowa State University*. 02 March 2008. <http://www.calpoly.edu/~rfrankel/magbac101.html>

Friend, Tim. "The Real Face of Cloning." 17 Jan 2003 *USA Today* 21 July 2008 <http://www.usatoday.com/educate/college/health-science/articles/20030126.htm>

Gleason, Paul. "Diving for Ancient History, Scientists Discover New Species: Finding the Unexpected 4,000 Meters Under the Sea." 23 Feb 2009 *popsci.com* 01 March 2009 <http://www.popsci.com/environment/article/2009-02/diving-ancient-history-scientists-discover-new-species>

Gonzalez-Teuber, Marcia, and Martin Heil. "Pseudomyrmex Ants and Acacia Host Plants Join Efforts to Protect Their Mutualism from Microbial Threats." 05(07) July 2010. *Plant Signaling & Behavior*. 02 Apr. 2016. pp. 890-892. <http://www.ncbi.nlm.nih.gov/pmc/articles/PMC3014543/>

Gore, Rick. "Dinosaurs." *National Geographic.* 183. No. 1. January 1993. pp. 2-53.

Gould, Stephen Jay. *Dinosaur in a Haystack: Reflections in Natural History*. New York, NY; Harmony Books, 1995.

———. *Wonderful Life: The Burgess Shale and the Nature of History*. New York, NY; W. W. Norton & Company, 1989.

———. *Rock of Ages: Science and Religion in the Fullness of Life*. New York, NY; The Ballantine Publishing Group, 1999.

Gray, Jonathan. "A Tomato Plant as High as a Three Story Building." (No Date) *Discourse and Disclosure*. 06 Jan 2007 <http://www.discourseanddisclosure.com/frontPage/tomato.htm>

Handrich, Theodore L. *The Creation: Facts, Theories, and Faith*. Chicago, IL; Moody Press, 1953.

Hile, Jennifer. "Snake Venom May Slow Cancer Growth, Studies Hint." 01 June 2004 *National Geographic Channel*. 21 Nov 2007 <http://news.nationalgeographic.com/news/2004/06/0601_040601_tvsnakes1.html>

"Historical Hurricane Tracks." 15 Aug 2006 *NOAA Coastal Services Center*. 12 July 2007 <http://maps.csc.noaa.gov/hurricanes/viewer.html>

Horner, John R. and James Gorman. *Digging Dinosaurs: The Search that Unraveled the Mystery of Baby Dinosaurs*. New York, NY; HarperPerennial, 1988.

Horner, John R. and Don Lessem. *The Complete T-Rex: How Stunning New Discoveries are Changing Our Understanding of the World's Most Famous Dinosaur*. New York, NY; Simon & Schuster, 1993.

Human Genome Project. "Cloning Fact Sheet." 29 Aug 2006 *genomes.energy.gov* 21 July 2008 <http://ornl.gov/sci/techresources/Human_Genome/elsi/cloning.shtml>

Humphreys, D. Russell, Steven A. Austin, John R. Baumgardner, and Andrew A. Snelling. "Helium Diffusion Age of 6,000 Years Supports Accelerated Nuclear Decay." *Creation Research Society Quarterly*. Vol. 41 No. 1 June 2004. 05 Jan 2007 <http://www.creationresearch.org/crsq/articles/41/41_1/Helium.htm>

Humphreys, D. Russell. "The Earth's Magnetic Field is Still Losing Energy." *Creation Research Society Quarterly*. Vol. 39 No. 1 June 2002. pp. 1-11. 05 Jan 2007 <http://www.creationresearch.org/crsq/articles/39/39_1/GeoMag.htm>

"Japanese Marine Park Captures Rare Shark on Film." 18 Aug 2015 *The San Francisco Globe* 16 April 2016 <http://sfglobe.com/2015/08/17/rare-prehistoric-shark-is-captured-caught-on-film-by-japanese-marine-park/>

Johnson, Phillip E. *Darwin on Trial*. Downers Grove, IL: Intervarsity Press, 1991.

Judson, Horace Freeland. *The Great Betrayal: Fraud in Science*. Orlando, FL; Harcourt, Inc., 2004.

Kaplan, Jeremy A. "Terrifying Sea Critter Hauled from Ocean's Depths." 30 Mar 2010 *FoxNews.com* 23 Oct 2010 <http://www.foxnews.com/scitech/2010/03/30/terrifying-sea-critter-from-oceans-depths/>

Kevles, Daniel J. *The Baltimore Case: A Trial of Politics, Science, and Character.* New York, NY; W. W. Norton & Company, Inc., 1998.

Krystek, Lee. "The Sperm Whale." (1998) *The Museum of Unnatural Mystery*. 20 July 2007 <http://unmuseum.mus.pa.us/spermw.htm>

Kuban, Greg. "Sea Monster or Shark?: An Analysis of a Supposed Plesiosaur CarcassNetted in 1977." (1997-1998) *TalkOrigins.org*. 19 Jan 2007 <http://www.talkorigins.org/faqs/paluxy/plesios.html>

Laino, Charlene. "Cloning for Cures: Cutting Through the Confusion." 29 Aug 2002 *MSNBC* 21 July 2008 <http://www.msnbc.com/id/3076915/>

Lewontin, Richard C. "Dishonesty in Science." *The New York Review of Books* Vol. 51 No. 18 18 Nov 2004 21 July 2008 http://www.nybooks.com/articles/17563

"Loch Ness Monster Look-alike Found." 11 Dec 2006 *The Associated Press*. 19 Jan 2007 <http://www.cbsnews.com/stories/2006/12/11/tech/main2247748.shtml>

Macrae, Fiona. "New Species of Leopard with Largest Fangs in Cat World Discovered." 15 March 2007 *MailOnline* 01 March 2009 <http://www.dailymail.co.uk/sciencetech/article-442309/New-species-leopard-largest-fangs-cat-world discovered.html>

Martin, Brian. "Scientific Fraud and the Power Structure of Science." *Prometheus* Vol. 10 No. 1 June 1992 pp. 83-98. 21 July 2008 <http://www.uow.edu.au/arts/sts/bmartin/pubs/92prom.html>

McClain, C.R. "Why is the Giant Isopod Giant?" 04 April 2007 *Scienceblogs.com* 23 Oct 2010 <http://scienceblogs.com/deepseanews/2007/04/why_is_the_giant_isopod_giant.php>

McGee, Glenn. "Primer on Ethics and Human Cloning." (2001) *American Institute of Biological Sciences* 21 July 2008 <http://www.actionbioscience.org/biotech/mcgee.html#primer>

McMaster, Joe. "In Defense of Intelligent Design." 06 April 2007 *Nova* 17 July 2008 <http://www.pbs.org/wgbh/nova/id/defense-id.html>

————. "In Defense of Evolution." 19 April 2007 *Nova* 17 July 2008 <http://www.pbs.org/wgbh/nova/id/defense-ev.html>

Mehta, Aalok. "Photo in the News: Rare 'Prehistoric' Goblin Shark Caught in Japan." 09 Feb 2007 *National Geographic News* 23 Dec 2008 <http://news.nationalgeographic.com/news/2007/02/070209-goblin-shark.html>

Midwestern University. "Why Were Prehistoric Insects Huge?' 08 Aug 2007 *ScienceDaily* 31 Dec 2007 <http://www.sciencedaily.com/releases/2007/08/070806112323.htm>

Miller, Kenneth. *Finding Darwin's God: A Scientist's Search for Common Ground Between God and Evolution*. New York, NY; Harper-Perennial, 1999.

Morelle, Rebecca. "Colossal 'sea monster' unearthed." 27 Oct 2009 *BBC News* 09 Oct 2010 <http://news.bbc.co.uk/2/hi/science/nature/8327208.stm>

Morris, Henry M. *The Twilight of Evolution*. Grand Rapids, MI; Baker Book House, 1963.

————. *Evolution and the Modern Christian*. Philadelphia, PA; The Presbyterian and Reformed Publishing Co, 1967.

————. *Biblical Cosmology and Modern Science*. Grand Rapids, MI; Baker Book House, 1970.

National Academy of Sciences and the Institute of Medicine. *Science, Evolution, and Creationism*. Washington, D.C.; The National Academies Press, 2008.

National Science Foundation. "Hydrogen And Methane Sustain Unusual Life At Sea Floor's 'Lost City.'" 08 March 2005 *ScienceDaily*. 09 March 2008 <http://www.sciencedaily.com/releases/2005/03/050307215036.htm>

Naval Historical Center. 15 Feb 2006 *Dictionary of American Fighting Ships and United States Naval Aviation, 1910-1995*. 12 July 2007 <http://www.chinfo.navy.mil/navpalib/ships/carriers/histories/cv41-midway/cv41-midway.html>

Neergaard, Lauren. "Scientists Find 'Devil-Toad' Fossil." 18 Feb 2008 *The Associated Press*. 24 Feb 2008 <http://www.msnbc.msn.com/id/23225938/>

"New Species Found in Colombian Forests." 02 Feb 2009 *CNN.-com/world* 01 March 2009 <http://www.cnn.com/2009/WORLD/americas/02/02/eco.columbiafrogs/#cnnSTCText>

"Nessie of Loch Ness." (No Date). *University of Norway Museum*. 05 Jan 2007 <http://www.unmuseum.org/lochness.htm>

Netherlands Chief of Hydrography. "North Atlantic Ocean, West Indies." (1993) *U.S. Defense Mapping Agency, Hydrographic/Topographic Center*. 09 July 2007 <http://maps.bpl.org/details_M8685/?srch_query=atlantic+ocean&srch_fields=all&srch_style=exact&srch_fa=save/>

NOAA Satellite and Information Service. 29 June 2007 *Search and Rescue Satellite-Aided Tracking*. 10 July 2007 <http://www.sarsat.noaa.gov/>

Obringer, Lee Ann. "How the Bermuda Triangle Works." (No Date). *howstuffworks.com*. 17 July 2008 <http://www.howstuffworks.com/bermuda-triangle.htm>

Olson, Steve. *Mapping Human History: Genes, Race, and Our Common Origins*. Boston, MA; Mariner Books, 2002.

"Orcinus orca – Orca (Killer Whale)." (No Date). *Marinebio.org*. 05 Jan 2007 <http://marinebio.org/species.asp?id=84>

"Organelle." (2008). *Cytokinetics*. 15 March 2008

<http://www.cytokinetics.com/glossary>

Owen, James. "New Rodent Discovered at Asian Food Market." 16 May 2005 *National Geographic News*. 24 Dec 2007 <http://news.nationalgeographic.com/news/2005/05/0516_050516_new_rodent.html>

Park, Robert. *Voodoo Science: The Road from Foolishness to Fraud*. New York, NY; Oxford University Press, 2000.

Pemberton, Mary. "Photo in the News: Rare White Killer Whale Spotted." 07 March 2008 *National Geographic News*. 08 March 2008 <http://news.national geographic.com/news/2008/03/080307-AP-whale-picture.html>

"Physeter catodon – Sperm Whale." (No Date). *Marinebio.org*. 05 Jan 2007 <http://marinebio.org/species.asp?id=190>

Powell, Corey S. *God in the Equation: How Einstein Transformed Religion*. New York, NY; Free Press, 2002.

President's Council on Bioethics. "Human Cloning and Human Dignity: An Ethical Inquiry." (Chapter Eight – Policy Recommendations) (July 2002) *bioethics.gov* 21 July 2008 <http://bioethics.gov/reports/cloningreport/recommend.html>

Ramm, Bernard. *The Christian View of Science and Scripture*. Grand Rapids, MI; Wm. B. Eerdmans Publishing Co., 1956.

"Reptiles of the Ancient Seas." (No Date). *University of Norway Museum*. 05 Jan 2007 <http://www.unmuseum.org/searepti.htm>

Ridley, Matt. *Genome: The Autobiography of a Species in 23 Chapters*. New York, NY; HarperCollins Publishers, 1999.

Roach, John. "New Monkey Species Discovered in East Africa." 19 May 2005 *National Geographic News*. 23 Dec 2007 <http://news.nationalgeographic.com/news/2005/05/0519_050519_newmonkey_2.html>

Rosenberg, Harold L. "Exorcizing the Bermuda Triangle." 12 May 1996 *Sealift* 24, No. 6. June 1974 pp. 11-15. 17 July 2008 <http://www.history.navy.mil/faqs/faq8-3.htm>

"Russian Ship Leave to Patrol Atlantic." 24 Sept 2008 *Kommersant* 06 July 2009 <http://www.kommersant.com/page.asp?id=-13285>

"Russian Sub Test-Fires Ballistic Missile." 25 Dec 2007 *Australian Broadcasting Corporation*. 27 Dec 2007 <http://www.abc.net.au/news/stories/2007/12/25/2127271.htm>

Schmid, Randolph E. "DNA Indicates a Greener Greenland." 05 July 2007 *USA Today*. 06 July 2007 <http://www.usatoday.com/tech/science/environment/2007-07-05-dna-green-greenland_N.htm>

————. "Three New Ancient Crocodile Species Fossils Found." 19 Nov 2009 *Yahoo! News*. 25 Nov 2009 <http://news.yahoo.com/s/ap/20091119/ap_on_sc/us_sci_odd_crocs>

Schnoor, Jerald L. "Fraud in Science." 15 Feb 2006 *American Chemical Society* 21 July 2008 <http://pubs.acs.org/subscribe/journals/esthag-w/2006/feb/business/is_fraud.html>

"Science team finds 'Lost World.'" 07 Feb 2006 *BBC News* 01 March 2009 <http://news.bbc.co.uk/1/hi/sci/tech/4688000.stm>

Shannon, Thomas A. *An Introduction to Bioethics*. 2nd Ed. New York, NY; Paulist Press, 1979.

"Scientists Produce Five Pig Clones." 14 March 2000 *BBC News* 21 July 2008 <http://www.news.bbc.co.uk/1/hi/sci/tech/676906.stm>

Smith, Simon. "The Benefits of Human Cloning." (October 1998) *Human Cloning Foundation*. 05 June 2001 <http://www.humancloning.org/benefits.php>

Sunderland, Luther D. *Darwin's Enigma: Fossils and Other Problems*. San Diego, CA; Master Book Publishers, 1984.

Tasaka, Hiroshi. "3 Strategies for Fusing Science and Spirituality." 28 Sept 2010 *The Huffington Post* 24 Oct 2010 <http://www.huffingtonpost.com/hiroshi-tasaka/3-strategies-for-fusing-s_b_737368.html>

"The Loch Ness Monster." (No Date). *Answers.com*. 19 Jan 2007 <www.answers.com/topic/the-loch-ness-monster>

"The Politics of Human Biotechnology." (No Date). *Center for Genetics and Society* 21 July 2008 <http://www.geneticsandsociety.org/article.php?list=type&type=59>

Touchette, Nancy. "Cloned Mice Have Genomic Flaws: New Findings have Profound Implications for Reproductive Cloning in Humans." 27 Sept 2002 *Genome News Network* 21 July 2008 <http://www.genomenewsnetwork.org/articles/09_02/cloned.php>

United States Coast Guard. "Coast Guard Helicopter Rescue Swimmer Manual." 27 July 2000 *Commandant Instruction M3710.4B*. 16 Jan 2007 <http://www.uscg.mil/ccs/cit/cim/directives/cim/cim_3710_4b.pdf>

———. "110-foot Patrol Boat (WPB) – Island Class." 06 Dec 2006 *Aircraft, Boats, and Cutters*. 16 Jan 2007 <http://www.uscg.mil/datasheet/110wpb.asp>

———. "HH-65A 'Dolphin' Short Range Recovery Helicopter." 06 Dec 2006 *Aircraft, Boats, and Cutters*. 16 Jan 2007 <http://www.uscg.mil/datasheet/hh-65.asp>

———. 16 Jan 2007 *Enlisted Rating Badges*. 12 July 2007 <http://www.uscg.mil/top/graphics/n02a>

———. 10 May 2007 *Unit Information: Station Fort Pierce*. 12 July 2007 <http://www.uscg.mil/hq/capemay/UI/STA%20FORT%20PIERCE.doc>

———. "USCGC Cormorant (WPB 87313)." 26 Jan 2007 *Sector Miami*. 12 July 2007 <http://www.uscg.mil/d7/units/secmiami/cormorant.htm>

University of Portsmouth. "New Species of Prehistoric Creatures Discovered in Isle of Wight Mud." 09 Feb 2009 ScienceDaily 01 March 2009 <http://www.sciencedaily.com/releases/2009/02/090209075822.htm>

"USS Gettysburg (FFG-58)." (No date). *USS Gettysburg Official Navy Website* 29 Dec 2008 <http://www.public.navy.mil/surflant/cg64/Pages/default.aspx>

Van Dam Shipbuilders. (2006). *85' Nordia Classic Staysail Schooner*. 02 May 2006 <http://www.nordia.com/y_cl_85ss_d.html>

Vogt, Peter. "Vent and Seep Communities on the Arctic Seafloor." (No Date). *Arctic Theme Page: National Oceanic and Atmospheric Administration*. 09 March 2008 <http://www.arctic.noaa.gov/essay_vogt.html>

Vuletic, Mark I. "In Defense of Evolution." (2003) *infidels.org* 17 July 2008 <http://www.infidels.org/library/modern/mark_vuletic/defense_of_evolution.html>

Wachbroit, Robert. "Human Cloning Isn't as Scary as It Sounds." 02 March 1997 *Washington Post* 05 June 2001 <http://www.washingtonpost.com/wp-srv/national/longterm/science/cloning/cloning6.htm>

Weiss, Rick. "Scientists Testify on Human Cloning Plans: Some House Members Vow to Seek a Legislative Ban on Controversial Procedure." 29 March 2001 *Washington Post* 08 June 2001 <http://www.washingtonpost.com/wp-dyn/articles/A7514-2001-Mar28.html>

————. "Human Cloning's 'Numbers Game': Technology Puts Breakthrough Within the Reach of Sheer Persistence." 10 Oct 2000 *Washington Post* 08 June 2001 <http://www.washingtonpost.com/wp-dyn/articles/A39671-2000Oct9.html>

Wertz, Dorothy C. "Twenty-one Arguments Against Human Cloning and Their Response." 01 August 1998 *Genesage, Inc.* 11 June 2001 <http://www.genesage.com/professionals/geneletter/archives/twentyonearguments.html>

Wheldon, Julie. "Jungle Secrets 52 New Species Found in Borneo's 'Lost World.'" 20 Dec 2006 *MailOnline* 01 March 2009 <http://www.dailymail.co.uk/sciencetech/article-423523/Jungle-secrets-52-new-species-Borneos-Lost-World.html>

Whitcomb, John C., and Henry M. Morris. *The Genesis Flood: The Biblical Record and Its Scientific Implications*. Phillipsburg, NJ; The Presbyterian and Reformed Publishing Co., 1961.

Whitcomb, John C. *The Early Earth: An Introduction to Biblical Creationism*. Revised Edition. Grand Rapids, MI; Baker Book House, 1986.

"Why the Loch Ness Monster is no plesiosaur." 02 Nov 2006 *NewScientist.com*. 19 Jan 2007 <http://www.newscientist.com/article/mg19225764.900-why-the-loch-ness-monster-is-no-plesiosaur.html>

Yeomans, Kate. *Dead Men Tapping: The End of the Heather Lynne II*. Camden, Maine; International Marine/McGraw-Hill, 2005.

Zacharias, Ravi. *A Shattered Visage: The Real Face of Atheism*. Grand Rapids, MI; Baker Books, 1990.

ABOUT THE AUTHOR

C. Kevin Thompson is an ordained minister with a BA in Bible Studies, an MA in Christian Studies, and an MEd in Educational Leadership. A former Language Arts teacher, he presently works as an assistant principal in a middle school. Kevin is the author of two award-winning novels, *The Serpent's Grasp* and *30 Days Hath Revenge – A Blake Meyer Thriller: Book 1*, and is a member of the Christian Authors Network, American Christian Fiction Writers, and Word Weavers International. C. Kevin Thompson lives a short ninety minutes from two different coasts in Florida where he celebrates all things Star Trek, and is a Sherlock Holmes fanatic, as well.

www.ingramcontent.com/pod-product-compliance
Lightning Source LLC
Chambersburg PA
CBHW020458260626
47156CB00006B/1772

* 9 7 8 1 9 4 1 0 5 8 6 7 1 *